The Farm

Julie Troutman

Fulton Books, Inc.
Meadville, PA

Published by Fulton Books 2022

ISBN 978-1-63985-122-5 (paperback)
ISBN 978-1-63985-123-2 (digital)

Printed in the United States of America

One could gauge the length of their life by the memories one retains. People knew they had lived a long complete life when some memories seemed only to be a dream. The pain, loss, lust, and love left them entirely in awe that they even made it through. If Ana Reed had known she would live so many lifetimes, maybe she would have kept a written record of each somewhere for her to remember each journey. She might have liked to remember the little things washed away by the waters of time. The only things she would never forget were the loves she had gained and the loves she had lost along the way.

*****

I know it will seem quite odd to be starting a journal this far along in the game, but I'm afraid time will steal memories I would rather not forget. I'm afraid many are gone already, but I will have to make peace with that. So as many do, I will start at the beginning. My given name is Deangela Dawn Reed—Ana for short. I've often wondered why my mother chose the most common deviation of the name. I have lived many lives already, but I should start with my first.

I was born in the mountains of Virginia. The Blue Ridge Mountains were rightly named as the sun made the ridges have a blue hue when one gazed upon them. The passage of the seasons allowed us to enjoy all the beauty nature had to offer. The spring brought the flowers; the fall, leaves; and the winter left the world in a blanket of white.

I never really understood how poor we were because love filled the void of finance quite well. My mother raised my brother and me. We lived in a rental too small for even a portion of our things. Mom held two jobs at most times just to make ends meet. When school was not in session, my brother and I would stay at my grandmother's house down the road. Anthony was eight years my senior, but he always found ways to fill my day with fun and laughter.

When Anthony had finished school, he decided he would join the military. He had an excellent work ethic and a drive for excellence. Anthony wanted to see the world and make a career of his service. I suppose he did, as he died in the deserts of Afghanistan. When my mother saw the military men dressed in their finest blues, she started to cry as she ran to the door. They showed the utmost respect for my mother as the news they brought ripped her heart from her chest.

It seemed that an assignment had not gone as planned. My brother and his team met their end in the line of duty. My ears rang from the screams that came from my mother. Her knees buckled, and only the arms of the man delivering the news kept her from falling to the floor. She began to pray. She began to beg the Lord for anything, for everything. Nothing came but grief and unbearable longing for the son she would never see on this earth again. This loss was the turning point for my mother and started her downward spiral into madness. She knew nothing but grief and pain.

There was never a father figure in our lives, and she was all we ever had. So her control was her only defense. She controlled every aspect of my existence. She made sure that every part of my life was as safe as she could make them. Activities that other children were allowed to do were entirely out of the question. I learned very early not to ask because she became so nervous and agitated at the very mention of unnecessary risks. I fell into the exact steps of fear that she walked. I never resented her for that.

Mom was always reading and had binders full of papers and notes that didn't interest me enough to go through. She studied folklore and legends from our region. She read every old ghost story she could find. She would even talk to the older folks. They told her remarkable tales of the mountain. Most believed there just wasn't anywhere quite like this place. One lady said she could feel the magic in the air, and being a young lady at the time, I could have sworn I felt it too. I never thought my mother's interest was much more than curiosity, but I soon realized how wrong I was.

My mother was searching for a way to heal her broken spirit. She loved me beyond measure. I was the light in her otherwise dark life. She had to keep me safe no matter the cost. She had to see what was out there in the dark empty void of life.

When I was nearing my fifteenth year, I walked down to my grandmother's house for the day. I never could have guessed that it would be many months before my mother would come back home to me. We had contact almost every day. Mother would call and ask about my day and explain it shouldn't be much longer now. Grandma would smile and encourage me in any way she could. The time with my grandmother was so special to me. We sat, and she told me of her youth and all the plans she had made that never came to fruition. She hoped my life wouldn't be the same as hers. She wanted to see me fulfill all my dreams on this earth. And I have done so several times over.

My mother's absence was difficult. Someone once said time would heal all wounds, and this was no exception. She did as she promised, and she returned to us. There was never really an explanation given to me, but I always assumed she had sought help for her grief. I could envision her in a white hospital gown in a sterile environment, recounting her loss. I imagined her healed and whole when she returned to us. I could have never dreamed of the change that awaited us.

Mother still cried from time to time. Just as she always did, she mentioned Anthony longingly, but her tears were not always in the foreground. Sometimes the stories she told of her firstborn were accompanied by a smile. Her pain had melted just a little. I was thankful for that. Her grip was still tight when it came to me, but I always did the right thing to keep her at peace.

When I was seventeen, Mom and I moved to a new house. This house was modest but much nicer than our old house. It was closer to my grandma, and that was nice. Mom never went back to her jobs, and to my knowledge, she never worked again. At the time, it never occurred to me to ask how she managed all this. But now I know why. She willed me not to ask. She willed me to accept our newfound life, and she wanted me to enjoy it.

School went as school often did—slow and tedious. I had a few friendships to speak of, but I enjoyed the education process. I soaked in new information like a sponge. I wanted nothing more than to continue my search for knowledge. I wanted to help the people who struggled. I wanted to be the light for someone else. With hard work and dedication, I achieved this.

I received my master's degree in social work. I decided to start my career by counseling at the local crisis center. My chosen career proved to be a gratifying one. Someone once said that if you chose a job you loved, you would never work a day in your life, and I found this to be true. I had my whole life mapped out. I would earn my degree, get a rewarding job, and then find Mr. Right to start my family. Well, two out of three weren't bad.

On a particular evening, I worked late and had plans to grab a quick bite on the way home. All I wanted to do was get home and get my shoes off. They were new and had rubbed blisters on my heels. My toes felt like they were in a vice. I knew these shoes had been a big mistake I wouldn't be making again. I was sure of that. The air was crisp, and the smell of fall was in the air. I slowed my car at the stoplight, and I decided that the shoes had to go. As we eased through the light, I fumbled with the buckle around my ankle on my left foot. I was able to get that thing off me, and I threw it on the passenger-side floorboard. Its mate would never see it again.

We traveled down a slight incline, so I decided to unbuckle my right shoe. I struggled with the buckle, turning my foot to get to the right angle. I took my eyes off the road for one second, and just that one second almost ended my life that day. My attention was slammed back to the road as my car veered to the right. My initial instinct was wrong as I jerked the car to the left. The harsh reentrance of the vehicle to the pavement caused a terrible reaction. I was thrown back out of the road and down an embankment.

My head hit the stirring wheel with such force I saw stars. The car came to a stop. The airbag deployed and hit me directly in my bleeding face. If the impact hadn't broken my nose, the airbag undoubtedly did. The highway happened to be a pretty busy section, so help arrived quickly. An ambulance took me to the hospital. I received six stitches, and my nose was to be set back into place. *Unpleasant* was a very understated term for it. However, the drama hadn't made it to the hospital yet, and there was no way to determine the personality I would get from my mother when she arrived.

As expected, my mother came in like a bullet. She demanded and screamed and cried. No one understood her bitchiness as her attempt to control her fear. She was loud and rude and undeniably horrible, but I had never been so glad to see her in my life. I had never had any serious injuries, so this accident was devastating to us both. Even though I was twenty-four and technically a grown woman, I clung to my mother with fierce determination. She immediately asked who was responsible for this, and when I explained it to her, she said everything would be okay. I knew that had someone else been at fault, she would have killed them on the spot.

When the doctor came in to talk to us, he seemed surprised.

"It's very nice to meet you. I'm Dr. Jonas, and you must be Ms. Ana's sister," he said.

"No, sir, I'm her mother," she answered fiercely.

He hadn't said anything out of the way, but that was the first time I realized just how young she looked. I was twenty-four, and she was fifty, but she didn't look it. She always looked young for her age, but she didn't seem to have aged in the same way other people her age had. She had the same face I remembered all my life.

The accident proved to be a breaking point for my already fragile mother. The very prospect of a shoe being my downfall was unacceptable, and she didn't care to let me know that. Finally, after many hours of recovery, I was allowed to go home. As the fear lifted a little, I did get a long lecture about the importance of not being distracted in a car. She sternly advised me not to eat, not to fiddle with the radio, and definitely not to try to undress while driving. I knew it was coming, but it still made me feel eighteen all over again. Yes, eighteen, because sixteen was just way too young to be responsible for your life in a vehicle.

Days passed, and I recovered fully just as the doctor said I would, but my mother had not. She pampered me until the word *smother* came to mind. I tried to explain that this was a freak accident and would never happen again. She would always say, "Your brother had an accident too." What could I say to that? I did my work from home for now. She seemed very pleased with that. She would often ask why I couldn't do it from home every day. It seemed like a way to save on gas and the wear and tear on my vehicle; but I knew it was that dark angel, fear, that fueled her questions.

One afternoon, as we sat with our evening coffee, my mother asked me a startling question.

"Do you want to know where I went?"

"When?" I asked, looking up from my cup.

"When I went away for a while and you stayed with Grandma."

"Yeah, I figured you would tell me sometime, but it doesn't matter now, Mom. That was a long time ago." I gave a slight wave of my hand. I didn't want her to worry about it.

"Yeah, it matters. It matters a lot. I just don't know where to start." She set her cup down and stirred at it mindlessly with her spoon.

I sat back in my seat and listened attentively to my mother. She seemed to be nervous, excited, and apprehensive. She had never lied to me. She had said things I didn't like, but she was always brutally honest with me. I had no doubt whatever she said was the truth. It might have been painful, but it was the truth in the end.

Rene

As Rene drove up the mountain, she felt both excitement and embarrassment. She couldn't believe she would go to these women for help, but she was also terrified not to go. She just had to know. She had to talk to her son. She had to know he was at peace and had forgiven her for not giving him a better life. Her embarrassment stemmed from the strict upbringing she'd had in a Pentecostal church. Their doctrine was straight and narrow: suffer a witch not to live. But there she was, seeking out counsel from the mountain witches.

Rural homes surrounded by farmland dotted the landscape. Neighbors could see other neighbors over the heads of their livestock. The gardens grew to perfection. Rene knew she was moving farther into the hills when the board fences turned to barbed wire and posts leaning precariously from side to side. Each parcel of land was an oasis. Each one was a world contained within rusty broken borders.

Everyone knew exactly where to find the Cox family. However, no one ever dared to go. Old wives' tales and stories told by terrified teens on a mission had led to everyone knowing exactly which places to avoid. Hell loomed before anyone who sought the mountain witches out. Rene drove with barely a glance to the left or right. Her destination was marked by many a night speeding through this same stretch of road. Many had always wanted to have an experience here but never did. No one had ever really believed that they would.

Rene drew in a deep breath and made a right-hand turn at the fork in the road. The width of the road was barely enough for a single car to pass. There was no dead-end sign to mark the inevitable end of real estate. Instead, the road made its way directly to the front yard of the Cox house.

An elderly lady hoed at the weeds in her flowerbed. Another sat in a rocking chair on the porch. She seemed to be evaluating the work the other was doing. Neither looked up at Rene's car, even though she was sure it was rare for them to receive guests. Rene threw her car into park and shut off the engine. She glanced around the yard to make sure they had no canine companion. Then she slowly exited my vehicle.

She moved to the front of her car and called out to the residents, "Ms. Cox?"

The women looked from one to the other, and the rocking chair dweller raised her hand. Then with a motion, she directed Rene to come closer. "Come on up here. Let us see ya."

She gestured to her, and Rene slowly moved closer. She stood in the yard at the foot of the steps and smiled politely at the gentle-looking ladies. The gardener Cox leaned her hoe against a porch post and joined her companion on the matching rocking chair. The chairs were well loved. (When referring to something that had outlived its purpose, Rene's mother would say that.) The smell of honeysuckle filled her senses. It was comforting and familiar.

"I'm sorry to bother you, but I was wondering if I might talk to you about…" Rene stammered to find the words and decided to spit them out. "About my son." It flew from her mouth like a viper's tongue, and she knew there was no going back now.

"You from 'round these parts?" the rocking chair Cox asked, totally ignoring Rene's comment.

Rene knew exactly how the older generation did business. This particular age group had to know one's lineage at least three generations back.

Rene politely answered, "Yes, ma'am, my name is Rene James. My people were the Reed family. My daddy was Robert Reed. Did you ever know him? He has passed now." She looked at them with a clear understanding that they never knew her daddy. Then she continued, "His daddy was Henry Reed."

"Yeah, now that name rings a bell. They called him Dewey, didn't they?" This recollection caused the gardener Cox to lean forward in her chair. Rene's visit seemed to have piqued her interest now.

"Yes, ma'am," Rene answered, thinking to herself that these women must be a lot older than she thought. They clearly knew her grandpa but not her daddy. Her father had been seventy-six when he passed, and that was five years ago.

"You said you had a question 'bout your boy? Let me just get right to it." Rocking chair Cox rose from her seat and took Rene's hand in hers.

She patted the top with her free hand like a mother consoling a child. Rene couldn't help but think how soft her skin was and how fragile the structure beneath was.

"If you have come seeking conversation with your child, we don't do that. Not that we can't, mind you, but we have found that the path has many false spirits. These spirits will, how should I say, jump the line and try to play the part of the departed. See, they only do this for mischief, but the impact on the living is real. Even if they say they are fine and happy, the search for the next conversation will be never-ending. There is never that last word you wish to speak to a loved one. People tend to seek them out to connect like death never separated them. I must say, young lady, that the spirit world is vast and your day of reconciliation will come. You will speak to him again, only not in this life. You must wait your turn to see him again."

She released Rene's hand and returned to her seat. This speech seemed to be one she had given before. It almost seemed rehearsed. Broken-hearted people would come from miles around to seek relief from the constant pain of loss, only to find that no relief existed at all.

As she returned to her seat, gardener Cox rang in, "No comfort will come from speaking to an imposter anyway."

The defeat and pain must have been evident on Rene's face. To her surprise, the two sat in silence, just looking at each other. She started to feel very uncomfortable. It was like she was in the room while a conversation was taking place, but the conversation was all about her. They communicated without a sound.

After the long uncomfortable silence, the first words were from Ms. Cox. "This one is different, Martha. Take her hand."

Rene now knew that Martha was the gardener's name. And Martha did just as her companion suggested. She rose and gently held

Rene's hand in hers for the briefest of moments. Then she released it and returned to the battered cushion of her chair.

"I don't feel no pain in you, girl. I feel fear. Why is that?" Martha tilted her head to the side as if she was trying to make out an odd painting she didn't quite understand. She said this with no judgment, only love and acceptance.

Rene wiped a tear from her cheek and tried to explain her immense fear to the best of her ability. "It really is about my son. It started that way, and then it turned into something ugly, something irrational. I fear for my daughter to the point of despair. I really don't know what to tell you other than that. I guess I thought I could find comfort if I knew he was still out there somewhere so that if something devastating were to befall my daughter, she would still be with me in some small way. I'm ruining her life. I know I am." Her tears flowed freely now, and she had nothing left to say.

"We know your people, Rene. We have dealt with you over the years many times. You all have always been fair in dealing with us. We feel we owe you for the sin we placed on your kin." Martha sat quietly, picking at a string on the front of her worn shirt.

Rene scrunched her brows in question, hoping she would continue.

"Many years ago, I won't say just how long, one of your kin came to us with a similar request. We were a little cocky at that time and thought nothing was beyond our capabilities. We were wrong. A grieving mother, much as yourself, wanted to speak with her son who had recently drowned in the river over there." She pointed through the heavily wooded area to her left. "All she wanted to do was talk to him. She wanted to make sure he was indeed in a better place, but we thought we could do better." A smug laugh escaped her lined lips. She never looked up from her lap. The two were like two halves of one whole.

Martha picked up the story and finished the sentences with ease. "There was another of us Cox girls at that time. Her name was Ellen. She was the youngest of us. She was such a good girl. Unfortunately, that turned out to be her downfall in the end." She swiped at an unseen irritant flying near her face. "Now you see, that's important for you to know, girl. The tragedy didn't just didn't happen to your family but carried over into ours."

Then the story switched narrators again and continued.

"We discussed how sad Mrs. Reed had been and how we believed our power reached even past the bounds of death. Even though we did exactly what we set out to do, it wasn't anything any of us wanted."

Silence followed, and Rene wondered when the next storyteller would begin. She held her tongue, and with much respect, she sat attentively.

"See, we explained that not only did we believe that we could connect her with her boy but that we could also bring him forth to the living again. She was entirely in our grasp. We wanted to experiment with our powers. We used her son and her grief as a board upon which to bounce our abilities. She couldn't contain her excitement. In our defense, we explained that we couldn't guarantee it would work or the consequences in the event that it did. It didn't matter to her in the least. All she could think was her son Marcus returning to her. She didn't think it through, and honestly, neither did we."

The conversation continued in this back and forth manner, like recollections of this memory came from the depths of one mind.

"We chose to do the procedure on the following Sabbath, and the days couldn't go by fast enough. 'Pride cometh before a fall,' they say, and yes, it does. The evening came, and we gathered right there." Martha pointed to a spot in the yard where a kettle hung on the braces.

"We filled the pot with herbs and soil and various other items we deemed necessary to reanimate a corpse. We had no idea why we thought we could do it, but it seemed to work with ailing stock and dying plants in our garden. The only thing we didn't consider was that these things were near death, not past the veil altogether. No life's blood had flowed through those veins in three weeks and two days. His body lay peacefully in the family cemetery up on Boone Road." She pointed to the right up the hill.

Rene nodded, knowing exactly where it was. It didn't occur to her at the time, but that graveyard was in terrible shape. Grass grew up around the stones, and some stones lay broken and flat on the ground. She couldn't believe someone would bury a seventeen-year-old boy in such a rough place. She knew that the passage of time wasn't a cause in this particular tale. The area was one of use, and nothing was strange about laying the boy in the presence of his recently departed relatives.

"The boy's mother joined us with items the boy prized. She brought a shirt that seemed as though he had just taken it from his back. These elements joined the brew we concocted, and we began our unholy chant to darkness. As one would imagine, the wind began to whip, and the fire raged around the kettle. We chanted until the wee hours of the morning. The only signs of success were the onset of the wind and the blue flames licking our brew. Finally, we decided we would send Mrs. Reed home. We assured her we would retrieve her in the morning and tell her any news.

"The sun broke through the barrier of the treetops. The fire jumped once from the confinement of the circle and died. We knew something had happened, and this left us with nothing but pride and astonishment at the depths of our power. We walked through the woods over the hill to the resting place of the boy. The very air seemed still and stagnant. No life was present other than our own.

"We made our way to the freshly covered mound and invoked more magic. The magic we did we didn't understand. We called upon the very essence of nature to undo what nature itself had done. It might seem anticlimactic, but this is the truth. We could hear scratching. Noises were coming from within the grave. Most would have been terrified, but we were excited. With a great burst of combined energy, we moved the earth from the mound with our minds to gaze upon the freshly hewed wood of the casket. The scratches turned to pounds. We lifted the unholy bed from the ground with but a flick of our hands.

"The top leaped from its frame, leaving broken nails in its wake. The boy jumped to his feet with no flourish or supernatural air and stared at us through milky flat orbs, the orbs that once housed beautiful blue windows to his soul. The absence of the blue was also the absence of the soul. The funeral clothes were dirty and damp from his earthen nap. They hung on his disproportioned frame. Death had expanded its structure in some areas and collapsed it in others. Death had made his body seem wrong. His mouth opened to expose a blackened hole. His teeth were only visible through a slimy black glaze that dripped from the corners of his frowning mouth. He cocked his head from side to side and grew silent. The groans and whines ceased in order to hear what he could no longer see. His nose was raised in smelling—the senses alive by the lack of the actual eyes to see.

"We stood in silence, looking at the abomination we had brought forth from the pits of the veil of death. No peace would be granted to his mother by this monster. There were no words of comfort to be spoken by it. Its blackened, voided mouth held no coherent thought. We agreed grief was better. But then the question was, 'How do you kill something that doesn't live?' Clearly, this thing housed no life. We could never allow his mother to see the abomination that was before us. We had agreed that if anything were amiss, we would tell her that the magic bore no results. The actual results were clearly beyond anything we could have dreamed.

"Elen's skirts rustled as she moved closer to me, only by an inch, mind you. This thing's attention was immediately drawn to her. With wobbly, unstable steps, he moved toward her. He stretched out his hands to guide his way. He made a terrible screeching sound, like a pig in a poke. She drew near me and tried to do a basic protection circle. We had done it many times to ward off animals meant to do us harm. He moved forward, spilling black bile from his mouth. The spell did not affect him at all.

"He grasped open air in hopes of obtaining his target. His wails sounded miserable. His voice was mute of any coherent words, only the constant pain of a creature not meant to walk the earth. We stumbled back, making our way to the gate, which seemed to be a mile away. No one broke and ran, but I must admit that it did cross my mind. His steps led him to stumble, and his head and limbs cracked across the markers of those who truly knew peace. He simply regained his footing and moved forward. As we reached the exit, we slammed it shut. We moved back, awaiting the creature's response to the barrier between us. He slipped his hands through the stems of the gate and flexed his fingers. He whined in frustration.

"We made it to the edge of the wood with a clear view of our victim. Our victim was and is precisely how we viewed him. He was an unwilling victim in this game—this game we played to prove our power. We wanted to ingratiate ourselves to everyone we knew. We wanted everyone to know how necessary we were to their lives.

"Ellen sobbed as Martha and I decided what we were going to do next. Ellen's eyes never left the abomination. Suddenly, through the opening, there was a streak of black. In her mourning dress, the boy's mother ran toward the gate. Martha and I never missed a step as we dragged her to the ground. We covered her eyes in an attempt to spare her the horror of her son. As I screamed that this wasn't her son anymore, she broke free. The same suit she had dressed him in was hanging from his shoulders. His hair fell into his eyes as it had always done. It was her boy in her eyes. Nothing would change her mind.

"I finally allowed her to look at her boy. I kept a firm grip on her arm and let her look. A mixture of tears and laughter filled her voice. The creature turned to her, and she reached for him. She was too close, and the corpse managed to grab her arm. The gate cut into her arm, and she pulled to free herself. The scream penetrated my very heart as she managed to retract her arm. No sound escaped her. No tears fell. She simply turned from us and walked, dazed, back into the woods.

"Ellen's tears turned to rage. She raised her hands and started to chant. Martha lent our energy to her chant. We had no idea of the magic she invoked, but our trust lay in her. We believed her to be the strongest of the craft even though she was the youngest. We asked nothing. Oh, we asked nothing. How I wish we had.

"The wind began to whip, and the very gate turned red from the scorching heat of the enchantment. Our energy was bound together like a knot. The thing fell to the ground and placed its hands over its ears. Its scream was that of rage. It bared its teeth in defiance. We grew louder and louder until our bodies lifted as one into the air. The last chant was clear and powerful. Our arms raised in unison toward the creature, and we sent all our power in his direction. A vibration was visible as it shattered the gate and the undead behind it. His corpse was reduced to ash as our bodies lowered to the ground.

"Ellen's body continued to crumble, and she lay motionless. Her slight frame held no life. There was no breath in her lungs, but the creature was no more. It had burned to cinders, and the wind carried its ashes to the corners of the earth. Unbelievably, we knew we could do nothing. We would have never tried. We laid her to rest up there under that willow tree. We wanted to be able to see her final resting place. We wanted to remember what pride will get ya."

Rene said nothing as the story unfolded. Yet as unbelievable as the tale seemed to be, she had no doubt that was exactly how it happened. Every word rang true—sad but true.

"The boy's mother, as we feared, never recovered. One month to the day, her husband found her hanging from the rafters of their hay barn," Martha said, finishing the tale. "Over time, maybe grief would have been easier, but what we did had no healing time. So we owe you something, Ms. Rene. We can't grant you even a conversation with the dead, but that's not really why you're here anyway, is it? I mean, to the heart of it all, that's not it, is it?"

— 🌱 —

Rene's Revelation

Rene stared at her for a minute, not really understanding her question. Of course, she had come to talk to her boy. Of course, she thought it would bring her some form of comfort. What else did they think she wanted?

"What else is there?" Rene asked, trying not to give in to a full-blown cry. "I just thought I could talk to him and know for sure he was out there." Shame rose to her cheeks, and the tears flowed to wash the color out.

"I don't think your boy is why you came at all," Ms. Cox said as she leaned back and began to rock back and forth in her chair. She crossed her ankles and laid her hands across her belly.

"Of course, it is!" Rene erupted. She felt almost attacked by the woman's unspoken accusation.

"I think you know there is nothing that would come from talking to him. I think you have a different goal, one where you try to figure out how not to have this happen again."

Rene didn't say a word. She only contemplated Ms. Cox's words and found her correct. She knew she would feel no different no matter how many times she spoke to him. The fear and guilt would remain. He was still gone. He was still dead, and nothing would change that.

"If you could ask anything of us, and knowing you would get it, what would it be?" Ms. Cox asked.

Rene smiled, thinking of a genie asking what your three wishes were going to be. She then remembered their story. As she recalled their power, she told them the truth.

"The one thing I want is the hardest to give. My greatest wish is for the fear to go away. The fear of walking a day on this earth without my daughter is overwhelming. The loss of my boy fuels my panic. You can't guarantee that, though, can you?" Rene looked from one to the other. She saw no smug confidence on their faces, and she knew this was beyond their scope.

"We could, child, but we won't. We will never dabble in the affairs of Mother Nature ever again, but we know those who will. There is no charge for their services, but there is for ours."

Rene gave them a look of defeat as finances were one thing she didn't have to offer.

"It's not your money we need, girl. It is but a simple kindness we require."

At this, Rene's attention was piqued again. There was a prospect of protection for her baby held in front of her!

"There needs to be some explaining to do. You said you were from round here, didn't ya? I'm sure you have heard of us Cox women all your life, right? The unholy act we brought forth in our tale to you was three lifetimes ago."

Somehow Ms. Cox's words were no surprise. Rene had no emotion about her revelation at all.

Ms. Cox continued, "We bucked nature and defiled it to its very core. We chose to go against the very basic laws she created. When we met that day, we destroyed the lives of so many. We destroyed a mother, whose only sin was her love for her son. We didn't go unpunished for the crime. We didn't only lose Ellen that day, but we lost our perceived greatness. We knew that there were forces more powerful than us in this world. The winds of death cursed us. As the life drained from the wounded mother's spirit, so did the ability for life to drain from us. Time carried us to weakness. It allowed us to become frail and hopeless, but it never gave us a reprieve. We came to discover that nothing made of this world would destroy us. We believe release will come from something other than what the vengeful nature has created, a being that can grant your request. It can give your child the gift of youth, health, and immortality."

Silence fell. This required a response, but Rene had none to give.

"We but know a name and a location. The details we leave to him. The only thing we require is the recipient of the gift must return to us and release us from our plague." Ms. Cox looked sad as she said these words.

"You can't mean what I think you mean!" Rene stood from her seat on the step.

"It's an act of kindness, really, releasing us from the prison of life and setting us free from the agony of eternal torture."

Then reality dawned on Rene. She thought, *This isn't true anyway, so what will it hurt to agree?*

She would like another lead to follow. She would love another mystery of the mountain to solve. She had to know this name. She had to have the next clue.

Rene returned to her seat and asked all the important questions—who, what, when, how, and where. To her surprise, the Cox women were not as forthcoming as they had previously been. They explained that there would be a binding contract between this mystery person and the Coxes and then between the Coxes and Rene. If, for any reason, the Coxes and Rene and her daughter failed to uphold their bargain within one year of the act, neither of them would live another day. The being would come and do the deed themselves and end both Rene and her daughter for the betrayal. But Rene believed no act would occur at all, so she agreed.

Ms. Cox rose from her seat and retrieved a notebook, where she wrote the details of their agreement. She made four copies—one for Rene, one for Ana, one for themselves, and one for the mystery person. Rene signed each.

At the bottom of the letter, almost like a PS, were the words "I, Rene Reed, am of sound mind, and I understand this contract as it is written." Rene signed all the copies again.

The name and location were written on a piece of paper and folded two times. As if there were twenty people watching, Ms. Cox handed it to Rene furtively. After slipping it into her back pocket, even Rene started to feel a little paranoid herself.

A handshake from one and a hug from the other were their parting gestures.

Richmond

As Rene made her way down the mountain, she smiled. She waited until civilization came to view to pull over and read its contents. It simply said, "Nickolas Brennon, Richmond, Virginia, the Seven Restaurant and Bar." Rene put the note into her console and began to think of all the possibilities this could mean.

She frowned at the location because it was a six-hour drive! She would have to think about this. She already knew her curiosity wouldn't let her ignore any of this, but she would have to figure some things out. The simplest thing, like gas money, was going to be a challenge. There was nothing extra after the regular monthly bills devoured her paychecks. She would have to think this through.

Rene put the note in her jewelry box, where all the most valuable things she owned were kept. Days went by, and she could think of nothing else. Rene folded and unfolded the paper until the creases were ragged. She thought of ways to make this trip happen, but even one day missed from work would create a hardship for the household. Rene found no peace from the constant thoughts. So she did what any poor person did; she applied for every credit card she could find. Finally, after several days, they began to arrive. She now had three cards from the three heavy-hitter companies, and she was feeling somewhat better. She had never been one to use a card because that was just another bill she would struggle to pay, but she felt like this was a necessary evil.

Rene planned her trip to Richmond and mapped out her route. Her only regret was that Ana would have to stay behind with her grandmother. Ana's school was still in session, and she loved school. Rene wouldn't take her away from something she loved just to chase down someone who probably didn't exist anyway. She planned to drive to Richmond, get disappointed, and drive back. The only expenses would be her gas and food along the way.

When doing some quick research, Rene found that the Seven really did exist. She found that the owner's name was indeed Nickolas Brennon. What kind of scam were they pulling? What could be the end game they wished to see? Maybe they were tired of people believing the mountain witches' lies. Maybe they wanted to teach people a lesson about seeking them out. Rene didn't know, but she was going to find out. She was determined to go back to the witches and do their deed if it turned out that they had made her go to Richmond for nothing. Nothing was just what she expected.

After getting Ana settled at her grandmother's, it was time to set off. Rene decided to use this trip as a minivacation. She stopped here and there, taking the time to smell the roses, as they said. Rene did regret the lies she had told her mother and Ana. She had convinced them that this was a training seminar and that she wasn't sure how long it would take. Rene was such an honest person that they never questioned her.

She explained that the hotel she worked for would give her extra training if she did well. As a housekeeper and front desk clerk, the option of moving up to hotel management was very appealing to her. This story was very believable to the unsuspecting pair. Life would proceed as normal for Ana, and if nothing else, Rene could mark this down as a great adventure.

She wasted no time when she arrived at her destination. She pulled her car right into the parking lot of the Seven. It was still early, so it was pretty quiet. She made a quick evaluation of her traveling state and decided a brush-up of her wind-blown hair and fresh lipstick would do wonders. She slipped on her one pair of heels and went inside for some well-needed dinner. She wanted to scope out the place, too, and she thought that there was no harm in killing two birds with one stone.

The Seven was very classy and elegant. Rene wasn't sure what she had been expecting, but this was a pleasant surprise. It was in an older building, so everything had an air of sophistication. Crystal chandeliers hung over the dining area. The wooden tables covered with fine linens lined the space. All the servers were crisp and neat. Everything seemed so elegant. Rene asked to be seated near the bar section so she would have a better view of the entirety of the space.

The first visit bore no fruit. Rene got the lay of the land and ate a very delicious meal. She hoped it wouldn't take very long to find the elusive Mr. Brennon. She decided to enjoy everything about this very unusual vacation. Her hotel was on a busy little street. Many shops and hobby stores were there for her to browse through. It was a charming older area of town. Somehow her thoughts always returned to her goal. She wondered what in the world was going to come of this. She couldn't wait to find out.

Every day Rene made her way back to the restaurant for dinner. On her fourth day of stalking, she noticed a man she hadn't seen before. He was standing behind the bar, flipping through the pages of a menu. He was very dapper in his navy-blue suit. After studying this man for a while, Rene was sure this was the owner. He seemed to be giving directions and had an air of authority about him.

She made her way up to the bar and placed herself close. She assumed her position and began to do the only thing she knew to get a man's attention. She stared at her drink as if lost in thought. She flipped her long auburn hair and glanced up from time to time. Bingo! He walked over.

"How are you today? Is there anything we can get for you?" he asked.

"Oh, no, thank you. I may need a refill," she said as she giggled and pushed her empty white wineglass toward him. Before she knew it, a beautiful lady set her drink in front of her with a huge smile.

"We are the Brennons. I'm Nick, and this is my wife, Victoria." He gave a loving look in his wife's direction.

"Call me Tory," his wife said, extending her perfectly manicured hand in Rene's direction.

Rene took it, and after regaining her composure, said, "Rene. Rene Reed."

The two looked at each other briefly before Nick asked, "You're new to our city, aren't you?"

"Yes, I am. I'm here on a vacation of sorts. Some ladies from back home said I might enjoy my stay here." Rene took a sip from her drink and took this time to reposition herself from her flirtatious posturing.

"And where is that?" Tori asked, wiping the bar down with a towel.

"I'm from way up in the mountains of Virginia, just an old country girl."

The silence seemed odd, but the conversation began quickly enough.

"How did you find our little piece of heaven?" Nick asked, holding his hand out, gesturing to their lovely business.

"Well, to be honest, those ladies I told you about said I should find this place and you." She sat staring in her glass, unsure what his response might be.

"These women wouldn't happen to be the Cox ladies now, would it?" Nick didn't seem to be unnerved at all.

"Yes." This is all Rene could say to that.

"Well, any friend of theirs is a friend of ours," the bubbly wife answered.

"I think maybe we should meet later in private to speak of any matters they felt like we could help with, don't you?" Nick said as he absent-mindedly dried a glass with a cloth. Rene almost thought he had a devilish glint in his eyes.

"Okay. I really don't want to be a bother. Whenever is good for you is good for me," Rene answered, trying to seem as though she wasn't dying inside to know what in the world was going on here. So how were these people connected to the backwoods Cox family? What common thread could there possibly be?

"How about ten, after the busy time is over here?" Tori seemed genuinely excited about the opportunity to have a guest.

"That's great," Rene answered. These people were not at all surprised by her presence. They seemed to have done this before. She could only imagine what the rest of the evening might hold.

Rene spent the rest of her evening in complete anxiety. She had no idea what direction the conversation might take. She really didn't understand the end game for the Brennons or the Coxes, but she planned to find out. However irrational the Coxes' delusion was, what did the Brennons have to gain? How were they connected to the fabric of her mountain? What strings would need unraveling to uncover the truth?

Ten o'clock finally arrived, and Rene took her seat at the bar. The couple emerged from the back room behind the bar right on time.

"So glad you came back." Tori smiled and patted her hand.

"Come on up," Nick said, gesturing with his hand to the staircase positioned against the back wall.

Their home was above the business, and it was nothing like she expected. In contrast to the dimly lit intimacy of the restaurant, their home was bright and cheerful. It had almost a sterile quality to it, having stark white walls and stainless steel accents.

The group settled in a very comfortable den. Rene could smell freshly cut flowers and the fresh scent of pine. Rene assumed it was an infuser as there were no flowers, and the pine scent must be a cleanser of some kind.

"We know why the Coxes sent you here, but we want to hear it from you." Nick blurted it out like it was the most natural thing in the world. "There isn't much of a reason to go a long way around either. Just tell us the truth. It will save us all a lot of time," he continued.

Not knowing exactly how much the ladies had told them, Rene just started at the beginning and ended with the fundamental core of the reason for her visit. She never wanted to lose another child, not ever, and if there were anything in this world to stop it, she would do it. Rene explained that the ladies felt they owed her for some sin they had done to her ancestors. She had to admit she took advantage of that when they offered to help her. Their guilt for their past wrongdoings had landed her with the knowledge. This knowledge could save her from more pain.

"So they didn't tell you anything about us? They didn't tell you exactly what you would get when you entered this agreement? I'm sure they didn't, or you wouldn't be here right now," Nick said, moving to refill all our glasses yet again.

"No, only that you could give me what I need."

"What you need and what you might want are two very different things. If you knew exactly what you were asking, I'm sure you would think differently about it."

"Can I ask you something before we go any further? Why, saying anything about this is real, would you do anything for the Coxes? How do you even know them? You don't seem to run in the same circles, to say the least." Rene moved to the end of her seat, hoping for an answer.

A smile appeared slightly on the faces of both Nick and Tori, and they took each other's hand. He stroked the top of her hand with his thumb as she looked longingly back at him.

"I know they told you they were from a different time. Well, so are we. Many years ago, while I was away at war, I received word that my beloved Victoria had come down with a fever. They didn't think she had very long and wanted me to come home to say goodbye if there was any way for me to do so. When I asked my superiors, of course, they said no, so I ran away. I became a deserter that day, but I would not let my Victoria leave this earth without saying goodbye to my only love. Luckily, we were not too far away from the mountain, so I got home pretty quickly. I found Victoria just as they said she was. She was on the brink of death. I loaded her in my father's wagon and took her to the Cox women. Everybody was upset that I had stolen her in the middle of the night, but I couldn't bear the thought of losing her. I had to try everything. Let's just say that the Cox women gave my Victoria a potion that could restore her. It was made from the ashes of a dead boy. The only thing they asked was that I drank it too. They asked us to stay there to see what would happen, and we did. Thankfully, Victoria was not in her right mind and not even conscious most of the time, but I was. I can't even begin to tell you how horrible it was. I knew I was dying. I thought those mountain witches had hexed us because I wanted to save her, but as you can see, they did save us.

"But there were consequences for this, as you might know. We will never grow old, and we will never die. We live on the life's blood of those who will. Modern times have given us resources to do it

26

more humanely, but it wasn't always like that. We are not the first of our kind, but we had no one to teach us the ways. The witches only wanted to see what their power could do. They were trying to find a way to bring back a loved one who had long since crossed that bridge of death. There was no saving their loved one, but they saved us. We would do anything for those ladies. We have done this before for them. They only help those who are truly worthy or those they think they have wronged in some way. We help anyone they send to us. We know the agreement you made with these ladies. We know what they asked you to do, and I hope for your sake and theirs that you will do it."

Rene felt as though she couldn't breathe. Her heart was pounding in her ears.

"Okay, so what you have described to me is…" Rene couldn't even bring herself to say the word. It was too crazy. It was totally absurd.

She spoke so quickly she barely understood herself. It seemed the couple had no trouble following her, though.

"We don't want to draw this out any longer than necessary," Nick said, sitting back comfortably in his seat. "If this is what you want for your daughter, we require she not go through it alone. We will first give you the gift, and when she is mature enough in both body and mind, we will grant her the gift," Nick continued.

"What? No, I'm not here for myself. I don't want it. I only want her to be safe." Rene felt panic rise in her body, and she jumped from her seat.

"If you want Ana to be safe until she has matured, then you will have to be strong enough to ensure that she is. If you take this gift, you will be able to protect her in ways you have never dreamed possible." Tori patted Rene's hand soothingly.

"You want forever with your baby. We can give that to you. When Ana is twenty-five years old, we will revisit this with her, but you must learn and grow in the gift until then. Give her the opportunity for a normal life, even if it is for a short time. Give her body and mind time to mature, so she is a woman and not a teenaged girl forever." Nick explained.

Rene soaked in every word they shared. She listened to every step of the process, which seemed to be quite simple that one would think it would be more challenging to change the very makeup of another human being. First, the gift's recipient would drink from the donor, and then the donor would drink from the recipient. Finally, death would come to the recipient, and they would be immortal when they awoke.

There were apparently many ways one could transform into an immortal. The change could be done by a spell, like with the Brennons' case, or by a bite, like what they'd planned for Ana and me. But there were also what Nick called nature's vampire. These were apparently very old vampires who just appeared in nature as an anomaly. No one seemed to know exactly how they came to be, but they were the most powerful vampires. Unfortunately, they were also the most elusive. Nick and Tori had never met or heard of anyone who actually knew any of these wonders, so that seemed a little sketchy to Rene.

Rene knew she would never risk Ana's life unless she knew the outcome firsthand. The idea of inflicting any pain on her child was unthinkable. Ana not only had to endure pain, but she also had to die. She had to die to live. Rene would have to know that her second child's mortal life was over. This unfortunate detail still had little effect on her decision.

"Now you go on to your room and think this through. You come back when you are ready. We aren't going anywhere. We have been here going on one hundred years, and we don't plan to retire anytime soon. So take your time and think of all we have said. You need to realize not only what you are giving your daughter and what will be taken from her as well." Tori smiled and stood as if to say, "You can go now."

Rene didn't remember any goodbyes. She simply got up in the haze of this information and left their unbelievable home. The night air hit her when she stepped onto the sidewalk. It seemed to open her up to the real world. She smelled the smells of the city. She heard the sounds of the few vehicles that passed on the street, and she went to her room to dream of a life where no death could touch her sweet daughter. She dreamed of the peace it would bring to herself. Would there be stability for Ana? Would there be any semblance of a normal life? A traditional family and friends would be stripped from her, but she would have a life. Nothing that could harm her would ever touch her. She would be as timeless as time itself. It was a simple decision. Rene had brought her into this world, and in this world, she would remain. Ana would know health, beauty, and life for all of eternity.

One might see Rene's decision as selfish, but she did not. She saw it as a way to end her own endless torture and ensure Ana's well-being for the rest of forever. Rene did think about it, as was suggested. She made list after list with the heading "Pros versus cons." The pros always outweighed the cons. Continuing a natural life would only lead to Ana's ultimate end, which was unacceptable. Whether by accident, disease, or the natural progression of the human condition, death would be her fate. If Rene must walk this path ahead of Ana, she would gladly do it. She would be the test subject for this experience. She would do this for her child, whether Ana realized how critical it was or not.

— ❧ —

Rene's Time

Rene took her place at the bar just like many times before. She wore her hair in a messy bun, and the beautiful auburn tentacles sprang loosely around her beautiful face. Her black pencil skirt and red blouse made her already-stunning figure even more alluring. She made no conversation with the men who wanted to make her acquaintance. She made it abundantly clear that she was not interested. Rene had one goal, and that was to secure this arrangement tonight.

As the Brennons made their way down the stairs, she really took the time to study them. She noticed the unbelievably perfect way they moved. Their every motion seemed planned as if they thought about every movement. In addition, their faces were absent of all traces of age. They appeared to be in their early twenties. Rene wondered why no one seemed to notice that they were not aging, but she figured it was part of their illusion to others.

These people were held firmly in the hours of their youth. They were perfection. Tori's eyes were such a unique shade of blue that they seemed violet when the light hit them in a certain way. Nick's face, so perfectly sculpted, could land him on the cover of any issue of *GQ* magazine. The first selfish thought crept into Rene's mind. She would never have the lines of age dance across her face, and her body would never be weak and undesirable. She took a moment to be grateful for that. Her time with the Cox women had let her see what damage the hand of time could do. She allowed herself a little pride and conceitedness. Surely it was okay to feel a little happy for herself too. As she stared at the two perfect people, there was no fear. Rene felt only excitement for their mercy.

"You ready?" Tori asked while flashing a beautiful smile.

"I am," Rene answered.

30

Tori took her hand and the hand of her beloved, and they ascended the stairs to their home. Rene smiled as she thought of how this must look to the lookie-loos in attendance. They might see it as some strange ménage à trois, but she really didn't care.

The couple had agreed that Tori would be Rene's maker, as she was more patient with the education process. Rene would be there for Ana when the time came. Rene would be the mother again and teach Ana the new way to live. Her first steps into this new life would be holding her mother's hand once again.

There was no supernatural ritual at all. It was as clinical and sterile as the environment Rene found herself in. Tori took her hand and led her into the stark white bathroom. The tiles shined like new money, and a clawfoot tub sat in the middle of the room. The white candles sitting upon their silver pedestals and the soft music played in the background lent themselves to seduction. Rene instantly relaxed in the artificial safety of the environment.

Everything about Nick and Tori lured humans to them—the perfect way they moved, their unbelievable perfection, and even their voices' tone drew the imperfect to them. One's subconscious craved a mere fraction of their grace. Just like how the captain of the football team or the head cheerleader seemed captivating to the average youth, so did these visions of perfection. One could only hope that they could learn the secrets they indeed must have to be as they seemed to be. It was but an illusion, Rene knew, but she craved it nonetheless.

Tori moved slowly. She touched Rene softly, as a lover would caress his virgin bride. She stood behind Rene and slowly slipped her hands around her waist. She freed her blouse from the confines of her skirt and, with ease, slipped it over her head. She put it on the dressing table neatly to keep the space free of clutter. Although uncomfortable, Rene simply stayed in her place. As she felt Tori unfasten her undergarment, she felt her face flush, and knots grew in the pit of her stomach.

Rene's upbringing was abundantly clear on the act of same-sex relations. This act was the unnatural one. It was utterly foreign to her. She had never had the slightest interest in this type of thing, but she found herself intrigued by it. As she reflected on this later, she found it amusing that her turmoil was not that an undead woman was undressing her but that a woman was undressing her. Tori wrapped Rene's hair and placed it firmly atop her head in a messy bun. Her skirt slipped from her frame, and she stood before this goddess in utter embarrassment. Until this moment, Rene never cared what anyone thought about her looks. She cared now.

As Tori disrobed, she couldn't help but look. Tori was perfect—utterly perfect. She had no stretch marks or cellulite, and there were no extra little bits of flesh peeking out from anywhere. Rene felt shame, guilt, and excitement as she took pleasure in her touch. She was exposed and vulnerable, yet she felt free and safe all at once.

Bubbles boiled from the top of the tub. A warm, comforting smell of lilac and lavender filled the space. Rene couldn't recall the tune, but she was glad to have it mask the thundering beats of her heart. Rene sank into the warm confines of the tub and felt relief that the billowy bubbles now covered her body. She soon realized Tori was moving in to take her place behind her. Rene found comfort that she didn't have to look at Tori during the process. She didn't want fear to envelop her.

Rene chose to remember all that was to come. If she wished this to be the fate of her child, then she wanted to know exactly what it would be. She had to know what the experience would feel like, both physically and psychologically. Would fear creep in and overtake her mind? Would she experience sheer terror? Would the pain be too intense for her to recover from it? She had to know if she was going to subject Ana to it. Tori offered to mesmerize Rene, but Rene chose not to do it. She wanted to remember it all. She wanted to remember the moment she left her worried mind behind and embraced peace.

Rene watched as Tori retrieved a silver razor from the tray by the side of the tub. She watched in terror as Tori ran the blade across her wrist and the blood danced across the water. Tori placed her hand on Rene's forehead and leaned her back against her shoulder. She put her bleeding wrist to Rene's lips and asked her to drink. Rene took the coppery liquid into her mouth. She made sure she took a sufficient amount. She didn't want to die and stay dead due to a technicality.

As Tori moved her wrist from Rene's lips, she held it for Rene to see what was to come. The wound from the bite of the razor's edge slowly sealed itself, and the bleeding stopped. Nothing meant to do her Ana harm would be able to touch her. Ana's own body would counter any attack formed against her.

Rene felt a soft kiss on the crease of her neck. The only warning was the grip on her tense shoulders and the sharp pain that seemed to radiate through her body. The blue wells of Rene's body sprayed forth the essence Tori craved. Rene tensed but didn't fight. She didn't scream out amid this ravenous encounter. Rene heard Tori moan and shake as if in the grip of an orgasm.

The world went gray, then black. There was nothing. There was no sense of anything as the life flowed from Rene's veins. Rene thought she heard a cracking sound when Tori withdrew her razor-sharp fangs from her flesh. The sound she heard was the sound the neck made when it had reached the apex of its flexibility.

Rene knew nothing, heard nothing, felt nothing after Tori released her from life.

As Rene opened her eyes, she found herself in a lovely white bedroom. The only color strategically placed were pops of baby blue, giving it a regal feel. She was clearly still at the Brennon home. The four-poster bed and down comforter seemed rich and luxurious. The artwork seemed older and was of baby blue and pink botanical subjects. Everything screamed class just as the Brennons themselves did.

Rene really felt no different than she did after a nice restful sleep. She rubbed her eyes and sat up slowly. Rene swung her legs over the side of the bed and stretched. Her muscles contracted then released, and she thought about the lack of pain from stiff joints. Her feet sank in a plush white area rug with blue and purple butterflies patrolling its borders. Antique sitting chairs sat by the window. A small side table adorned with a vase of beautiful flowers sat between them. The fragrance filled the entire space.

Rene noticed an envelope on the dresser with her name written perfectly on its front. Rene looked for her reading glasses but didn't see them anywhere. She opened the letter, and to her surprise, she could see it quite well. The letter said:

Rene,

Good morning.

I hope this finds you well rested and happy. Nick and I are at the bar and will return shortly. Feel free to make yourself at home. Help yourself to anything in the fridge, and I put some clothes out for you. The only thing I ask is that you don't leave the apartment just yet. I'm sure you understand.

Tori

Someone had covered the mirror, and Rene wondered why. As the cloth fell from the reflective surface, Rene could only stare at her reflection. The reflection was both her and not her all at once. Her hair was once again full and lush. The ringlets seemed full of life, and the red of her youth had returned. As she had aged, time had dulled its luster, but now it had returned even better than before. Although the basic structure of her face was the same, her skin radiated youth and health, and her brown eyes were now alive with vibrant gold flecks. She was, as the Brennons appeared to be, perfect. But this was all to lure in her prey. Her perfect appearance and soothing voice would be the hook used to reel them in.

Rene was pleasantly surprised to find that not only could she eat regular food but that it was even more delicious to her. There was no ravenous hunger like the movies suggested. Rene was also thrilled to realize that she had no desire to rip the throats out of every human she saw. Wow, the film industry sure had that wrong! Actually, the thought of drinking blood was still kind of gross. Rene felt no different than before. She only felt stronger and healthier than she ever remembered feeling before. "So far, so good" was the attitude she took. She had to. It was now too late for any regrets.

Tori and Nick wasted no time versing Rene on the ins and outs of her new life. All the myths were rendered false except for the basics: "Death will come to our kind through the destruction of the heart or the separation of the head from the body." Rene had to think that this was a little funny because that should be avoided by pretty much anybody anyway. The aversion to the sun—a myth. Only surviving on the blood of humans—a myth. Being telepathic—a myth. If someone happened to be clairvoyant before the change, their abilities would be heightened after the change. But it seemed that literature and cinema still got a few things right. They were strong and fast, and they had incredible beauty.

Rene wanted to go home, and this desire motivated her to learn quickly.

Tori explained the art of mesmerizing humans and the possible reasons for doing it. Rene could mesmerize people to do her bidding. She could also control what she chose them to remember. Circumstances could arise where that could be a helpful tool. She would have to appear as if she was aging appropriately. She would have to change people's perception of her if she planned to stay in one place very long. She had lived in her small town all her life, and she didn't plan to leave, not ever. This time away was the longest she had been away from her mountain, and she was anxious to return. The mountain always called its children home.

Rene decided to play the part of Robin Hood in her new life. She would steal from the wicked and give to the poor, which just so happened to be her family. Rene would mesmerize the evildoers in the area and find joy as they handed their ill-gotten gains to her. She and Ana would never have to struggle again. She would never have to say no unless she needed to for moral reasons. She wanted Ana to have all she needed and most of what she wanted but didn't want her to feel entitled to anything.

Rene believed she would be doing the right thing, taking from these sleaze bags. The more money she took, the fewer drugs they could make. She felt no guilt when she read that some drug dealer was found dead by the local police. Usually, death resulted from not being able to pay a kingpin. No working girl would be willing to work for a pimp who couldn't supply her with drugs or a place to stay. All that took money, and Rene would take it all. She would leave nothing in their pockets when it was time for her to pay her bills. Her shakedowns would be ruthless.

Rene understood she could survive on the blood of animals, but she would need human blood every so often. She could get it one or two ways. She could go into the blood banks and take some, or she could simply feed. If she chose to feed, she would have to be very careful in listening to the heartbeat. She could never take the last drop of human blood, or suffering would follow. The last drop housed all the pain, depression, and loss of the person to whom it belonged. It took a very long time to overcome the donor's powerful feelings. Rene could also take from a donor only enough to sustain her and mesmerize the donor to forget about the incident. Rene never planned to kill a human being if she could help it. She would take from the banks, or she would feed and blank them out.

There was really no significant amount of insightful wisdom to be gained from the Brennons. The two had no maker, so they could only pass along the information they had gleaned over the years. It was all Rene had to go on whether it was right or wrong. Thus far, Nick and Tori had managed a very long life, so she believed they knew best. Tori decided Rene had learned all she could from them, and if she agreed to stay in contact, she could go home.

Rene's Return

Rene secured a new house for her and Ana and happily lived a boring, uneventful life. Ana progressed and flourished in her academic studies. Rene's tight rein on Ana's social calendar kept her safe and without bonds to many people. She must keep Ana focused on anything but love and marriage and children. She constantly preached the importance of independence. She would say Ana only needed a man to mow the yard and open jars. If she made enough money, she could hire someone to get that done. Only one thing still plagued Rene. It was her agreement with the Cox ladies. She never once considered reneging on her promise, but she really didn't want to follow through.

Rene had a year to fulfill her agreement with the Cox ladies, and as difficult as it would be, she was wholeheartedly going to fulfill her promise to them. Rene was the kind of person who didn't procrastinate. If there was a job to do, she would just do it and get it out of the way. She planned to make her trip back up the mountain as soon as possible and release those lost souls. They were kind and merciful to her, and she owed them nothing less. She would do as she agreed and end their torture.

Two months passed, and Rene slowly made her way around the winding backroads. She barely glanced from the road as she tried to keep her mind from the task ahead. She saw nothing beautiful on this trip. She only saw the path in front of her. As she exited her car, a feeling of dread and excitement filled her. She didn't quite understand the excitement. Her stomach was in knots, but her heart cried out for something. She felt an emptiness that she couldn't explain.

She took the stairs, slowly counting each step before she reached the door. Martha opened the squeaky hinged screen door and motion for her to come inside.

"Well, I see you followed through," Martha stated simply.

Rene followed her into the sitting room, where the other Cox woman was sitting. She sat beside an old potbellied stove glowing almost red from the heat trapped inside. She turned and smiled at their very unusual guest. Martha took her seat next to the fire, and Rene found a seat on an old Victorian settee. The fabric was so threadbare that Rene was afraid she would damage it by just sitting on its edge. Everything in this house was antique and battered from years of use. Rene wondered what stories each piece could tell if they were capable of speaking.

"You're the first to come back besides Nick and Tori. That says something about you. You are truly beautiful in this form, my dear, so very lovely."

Rene blushed from a strange sense of embarrassment. She had never taken compliments well, and this one was even more uncomfortable.

"Can I ask you something?" said Rene. She had so many questions she would like to ask, but this one was the one that plagued her most. "Why didn't Tori and Nick do this thing you're asking of me? You have waited and suffered for such a long time. It seems they could have ended it long before now if their love was, as they say it is, for you." Rene sat up straighter in her seat and waited for their response.

"You see, we are their makers. We gave them this immortal gift and, in doing so, rendered them powerless to help us. Those of your kind can't harm their makers. You indeed will never be able to end the one who placed the immortal kiss upon you. It is the fabric of the magic. It's past anything that we even understand." Martha's answer was plain and simple and sad.

Rene nodded as if this made perfect sense. She knew nothing was out of the question in this strange story she found herself. She began to understand her unusual feeling. Tori had explained the draw of human blood, but Rene had only ever taken from blood banks and animals until now. Her gums seemed to ache as her fangs wanted to break through and do their awful job.

"As you can imagine, I don't have a clue about what I am doing."

"You are a step closer than anybody else has ever been just by showing up. We are so grateful for that."

"I don't suppose you all changed your mind since last we spoke?" Rene was half-heartedly serious about that.

"Oh no, we are so done with this torture. If you can bring us peace, then please do it." The quieter Cox finally spoke.

"I don't know what I need to do. I was hoping you would know what I need to do." Rene was hoping for a relatively humane answer, but that wasn't what she heard.

"Violence and blood started our curse, and only violence and blood will end it. As we are drained to the point of death, we will feed the curse that lives in you," Martha explained.

Rene didn't see her condition as a curse, and in all her existence, she never did. Instead, she viewed it as the ultimate gift.

Martha moved to take the hand of her dearest friend. "We have been through it all, you and me. I have no doubt that if there is anything after this, we will face it together. I love you beyond measure, Carolyn, and I will see you on the other side."

Tears dampened the eyes of this brave soul as she spoke her final farewell. Not many people could get this chance to say goodbye. This fact was, in a small way, comforting.

The woman who Rene now knew was named Carolyn wiped tears from her cheeks. Rene understood all too well that they were not afraid of dying but of being separated. This moment was the first time they had no idea what was to come next in their long lifetimes. Their endless mundane days of pain were all they knew. Now a new path lay ahead. This was an unknown road they were now to travel.

Rene stood and walked over to the ladies and put her hands on their shoulders. It was odd that she wanted to comfort them when she would be their end. She was here to take their lives.

"We're ready," Martha said, taking a deep breath and putting on the bravest smile Rene had ever seen.

Everything was as natural as breathing to Rene. Her fang broke through her gums and took their natural place. Rene turned Martha and stared into eyes lined with and full of pain.

"You will not be afraid, and there will be no pain. Do you understand?"

Martha nodded, and Rene held her in a loving embrace. She nuzzled her neck and breathed in her sweet smell. Then nature took over, and Rene's fangs penetrated the paper-thin skin of the older woman. Martha never made a sound. Her body only slumped in Rene's arms as she took all but her last drop of life's blood. Rene stopped before she supped from the table of death. She lay Martha gently onto the settee and looked at Carolyn. The latter had no fear in her eyes. On the contrary, there was longing and hope. Rene mesmerized her just the same, cradled her gently, and took her life.

Rene fell to her knees as the rush of their essence filled her, and she felt the most extraordinary euphoria she had ever known. Tears flowed as she tried to breathe. The guilt seemed to lessen due to the total completion she felt. The ladies wanted this so badly. She had to end their suffering and complete her agreement with them. The ladies wanted to end their suffering, and briefly, Rene hoped she would never want to end hers, with no way out.

Rene did the respectful thing. She placed their bodies underneath the willow tree to rest beside their beloved Ellen. She knew they would want that, and she wanted to use this spot as a way to never forget what pride would get you, as the ladies had once said to her.

She made her way home without as much as a backward glance in her mirror. She had upheld her end of the bargain, and Ana was now truly safe. Everything she had done or would ever do was for her child. This act of kindness was no different.

Ana's Reaction

As Rene finished up her unbelievable tale, Ana just sat quietly, wondering what had sent her mother over the edge. Had she gone crazy? Had she completely lost it? Ana knew her recent brush with death was hard on her mom, but this?

Ana's training as a counselor kicked in. It was challenging to counsel one's own parent, that was for sure, but she knew she couldn't let anyone hear her mother speaking like this. They would lock her away in a looney bin!

Ana took a sip from her water bottle and covered her feet up with a blanket, which always seemed comforting. "Mom, I don't really know what you want me to say here." She had decided that the direct approach was the best way to go. "You are sitting here on this couch, in our house, expecting me to believe you are a vampire. Do you understand how crazy this sounds?" Ana couldn't lose her cool here. She had to remain calm. "I'm not saying you're crazy. I'm just saying the story is crazy."

Rene smiled as though she had expected just this response from her level-headed daughter. "Don't try to analyze me, Ms. Ana-fo-Lana." Ana fo Lana was a pet name Rene used when trying to discipline Ana without being too harsh.

"Oh, I'm not. This is outside anything we've ever learned. I wouldn't even know where to start to analyze this." Ana's tone was a little more panicked now.

"Ana, have I ever lied to you?"

"The scary part is that I don't think you believe you are lying." Panic ran freely in her words now.

Rene could tell Ana was really scared. Of course, she didn't want her to be afraid for her, but she had to let her feel however she was feeling.

"Look at me, baby. See me." Rene stared into Ana's frightened eyes and revealed her true beauty for the first time.

Ana jumped back in her seat. She clung to the back of the couch as though she could rip it free and protect herself with it. This was her mom. Ana could depend on her. What was going on here? What was she seeing? As if she was seeing the world through new eyes, she saw her mother. She *really* saw her mother. With the veil now lifted, she could finally see what her mother had been hiding.

The lines of age were gone from her mother's face. Her hair glistened and shown in a way Ana had never remembered to have happened before. Rene's eyes, even though they were similar to Ana's, were not.

Ana stared into the face of someone she had never met. She saw a version of her mother that only the people of her youth had seen. The only exception was the eyes. The eyes were new. They were not anything that had inhabited a mere human. They were perfect and oddly unsettling at the same time. Ana just sat there and didn't have words to convey her shock.

"It's okay, Ana. It's going to be okay, I promise. Don't be afraid. Don't you dare be afraid of me!" Fear reigned supreme in Rene's heart. She never even thought about Ana being afraid of her own mother. She loved Ana with all her might, and she couldn't bear the thought of her daughter being afraid of her in any way.

Ana slowly moved forward. She placed her hand on Rene's cheek. Rene melted into her touch, kissing the palm of her hand, as she had done when she was a child.

"Mom, what is going on?" Ana began to sob as she spoke.

"Don't cry, baby. I did this for you. I did all of this for you."

Ana sat and tried to remember precisely what Rene had said. She had thought of nothing but curing her mother of the mental illness she clearly had. She hadn't really listened to the story. Instead, she had been rummaging through the textbooks in her mind, trying to recall similar bouts of this particular delusion. She found she wasn't familiar with any. So what had her mother said?

"I don't know how to help you, Mom." Ana sniffled as she spoke

"That's just it. I'm here to help *you*. Don't you understand? You can be like me now. You don't have to grow old. You don't have to die. I have seen to that." Rene seemed so excited. She had waited so long to do this for her baby, and now was the time. Now she could give her this special gift.

"So you're telling me you're immortal. You're telling me you are like the TV vampires. All blood and teeth. Running around, killing people. Is that what you're telling me?" Ana calmed down a little bit. It was all so absurd that she decided she would just take it one step at a time.

"Partly, yes. I am immortal. I do need to drink blood but not like you think. I can drink from blood banks or animals, and there is no killing of anybody unless it's called for. A lot of what we have read and seen in the movies are not true at all. Our kind is just another version of a human being. We just live a really, really, really long time, like forever long."

"I can see there is something different about you that is obvious, but to have me believe in vampires is a whole other thing. So what else can you do? There have to be more amazing things than this mesmerizing and looking half your age. Prove me wrong, Mom. Prove to me we aren't both insane."

Rene slowly stood. Then in a blink of an eye, she was gone. Ana shifted one way then another, looking to see where she had gone. Her mother appeared in the kitchen doorway, holding a large kitchen knife in her hand.

"Okay, Mom, let's take a moment here. What are you doing with that knife? How did you get there so fast?" Ana stood up, preparing herself for defense of some kind. She could never imagine her mother hurting her, but she stood five feet away, brandishing a long blade.

"Oh, sit down, Ana. I'm not going to hurt you. Have you gone crazy now?" Rene smiled, trying to lighten the mood of the now tense room.

"What are you going to do with that knife?"

"You'll see." That was all Rene said.

Rene took her seat on the couch and produced a kitchen towel from under her arm. She slowly drew the blade down the length of her forearm. The blood seemed to gush from its depths. Ana screamed and tried to grab at the wounded appendage as the towel soaked up the blood pouring down her fingertips.

"What are you doing? We have to get you to the hospital, now!" Ana screamed frantically, trying to drag her mother from her seat.

"Just watch," Rene said, staring at the wound on her arm.

Just as that time long ago when Rene had watched Tori's wound close quickly, so did Rene's wound now close just as quickly. The slit closed itself perfectly, and the flow of blood stopped.

"We are fast, strong, and nothing can hurt us," Rene explained, taking her daughter's hand in hers.

"This is what I've been waiting for. I just want you to be safe, my baby. I don't want anything ever to hurt you again. This car accident was minor, but it could've been tragic. I can't risk anything like that happening again."

Ana couldn't cry. She couldn't laugh. She couldn't do anything but stare at the perfectly healthy arm in front of her. No large cut was visible on her mother's skin. There was nothing to show that her mother had just taken a knife and sliced open her vein.

Ana was terrified. She realized that her recent brush with death had been devastating to her mother. She knew her mother had an unreasonable need to protect her, but whatever this was, it was too much. Ana now believed something was going on. She just wasn't sure what it was.

Could she believe her mother was this thing she claimed to be? Could she believe, even though she could see, that her mother was anything less than immortal? Ana had watched her mother move so quickly that her mind couldn't even register the movement. She had seen her mother inflict a life-threatening wound on herself, yet there were no traces of it moments later. Ana had seen her mother transform from a middle-aged woman to a young, vibrant woman in a matter of seconds. She had to believe. She had to believe something, or she was a victim of mass delusion and was a crazy as her mother appeared to be.

Even though this story was a product of her mother's damaged mind, Ana wanted to know more. She was fascinated by the thought. Ana had always been a fan of the supernatural. She read every book and watched every B-rated movie she could find to feed her addiction. She found this particular brand of villain to be the most appealing. They were, after all, beautiful and ageless. There was a sense of seduction about their very being, and every product of this curse was immensely loyal to the ones they loved.

As there was only Ana and her mother, she found this to be the most alluring part of all. She wondered what it would be like to have a love like that. She always sided with the vampire in all the movies she had watched. She wanted them to get the girl and ride off into the sunset, as it were. That had never happened. Death was always the reward for their undying love.

Ana shook herself back to reality. She was a woman of science, and this definitely wasn't science. This was fiction. Nothing was immortal, and even inanimate objects found decay at some point. Science was rational and current. Magic and spells and raising the dead were thought of by the more flamboyant of society. Most of this part of society remained hidden so others wouldn't believe them to be crazy. Nobody of any substance would dare admit to such nonsense. Yet here, Ana found herself confronting it. She found herself faced with irrefutable data. Believing was seeing, and seeing meant truth, so she must admit she had seen all the things she had seen.

Ana needed little persuasion. Her response was not at all what Rene expected. She was curious, and somehow her need to learn more was overpowering. Being a woman of science lent itself nicely to pursuing a rational explanation. Yet down deep in her soul, Ana knew no reasonable explanation existed. She had seen the wonders of her mother, and her excitement grew as she thought of the possibilities. She played the tape like a film in her mind. She saw herself transformed into this perfect version of herself. Her mother's fear had long since rooted itself into her soul, and she found herself excited by the thought of safety.

Nothing would harm her, nothing would control her, and most of all, nothing would frighten her again. But of course, she would find this to be untrue.

Rene went back through the particulars of her story. She revisited her transformation, allowing Ana to take it all in. Ana needed to be very aware. She needed to realize death would come to her but that she would live again. Rene wanted her to really understand that part of it because no one was ready for that. Rene could still hear the snapping sound her neck had made when her life had ended. Ana would never have to endure that memory because Rene would make sure she was safely tucked away in her mind when that time came. Nick would ensure a peaceful transition. He would give her comfort in her final moments as a human. As false as it would be, that comfort was mercy.

"What do we do now?" Ana asked, gripping her cup so tightly her knuckles turned white.

Rene smiled and patted her daughter's hand gently. "We don't have to do anything this very second."

She understood that, like herself, Ana didn't like to procrastinate. She could see the excitement in her daughter's eyes, and it reminded her of a time long ago. Rene would read Ana a bedtime story, and Ana would seem lost in its pages. That was what made Ana so great at her job. She could not only sympathize with her clients, but she also empathized as well. She could easily slip into the lives of anyone she knew. She could take on this new life with a vengeance. She would excel as she had always done.

"Let's take a little time. Not too long, but a little. Don't be surprised to find yourself wrapped in a bubble wrap or a suit of armor, though. Just saying." Rene laughed as she pictured it. She could just see Ana in a suit of armor or wrapped in bubble wrap, her arms held out 'cause she would be unable to move very well.

"Whatever you think is best. I'm still in shock, I think." Ana returned her mother's smile.

"Do you want me to do something about this?" She pointed down her body as if she was asking her permission to go back to the way Ana saw her before.

"What would be the point in that? I already saw you now. You do that thing to everybody so that they see you as you want them to?" Ana asked, genuinely curious.

"Yep, I just have to do it once, and I will age gracefully in their eyes. Of course, I know I will have to make them forget how long they have known me at some point, but I will cross that bridge when I come to it. You hungry?" Rene asked, moving the cups from the table.

"Question is, are you?" Ana said with a mischievous grin.

Rene knew she would be the butt of a lot of Ana's jokes. The meaning was a little morbid, but Rene had a morbid sense of humor, just like Ana.

"You are too funny. Hahahaha." Rene rolled her eyes and made her way to her duties in the kitchen.

Ana and Rene sat down to some meatloaf, mashed potatoes, and green beans. It had always been Ana's favorite comfort food. Even though she had made it several times, with her mother instructing her every step of the way, Ana never got it to turn out as good as her mom's.

They never said a word about the hours they had spent on the couch, talking. Instead, they talked about normal, everyday things. They spoke about Ana's job and how frustrating it was to try so hard with so little result. Ana looked up from her plate with a newfound expression.

"I could really help people if I…you know," she said, looking up and down her mother, trying to make her understand.

"Yep, at the very least, you can persuade people to do whatever it is you think they should do. At the most, you can just take out the problem altogether."

Ana had often thought of how nice it would be to inflict the pain on the parents of the abused children she saw every day. She thought about how nice it would be for them to be afraid and weak and hopeless. Any form of torture wouldn't be enough. Some of these people were actual monsters.

The children were innocent. Their eyes told the story of how damaged they were. Physical clues were visible to an onlooker, but the internal scars were the most dangerous. These scares twisted and marred their soul until there was nothing but a mirror image of the monster that abused them.

Ana thought this would be the reason she took on this new role. It wouldn't be for herself or even to unburden her mother. It would be to punish the unpunishable. She could terrorize them in their dreams and their waking lives. She could show them what hell really was. She couldn't have dreamed of anything more perfect. She didn't need any more time to think. She wanted this power. She had to have it.

Ana ran down the stairs like a teenage girl. She yelled for her mother until she poked her head out from the kitchen.

"What in the world is your problem?" Rene asked, drying her hands on a dishtowel.

"We have to do this! We have to call those people and do this! I don't need to wait!" Ana almost screamed it like an order.

"What in the world has you in such a tizzy? We can call them. Just settle down." Rene sat down on the couch and patted the cushion, indicating where she wanted Ana to sit.

Ana sat and began to explain all the reasons this was important for her. She wanted her mom to see that she wanted to be extraordinary. She wanted to be more than human. She needed it. The kids she tried to help deserved it. She could do so much more with these abilities than she ever thought possible. She could actually save some of them and not have to sit idly by and watch them fall. These kids could escape both nature and nurture if she could intervene.

Rene sat quietly for a moment. Then her selfish side began to rear its ugly head. She didn't care why Ana wanted it, not really. All she wanted was for her child to live. She wanted her safe. If Ana could do some good, then okay. She really didn't care about anything but her child. She would take this ball and run with it.

"Okay, I will call them a little bit later. They work nights, so they are probably still resting, but I will call. Don't you have work today? Is your sick leave over?" Rene couldn't help the sound of disappointment in her voice. She liked having Ana safely at home with her, but she knew she had to let her go some time.

"Ugh, yes," Ana said while bounding back upstairs.

She threw her hair up in a high ponytail. She slipped on black dress pants and a nice crisp white button-down top. On her feet, she wore black flats, no buckle required. She was quite certain she would never even drive above the speed limit again until it was safe to do so. She hugged her mother and went to her office. She dreaded going back into the same old drama, but she knew she would be changing that very soon.

Her first case of the day was Byron Talbot. He was a perfectly adorable six-year-old boy. He had recently lost his two front teeth, and nobody thought it was strange that they fell out at exactly the same time. Ana did. She knew that brute of a father had knocked that poor boy's teeth out in an attempt to get him to move faster or talk louder or just be better, whatever the case might have been that day. She wanted nothing more than to knock out his stupid teeth, but she had to remain professional. She could help no one if she was unemployed by the state of Virginia.

"So how have you been doing, Byron?" Ana asked, taking a lollipop from her cup and handing it to the boy.

"He's just fine," his father answered for him. "I don't know why we have to keep coming here. Y'all don't do a damn thing."

"First of all, Mr. Talbot, I was speaking to Byron. Secondly, just what do you think we need to be doing?" Ana asked, sending the clear message through her body language that he didn't intimidate her in the least.

"You're supposed to be helping us get this brat under control. He is always running that mouth and leaving his shit lying all over the house for us to fall over and kill ourselves. You ain't done nothing. And what about the stamps you said we was gonna get? How are we supposed to feed these kids without more stamps?"

Ana knew he meant the EBT card the government provided to families for food, but this asshole had lived off the system for so long he still referred to them as stamps. She wanted to suggest the unthinkable, that they get a job, but she didn't. She wanted to suggest they not have more children than they could afford, but she didn't. She simply said she would look into it.

"Ah, hell, you say that every time. This is a waste of my time and taxpayer money if you ask me." He sat like he had won some unspoken, battle glaring at Ana.

"And what would you know about that?" Ana muttered under her breath.

"What did you say?" Talbot leaned up in his chair, gripping the arms tightly.

Ana couldn't hold it in. Management had spoken to her many times about her blunt rudeness, but this time, she just couldn't hold in her rage.

"You would have to pay taxes for that to be your problem, now wouldn't you, Mr. Talbot? You think we are dumb here, but we are not. We know exactly what you are doing to this boy, and if I can do anything about it, I will. You don't scare anybody, Mr. Talbot, nobody except this little boy. I assure you I am not six years old, and you don't scare me at all." Ana slammed both fists against the desk as her bottom lifted from the chair. This outburst had happened much quicker than usual. She felt the fire running through her veins as she thought of smacking his face off his skull.

"You ain't nothing but a stuck-up bitch. I hope you don't think you scare me none 'cause you don't. This is my kid, and I will raise him the way I see fit. Do you understand me?" He was so mad he shook when he spoke, and he met her stance of defiance.

"Let me explain something to you, you loudmouth bully! That child might be yours legally, but let's see how fast the state of Virginia can change that. Piss in this cup." She slapped a clear white cup in front of the man. He stood in complete shock.

"You can't make me do that, bitch! That ain't part of the deal!"

"We don't have any deal, Mr. Talbot. I'm here to ensure the safety of the boy, nothing else. Maybe some time away may be just what the doctor ordered. Don't you ever think you're going to jump up in my face. I'm the wrong one. Do you understand me? Now, Mr. Talbot, take the cup and go collect that sample. Byron won't be leaving until you do."

Talbot swiped the cup from the table and left the room. Ana was sure he wouldn't have done it, but the fate of the child services check was on the line. Maybe he thought nothing would show up. Perhaps he thought the gods were on his side. They were not.

Byron didn't have to go home with that monster that day, and social services removed Byron's siblings from the home within hours. Ana handpicked the foster family that would take them in. They were a very decent family with grown children of their own. They wanted to ease the suffering of lost children, and Ana found that they really did.

Day after day, Ana encountered more of the same. One after another, children came in front of her—dirty, starved, and lacking basic love and care. Unlike the Talbot child, Ana couldn't save them all. She had to watch as they continued to survive and never thrive as they should have. She saw teen girls who thought the attention they received from their mom's significant other was love. They didn't understand it was molestation. Any attention was better than none at all. Usually, no amount of explanation would suffice. The girls were just glad somebody wanted them, even if it was the sicko living with their mother. Ana had to let them go. She couldn't get them to tell the truth. The perverts were free to keep abusing.

Every evening, Ana would retire to her office and prepare for the coming day. She relied on her schedule book entirely. There were so many children in need. There were so many home visits, and she handled them all. She felt an unquenchable need to personally handle each case as if it were her only case. That was impossible. There were just too many. Some would fall through the cracks, and she had to be sure the ones that did slip through were strong enough to pull themselves up again.

The youngest and most abused had to be her priority, but how did one choose? How did these seasoned vets of the system simply watch? How did they do nothing? How was the rage of injustice not devouring them every second of the day? How were their dreams not plagued with visions of the innocent in the hands of the guilty?

Ana wasn't built that way, not at all.

Ana's Chance

Many weeks passed, and Ana grew more impatient with every passing day. Her mother tried to explain that Nick and Tori had lives too. They couldn't just drop everything to be at her beck and call, but Ana was spoiled and used to the right-now version of things. She had almost given up her constant whining on the subject when her mother gave her the news.

Nick was coming. He would be there on May 7, and Ana couldn't wait. She felt like a schoolgirl waiting for her prom date to arrive. She had not ever experienced that, but she thought that must be how it felt. This man came to take something from her that she could never get back, just like the virgin prom dates of the willing young boys that accompanied them. Now all she could do was wait for four more days. She was sure she would never make it. She might explode with anticipation. But she did, to her surprise, make it. She did not die from being denied the "right now" of it all, and she was over-the-top happy.

May 7 was a Saturday. It was a beautiful spring day, and everything was coming alive after its cold winter's sleep. The irony wasn't lost on Ana that as everything else struggled to live, all she wanted to do was die. She wanted to be free of the mortal coils that were wrapped around her like the coils of a viper. She wanted to be free. No pain, no struggle, no fear would be her reward for one night of suffering, and she could spare many children many days of suffering afterward. It was still her main objective, but she did find herself wondering what it would mean for her life in the long term. Would she be happy in this new life, or would the endless days weigh her down after time? She didn't know, but she was soon to find out.

Ana stood at the living room window, watching each car as they drove past the house. Rene smiled, remembering the way Ana would search the skies on Christmas Eve in hopes of catching a glimpse of Santa.

"Deangela Dawn, move away from that window. You know Santa won't come if he sees you snooping." Rene scolded, waving a spatula about in the air.

"You are so crazy," Ana said, rolling her eyes. She did, however, move away from the window, just in case.

"Help me set the table."

"K," Ana said, taking the good dishes from the cupboards. She really could think of a lot of things she would rather be doing, like staring out the window, but she did as she was told. She always had.

Setting the table and wiping down the countertops did just what Rene had hoped it would do. It passed the time. She heard the sound of the engine of an expensive foreign car slowing down at their driveway. There was no stopping Ana this time as she ran to the door. Nick had barely closed his door when she popped out onto the porch.

Rene walked up behind Ana and said, "Shut the door. You're letting the flies in." Then she greeted Nick, "Nick, I'm so glad you came. This girl is driving me crazy. Come in, come in."

The Southern charm oozed from Rene's lips. Nick was on her playground now, and it would be nice to show him some hospitality for a change. Tori and Nick had gone above and beyond to make her feel welcome, and so would she.

Sometimes, when Rene spoke of Ana, she made her sound like a ten-year-old child, maybe eleven, instead of a beautiful woman of twenty-four. Nick was somewhat shocked by this revelation. He studied Ana as if she were some new alien creature.

"I thought you said Ms. Ana was a baby. She is no baby, as far as I can see." Nick took Ana's hand, kissed it lightly, and hugged Rene tightly.

"Well, she's my baby and always will be," Rene answered.

They made their way to the living room, where Nick sat down and sighed loudly. "You wouldn't think we would get tired, but we do. It's not the same kind of tired as a mortal, but it's still being tired. It's a long drive from Richmond to your beautiful mountain."

This had once been his mountain, too, but time had taken a portion of his ownership. The big city was now his home, but Rene suspected that this mountain would always live in their hearts. Mountain life was simpler, a little less fast-paced. Rene appreciated that.

"Something smells delicious." Nick made an exaggerated smell face.

"I just threw some pork chops on and a little biscuit and gravy. I thought you might want some breakfast for supper. I don't think y'all do that much where you're from." Rene smiled as she acted like it was no big deal at all to whip up this table full of food.

"I couldn't tell you when the last time was. I can't wait. I'm starving."

"Well, let's go fix you a plate. Can't have you starving to death. Tori would kill us all."

Ana gave her mother an exasperated look, not knowing how Nick would take it.

Nick ate two biscuits smothered in hot sausage gravy and a large bone-in pork chop. He had two slices of tomato and some homemade blackberry jam from last year's harvest. He seemed very satisfied with his meal and patted his belly to emphasize that fact.

"If I had known you could cook like that, we would have tried to persuade you to say on at the restaurant." Nick smiled, knowing full well she would never forsake her mountain.

"Just some old biscuits and gravy, not nearly fancy enough for your ritzy ditzy customers." Rene blushed.

"You might be surprised," he said as he pushed his chair back, letting his tummy have more room.

"Let's go to the living room and rest awhile," Rene said, already starting to clear the table.

"Can I help you with that?" Nick asked, showing his Southern manners.

"Oh, no, it's nothing. I got it. You and Ana get better acquainted. It won't take a second to get this all sorted out."

Ana and Nick found their places in the living room, and Nick began to speak.

"Do you have any questions at all?" Nick asked. He had made himself very comfortable at his end of the couch.

"I don't think so. I think Mom has answered pretty much everything."

"She said you could do that thing that won't make me remember or feel anything. Is that what you're going to do?" Ana asked.

"If that is what you want me to do, that's what I will do," Nick answered very matter-of-factly.

"I think so. I'm not as brave as my mom. She is kind of a sadist like that." Ana giggled, trying to lighten the mood.

Nick smiled and took a sip from his coffee. He knew Ana was terrified. He could feel her heart beating like a drum. The sound was deafening. Nature made him crave the adrenaline that fear produced. His palms were sweaty, and his mouth watered even after the amount of food he had eaten. He wanted nothing more than to taste her. He wanted to feel the warm copper flowing into his mouth. His attention span was minimal, so he was glad she didn't ask many questions that would have taken clear thought to answer.

"I just want you to know that I'm not doing this just for myself. I want to do good with the gift. I want to help people. I think I can. Don't you?" Ana looked at him as if she were begging for confirmation.

"Your mom told me why you wanted the gift. I think that is the most selfless reason I have ever heard. I believe you will do great things, Ms. Ana. I truly do. Tori wanted to come for this visit, but the show must go on. It would be chaos if we were both gone from the restaurant at once. There would surely be fire, flood, or some other natural disaster." Nick laughed, recalling every other time they tried to leave and having something crazy happen.

"I wish she could have too, but maybe I will get to meet her someday. We will have nothing but time now, will we?" Ana thought about this for a moment and realized she would have all the time in the world.

Rene joined the two in the living room and sipped on her hot coffee, offering to refill theirs if they needed it.

"Do you want to do this now?" Nick asked. He didn't want to sound pushy, but he really didn't know how much longer he could stand her pounding heart without going crazy.

"Now?" Ana asked, growing a little anxious but excited all at the same time.

"Yeah, no time like the present. Isn't that what they say?" Nick quoted, acting as innocent as he could.

The predatory nature was in full force at the moment, and he was doing his best to keep the beast at bay. Nick knew Rene felt Ana's quickened heartbeat. She had no desire to drink from her daughter, so it didn't affect her in the same way. However, Nick knew his role in this play and was overly excited to play his part to the fullest. He and Tori didn't partake in human blood often, but he did enjoy it quite a bit. Tori knew he could have a problem controlling his hunger, so she encouraged him to seek other sustenance most of the time.

"I fixed up the library for you. If that's okay, Ana." Rene took her child into her arms and hugged her so tightly she thought she would squeeze the air straight from her lungs.

"Mom, not so tight," Ana said as she hugged her mother back but tried to wiggle free at the same time.

"Sorry, I'm just so happy and scared. It is all new to me too. Who would have ever thought I would stand by and watch as a man took my baby into a room to kill her? I'm the original smoother mother." She stepped back and stared at her daughter.

"What?" Ana said, straightening out her hair and feeling very uncomfortable.

"I'm memorizing your face," Rene said as tears weld up in her eyes, threatening to spill over onto her perfectly sculpted face.

"Oh, no, there will be none of that business," Ana said, moving down the hallway to the library door. She was afraid her mother would chicken out and Nick would listen to her.

The library was really just a room with several store-bought bookshelves lining the wall. There was a desk and a filing cabinet, but calling it a true library was a little bit of a stretch. Ana's mother had put down a beautiful red plush rug in the center of the room. No doubt to hide any blood that might get on it. She had candles burning, which was something she rarely did. She was always afraid of the fire associated with an open flame. Ana could smell lavender and lilacs. She didn't know where it originated. Nick sat on the carpet and held his hand out to Ana. She joined him willingly.

Nick stared into Ana's beautiful blue eyes and said, "No pain, no fear."

Ana instantly relaxed. She could still feel the soft carpet under her bare legs and smell the smells of the room, but she had no fear. Nick gently laid her on her side and snuggled against her back. He traced her shoulder with his finger moving up and down the crease of her neck. He breathed in her scent, which was honeysuckle and roses. His body began to tremble, and his gums ached. He knew he couldn't hold this position long, or he would lose control, and he didn't want to. He placed soft kisses up and down her neck, and he felt her lean into them as a lover would. She exposed her flesh to him in such a way that he could no longer divine right from wrong. All he wanted was to have her essence fill him. He wanted to taste her glorious bounty.

He opened his wrist with his now elongated fangs and fed her from his depths. She drew in the droplets willingly with no hesitation. She had no desire to break free. She licked and swiped her tongue along the wound as he pulled it free from her lips. With one fatal bite, he drank from her. He nuzzled and cooed as a babe suckling from its mother. He gripped her wrists and pulled the very life from her veins. The last drop came too soon, and he released her from his grip before it pulled him into death's grasp.

Nick lay with Ana for a while, trying to regain his composure. He took no time to complete the task. He took Ana's fragile neck and snapped as if it were a branch on a tree. He resumed his position behind her and closed his eyes to rest. Ana would awaken soon, and she would need him and her mother. He was lucky to have Rene to help him. He didn't like the feeling of another person's life being in his control. He didn't want that kind of power over another human being. She was no longer a human being, so that was a plus. Ana would awaken a goddess. A vigilante out to seek retribution for the weak. He had created a superhero, his very own supergirl. He smiled as peaceful sleep came to him, with Ana nestled lovingly in his arms.

Rene waited not so patiently in the living room for any word about Ana. She waited as long as she could before she couldn't take it anymore and decided that she'd had enough. She lightly knocked on the library door. Although Nick was peacefully sleeping, he stirred at the sound. Then he quietly slipped his body from his new creation and left the room.

"I was starting to get worried. How is she?" Rene said impatiently.

"This takes time. Everybody is different at this stage. Some wake within hours. Some might take a few days to be fully awake and active. You just have to be patient. Do you want me to put her to bed?" Nick said, understanding Rene's apprehension.

"I got her," Rene said as she entered the room and gently scooped up her daughter in her arms. When Ana was young, after falling asleep in front of the TV, Rene would carry Ana to bed.

She dressed Ana in her favorite fuzzy PJs and tucked her in tightly. Rene was unnerved by how Ana looked just lying there on her back. She looked like she was waiting for the undertaker. All that was missing was the creepy way they folded the dead's hands on their bellies. That had always given Rene the willies. She gently turned Ana on her side and propped her pillow under her head comfortably. Now that was much better. This position was Ana's natural sleeping habit, and Rene should know, as she checked on her throughout the night many times. She would often come in just to see if Ana was still breathing. Ana hadn't been as young as one might have wanted her to be the last time Rene stalked into her bedroom unannounced. Rene had always done it and probably would always do it even if she had to steal a key if Ana decided to move away. Rene did this for her own sanity, not for Ana's sake, but still, she would continue her rituals for as long as they lived. Thankfully, that would be forever.

As Rene made her way back downstairs, she smelled fresh coffee. Apparently, Nick had made himself at home after his nap and made some. Rene poured her a cup and smiled when she realized what she was drinking. It was the potent Death Wish coffee, and she found that to be an appropriate choice considering the circumstances. When the first drop of the hot liquid hit her tongue, she could almost feel it hit her soul as well. This day had drained her both physically and mentally, but it was almost over. Soon they could find peace.

Rene didn't want any details, but Nick offered her the basics to ease her troubled mind. He explained that Ana was calm and at peace during the whole process. Ana had felt nothing. That detail did bring Rene comfort. Now all she had to do was wake up. That was the most critical part. When panic started to creep in, Nick would reassure Rene. He would tell her everything was exactly how it was supposed to be. He coaxed her to relax.

Nick and Rene decided to gather all the snacks in the kitchen, some leftover biscuits and blackberry jam, and surf the movie channels. Channel 300 played a new movie every Saturday night. They decided to check it out. Strangely enough, it was the blockbuster hit of the previous year with that gorgeous Cruz and Pitt. The movie followed the life of one of the two characters. Rene and Nick laughed and gagged a little at how the industry portrayed their kind. Some things were spot on, while others were gross misrepresentations of the vampire species. Misinformation like this had both protected and put a bulls-eye on an entire group of people. Humans tended to fear what they didn't understand. They attacked their own kind for the slightest differences. Nick believed this would be their downfall. He had no idea how right he was.

Rene climbed the stairs once more, as she had done all through the night. She looked in on her sleeping angel. This time, Ana wasn't as Rene had left her. Instead, she lay stretched out on her back with one leg thrown over the covers. Her arms were wide on each of her sides like she was waiting on a big hug. A tiny bit of drool seeped from the corner of her mouth. Rene could now breathe. She knew Ana would awaken soon, and she could begin her new life as an immortal. Rene found there was no karmic punishment designed just for her. Everything had gone just like it always had gone—perfectly. she ran downstairs to tell Nick the news. She didn't have to say a word, and Nick knew.

"I told ya," Nick said with a smug attitude, leaning back on the couch.

"Yeah, I wasn't worried," Rene said as she hurried to the kitchen to make her baby's favorite breakfast—French toast, sausage, and eggs.

The breakfast sat untouched well past lunch before Rene heard stirring from above.

"I wake up now," Ana whispered just as she did when she was a child.

Rene had a fear that Ana would stumble down the stairs in her sleepy state, so being a good mother, she always required Ana to let her know when she was ready to come down.

Rene raced up the stairs and burst into the door of her baby's room. She found Ana standing in front of her mirror, which hung on the closet door. The sun poured through the window, making Ana's long blond hair shine like corn silk. Rene could see through the reflective glass the perfect version of her daughter. She never imagined Ana could be more beautiful, but somehow, the magic had made her even more devastatingly lovely. Her eyes were huge, and the blue was the color of the bluest ocean. The same golden flecks as her mother's danced around the iris. Her cheekbones were prominent, and her lips were full and ruby red. Her skin was radiant and ivory white and glowed with health and youth. Rene felt as though she was watching the birth of her daughter for a second time.

Ana turned and squealed like a child. "It worked!" she screamed.

"Why, of course, it did, silly girl. I wasn't worried at all." Rene waved her hand in the air as if she were shooing a fly.

Both ladies turned to see Nick leaning against the door frame, rolling his eyes.

"Yeah, yeah, she wasn't worried at all," he said, exaggerating every word. "Immortality looks good on you, Ana. Quiet lovely, I must say." Nick reached for Ana's hand and leaned in to kiss her cheek. The formality of strangers was not needed anymore.

"I don't know what to say. How can we ever repay you?" Ana said, returning his kiss.

"I'm just glad it all worked out. No thanks necessary," Nick answered, seeming a little uncomfortable by the outpouring of gratitude.

"I don't know any more than you do about how this all works, so I'm just glad it all worked out the way it was supposed to. I am a firm believer in that. Nothing will happen or not happen that wasn't in the cards anyway. So all I can say is, can we eat now? Your mother has all this food down there and wouldn't let me have anything but chips." Nick turned and started to stomp back down the stairs. He acted like a spoiled brat, but Ana thought it was kind of cute.

Ana and her mother stood and stared at Ana in reflection for a few more minutes, and Ana found some sweats and a T-shirt to put on. It wasn't much of an improvement over the PJs, but it was comfortable. They followed Nick down to the kitchen and reheated the food. They were all starving. This breakfast was the best food Ana had tasted in her life. She seemed to be able to dissect every ingredient in every dish. The maple syrup was sweeter than any she had ever tasted. Everything was perfect.

Nick asked Ana when she wanted to try the other form of sustenance. He thought it was best to get the heebie-jeebies out of the way. Some baby vampires found this to be the most challenging part. He hoped Ana would take to it well, as it was a needed inconvenience.

"Can we let the food settle for a while? I don't want to lose all that hard work Mom did to make it." Ana made a snarling face as she spoke.

"We can, but you will have to do it soon. It is how you finalize your transformation. There is no other way but by taking the blood of a human. I'm sorry about that." Nick really did seem to be sincerely sorry.

Rene wasted no time going into the kitchen and filling a red cup half full of the thick unfamiliar liquid. She even snapped on a lid and gave her a straw to make it more palatable.

"Here ya go. It's not that bad. Really, it's not. Just swallow it down fast like that nasty cough syrup you don't like." Rene handed her the cup and stood with arms crossed, all but tapping her foot like she did when Ana was a child and didn't want to take her medicine.

Ana did just that. She slipped the lid back so it would be quicker and downed every last drop. She didn't give her taste buds time to register that this wasn't normal. She gasped air back into her lungs and handed the cup to her mother.

"There, it's all gone," Ana said in her best six-year-old voice.

Rene smiled and showed the empty cup to Nick

"Well, we have a professional vampire here, don't we?" Nick beamed like a father witnessing a new talent from their child.

"I can do that," Ana said with a stern determination in her voice.

"Never doubted you for a second." Her mother puffed out with pride.

Nick stayed until the following Wednesday. He had to get back to the restaurant and Tori. Ana and Rene could see that Nick intensely felt her absence. Their bond was so strong Ana didn't even understand it. Rene really couldn't either because the children's father could not and would not bond with her or their children. Nick filled in all the blanks with Ana and did his best to prepare her as best he could for anything that might arise. Ana couldn't have been more grateful, not only for his loyalty but also for his willingness to help two people solely based on the word of two mountain witches. Ana was thankful that this was a friendship that would last an eternity. She would need those now.

Ana's Normal Life

Ana couldn't miss any more work, and the following Monday was a workday. She promised her mother she would come home if anything felt funny. Rene knew how she had been around the general human population, but this was different for every baby vampire. Her fear had switched gears since the transformation. She thought of every possible scenario where this could go horribly wrong. What if someone pissed Ana off, and she just ripped their arms out of the socket? What if she moved too quickly and someone saw? The worst was, what if someone cut themselves and she fed on them? What then? What would they do then?

"Mom? Mom? Earth to Mom," Ana said, waving her hand in front of her mother's face. "You have to calm down. I'm going to work just like always, and I will be home at six thirty, just like always. If I'm going to be late, I will call."

"You will call me every chance you get. That is what you will do, Ms. Sassy Britches." Her mother swatted her twenty-four-year-old behind as she left the house.

Ana opened the door of her mother's Honda and made a mental reminder to go car shopping. Her car had was totaled in the accident, and she hadn't taken the time to find a new one. She had a long list of things to do, but she would take one thing at a time. First, she had to get through this day. Then she had to see how it would go with her newfound abilities.

Ana pulled into her regular parking spot and made her way inside. She casually spoke to some of her colleagues and noticed them giving her a peculiar glare. Ana smiled as she thought of them gossiping about the work she clearly had done. The nosey Betties in her office would hint and probe her about where she had been. Ana would gladly tell them the truth. She would tell them she was feeling a little under the weather and that the doctor recommended she stay at home for a few days. That was not a lie because that was precisely what her mother mesmerized the doctor to write on her note. They then would say how they couldn't believe how Ana lied. She found some morbid satisfaction in that thought. She had never been one to care about other people's opinions, and she was sure she wouldn't start now.

Ana's first client was due at nine thirty, so she began to read over her file and sip her delicious iced coffee frappe, something she bought at the coffee shop. She nibbled on a lemon-filled donut, of which her mother would surely disapprove. Rene tended to frown on anything unhealthy unless she prepared it herself. Somehow she figured it had to be a little better for you if it was homemade. Nine-thirty came and went, and her client never showed. She put a note on the top of the file with an oversized paperclip. She shoved it in her "to be looked at by the end of the day" pile. She retrieved her ten thirty appointment and readied herself.

Dayla Vanjoy strolled through the office doors and ten thir-ty-five, chomping on a piece of gum and reeking of cigarette smoke. She had her hair pulled back in a banana clip. Ana didn't know they still made those 80s nightmares. It was so tight it looked like it might pull from the roots at her temples. The front was poofy, a true sign of the all-powerful rocker chick. The only thing missing was the denim mini skirt and the rocker tee of choice.

Dayla had on her waitress uniform from the local greasy spoon and seemed to be in a hurry.

"Ms. Vanjoy, glad you could make it, but where is Tony?" Tony was the son of Dayla, and it seemed there was always some reason he couldn't attend these court-mandated sessions.

"If I have told you once, I have told you a thousand times. I can't just bring him all willy-nilly. I have to be at work at twelve. I wouldn't have time to drive him all the way back to the sitter now, would I?" Dayla glared at Ana, swinging her boney leg as if she were completely put out.

"We have discussed this over and over, Dayla. If you don't bring Tony with you, I can't tell the judge he is fine. I'm not going to do that. I understand you have a job, but so do I. And seeing Tony is my job. The judge ordered it. If you want to keep your son, I suggest you follow the rules." Ana wanted to add, "for once in her life," but she refrained.

"Now you listen here…"

Blah blah blah was all Ana heard. She knew the drill. Dayla would say something like, "He is my child. I know what's best for him" or "I'm doing the best I can here. He is just fine." Either way, Ana wasn't going to accept any more excuses from this junky whore. There had never been signs of physical abuse, but the school was concerned about his hygiene and proper nourishment. I was concerned with the damage it was doing to his developing mind and his own sense of self-worth.

"I'm just going to lay it out there for you. You need to call into your job today, and you need to have Tony in this office by one o'clock, or I will have DSS at your door today. I can't be any plainer than that. So if you want to keep that check—I mean, your son—you will have him here. Do I make myself clear?" Ana stood and held her arm out, suggesting she leave and get the ball rolling.

"You ain't never worked a day in your damn life, you snooty bitch. I don't work that kid don't eat, and you don't care. Oh no, you don't care." Dayla stomped from the room, slamming the door behind her. Ana knew there wasn't a snowball's chance in hell she would see them by one. She would follow through on her threat, though; she could count on that. She put a paperclip on that file and stuck it in her "to be done after lunch" pile.

Ana called home intermittently throughout the day. She wanted to keep her mother at peace because one thing was for sure: she wasn't above coming right on down to the office if she didn't call. One right after another, the clients filed in, three before lunch and two after. Only one seemed to be positive. The father had petitioned the court for custody of his daughter, and instead of just leaving them be, the court ordered weekly visits. That would have never happened if the mother had custody. It didn't happen when that particular child's mother had custody and beat that child within an inch of her life. Her father stepped in and stepped up only to be watched and criticized for caring for his child. Ana wondered if it would have been the same if it were a male child. She believed it wouldn't have.

Ana looked at her watch and noticed it was almost five-thirty, so she better wrap it up for the day. Two files remained on her desk, and she wholeheartedly meant to see to them. She called DSS and explained the situation with Tony, and they made arrangements to go to the home. She knew the outcome would be Tony's removal. He would be better off anywhere. She looked at the file of the nine thirty appointment. Marci Patterson was the child's name. She was thirteen years old and in a terrible home situation. This was the second meeting they had skipped out on, so Ana gathered her things and began to call the home. She looked in the files and found work numbers for the parents. She tried the mother's workplace first.

"Hello, this is Ana Reed. I'm calling to speak to Mrs. Patterson. Is she available?" Ana was as professional as always. Of course, the business didn't need to know her business with Mrs. Patterson, so she didn't give it.

"Ain't no Patterson works here no more. She used to, but she was a no-call, no-show two days in a row. Boss figured she quit or something," the youth answered.

"You wouldn't happen to know how I could—" Ana didn't get the chance to finish when the receiver went dead. She growled in frustration and gripped the phone and stared at it like it was the wrongdoer. "Okay, that was a bust," Ana said.

She was talking to herself now. She was sure she was going nuts. She dialed the second number.

"Hello, my name is Ana Reed. Is there a Mr. Patterson there today?" Ana asked, regaining her professional tone.

"No, he's out sick, ma'am. He's been out a couple of days. Is there something I could help you with?" a very nice man asked.

"Could you tell me if they still live up on River Run Road?" Ana knew she was pushing it, but he seemed willing to answer.

"Yeah, I reckon they do. I haven't heard nothing different. Is everything okay?" he asked, realizing he might have betrayed some sort of trust with Mr. Patterson.

"Oh, no, no, he just missed a meeting or two, and I was trying to catch up with him." Ana tried to sound as nonchalant as possible.

"Okay, if you see him, tell him we need him on the job as quick as he can. We are getting behind here."

"Will do, and thanks so much." Ana drew out her words with her best Southern charm.

"You're welcome. You have yourself a good one," the nice man said as he hung up the phone.

Ana made a choice that day that would haunt her for the rest of her life. She decided to go home and follow up the next day. She would regret that decision. Marci Patterson's body was found at two forty-two the following day by some hikers up on the trails. Her body was nude except for one pink sock. She had been strangled and sexually assaulted. Marci's mother hadn't been in for several days, but Marci had been deceased less than twenty-four hours. Ana's pain turned to fury. She had never felt such rage in her life. She wanted to kill the person who had taken this young girl from the world.

Although Marci was thirteen years old, her body was the size of a nine- or ten-year-old child. Her social interactions were strained and highly dysfunctional. Marci was bullied and harassed by her peers, who viewed her as poor white trash. Marci did reasonably well in school but never excelled. Her teachers had little to say about her, and Ana believed it was because they didn't take the time to check on her. They didn't have time to be bothered with a lost cause. People in authority felt it was above their pay grade to do very much regarding a seemingly lost cause, and it sickened Ana. The people in charge of this child eight hours a day had to have seen her condition. They knew the pay rate when they took the jobs they chose. If their job was such a burden for the pay, they should have made a career in another field.

Ana knew she had to get out of the office. She knew she wouldn't be able to control her rage. She worried about what she would do if anyone were to upset her anymore today. So she rearranged her schedule for the day. She could make her calls from home. Ana's boss could see this wasn't a good day for her, so she insisted she take the day off and collect herself.

"That's the most challenging part of this job, Ana. You can't save them all. We can only do our best, and you did that. No one expected any more than you did. We have all been where you are right now," Mrs. Baker said she empathized with Ana because she had been there several times in her many years on the job.

"My head knows that, but it's my heart that doesn't. She might have still been alive had I gone after work. Maybe I could have stopped it." Finally, Ana broke down, and the tears flowed like rain.

"Or maybe you could have died too. We don't know who did this horrible thing. What we do know is whoever did it is a monster. You couldn't have stopped them, and I'm afraid they would have hurt you if you'd tried." Mrs. Baker rubbed Ana's arm in a comforting manner, but nothing would have soothed her. Ana knew she could have stopped it. She knew she was the monster who could have protected that little girl if she hadn't wanted to go home.

"I will get my work done today. I will be in the office first thing in the morning. It is just a rough day today, but I will be okay." Ana gathered up her things and said her goodbyes.

Ana and her mother were as thick as thieves, and Ana called her immediately from the car. Ana told her mother about Marci and all the terrible things she knew so far about the case.

"You just come on home now, baby. We will sit down, have some coffee, and talk this out. Then you can give yourself a little break before you make your calls." Rene had a solemn tone to her voice, and Ana found it interesting.

Ana threw her bag down on the table by the door and flopped down on the sofa. She wiped at her eyes that were semi-swollen and still wet with tears. Rene came from the kitchen with two steaming cups of coffee, two sugars, and some cream, just like Ana liked it.

Rene took her place at the end of the couch and patted her daughter's leg. "This is a hard one, baby girl. You got this. You have to snap out of these feelings of guilt. It wasn't your fault. We will do whatever you want to do together. I will help any way I can."

Rene had never seemed so intent on anything. Ana just sat there a moment before she realized what her mother meant.

"What can we do? I don't even know where to start," Ana said with a look of defeat in her eyes.

"Well, about that, I called Nick," Rene said.

"Nick? Why?" Ana said in a perplexed manner.

"You said that the reason you wanted this gift was to punish the guilty. Well, whoever did this to this child is definitely guilty. They need to be punished. But I don't think anything the law could do to them would be good enough. Do you?" Rene said with a little bit of the devil in her eyes.

"What did Nick say?"

"He said to use your gift. He asked that you be very careful to maintain your secret, but he agreed that it was now if there were ever a chance to do good with this gift. He said to follow your heart and let nature guild you. Nature is a good leader if only you will follow. I'm not sure what he meant by that, but he assured me you would when the time came," Rene relayed.

Ana wiped the tears from her eyes and took a deep breath.

"He said your emotions were in overdrive. He said to try to control them as best you can. Tori was there too. She said you had all the tools to find not only who the culprit was but to punish them with all they deserve. She would be the hunter, not the prey. Tori said to start at the beginning of the end of this child's life and work your way backward to find her killer. It would be easier than you think. She said to get a lick in for her too." Rene smiled as she explained their instructions.

"Will you go with me? I mean not right this second but when I get through with my calls." Ana was almost pitiful with her request.

"Like you even have to ask?" Rene answered.

Ana was quick with her work but not neglectful. She arranged meetings and did check-in calls. She was excited to get started. She imagined the scene was still teaming with officers, so there was no use to get there in a big hurry. Ana found herself unexpectedly calm by the time she finished up. For once, all the calls were routine, and all were cooperative. She was thankful for that. She changed from her work clothes to a pair of faded black jeans and a gray T-shirt. She grabbed a black hoody from the coat closet and set off to find her mother. Rene was sitting on the swing on their front porch, patiently waiting. She was wearing khaki cargo pants and a nice polo. Her hair was pulled up in a ponytail, as was Ana's.

"Let's roll," Rene said, keys in hand.

The two parked the car and walked through the heavily wooded area adjacent to the well-marked trail. They heard the officers speak about the lack of evidence and the gruesome scene they had found. Their acute hearing was their advantage. They knew when the officers were on their way out for the day. Their lack of enthusiasm aggravated Ana, but she'd had enough of them all. They chose just to leave when their shift ended instead of search for more clues. However, this would work in favor of the two amateur sleuths.

Ana was careful not to disturb any police tape or the evidence cards placed randomly around the scene. There were hundreds of footprints and even an empty candy wrapper lying nearby. Ana was sure some desensitized police officer, well past his use-by date, stood and ate a candy bar in the same spot where a little girl was brutally murdered. She could almost see his annoyance and boredom as he waited in the hot sun. Ana hoped she would never lose her fire for justice.

"What do we do now?" Ana asked her mother. She was at a loss about the next step she was to take.

Rene closed her eyes and put her finger to her lips to silence Ana. She stood as if in a trace face tilted to the sky. She allowed the environment around her to lead them in the next direction.

"All I can smell is the blood," Rene finally said.

Ana adopted her mother's trance-like state. She took in every sound and every smell around her. She allowed nature to feed her senses. She began to leave the general area and walked forward and back, to the left and the right. She moved back to her original front-facing position and moved forward.

"I think we need to go this way. Can you smell that?" Ana asked her mother.

"Yeah, it's faint, but I do." Rene looked surprised by her revelation.

"The blood is strongest here, then nothing in any direction except straight ahead." Ana pointed her finger straight ahead of them down the path.

"He brought her down this way, I think." Ana still wasn't sure, but it was all they had.

Rene and Ana began to follow the metallic smell of the blood. It seemed that the farther they had gone, the more pungent the smell. Ana tried not to think about poor Marci bleeding as he carried her body down the path. Ana only hoped she was dead and at peace when he dumped her body in this lonely place. Ana knew she was injured badly, so maybe she was, at least, not conscious of the abandonment. The trail bared to the right and crossed a stream into the heart of the wooded area. Ana wasn't sure exactly where they were now, but she wasn't stopping, not yet. Minor signs not visible to human eyes were everywhere along the trail. Ana flexed her new eyes to see them all. She saw small fibers caught in the branches of low-lying branches. She saw the blood droplets on the fallen leaves. A new smell mixed with the old. It was a familiar smell of cologne, but Ana couldn't place it.

"I smell it," Rene said while picking up her pace.

The wooded area stopped as soon as it had begun, and Rene and Ana were staring up at a guard rail. They climbed the bank and saw they were right beside Highway 58. It was a rural section of the highway with not much traffic. Ana's heart fell. She thought they had lost the trail.

"You're not giving up that easily, are you? I didn't raise no quitter." Rene pushed Ana in the center of her back for encouragement.

"Not too sure what to do now. Are you?" Ana said, hands on her hips, looking up and down each side of the road. A huge rock sat in a pull-off area, and Ana took a seat. "What's your plan, Stan?" Ana asked her mother, throwing her hands in the air.

"First thing we are not going to do is to stop now. We have lived here all our lives. Let's think about where we are a minute. What's close by?" Rene said with the same hand on the hip stance.

The two thought for a moment, and both said nothing. There was nothing close by to this. It was miles to the next house and no business or anything around.

"Okay, all we can do is work backward from here. First, we can go this way and see if there is anything. We can see if we can't find the scent again." Ana had a new determination now.

"Can we at least go get the car? We can stop here and there and check." Rene wiped at her brow as if to say shew she was tired, even though Ana knew she wasn't.

"Well, duh," Ana said, rolling her eyes and climbing over the guard rail again.

When they were back at the car, it took them a minute to figure out how to get where they had been by car, but they managed to figure it out. They stopped at the rock to make sure that it was indeed the same rock. Then they began moving slowly up the road. The car didn't exceed thirty miles per hour, as Rene and Ana held their heads out the window like old dogs out for a joy ride. Miles went by with nothing until a small country store came into view. Neither remembered it because mainly trout fishers and hikers stopped there to buy snacks. The occasional lost soul on the parkway found their way there for directions, but it wasn't a regular stopping point for most locals.

"Let's see what we got here," Ana said, hopping out of the car.

The old country bell rang as they pushed in the door. It was a loud doorbell from a different time. Rene began looking around at the various outdated snack cakes and melted candy bars. Ana took bottled water from an ice barrel long since depleted of ice. All that remained was tepid water in which the bottles floated. Rene opened a small cooler and immediately closed it. She and Ana held their noses. If there was anything worse than the smell of rotten fishing worms, Ana didn't know what it was. It was terrible before her extraordinary nasal abilities. Now it was unbearable.

"Oh yeah, been meaning to clean that out. What can I do ya for?" an older man said, coming from the back room, where Ana could see a recliner and hear a TV blaring in the background.

"Just been out riding today. Thought we would stop in and get us something to drink," Ana said, producing the water bottle from her arm.

"Sure thing. Let me ring that up for ya," he said.

Ana produced two dollars from her pocket and said for him to keep the change. Ana looked at Rene for any suggestions about what to do next.

"It has been a long time since I been up this way. It sure is pretty up here. My cousin said he was going to bring his girl up here to fish, but I can't remember for the life of me where he said they would be." Rene started walking to the counter. She had a big smile and did all the things a woman did to get her way. She acted super interested in anything the man had to say. She hung on his every word. Her behavior left him agreeable to having a conversation with the two lovely young ladies.

"I ain't seen nobody much today. All week, really. I just had that one couple come through yesterday, I think. Yeah, it was yesterday 'cuz the president was on the TV. I just don't know about that president of ours." He shook his head as if whatever the president spoke about was not in line with his political views.

"You know what? Maybe he said he was bringing that new girl-friend of his, Ana," Rene raised her eyebrows in a la-di-da manner.

"Well, she must not be as classy as you two are. That place they was staying at is all run-down. It needs to be done away with, if you ask me," the man said, shaking his head with disappointment.

"Oh, no, ewww, she sounds a little trashy," Rene said, holding her hand over her heart.

"Well, I don't know about that, but that old cabin is shabby like I said, and a woman like you wouldn't be caught dead in there," the man continued.

"Where is it?" Rene said, acting very conspiratorially.

"It's that old cabin up on Deer Camp Road. You know, where old Bucky used to stay before he got locked up back yonder." He pointed out the window up the road. "'Bout three miles up there on the right-hand side of the road. It's bad up there. Probably can't get a car up in there too easy," he said.

"Well, I'm glad you warned us. We sure don't want to run up on that." Rene giggled.

"You two better be getting on back home soon. It's gonna get dark, and people get turned around up here all the time." He stood straighter as if he was giving the soundest advice ever.

"Yeah, we sure will. Thanks so much. We will come back next time we go through here," Ana said, rushing to the door.

"You do that, pretty lady," the man said, staring at Rene the entire time.

Ana and Rene quickly got back on the road. They headed in the direction the old guy pointed. They drove five or six miles and decided that either they had missed the turn or the old man was senile. They found the closest turnaround spot and headed back toward the store. They drove slowly, looking at every slight turn they could find. Finally, a low-hanging tree branch camouflaged a home-made sign that said Deer Camp Road. Ana moved up the road a little bit farther and parked the car. They crossed the road quickly and ran up in the woods to find the hunting cabin.

After walking for about ten minutes, they saw the cabin up ahead. It was more of a shack. Rusty tin covered the roof. Several windows had plywood where the glass should be. The old chimney had several bricks missing. It reminded Ana of a child's missing teeth. Ana made a face at her mother as she smelled something similar to the decaying fishing worms. Rene shrugged. Ana motioned to her mother to come on. Rene joined Ana, and they moved stealthily to a window with the actual glass still in the frame. A man sat in a kitchen chair, with his head lying in his arms. He appeared to be sleeping until Ana saw the half-emptied liquor bottle on the table beside him. There was no glass, so he must have been chugging it straight from the bottle. Ana couldn't see the man's face, but it sure did look like the Patterson man from where she stood.

Rene pointed around the side to show Ana she planned to go around for another look. Ana nodded. She glanced over to where the driveway once had been before grass and potholes filled with water took it over. A beat-up old Pontiac was sitting there. The car looked almost as shabby as the cabin, but she went to take a look. The closer she got to the car, the stronger the pungent smell permeated from inside. She got two distinct odors. One was like dead worms. The other was blood Marci's blood.

"Psst psst!" Ana whispered, waving for her mother.

"Psst, really? God, what is that smell?" Rene held her nose for emphasis.

"Marci and I suspect there is something in that trunk," Ana said, patting the trunk with her hand.

"I'll pull the latch," Rene said, slowly opening the driver's side door.

The overhead light blasted on, and Rene wasted no time hitting it with her fist to extinguish the light. She found the latch, and the trunk lid released with a low popping sound. Ana held it closed until her mother rejoined her in the back of the car. There was no way she was going to open it without her. Ana slowly lifted the lid and peeked with one eye open into the darkness of the trunk. The sun was starting to set, making the whole thing even more creepy. The smell rushed out to meet them, and they were staring into the dead eyes of Marci's mother. It appeared she was brutally beaten, and there was one bright red line circling her neck. There was no more blood to spill from her lifeless body. She had bled out in whatever hellhole he had killed her. Her milky white eyes stared aimlessly into the evening sky. Ana turned and was almost sick from the sight. Rene gently took Ana's hand from the trunk lid and closed it quietly.

"Let's do this," Rene said. There was no sickness or remorse in her words, only revenge. There was no doubt the man in the cabin was guilty. He carried his proof with him in the trunk of his battered old car.

They didn't try to be quiet anymore. Instead, they stomped like two women on a mission to the front door of what was to be the last thing he would ever see. Ana kicked in the door solely for added effect. The man groaned a little, and one arm slipped from the table, but other than that, nothing. Ana ran over to the chair and kicked it over. Patterson spilled out onto the dust-covered floor. His head bounced off the floorboards loudly.

"Well, shit," Ana said, very irritated about his lack of conscious-ness. "What are we supposed to do now?" She looked at her mother as if she knew exactly what to do to sober up a drunk before she could torture and kill him.

"How in the world do I know?" Rene said, matching her daugh-ter's irritation.

Ana kicked the man's leg. "Hey, you piece of shit! Wake up!" she screamed, kicking him again in the gut.

He groaned a little and rolled over to his back. Rene picked up an old water bottle and poured it into his face. This did perk him up a little. He began to swipe at his face and muttered incoherent curse words under his breath. Ana reached down to his overly long, greasy hair and sat him up. She smacked him two times hard across his face causing his lip to bleed.

"What the fuck you doin'?" he said, beginning to come around.

"What you got out there in your truck, Patterson?" Ana said with a smart-aleck tone to her question.

This seemed to wake him up. He wabbled his head, trying to open his eyes to see who was talking. Ana, gripping his hair firmly, began to shake his head violently. She could hear his neck pop and crack. She didn't care if it broke, but she wanted to make him suf-fer a while first. His eyelids finally pulled free from each other, and he found him staring at Ana Reed. Patterson had only seen Ana once, but he knew instantly who she was. Ana had threatened him and his wife the last time they had to take the kid to her meeting. She told them she would take Marci, and they would never see her again. He smiled.

"What are you smiling at, you worthly, spineless shit!" Ana emphasized each word with a punch to the center of his face.

"I will fucking kill you!" he screamed, almost fully alert now and scrambling to free himself from her grasp.

"Oh, please try. I want you to. Let him get up, Ana. Let's see this boy hit somebody that will knock the hell out of him." Rene went to her child's side. She instantly resumed her role as a protective mother when this useless thing threatened her child.

"Oh, by all means, get up. Let's do this thing!" Ana released his hair, and he wobbled to his feet. Unfortunately, this wasn't nearly as fun because he was too drunk to know what was happening.

Patterson took a swing at Ana, who quickly reflected his blow.

"Oh my god, is that all you got?" Ana said, tormenting him.

Patterson stumbled forward, and Rene kicked his feet out from under him, and his face met the floor once again. Blood spurted from his nose and mouth as teeth flew out. Rene laughed out loud. She didn't even try to stifle it.

The wounded man staggered to a sitting position. He was struggling, and Ana thought it was funny how little he could take. This man had raped and killed his own daughter and was carrying his dead wife around with him was defeated with a couple of kicks and a punch or two. What a weak, pathetic textbook narcissist he was. If given a chance, Ana was sure he would blame the dead for making him kill them. That was the trick of the narcissist. It was never their fault. It is always because their mother didn't love them enough, or their father beat them. It was always somebody else's damn fault. What had Marci done to warrant his wrath? What had she done to provoke him?

Ana was a little hard on her stance for the mother. She knew the child had no choice but to remain in an abusive household, but Ana was sure this wasn't the first time the mother had suffered at the hands of this pig. Yet she chose to stay. She continued to give him another chance until he killed her little girl. Ana really had no sympathy for the rotting corpse in the car's trunk. Ana felt that the first time a woman was mistreated, she was a victim. The next she was an accomplice. She might have been taken off guard the first time, but any time after that shouldn't have come as a shock. Sadly though, the children paid the price most of the time.

Ana felt a raw, primal feeling building in her chest. Her face tingled, and it felt as though he had managed to hit her when she hadn't seen it. Her mouth was aching, and her skin twitched.

"Mom," Ana said, holding her hand against her cheek, signaling she was in pain. "What's happening?" Ana turned to let her mom see her face.

As Ana looked at her mother, she saw a whole new person standing in front of her. Rene's face was fuller, and her eyes glowed with a golden glow.

"Don't be afraid. This is what happened." Rene opened her mouth in a terrifying smile. Her beautiful incisors had grown into razor-sharp daggers in her mouth. It reminded Ana of every horror movie she had ever seen, and she started to back away from her mother.

"I don't know where you're going, but you might want to look in that mirror if you can see in it," Rene said, approaching her frightened daughter slowly.

Ana found a dirty rag on the edge of the sink and cleaned the disgusting mirror. What she saw was both horrifying and so cool all at once. Her face was fuller. Her eyes glowed with the same golden hew as her mother's. Her mother had spent a small fortune on her perfectly straight smile. The perfection the orthodontist tried so hard to achieve was something else now. Fangs protruded from her red swollen gums, and a tiny trickle of blood seeped from the wounds. Ana brought her fingers to her mouth and touched the points of her murder blades.

"Ana, get your fingers out of your mouth! This place is nasty!" Rene pulled her hand from her mouth.

"What do you think I'm going to catch? Mouth cooties?" Ana said with a wink.

"It's just gross. Don't," Rene said in a scolding tone.

When Patterson could actually register what he saw, he quickly hurried backward. He cleared the dirt with the seat of his jeans. His eyes bulged from their sockets, and his breath was quick and panicked. His heart pounded in his chest, and Ana could smell his fear. The closer she moved toward him, the faster the rhythm of his heart. He begged, as Ana was sure Marci had, for mercy. There would be none here today.

"I'm going to show you the same mercy you showed your sweet daughter. I'm gonna let you cry and beg. Did she beg you? Did she beg you to stop hurting her? I bet you liked that, didn't you, you sick bastard!" Ana reached down and, with one move, stood him up by his neck to face her.

"How does it feel to be afraid? How does it feel?" Ana screamed, not realizing she was squeezing out any air he might have to answer her. She loosened her grip so the creature could lie to her. "Tell me how it was her fault. Tell me how she teased you all the time. Tell me how her thirteen-year-old self asked for it!"

Ana was losing it now.

"No, don't tell me nothing!" Ana screamed as she sank her fangs deep into his throat.

She had never done this before, but she let nature guide her in her method. She sucked and drank from this scum. She tried not to think about what she was letting enter her body. She wasn't concerned about it being human blood. She was worried that this pedophile's blood would corrupt her body with his filth. She felt Rene's hand on her shoulder and felt a jerk as her mother's fangs sank into the other side of his motionless neck. Ana believed him to be in shock, like a zebra getting eaten alive by the lion. Ana felt Rene pull away, and Rene gently pulled Ana from her prey.

"No, Ana, not the last drop. Stop now. He's as good as dead," Rene said, coaxing her away.

Ana pulled away as instructed and let the disgusting thing fall to the floor. Rene pricked her finger with her fang and rubbed a tiny droplet of blood on the marks they had left on his skin. Ana watched as they closed.

"Now we make it look like an accident," Rene said. It almost frightened Ana how her mother knew just what to do in this situation. Ana guessed all the investigative shows she had watched had paid off.

The two killers fashioned a noose from a piece of cloth they found in the corner of the room. It appeared to be the remnants of a sheet. After putting the boot prints of the psycho's boots on the kitchen chair seat, Ana laid it on its side in the middle of the room. They tossed the noose over a beam in the ceiling of the room. Ana hoisted the dead man's body up, and Rene slipped the noose over it. They stood and watched as the last bit of life left his body. They removed all traces of their having ever been on Deer Camp Road and left the same way they came.

Neither spoke on their trip home. The two went to their separate bathrooms and showered. Both washed their clothes to rid them of the smell of that wretched man. They made their way to the kitchen for a late diner.

Neither Ana nor Rene spoke of that day ever again. They both knew that there would be many more days like those if the need arose. Ana felt it was her duty, and Rene felt a duty to her child. She would follow her through the bowels of hell if need be. She would hold her hand through it all. Ana could feel her mother's loyalty to her now more than ever, and she knew this changed the dynamic of their relationship forever.

Not only was Rene Ana's mother, but she was also her best friend. Rene was Ana's confidante, conspirator, advisor, and partner in crime. Ana was sure this would be an eventful ride, but she knew Rene would drive. Marci Patterson could rest in peace now, and whether her mother rested was of no concern to Ana.

Rene and Ana made sure the police knew a general location to find Patterson. His guilt had been too much, they would say. He just couldn't handle what he had done. He committed suicide. Oh, what a tragic loss. He must have needed help, they would say. Someone should have noticed, they would say. Who saw that Marci needed help? Who noticed that she was suffering? No one, but that was okay. Ana had issued punishment, and it felt so good.

The Working Years

Sometimes one learned to control the beast inside, but other times, the beast broke free to control them. Ana had to learn to reign in her demons from time to time and dole out punishments that fit the crime. It would have been easy to simply end the lives of those who were guilty of minor infractions, such as neglect or parental laziness. However, Ana felt those children deserved their guardians to have a chance. The ultimate punishments were reserved for the monsters that refused Ana's particular brand of rehabilitation. After sessions in her office with families in need of adjustments, Ana would take the adjustments to them. While the children slept peacefully in their beds, Ana would strike terror in the hearts of those who simply refused to get it.

Mr. and Mrs. Josh Thompson slept in their pristinely kept bedroom within their perfectly designed home. *Home* was a strong word to use. It was just a house. A home was where one felt safe and free to be themselves. This was more of a museum of finely crafted art and furniture that seemed to have never been used. Nothing seemed to be out of place. There was no dust on any surfaces and no stray cobwebs in the corners. Ana walked up the stairs to have a little talk with one of them. Ana knew this was the mask of a highly dysfunctional man.

Josh Thompson demanded complete perfection from both his wife and two children. Any small detail that wasn't in his eyes up to standard was met with swift extractions of basic human comforts. For example, the children would have to go days will nothing to eat. He called these fasting punishments. These punishments were designed to make them grateful for the little things. The children's fear ran so deeply in their core that they didn't dare partake in meals at their school. They feared that somehow he would know.

He forced his daughter to attend school unbathed and with no change in her clothing for a week because she had gone in a less-than-perfect presentation to a company picnic. She had the nerve to play and soil her lovely outfit. Her disheveled appearance mortified Josh. He thought his lesson would teach her to value cleanliness. The eight-year-old child had suffered ridicule and horrible teasing from her classmates. This was when the school called for assistance.

Ana had a plan for a little harmless retribution. Well, Josh might not see it as harmless, but he could rest assured it was the lesser of two evils. Ana stealthily made her way into the couple's bedroom. She crept over to Josh's side of the bed and knelt down to eye level with the bully.

"Wake up, sleeping beauty," Ana whispered. She covered his mouth as he jumped from being startled from sleep. She stared into his eyes.

"You will follow me quietly. Do you understand?" she whispered.

Mrs. Thompson stirred a little but rolled to her side and resumed snoring. Josh exited the bed and followed Ana down to the farthest corner of the house.

"Have a seat." Ana smiled, patting the back of the perfectly placed media chair.

Josh did as instructed, of course. Ana's mind-altering gaze left him no choice but to comply with every request.

"Now we are going to have a come-to-Jesus meeting. First, I want you to understand I have counseled you, instructed you, and all but begged you to do better for your kids. I know you think your way teaches them discipline, but teaching them fear is what it's really doing. You have an intense desire to keep up with the Jones. Isn't that the correct metaphor? I'm here to show you that a little imperfection is normal and makes the world a much more interesting place. You don't have to be just like everyone else, and you sure don't have to try to be better than anyone else either." Ana liked to explain why before she explained how she planned to fix the situation.

"Here's what we are gonna do, okay? You will lighten up on the kiddos, and you will follow the same rules as having been applied to them. You will go to the office every day this week wearing the same suit and no shower. You won't even shave. You will fast for three days. Well, you better drink some water. We wouldn't want you to dehydrate now, would we? You yourself believe this will do wonders for one's attitude, so we are gonna test that theory. You will see that this is extreme and that there are much better ways to correct your babies."

The Thompson family believed Josh had lost his mind. His outward appearance was so important to him, and he was looking a lot like a homeless person. Ana went out of her way to go by the locations he would be. She giggled. If this had gone on much longer, Ana was sure the family would have started making preparations for his stay at the local mental institution.

Ana's next visit with the Thompson family was completely different. Mr. Thompson did apologize for their less-than-professional appearance. They were all comfortable and Ana could see swimsuits under their baggy clothes. They were heading to the local water park for a family day. Ana couldn't have been more pleased by the outcome. After six months of weekly visits, Ana cleared them from future visits. She knew the transformation from strict authoritarian to sane, caring parent was complete.

Only once did Ana's strategy have an unwanted conclusion. Through no violence of her own, one client found themselves on the wrong side of a bottle of sleeping pills. Ana had entered the home, as she had done many times before. She spoke with Helen Ramzie, the grandmother of the child in Ana's care. Ana explained that Helen needed to relax. Helen wasn't a bad woman. She was very religious. Everything that went against the church's doctrine was deemed immoral and wicked. Ana had never thought her visits would haunt the woman so much. She had mesmerized her as she had done all the others, but the woman became convinced a demon was trying to possess her. To save her soul, the woman took her life. She left the demon nothing to inhabit.

Ana felt terrible about the outcome but thought if the woman was this unstable, she didn't need the child anyway. The little girl went to live with cousins who had two daughters of their own. The rest of her childhood was full of sleepovers and regular teenage pranks but no religious persecution. Ana watched the progression of her life. She left the mortal plane in her seventy-second year. She passed quietly in her bed. She left behind four children, to whom she had given wonderful lives. Ana could envision her husband waiting for her at the gates of paradise.

This was why Ana did what she did. These were the results she longed to see. Ana had the opportunity to see the lives play out from youth to the end. Sometimes, she patted herself on the back when one of her charges led extraordinary lives. She found the same pride in those who led regular lives too. She loved them all as if they were from her own flesh. She could not have children of her own, but she had thousands to call her own. When loss came, she grieved. When success happened, she celebrated. Ana felt wholly fulfilled. She felt nothing had been denied her.

Ana and her mother developed a bond that only grew stronger with the passage of time. Whatever Ana deemed necessary, Rene never questioned. Instead, she took up the task with pride. Her only goal in life was to make Ana's life count. Ana was crucial to these children, and Rene felt a little responsible for them. She enjoyed learning all the ins and outs of the system but didn't like how difficult the state made it for a regular worker to enact change. Rene wasn't a college-educated person, but she took her life experience and mixed it with Ana's degree. They made a dangerous team.

Ana loved her mother like no other. Her mother's gift to her was something she could never repay. Her mother had taught her everything about life and showed her many ways to help those she tried so desperately to save. Not only did they work together in the field, teaching the lessons, but they also spent endless hours poring over regular interventions for the families. Ana was grateful for her help in every aspect of her life.

Kat

Throughout Ana's life, she chose her relationships carefully. She understood the cost of friendship. Over time, the mortal walk of all acquaintances would end, and she would be left to grieve the created void. Fear was the driving factor in her decision, but sometimes one couldn't help with whom they bonded. Ana met her friend Kathlene Rogers while Kat was going through a nasty divorce. She offered to counsel the father of one of her children, which he refused. Kat was fifteen years Ana's senior, in human years. The two spent hours sitting around Kat's kitchen table, gossiping about one thing or another. Ana loved her time with Kat's two children and loved them like her own.

Kat had a son by the love of her life, but this was not to be. He passed away when her son was but a baby. Her daughter had another father, and he didn't do as well with parenting as anyone would have liked. Kat had many relationships and tried so hard to make them work, but there seemed to be problems with them all. Kat needed Ana, and she needed Kat. Ana lived vicariously through her. She watched as she struggled with love and helped when she could with the children, which were Kat's world. Ana was always intrigued about how much life could be squeezed into a few short years, and Kat had managed to do a lot of living.

Ana would often think about the ramifications of her friendship with Kat. As the years rolled on, Ana saw the effects of time on her friend's face and her very soul. Kat often spoke of those whom she had lost to death. The pain in her voice was the very description of grief. Sometimes the panic rose like bile in Ana's chest. She wasn't ready, nor would she ever be ready to let her go. Ana would never lose her mother, and it was a blessing when her grandmother had passed.

Her grandmother had suffered for a very long time, and her escape from the pain was truly welcome. Kat was Ana's closest companion, and she didn't want to ever lose her.

Ana decided to speak to Kat about the change. She decided their friendship was worth letting her know. Ana went to Kat's house as she had done many times over the years, but this time was special. This visit could save her life. They engaged in their regular banter and consumed entirely too much coffee. Kat knew something was up. She waited and waited for her friend to open up to her.

"So you gonna tell me what's got you so messed up?" Kat finally asked.

"Why?" Ana answered very nervously

"Ah, hell, we have known each other too long for this. What's going on? The quicker you tell me, the faster we can figure it out!" Kat had zero patience and became more irritated as the moments went by.

"Got something to show you." Ana stood and pushed her chair back under the table.

Kat looked at her with a confused expression on her face and tilted her head like a puppy trying to figure something out.

"I don't want you to die," Ana simply stated.

"Well, that's good 'cause I don't guess I was planning on it anytime soon." Kat shifted in her seat but still giggle a little bit.

"No, you don't get it. You are my best friend, and I can't bear the thought of you *ever* dying." Ana emphasized the *ever* part.

"You are starting to creep me out. What's going on, Ana?"

"There is really no good way to tell you how badly I have been lying to you. I guess the only way is to show you." Ana had mesmerized Kat many years ago so she wouldn't question Ana about remaining young and beautiful. Ana had always felt guilty about lying to her friend.

Ana stepped close to Kat and looked into her beautiful green eyes. "See me," she whispered.

Then she stepped back so Kat could have a better look. Kat only stared at her. All the color drained from her naturally rosy cheeks. She said nothing.

"Are you okay?"

"Hell no, I'm not okay! What in the world is going on here? How did you do that?" Kat jumped out of her chair and moved quickly to the far side of the room.

Ana moved slowly back to her seat. She wanted her friend to feel comfortable as she could during this discovery.

"Let me explain. It's not a trick, and I promise I can explain if you let me," Ana said calmly.

Kat took her seat tentatively. Ana slowly explained how all of it had come to pass. Cup after cup of coffee drowned the words as she spoke them. Kat really was her soul sister, her best friend. She had no judgment in her eyes.

"That's a lot," Kat said, resting her face in her hands. "That's a lot to take in." She was in shock but processing it all slowly.

"I know, but what I'm trying to tell you is, I can do this for you." Ana was pleasantly surprised by her response so far.

"Do what for me?" Kat asked, looking at Ana like she had completely lost her mind.

"You can be like me. You don't have to die, Kat. You can be just as you are, forever."

Kat sat quietly for a moment and smiled. "Nah, I'm good. I have had a hard life, girl. I want to get out of here someday and see my mom and the only man I will ever love. You can't really get that, but someday you might. I'm thankful for every little bit of time, but I will be grateful for the release from it too. I miss my mom. I miss so many people who are gone. I think I would rather go be with them," she said this with great sadness in her voice.

Ana couldn't believe what she was hearing. She never thought Kat would say no. She never fathomed a time Kat would give up, but here it was. Tears welled up in Ana's eyes, and she pleaded her case again. As she spoke, Ana realized how selfish she sounded. She wasn't just doing this for Kat; she was doing this for herself. She didn't want her to go, so she was willing to see Kat suffer and miss her loved ones forever. It wasn't fair. Would we turn the entire world not to feel the pain of loss? That wasn't reasonable. Kat had children and someday grandchildren. Would we turn them all in order not to lose them? Again, the answer would have to be no.

As the tears found their way down Ana's cheeks, she respected Kat's decision.

"I can take all this away, Kat. I can make you not remember anything we have talked about today. I can make you see me as I was before. You don't have to know this, but I will have to ask you if you want me to readdress this again someday. Like, if you get sick or for any reason you say. I will come back, and we will have this whole day again. Then we can see if you still feel the same." Ana's heart was breaking, but this was the only way. She needed hope. Maybe this way, Kat would change her mind.

"You can, but I don't believe time will do anything but make me want them more. You can try. Just make me forget, okay?" Kat knew she couldn't handle this secret. She knew she might have a weak moment and choose something she could never take back.

Ana moved over to Kat. She cried harder as she put her hands on Kat's tear-streaked face. "Forget all you have heard today, and don't see as I am but as I should be. Then when you awaken, you will be laughing and believe the tears came from joy."

The years passed, and Ana listened to the stories Kat told. She listened to how much Kat missed her mother. Kat always checked the sky for butterflies, which she believed was a sign that her mother was near. Kat drifted off into memories of her late husband when she heard anyone playing guitar. She often spoke of his talented ear for music. Kat told of the reunion she would have with them someday.

Ana planned to ask Kat again later in her life, but she wouldn't get that chance. Kat was a youthful spirit, and age hadn't touched her how it had other people her age. Ana believed she had time. The urgency wasn't there. At the age of sixty-two, Kat was a rare blood disorder victim, and there was no time to save her. She left this world within hours of her admittance into the hospital. Ana had truly believed she would be okay. Kat was tough. She never had more than a common cold in her life. Ana hadn't rushed to her side.

When the call came that Kat hadn't made it, Ana was in shock. Her elevated emotions crippled her. The very breath she took caused pain in her chest. She and her friend had been like one person. If one felt joy, the other celebrated their happiness. If one experienced pain, the other felt the same. The bonds of their connection were unbreakable, and now Ana's other half, her soul sister, was gone. Ana would have never changed Kat without her blessing, so Ana chose to find joy in Kat's happy reunion. For the first time since Ana's transformation, she knew no such reunion awaited her. She would forever mourn the loss of her human companions. She would always bury the ones she loved. She vowed never to get that close again. She would allow only those with her gift inside her circle.

Ana would whisper messages to her friend into the wind. She hoped they would ride the breeze to reach her. The wind appeared to be an excellent messenger because signs appeared that gave Ana comfort. Butterflies landed unnaturally on her cheek, and there were always feathers in her path. Each time Ana smiled and knew her friend would never be truly gone. Ana would remember and treasure every moment she had with Kat, and she would never forget the meaning of a true friend.

Life Goes On

A na never fully recovered from Kat's passing, and she did just as she planned. She developed close relationships only with those of her kind. There was safety in that choice. Kindred spirits found their way into her life, which lessened her grief. Ana became more aware of the senseless cruelty of the human species. She watched as humans fought terrible wars over nothing more than control. Those in power were ebbing closer and closer to a place from which they could never return. People grew desensitized to death. To some, killing was nothing more than a sport. Great numbers of humans washed their hands in basins of blood just to prove a point.

The cruelty of nature only matched the cruelty of humanity. Nature waited and watched as humanity tried to destroy all she built, one by one. Time after time, nature found remedies to counter the ignorance of man. How many times would she have to save them? How long would nature tolerate human ignorance? Great numbers of nature's creations were being destroyed due to man's insatiable appetite. Nature's own beauty was raped and pillaged for that one great snapshot. Beasts that lived from day to day in complete balance were pushed to extinction. Why did man continue to believe they were so superior? Why did they feel the scales should always tip in their favor?

The air was so polluted that the very earth's protection eroded in the sky. Nature's tears melted the glaciers, and the seas rose to meet man, yet there was no response. The very core of human survival was under attack, and their focus lay in the paper currency that wouldn't even warm them when it burned. As man mixed the elements to kill one another, nature did nothing to stop it. Each segment of the world designed its own destruction. Life was too fragile for this level of hate. Ignorant reasoning to destroy one another eventually would kill them all.

In nature, creatures didn't hate because of outward appearance. They were not bothered by the choices of other beasts if their choices did not affect their lives. They never attacked only to make another comply. They killed to eat or protect their lives or the lives of their offspring. The human race found many reasons for their treachery.

It wasn't a quick demise, as anything successful wasn't. It was slow and had no mercy. The chemical warfare countries released into nature's water and air were not contained inside any borders. It passed through the very bodies of those it was meant to destroy. It crossed the seas in its waters and made its way from the guilty to the innocent with ease. It left in its wake sheer destruction. The essential functions of man were rendered useless. The lungs hardened, and the blood boiled in their veins. Their weakened hearts ceased to beat. Man created no escape plan. No remedy existed for their own creation. It grew like a parasite until nothing could control it.

The immortals watched the devastation. They planned and prepared for the inevitable end of humanity. The essence of man was the ultimate sustenance for the living dead. Other creatures would suffice, but the human blood was complete. Human blood housed immortal power, and merely surviving was not an option. No empathy reined in the hearts of the immoral for the human race. There was only a problem, and this problem needed a solution.

Ana knew something big was coming, but she didn't realize just how big it would be. She watched the news that continuously played twenty-four hours a day. It described a terrible infirmity that killed in great numbers. No one took the blame for the plague. Everyone blamed one another for the invasion. Ana believed it was a mixture of all their plots that had joined together to create the ultimate weapon. She talked to her mother at length about the possibility of this creation mutating into its own version of death. How ironic would it be if all the planning in the world started planning on its own? The artificial intelligence created by man learned to reason. Why couldn't this living element do the same?

Day by day, the broadcast became more desolate. Humans recorded more deaths than at any other time in history. Mutations arose, just as humans found breakthroughs to defeat it. This foe did what humanity did not do. It learned to protect itself. It learned to evolve and create structures within its own makeup to survive. What foe was there that could mutate and thrive while a whole species died?

Ana bounced down the stairs in her running shoes. Rene stood drinking her morning coffee. She swore that, without it, she couldn't function at all. Ana felt the same, so she quickly poured a cup for herself.

"Any good news today?" Ana asked, pointing her cup toward the TV.

"Nope, never," Rene answered.

"Looks like they could figure this out," Ana said.

"Don't look good right now," Rene said.

"Yeah, I know, but what are ya gonna do?" Ana said, tightening her shoelace.

"Ready to run?" Rene said.

Ana took a big drink from her cup and put it next to the sink for her next cup. The two started out the door and toward the park. It was their usual route. They loved to run there. The park was full of families enjoying a nice, mild day. Kids played in the sand piles and on the swings. Mothers sat on the benches, watching them for any signs of danger. It always reminded Ana of mother geese protecting their goslings, ready to flog and bite any intruder on their children's space. But something felt a little off today. Ana couldn't really put her finger on the feeling. She noticed her mother scanning the area as though she felt it too. She was another mother goose, and she would do more than flog any intruder.

Ana and Rene stopped dead in their tracks as they heard three popping sounds. They rang through the park, like fireworks, as they were sent into the sky. Yet there were no fireworks. They looked from left to right until they found the origin of the sound. A young man about nineteen or twenty stood there, holding a small-caliber handgun. He began to empty the contents into the air. The metal landed in various bystanders' bodies with a thud. Ana ran as quickly as she could without activating her vamp speed. Rene was right on her heels. They took the man down as the last bullet flew from the barrel, missing Ana by inches. Rene held the boy in place on the ground, and Ana threw the weapon out of his reach.

Ana rolled the boy over onto his back and noticed blood coming from his nose. Then blood trickled from the corner of his mouth. Ana knew they hadn't caused this much damage to him; they had just knocked him down. Blood then rolled from his eyes like rivers of bloody tears. He struggled to breathe. He gasped like a fish out of water, and Rene moved him to his side to help clear his airway. Nothing would save this young man from this attack on his body. The killer was silent and attacked him from the inside out. They watched as he drowned in his own blood.

"What the hell?" Ana said.

Rene moved slowly away from the boy. She watched as the crowd slowly came out of their cover.

"Let's go," Ana said.

The two moved so quickly they were sure no one saw them leave. They rushed home and turned on the TV to see what had just happened. Ana changed out of her soiled clothes and poured herself another cup of coffee. She knew this would only cause her jitters to worsen, but she wanted the hot beverage to comfort her. Rene did the same. They sat like silent statues in front of the messenger of doom, as they now referred to the news broadcasts.

"Murder was on the mind of Christopher Mills today at Honey Suckle Park. Mills opened fire, killing two and wounding one person. He may be the victim of the strange illness afflicting many across the country. New terrifying symptoms are arising daily. Doctors are at a loss as to what mutations may occur. More to come later, at six," the broadcaster announced.

Ana continued to watch the channel as they reported one story after another. Each story was more brutal than the next. This seemed like something from a terrible movie. People were committing unthinkable crimes or just falling dead in the street.

"We have a special report from our man on the street Patrick Robins," the broadcaster said.

"Yes, thank you, Regina. The community is in a panic right now as hundreds of calls come into 911. EMS is overwhelmed, and local fire department personnel are being sent to handle the overload in calls. Police units have been called to several domestic violence situations and some acts of nothing short of terrorism in the area. The public is urged to shelter in place, and if any symptoms arise in the home, the public is encouraged to seek medical assistance. Isolate the infected person and use extreme caution. Strange, violent outbursts and feral behavior have been observed."

The broadcast flashed from frame to frame. One man lay burning in the street after dousing himself with gasoline and striking a match. A woman knelt screaming by his side. Another showed a woman in a sundress being mowed down by the police as she welded a large butcher's knife. Several clips were of people with blood pouring from their eyes and ears stepping into traffic. Finally, a lady stumbled down the street with what appeared to be a baby doll dangling from her arm. Ana could only hope it was a doll. Ana turned from the screen. She could bear no more.

"What is going on?" Ana asked.

"I have no idea," Rene answered.

The phone rang, and Rene immediately answered.

"Hey, Nick," Rene said.

"Hey, I know you have been watching everything that has been happening. Don't be alarmed, okay? We have all this under control. The people our kind have placed in charge have asked that we come together for a while until this is all over. The Virginia District is to meet here in Richmond. You will need to get on the road quickly. Don't bother to pack. We have all you will need. Just get moving. Now," Nick said. He wasn't making a suggestion. He was instructing his children.

"You want us at the Seven? Is that good?" Rene asked.

"Yeah, just get moving," Nick said.

Rene didn't have to tell Ana twice. They both grabbed their purses out of habit and headed for the door. The drive was terrifying even to the immortals. Vehicles sat on the sides of the interstate and some in the middle of the interstate. Humans walked aimlessly in the middle of the heavy traffic. One man wore one shoe and was disheveled and bleeding. He fell graveyard dead on the centerline, and the traffic never slowed their pace. Rene and Ana had no idea where everyone was going, but they had a clear destination for themselves. Nothing was going to slow them down. Neither woman was sure what was to come, but they trusted their makers to the fullest.

Four hours of strategic driving ended with a stop in the parking lot of the Seven. They quickly gained entrance with a single knock.

"So glad you got here safely," Tori said, hugging Rene tightly.

Nick kissed Ana's cheek and held her hand tightly.

"Let's sit and get you caught up," he said, leading the ladies up to the apartment.

The group poured some drinks and sat on the plush furniture that Tori had definitely picked. This room was white and pastel. Of course, no man would pick this décor, but it was beautiful and elegant. Everything matched to perfection. Ana was almost afraid to touch anything. She didn't want to mess anything up with her clumsy nature.

"You two don't need to worry. That's the first thing. Our leaders, whom we call the council, have everything under control. They have seen this coming for a very long time. They have made arrangements for our species' survival. The plan may seem drastic, but it's the only way," Nick began to explain.

"I don't like the sound of this," Ana said.

"Yeah, we didn't either in the beginning. The human race is on its way out. That's clear. They have destroyed themselves with this chemical warfare. Our kind has been working to ensure their survival for our use, not out of kindness to them. We rely on the essence of man to remain strong. There was no choice but to do what had to be done here. Great systems have been devised to house the strongest of humans. Genetically superior specimens will survive due to our intervention. These systems are called dome farms. Immortal beings will be allowed to feed and utilized these farms. The council believes this is a small price for the human race to pay to ensure their survival," Nick explained.

"So to 'house,' you mean to detain?" Ana asked.

"These people were doomed to die a terrible death. All walks of life are represented within the domes. To live meant to live this way. No one would choose death. I don't care what they say. No one would choose death," Tori said.

"What exactly is happening to them?" Rene asked.

"The chemicals they released have slowly attacked the bloodstream in humans. It caused the blood to thicken in the brain and for tumors and clots to form. This causes the brain to misfire as it tries to counter the attack. This is why you see the erratic behavior. Others die from pneumonia-like symptoms. That's why they didn't detect it for so long. We knew something was wrong with the blood a long time ago. The remaining few are protected now, living in the domes. The air and water are filtered and cleaned to ensure their survival. The greatest minds of many generations have come together to guarantee success," Nick explained.

Ana couldn't respond because she didn't really feel guilty. Humans had done this to themselves. They allowed greed to destroy them. She was witness to the end of an era. As the Southerners had done hundreds of years before, she watched as a way of life ended and a new one began. Even though this came gradually with the first symptoms and deaths, the second wave was violent and moved across the earth like the aftershock of a great earthquake.

"We will be fine here for as long as it takes. We have been preparing for this since we first learned about it. I know you are wondering why we didn't warn you. We didn't want you to panic. We have it all under control. We will stay put here until the council tells us what to do next," Tori said.

Tori showed the ladies to their rooms. Rene stayed in the room she had once called her home. She fondly remembered her time here during her transition. No matter how long it had been, it still felt like coming home to your parent's house for Christmas vacation.

Ana settled into the room down the hall from her mother. She was pleasantly surprised to see everything was just as Tori had said. Everything was perfect. She opened her closet door to find a full assortment of garments for any occasion. There were many pairs of designer shoes on the rack and comfortable shoes as well. Ana knew the more casual ones would get the most use. Her drawers were full of everything she would need. She began to realize their stay would be extensive. Tori had even selected Ana's favorite colors. The walls were a soft yellow, almost a golden tone. Sleek, rich violet fabric covered the windows, and the bedding mirrored its class. The room was elegant and regal, just as Ana would have described Tori herself.

Richmond Life

Ana and Rene remained welcome guests in Tori and Nick's home for a very long time. Thousands perished every day, and all the immortals could do was watch and wait. Nick attended meetings with the council. He brought back details of the progress that immortals had made. The evolution of man took thousands of years, but the destruction did not.

News broadcasts kept Ana informed. Twenty-four-hour coverage documented the fall of an entire species. The network one chose to watch decided which version of the truth one would hear. One network leaned heavily to one side of the political podium, while the other tilted just as far in the opposite direction. Stubbornness never allowed either to admit defeat. Both sides would rather die than come together, even in the face of such a worthy opponent. Politicians were not the answer to anything. The doctors and scientists were not fast enough to stop the speed of this monster, so what did a suit think they could do?

Ana grew to know every anchor that remained on her channel of choice. Over the years, she watched as work colleagues mourned the loss of their fellow work family members. No one was immune, and no one was safe. The one anchor who had remained since the beginning was Ric Robins. Ana felt there was a little something off about that. He never missed a day and never seemed to suffer even a symptom, suggesting he was infected. Every original person at the network was dead, but there stood Ric every day. He appeared to be as healthy and strong as he had the first time she had seen him. He had a little salt-and-pepper hair at his temples that seemed new, but other than that, he was fine. Boredom caused Ana to focus more energy on that than was needed.

Ana found it sad that every child she had saved was gone. Either by age or the effects of this illness, they were all gone. Her life's work was over. She wondered what she would do now that there were no humans to save from the brutality of one another. Many would have to find new paths in this new world. There would be no need for many occupations. Doctors, lawyers, and many high-paying jobs were now useless. She would have to think about it for a while. She knew she would have to find something to make her feel useful, or why even bother living for eternity?

As the cities emptied of their residents, Rene and Ana enjoyed visiting every building in the area. They first visited common tourist places, like museums, libraries, and art galleries. Then they thought it might be fun to snoop through the mansions and unique homes in the area. No one was left to live in these structures anymore. What had once been a sign of wealth and power were now nothing more than empty shells. The two never invaded the space of people hanging on to life, but these spaces were growing harder to find. So they made up a game. They tried to guess what the people did for a living, what their names were, and how old they had been. They would then snoop through all the personal items to find the answers. Ana never got it right, but Rene was surprisingly good at the game.

Ana remembered where they found the last living human outside the farms. As Ana and Rene walked up into the yard, they heard someone coughing. As they opened the front door, they asked if anyone was home. They knew they were because they could smell the horrible stench of death coming from them. Ana walked down a narrow hallway to a back bedroom. Inside was a woman of maybe thirty-five lying on her bed. She was frail and pale as a corpse. Her eyes were closed, and her breathing was labored.

"You have to get out of here. It's not safe," the lady whispered.

Ana was shocked that the woman could even form a sentence, and she was impressed by the woman's concern for her safety.

"You just rest now. We will be fine. We will stay right here with you, okay?" Ana said, pulling the sheet over the woman's bare leg.

The woman moaned, and Ana felt so sad for her. She wished the dark gift could cure this illness, but for some reason, it couldn't.

Nick had said that since this was a man-made thing, he believed this was why their gift couldn't help the infected. This woman deserved better than to die alone. Finding anyone alive in this world today was unlikely, and the two agreed this would probably be the last they would ever see.

They would stay with her until the end. Watching a mortal death was always sad, but the thought of something awaiting her after this was wonderful. She would experience what Ana and Rene never would.

Ana offered the woman food and drink, but the woman could not take either. The woman's inability to breathe was sickening. Ana tried every position she could think of to ease her suffering, but nothing helped. She wiped the sweat from her brow and talked to her. She didn't really have anything to talk to the woman about, so she just talked about anything. She spoke about the recent weather and how the sunset made it look like the sky was ablaze. Every so often, the woman would smile as if she could see just what she was describing. Ana covered her with blankets when the tremors shook her body. Then she would take the covers off when she would seem too hot. Ana and Rene did anything they could to help this person they had never met.

Blood began to pool in the woman's eyes. Ana knew it wouldn't be long now. As the woman's suffering intensified, Ana wanted to end her pain. Rene did not. She believed this woman deserved to fight to the end. Rene saw this woman as a warrior, and she should have a warrior's death. She should go down on her feet, not on her knees. The woman's eyes closed, and peace found her. Ana cried and felt a sense of defeat. Ana knew this was the end of the world as she had known it, even though it had been gone on for a long time.

Rene and Ana walked outside to see where they could lay this unnamed woman to rest. As they made their way to the back of the house, they noticed an old play structure. It sat like a temple to the youth of the past. Ana saw two mounds of dirt that seemed to be out of place for the area. There were two homemade crosses, which marked the graves of what appeared to be children. Between the two was a plaque that read, "Here lie the bodies of Christopher Allen

Creed, age eight, and Ethan James Creed, age eleven, beloved children of Amilia Lenore Creed. May we meet again in paradise."

The nameless lady now had her identity restored, and Ana was thankful.

Ana and Rene made another marker and plague. It read, "Here lies the body of Amelia Lenore Creed, mother of Ethan and Christopher Creed. May she find peace in the arms of her family."

Rene and Ana locked her house up as though someone would be breaking in to steal from the family they had grown to love. The two headed home with a sense of satisfaction. They had done a good thing for the lady, and they wished everyone could have that.

"Hey, we were beginning to think you ran away," Tori said.

"Nah, had a rough day. There was this lady, and she wasn't doing good. She had the sickness, and we stayed with her until she passed," Ana said.

"That's terrible but so cool that y'all was with her. I never liked it when people left here alone," Tori said.

"What are y'all doing today? Did you need us for something? Was that why you thought we ran away?" Rene asked, trying to get off the depressing topic.

"Well, the council has something fun for us to do for a change," Tori explained.

Nick came walking down the stairs like a reject from the *National Geographic*. He wore cargo shorts, a button-up khaki shirt, hiking boots, and a floppy Aussie hat. The women tried not the laugh, but it was definitely hard.

"What in the world are you wearing?" Ana asked, snickering.

"This is quite appropriate for the day, I assure you," Nick said in his best Aussie accent.

All three women laughed out loud this time.

"Okay, what are we doing that you have to be dressed like the crocodile hunter?" Rene said.

"It's a surprise. Everybody load up and let's go," Nick said.

Everybody piled into a soft-top jeep that was sitting in the driveway. This vehicle was clearly an extension of Nick's costume for the day. The trip was short, and it didn't take long for the ladies to figure out where they were going. A half-moon-shaped sign sat lonely and abandoned on the outskirts of town. It said, "Richmond Valley Public Zoo." Immortals had taken great care to ensure the remaining humans' safety by keeping the deadly predators under lock and key. Their time for captivity was through, and they deserved to be free. A different predator was in charge now, and bars would contain those who dared to enslave the beasts.

The animals remained reserved and skeptical of their caretakers. They had grown accustomed to their presents, but they sensed the danger the immortals presented. The group respected their fear and opened the enclosures and moved out of the way so the animals could venture into freedom. Ana found great satisfaction in the release of the great animals. She watched as nature reclaimed her children. One species after the next was moved outside the confines of their prisons. From the great to the small, all were set free. Each animal was given ample time to clear out, and then the next would be freed. Great elephants wandered slowly down the once-busy street. Lions took to the hills at full force. The eyes of the great beast were full of wonder at their new surroundings.

The last to wander free was the greatest of the primates. As the adult silverback lumbered out, he stood tall and struck his chest in domination. Even though he had never experienced freedom in the wild, he now welcomed it. This environment wasn't one he would have known in nature, but it was now his to survey. Offspring of the great king held tightly to their mothers, barely glancing up from her fur. Ana couldn't help but remember the passage "Where ever thou goest, I will follow" as the group, in single file, ventured into their new normal. Every door was disabled, and the outer gate was removed entirely, just as the council requested. It was a show of solidarity from one beast to another.

Ana took a moment to let it all sink in. Everything man shrove so hard to control had flipped the script in the end. Even the animals enslaved for human pleasure were the last to stand freely in the sun. Confinement was reserved for the guilty, and in this case, that was man. Certain groups of humans knew the terror of imprisonment. Some knew enslavement in the cruelest ways. However, this was not the case for all of humanity. The powerful never knew suffering, as did the weak. In a way, this seemed to be justice for all those wronged by the actions of others. The powerful and the weak were the same now.

If the truth were told, there were no powerful humans left alive. The only ones who could truly survive were those who knew how to survive. To Ana, the ones who suffered injustice in life seemed to be the most resilient. They seemed to be more able to adapt to anything life presented them. Ana chose to believe that the most horrid of humanity had been erased. Those who remained were those who never stood a chance in the mortal world. The poor, the weak, and the powerless were now the ones to rebuild the human race. What a powerful breed of man this would be, sired by the very men the powerful meant to hold down in poverty and suppression. The offspring only existed for the consumption of the immortal. Ana couldn't help but cheer for the human race's success. She hoped they would be greater than they had ever dreamed.

Going Home

Ana grew accustomed to this new way of living, but she still missed the old. Her kind now populated the earth, and no one had to hide or be conscious of their unnatural behaviors. She met many good friends who shared her interests. Ana tried many new things. She wanted to feel relevant in this new world. Rene told her many times just to enjoy herself. There was no sense in wanting a project all the time, but Ana wasn't built that way. She felt a drive to accomplish things and a need to help others. Tori and Nick supplied their every need. There were always fresh blood bottles, and every new device one could imagine. Tori loved to shower Rene and Ana with gifts. She wanted their lives to be comfortable and easy.

Rene knew they couldn't stay in Richmond forever. Ana needed more. She needed something to do. So Rene decided that they would go home to the mountain if Ana wanted to go. They would see what remained of their old lives and start to build a new one.

"Good morning, angel face," Rene said.

"Good morning," Ana answered.

"Hey, I was thinking about something. How do you feel about going home? I understand if you don't want to, but we could just go and have a look-see. What do you think?" Rene asked, pouring Ana a cup of coffee.

"When can we go? Do you think there is anybody there?" Ana asked excitedly.

"I don't know, but there will be two when we get there," Rene said.

"Sounds good to me," said Ana.

Ana almost felt a sense of relief at the thought of home. She couldn't wait to go. Nick and Tori had gone to a council meeting in

New York for a few days, so Rene called them to let them know their plans. The adoptive parents would miss their baby birds but wanted them to spread their wings and enjoy all the world had to offer. They told them many times that Richmond would always be their home. They encouraged them to come back anytime they wanted to come, day or night. Rene really did feel like a child when she spoke to them, but something was comforting in it too.

The groups that chose to be family in this new world were tight. Their bonds were unbreakable. It was rare that actual blood relatives remained together. Rene and Ana counted themselves blessed to share the gift of forever. The two packed the most vital of their acquired Richmond possessions and loaded them into a bright-yellow hummer. Ana would have never chosen such a vehicle in her old life. It was expensive to buy and costly to keep fueled up, but now it didn't cost a thing. The council maintained the roadways and kept the fueling stations open at all times. It was a given that these things were just there. Ana never wanted to take it for granted, though. She knew how quickly the world could change. She had seen it already.

Ana learned all she could about anything she could, but gas refining was well beyond her level of interest. She would just hope others stayed motivated enough to keep her tank full. The drive back to the mountain was enjoyable. There was little traffic on the roadways nowadays. It was beautiful to see the terrain change from city to rural as they traveled. Ana could smell the difference in the air. The immortals went to great pains to keep the comforts of humankind available, but Ana noticed the small things they had let fall to the wayside. Grass grew wildly in the medians, and tree branches hung over the roadways. Humans would have seen great danger in these things, but the immortals had no fear of them.

Ana watched out the car window and saw several immortals traveling or working on different projects along the way. Immortals used the fueling stations just as they were always used. Travelers refueled their vehicles and themselves. Immortals stopped for bottled blood or human snacks. There were even snacks made for immortal consumption. Ana often laughed at the names given to these new products. Items that resembled human chips had names like BBQ

O chips or sour cream and onion A chips. They baked the essence of man into the chip. It was ingenious, really. Ana would have never thought of it, that was for sure.

There was no currency in this new world. Everything ran on the honor system. There was never a need to hoard items as they were always well stocked and accessible. Ana wouldn't mind traveling and helping replenish supplies sometimes to contribute to the process. That would be something she could do to feel helpful. She made a mental note of that. She was amazed by how much preparation had gone into every aspect of daily life. The last hour or so of the trip was exciting, and Ana could hardly wait to be home.

"I was thinking…," Ana said.

"Oh no," Rene said, smiling.

"Very funny. I thought we could clean up around here and get it livable again. Maybe fix up some of the more touristy places, and people might want to come here to visit again," Ana said.

In the end, the mountains had become a destination for retirees and tourists for some time. Great numbers came for miles around to see the leaves changing in fall. They gathered for great conventions of local music. Bluegrass was the music of choice in this region, even though Ana didn't care for it much. Others called it a violin, but it was a fiddle. In the mountains, people played better than those classically trained. People in this area did what they called playing by ear. They needed no graph-lined paper with notes written on them. They played from the depths of their soul. Ana was sure some immortals still played the old-time bluegrass music. She would see whom she could find to revitalize this important local history.

"I think people would come. It is so beautiful here, and a lot might have missed it. You might be on to something, Ms. Ana Fanna," Rene said.

She always had a way of coming up with some unique, slightly irritating variation of Ana's name. Ana always smiled and showed the respect her mother had earned, even though she wanted to roll her eyes in irritation.

"It really is beautiful. There aren't any big attractions close by, so you're right. A lot might have missed it," Ana said.

"There is the attraction," Rene said, holding her hand up to the windshield. She pointed to the mountain.

"Totally agree. We will brainstorm this and figure it out. It will be a fun project for us," Ana said.

"It will take time and hard work, but all we have is time, right?" Rene asked.

Ana leaned back and enjoyed the rest of the trip. She felt surprisingly whole again. Even if it was the mountain, something to save was still something to save.

As the house came into view, Ana felt a warm, pleasant familiarity wash over her. Even though Richmond had been their home for a very long time, this was home. The feeling was like a warm hug or wrapped in a cozy blanket on a cold day. A certain sense of safety and belonging came from nowhere else on earth other than returning to the place you were raised. Ana and Rene walked into their home as if returning from a week's vacation. They threw their purses on the counter and plopped in their usual spots on the couch. The house smelled musty and maybe a little damp. Many years of dust had accumulated on every surface of the home.

"First things first, we have to clean this place up," Rene said, slapping the couch cushion and watching the dust fog the entire space.

"Ewwww, yes. Gross," Ana said.

Rene went around the house and opened every window and door. Electricity was on in every dwelling with a switch box, so the ceiling fan spun at full blast. It blew all the stagnant air out of the house. It made it seem better almost instantly. Rene walked into the kitchen to find Ana staring at the stainless steel refrigerator. She wrinkled her nose and stuck her tongue out.

"I can't even imagine what's in there," Ana said, pointing to the container of nasty smells.

"How about we push it onto the porch, throw open the doors, and run? Let it air out a while before we tackle the cleaning?" Rene suggested.

"Still doesn't sound fun, but what choice do we have?" Ana said.

Rene and Ana slid the fridge out onto the back porch with no problem. The two picked it up by the corners and set it into the yard.

"On the count of three, open, and run," Rene said.

She grabbed the fridge side, and Ana grabbed the freezer side.

Rene yelled, "Three!" Then the two opened it and ran just as they had planned. Apparently, the years had killed the bacteria that caused the rancid smells they expected to find. However, it still needed to be cleaned thoroughly. The next vital thing was the bathrooms. That was a quick process. Bleach, scrub, and rinse was the strategy to get them all spick and span. Rene and Ana decided to go to the nearest Pickup for supplies soon. That was one tricky thing. Supply and food stores were spaced far apart from one another. Human food wasn't a necessity, so it was considered a luxury.

Rene would have a two-hour trip to the closest Pickup, which was what they called these locations. One could find anything they could possibly want. They just had to go a little way to find them. If you needed something that wasn't in stock, all one did was ask for it. They guaranteed it in thirty days. Everything was in season some-where in the world. Just as Ana longed for her old life in the DSS, so did the everyday immortal. Those who enjoyed buying and selling goods still enjoyed it. They enjoyed making people happy with new things to try. They enjoyed being able to fulfill someone's desire, even if it was for a wine they hadn't tasted in a while.

An immortal would simply mesmerize humans in the old world to gain entrance into elite places or obtain rare things. This was much easier, and Ana felt better about it. Ana always felt like she was just stealing when she took whatever she wanted. She was just stealing. Ana liked it being free much better. Humans worked hard for what they had. Who were they to just take it from them? Rene had explained that taking it by asking was better than what some did to acquire what they wanted. That went for both humans and immortals alike.

Ana was a grown woman at the time of her change, but she always wanted to go to Disney World. She thought how much bet-ter it would be since there would be no long lines and crazy prices to pay for the experience. She loved the parks, and she was glad other immortals did as well. They kept the dream alive for everyone. The beloved characters remained forever beautiful in their uniquely designed kingdoms. Immortals continued to do the things they enjoyed in their previous lives. Great movies and music were not lost to the loss of the human race. The immortals carried on the arts. After all, they were once humans too. Ana did miss the children, but it was an evil that couldn't be avoided. Ana and Rene planned a trip to their local farm to check out the setup there. Ana didn't enjoy going as much as Rene did, but she would go every so often that her mother wouldn't worry about her lack of "fresh food."

Ana woke early the following day and started making plans for her day. Rene was going to the Pickup, so Ana had time just to mess. Shorts, a T-shirt, and running shoes were the attire for the day. She thought a run would help her focus on the schedule she needed to make.

As Ana jogged casually through the neighborhood, she stopped here and there to clear debris from her path. Basic clean-up was the first order of business. The only sounds were birds chirping, and Ana could hear a dog barking somewhere in the distance. This was such a peaceful place. She turned and made her way back home.

She saw a truck sitting in the yard of the house next door. She decided that would be a great work truck. Ana was surprised to find the keys still in the ignition. The truck hadn't been sitting very long because even though the motor protested, it began to come alive.

Rumble, rumble, rumble, the truck growled, but then the steady hum of the engine replaced its coughing sounds. She was pleased to find almost half a tank of fuel as well. This day was starting great so far.

She let the truck sit and idle while she snooped into the shed beside the house. She found a rake and a pair of shears. She popped into the neighbor's garage and found another rake, a hoe, and a shovel. A floral pair of gardening gloves would be an excellent addition to her wardrobe. The gloves were not necessary but would keep her hands clean and dry. She had a great collection of working gear. She had never really done yard work before, as her mother always hired the little Kerns boy to do her gardening. Ana saw a practically brand-new zero-turn mower sitting in an open garage. She thought that, through trial and error, she could figure out how to operate it. That proved harder than she anticipated, but eventually, she mastered how to stop and go. She decided home was ground zero and that she would work her way out. Ana cleared tree limbs from the yard, and years' worth of dried leaves gathered and piled in the middle of the asphalt street to burn.

As evening approached, Ana sat under a freshly pruned tree, drinking a cold drink. She oversaw the fire. She made sure she was aware of where the embers were landing. She heard the rumble of a vehicle coming her way. She assumed Rene was returning from her trip, but it wasn't the exact vehicle she had left in this morning. Rene tended to change cars like others changed their socks. An orange Dodge charger came around the bend. Ana quickly realized her mother couldn't haul all their things in this sporty car. The car slowed, and the motor pulsed like a heartbeat.

Suddenly, Ana realized who the driver was. It was her long-time friend Kimmy Coleson. Ana had met Kimmy many years before. She was sitting in Ana's secret spot on the river. She regularly visited her spot to decompress from a complex case or some other disappointing occurrence in her life. As it turned out, so did Kimmy.

"Hey," Ana said, walking up to the picnic table she thought was hidden from the rest of the world.

"Hey," Kimmy said, wiping a tear from her eye.

"I'm Ana Reed, and you are?" Ana asked.

"Oh, Kimmy. Kimmy Coleson. Nice to meet you," Kimmy answered.

The two sat for hours on that old picnic table and chatted about first one thing then another. Ana learned of Kimmy's recent breakup with the love of her life. They simply referred to him as Satan. Satan, it seemed, had a terrible habit of using women and throwing them away without a second thought. He had used Kimmy for a place to stay and all the other benefits having her around provided. Kimmy never let him know what she really was. Of that, Ana was thankful. The world didn't need an immortal ass hat like that. He was a terrible human and would have been a vicious immortal. Kimmy wholeheartedly agreed with Ana's assessment. She had given him everything a man such as himself could have dreamed of having. He had a new Harley in the driveway and a new 4 x 4 pickup in the garage.

She paid for every tattoo that he wanted to get, and those things were not cheap, as Ana was to find out.

Kimmy had found out he saw not just one but several other human women. Her first thought was to blame the woman. Then she realized they had just been fooled by him, the same as her. So she decided to cut all ties with this loser and return home to the mountain. The mountain was always a reliable shelter from whatever storm came one's way. Ana and Kimmy decided that very day that they had found their new best friend. They met regularly by the river to update one another on any new developments in their lives. Ana loved Kimmy's free spirit and love of life. Kimmy was also one of the most beautiful immortals Ana had ever seen. She reminded Ana of the Cartoon Character Betty Boop. She was short and curvy, which always garnered her attention from both immortal and mortal alike.

It was seriously intriguing to Ana to listen to Kimmy's stories. Ana had only had one serious relationship in her life, which was when she was in college. She dated a boy for a grand total of eight months. She had chosen to have a physical relationship with this boy, as she just knew he was the one. It turned out he was not. Shortly after his conquest of Ana, he moved on to pursue another. Ana was heartbroken but learned to deal with the betrayal. She never gave her heart freely to another again. Physical relationships were easy, and Ana never cared even to know their names. They were usually just food with a bit of extra on the side. No human named a steak before they ate it, so neither did she.

Kimmy was a sucker for love and dreamed of her happily ever after. Ana hoped she never lost her innocence on that matter. Ana came close to having a relationship once with a man of her own kind. He turned out to be a much better friend than a life-long companion. She did enjoy the no-holds-barred approach to sex. She was free to be herself. She didn't have to worry about the fragile human male body or their ego. Wild, rough, and wickedly fun was the order of the day when Jerod came to town. Ana didn't mind because that was all she wanted from him anyway.

"Girl, what brings you this way?" Ana said.

"I was just heading down to Myrtle and thought I would swing by, just in case you made it back this way," Kimmy said, hugging her friend tightly.

"No place like home," Ana said.

"True story, kinda quiet around here," Kimmy said. She stood back, hands on her hips, surveying the deserted neighborhood.

"Yep, that's what I was thinking too. We are gonna fix it up, and maybe people will come to visit up here again," Ana explained.

"That is so cool! Who's we?" Kimmy asked.

"Just me and mom so far. But hey, why don't you stick around for a while if you don't have anything monumental planned?" Ana asked. She loved Rene with all her heart, but it would be nice to have another female to talk to.

"I'm not in a hurry. I really was just going to have something to do," Kimmy answered.

"Awesome! It's gonna be a lot of work, but what are we doing anyway?" Ana said.

The two walked around the neighborhood, and Ana showed Kimmy her notebook filled with ideas. After that, Kimmy was totally on board. Even though Kimmy strayed from the mountain from time to time, the mountain was just as important to her as Ana. It was her home, and she wanted it to be alive again.

Rene pulled into the driveway, and the girls instinctively stopped what they were doing to help unload the van she had brought home.

"Kimmy, it's so good to see you!" Rene squealed.

"So nice to see you too. I hope you don't mind me just popping by. I didn't know if you were here," Kimmy said.

"Don't be silly, girl. This is your home. We love seeing you. We have missed your face," Rene said.

Ana's mouth began to water as they emptied the bags. Her mother must have cleaned out the Pickup. She had absolutely everything. There were items for a seafood boil, and Ana couldn't wait. The girls helped Rene prep for dinner. Kimmy fixed her famous strawberry cheesecake. By the end of the evening, they were all so stuffed they couldn't move.

Few networks remained these days. Rene and Ana enjoyed a little news and a movie from time to time. The report was no longer full of morbid depression. Reconstruction and ideas for new ways to enjoy this new life were rolling. Most were nothing more than infomercials for coming attractions. There would be a freak motor vehicle accident every so often, but it always concluded with the immortals laughing about their dumb luck. No death, no disease, and no fighting among neighboring lands were ever recorded because they just didn't happen.

If an immortal met the true death, no one would be so crass as to publicize it. That was a private matter reserved for the closest of one's acquaintances. It was tragic and too horrible to even speak about, so no one ever did. Ana made a mental note to send in information about their little slice of heaven. With the three of them on the project, morale was high. As the months passed, the streets were clear, and everything was clean and fresh. Ana discussed different business ideas that she thought might bring people into the area. This would definitely require help, and Ana was determined to get it. The immortals, like the humans, lived with a pack mentality. They preferred to live in social groups. This place wasn't everyone's cup of tea, but Ana knew others felt the same as she did. They would thrive in this peaceful environment.

Ana sat many evenings preparing her announcement for Channel VAA (or Vampires across America). She wanted to get it just right. She thought that having Kimmy deliver the message would be best. Kimmy was spunky, energetic, and beautiful—all things Ana felt were lacking in herself. Kimmy argued this undeniable fact but agreed in the end to make the announcement. The broadcast day had arrived, and Rene, Ana, and Kimmy took off on their mission. Kimmy was perfect, just as Ana knew she would be. A live interview with Kimmy enhanced Ana's prerecorded story. Kimmy then did the unthinkable. In the middle of the interviews with the handsome Ric Robins, she threw Ana under the proverbial bus.

"Yes, Ric, without my partners, none of this would be possible," Kimmy said.

"Oh, and who are your partners, Ms. Coleson?" Ric asked.

"Come on up here, Ana," Kimmy said, standing and holding her hand out to Ana.

Ana shook her head violently, but what was she to do? This was live TV, and the camera was already on her terrified face. Ana moved slowly to the stage, and a stagehand quickly brought her a chair. Ana knew she had to be as welcoming and friendly as possible, not her typical traits. She had a resting bitch face, and she knew it.

"Welcome, welcome, Ana. So are you the mastermind behind this project?" Ric asked.

"Thank you so much, but this is truly a group effort," Ana said.

Her face was as red as a beet, but she struggled through. She was so embarrassed to be in the limelight. This was definitely Kimmy's thing and not hers. Rene was thankful she had stepped out, or she had no doubt she would have been dragged up there too. Ana did get a little more comfortable as she talked about their little town. She was so passionate about it her words flew from her. She described the mountaintop music arena while clips played to show the area's beauty. Wild ponies ran in their sanctuary. Ana couldn't imagine anything more beautiful than the majestic beasts. Ana made sure to show all the lovely places for people to stay when they visited. Ana explained the need for others to come and help in the restaurants and different areas they might have an interest in. She was so excited to get the word out.

"This place is so lovely. To tell you the truth, I had never heard of it before. I can't wait to visit, though. I hope I get a full tour," Ric said.

Kimmy finally took over the interview. "This place is a romantic spot for a getaway or even a permanent residence. My family believes in the power of our mountain. It is relaxing and offers all the seasons. There is no boredom there, that's for sure. From one day to the next, we just look outside to check the weather. That tells us what our plans will be for the day," Kimmy said.

Some might think the changing seasons aren't a big deal, but the fight to overcome boredom was real to a vampire. Immortals have to work hard to overcome it. After a while, one had seen it all and done almost anything they were interested in doing. Mundane existence was horrible. The mountain offered deviation every day. Ana thought this would be appealing to some of the older immortals. Just a slight difference, like the weather, would help with the flow from day to day. Those who lived before technology ruled the world would be nostalgic for their old lives. The mountain was kind of stuck in a simpler time. That was rewarding in its own way. The people of Oak View, Virginia, could hold on to innocence and peace a little longer than the rest of the world.

"I can't wait to come to check it out, Ana. This place sounds so perfect. I think you will get a lot of traffic up there on your mountain," Ric said.

"Everyone is welcome. We encourage everyone to come on up. Feel free to give us a call if you have any questions," Kimmy said.

Ana's and Rene's numbers rolled across the screen, and there it was, the beginning of their new lives.

The broadcast played for several days. The calls were slow to start, but the interest was definitely there when they did. Saturday welcomed the first visitors. Adam and Cecilia Pike were to arrive. Ana and Rene planned to put them in the old Nathan Dorady house. The house was an old plantation house that had stood the test of time. It was a massive home with movable panels leading to hidden rooms. The cellar was a makeshift dungeon used to house the unruly, unwilling workers. This was a horror of the time in this area. Ana felt that people, especially ones who lived during that time, might enjoy going back in time in a way. Ana made sure the oil lamps and actual paper and pens were available to the guests. She thought it gave it a more authentic feel.

Journals written by the original owners of the plantation were available for the visitors to read. Ana found it interesting to learn how they lived. She hoped others would like it too. Ana had heard it said before that a person died twice—first by their mortal death and the second the last time someone spoke their name. Ana hoped the journals would postpone the second death for Nathan and Dally Dorady. She felt as though they were friends after her dive into their lives. Some things were beyond her scope of understanding, but she simply agreed to disagree with their choices.

Rene would prepare the meals for the guests. Ana's job was to chauffeur the visitors around and let them see the area. Saturday would be a lazy day, as the couple had traveled quite a distance to get there. Ana knew downtime would be needed. She showed them the home in which they would stay. She encouraged them to tour the grounds and call if they needed anything. Rene had prepared their lunch and left it in the kitchen. She had pot roast, potatoes, and onions simmering in the slow cooker. A pineapple upside-down cake was to be dessert.

Rene hoped they enjoyed her efforts because nothing pleased her more than others enjoying her cooking. She prided herself on being somewhat of an amateur chef. To our surprise, the Pikes wouldn't hear of them not joining them for dinner. The group decided to make it an event and dress for the occasion. Kimmy, Ana, and Rene wore beautiful dresses. Kimmy had so much fun fixing everyone's hair and makeup for the evening. Cecilia explained that people used to always dress for dinner. It was a sign of respect for the person responsible for supplying the meal. The Pikes explained how it was rare to receive guests, so something like this would have been a huge deal. Adam said he resented the way humans had gone out of their way to separate themselves from others at any opportunity. Children taking their meals in front of the television or sitting with their noses in their cellular phones was horrendous to him. No wonder there was no sense of consolidation with the humans. They fought it at every turn.

The immortals needed inclusion, and they welcomed the opportunities gatherings provided. They wanted to feel like they were part of something. New conversations, new hobbies to learn about, or just new faces were always pleasant additions to their forever. New was hard to find, especially among the older immortals. Ana didn't have that to worry about yet. The evening came to a close, and Ana felt a kinship with this couple. She felt like she had made two wonderful new friendships. Tomorrow was another fun-filled day to get to know them better, and she looked forward to it.

"Today, as we go up the mountain, I thought I would show you the restaurant we are hoping to get up and running. It's so beautiful we feel it's a shame for it just to sit and not be enjoyed," Ana said.

Rene had a sign commissioned. On the sign was the mountain in all its blue ridged glory and trees with the leaves in many shades of oranges and yellows. Nestled in the middle was the name the Mountain Seven. Rene and Ana felt this paid tribute to Nick and Tori in a small way. They had carried part of them home to the mountain with them. The couple made their way inside, and there was an audible gasp.

"This place is fantastic! I love the rock and the waterfall. It is so lovely. The logs make the place all warm and homey," Cecilia said, wrapping her arms around her shoulders.

"We just love it. We hope enough people will enjoy it to keep it stocked and running. Everything is top of the line in here. It would be easy for someone so inclined to come in and just start cooking," Ana said.

Adam hadn't said a word since they walked inside. He was assessing everything, but he seemed to be paying attention to the bones of the place, not the fluff.

"You know what, Ana? This place would really be something special. We have traveled to every corner of the world. This place is as unique and beautiful as any I have seen. Wouldn't you agree, dear?" Adam asked.

Cecilia nodded her agreement.

"I know some people who might be interested in doing this project with you. I know many who would love the tranquility of this area. So if you want, I could give them a call. They could come up and just see what they think, if you agree that, of course. This place could be great again," Adam said.

"Well, I'm not sure anyone would have ever called this place great, but us mountain folks are a rare breed. Either you love us, or you hate us. There is no in-between," Ana said with a giggle.

"I would love to be an honorary mountaineer," Cecilia said.

"You are officially in the club. Your one of us, one of us, one of us," Ana chanted.

Adam began making a phone call before he even left the building. The conversation came back around to the area's future success all day. Ana was so excited to hear all the great ideas the newcomers had. They came up with ideas she had never thought about before. Sometimes it was nice to have a fresh set of eyes on a project after all.

Kimmy's Gone

Everyone had a wonderful evening, as they had every evening thus far. Ana could tell Kimmy was getting antsy, as she did when she was stationary for too long. Ana knew she would be pulling out again soon. Kimmy was a free spirit, and she liked to travel, meet new people, and see things others only dreamed of seeing. She had stayed for six and a half months, so it was time for her to go for a while.

"Hey, lady," Kimmy said.

She was dragging two big bags and her tote-sized purse down the stairs. She was always prepared for anything. She always reminded Ana of the lady with the carpet bag in the movies, who pulled out ten thousand things from her endless supply, or Santa's magic sack that held every child's Christmas toys. Ana ran to help before she dropped everything.

"Good morning, sunshine. Is it time for you to jet for a few?" Ana asked

"Yeah, just for a little while. I will roll back this way before you know it," Kimmy said, making a click-click sound with her tongue.

Ana and Rene hugged their dear friend and said their goodbyes. No one was sad because they knew she would be back just as she promised. That was another thing that was good about being immortal. There was always tomorrow.

Kimmy pulled out, stomping the accelerator on that vicious V8, and let it roar its goodbye too. She knew her way to the ocean even with her eyes closed. She had stops to make here and there, but the trip that used to take five hours now was three and a half. She was glad the lanes of traffic were drastically reduced. She put the pedal to the metal, just as she had always done. She was always on a mission, even when it could be fatal. Now she just cruised along, enjoying the ride. Every once in a while, an animal might jump from the bushes in her path, but they were no match for her vamp reflexes. She would simply slow, swerve, and resume speeding.

Kimmy smelled the ocean air long before she saw the endless blue. She heard the familiar call of the gulls. This place had always provided Kimmy with a sense of calm, unlike anywhere else in the world. Her mind could relax. She didn't have to think about anything but the sun on her face and the sand between her toes. Kimmy thought there was no better therapy in the world. She knew there was another reason she loved the ocean. Nothing on land could touch her speed or power, but the sea was different. The ocean depths had creatures no one had even heard of before. She could almost feel how vulnerable humans felt as she stepped into the murky waters. She imagined the great white deciding she looked like fair game. Her heart would pick up speed as she scanned the waves. This was her way to get the elusive adrenaline rush. They were hard to come by when such a limited number of things could harm you.

Kimmy spent three days on the beach. She ate and drank and enjoyed the silence. She took time to talk to several passersby that wanted to make her acquaintance. She enjoyed the fresh seafood and the bartender's tropical drinks, which he seemed always to be handing her. He was a cutie, so she allowed his attentions.

"Can I sit?" a voice asked.

Kimmy shielded her eyes with her hands and lifted her head to see the speaker.

"Sure, come on," Kimmy said.

She sat up and started straightening up her things as if the whole beach wasn't enough space for this one tiny person.

"I'm Lana Sparks," the young woman said, extending her hand.

"Hey, girl, nice to meet you. Kimmy Coleson," Kimmy said with her award-winning smile.

Lana got comfortable on her towel, slipped off her shades, and took a swig from her water bottle.

"It is beautiful today. When I saw you over here by yourself, I thought no since in both of us being alone, unless you wanted your privacy. I'm so silly I never even thought of that," Lana said.

"No, you're okay, girl. I have been here for days. I could use somebody to hang with for a while. Where you from?" Kimmy asked.

"Washington, DC. What about you?" Lana answered.

"Way up in the mountains of Virginia. You know what they say about the girl and the mountain, and the mountain and the girl, right?" Kimmy asked.

"I think they say that about everywhere," Lana said.

"Well, must be true about me 'cause I can't get that mountain out of me for anything no matter where I go," Kimmy said.

The two assumed their lounging positions, and Kimmy took the earbuds out of her phone so both could enjoy the music. Lana and Kimmy had a great time just chilling on the beach or poolside. They picked up so many beautiful shells, but Kimmy always threw them back into the sea. She thought they deserved to stay there. If she found a unique one, she would take it back to Ana and display it somewhere. She always thought about Ana when she was away. She called almost every day just to see if she had missed anything exciting. Ana always had a list of projects she was tackling and good news about things she had finished. Kimmy loved that about her.

Lana suggested the two get all dolled up, as she called it, and hit a local club. Kimmy didn't see why not, so they spent the afternoon trying to decide which outfits to wear and how to style their hair. Kimmy chose to be comfortable in her powder-blue country lace short dress, while Lana went a more risqué route. She wore a skin-tight burgundy number with four-inch heels. Kimmy didn't need to do all that to get anyone's attention. Lana didn't either, but she was a little insecure. The place was really bombing tonight. Kimmy hadn't seen this many people gathered in one place in a long time, and it was nice. Everyone was beautiful, healthy, and forever twenty-five. There was no one here that Kimmy would refer to as a four. They were all solid nine and a half.

The girls danced and danced and danced. They drank way too much and took a break to eat some real food. They washed it down with some BB or bottled blood, as it was called. Lana had several potential suitors for the evening. Kimmy enjoyed watching them fall all over themselves for her attention. Kimmy tended to find someone she connected with and hang with them for the night. The lucky man of the evening was seriously gorgeous. He had shoulder-length dark-brown hair, his skin was bronze, and his smile was contagious. His eyes were so dark you would almost think they were black until you saw the hint of gold in them. Kimmy liked the view with this one, but not enough to remember his name. She was sure it was Brad, Chad, or something ending in an -*ad*.

"Hey, I think I'm gonna call it for tonight," Kimmy said.

She had to scream for Lana to hear her over the music, but Lana nodded her understanding.

"See ya in the morning then?" Kimmy asked.

Lana nodded her understanding again, even though Kimmy wasn't sure she did understand.

The delicious Brad, Chad, or whatever his name was offered to escort Kimmy home as any gentleman would, but Kimmy was really not feeling all that rolling around tonight. Even though he was the ocean's Adonis, she would have to pass. She made her exit gracefully.

It was kind of far from the house she was staying in, but it was a beautiful night, and she would enjoy the walk. She did choose to hit a few back alleys to shorten the journey. The alleyway at Luna Street was particularly dark and ominous, but Kimmy had no fear of anything. She hadn't feared anything in a very long time. Tonight wouldn't be the night she started. As she walked, she could hear her rhinestone thong shoes as they *flip-flopped, flip-flopped*. Her charms on her bracelet seemed to be extra loud as they pinged together in rhythm with her steps. Her mind wandered to the next day's plans. That was probably why she didn't hear the footfalls behind her.

As stealthily as a cat approaching its prey, someone eased up behind Kimmy. Unfortunately, she was too late in her acknowledgment of the stalker. He was fast, and he was deliberate in his actions. He quickly grabbed the sides of Kimmy's head, and with a sudden jerk, he snapped her neck. Although this wouldn't kill her permanently, it did render her unconscious. She dropped her bag in the alley as he lifted her into his arms and made away with her to his awaiting vehicle. Kimmy hadn't prepared for anything like this. She had never even heard of such a thing, so how could she prepare for it? No human could have ever been strong enough or fast enough to subdue any vampire, and now that they were all secure, it wasn't an issue anymore.

Kimmy woke to find herself in a very damp and dimly lit basement. Well, she believed it to be a basement. But she wasn't sure of that. Kimmy found her wrist and ankles secured by silver chains. No matter how hard she struggled, she couldn't break them. She had never seen anything she couldn't manipulate or break in one way or another. She hoped she would have better luck with her captor.

Ana's Farm Trip

While Kimmy frolicked on the beach, Ana continued her work. She oversaw every aspect of the renovations to the buildings and landmarks in her town. She absolutely loved the group of women who chose to open the Mountain Seven. Two seasoned chefs and several veteran servers had turned the place into a welcoming place for all the travelers and new residence of the area. The jobs they didn't really enjoy in their mortal life were now their passion. They went the extra mile to make everyone feel like family. They greeted everyone by name upon arrival, and if they didn't know their names, they would by the end of the meal. Patricia and Emily were locals, Janis was from New York, and Dawn was from Georgia. The younger crew members were Amilia, Chelsea, Brittney, and Mylie. Ana loved them all.

She knew it was time to make the trip to the farm. She was feeling a little off lately, and Rene encouraged her to go. The fresh blood always rejuvenated her, so she was ready. On the morning of September 6, she woke with no idea this day would forever change her life. Rene and Ana drank their morning coffee and had a light breakfast. Then they decided to take the bikes up the mountain to the farm. Ana had learned to ride on a small dirt bike and eventually grew into the purple Harley she now sported. It was a Softtail with a springer front end. Rene decided that she would learn to have something else to do together. Her bike of choice was a pearl white Roadking, with angel wings painted on the tank.

The two wore their leathers and gloves but didn't see a need for the cumbersome helmets the mortals had worn. Ana liked to feel the wind whipping through her hair, even if she did eat a bug or two along the way. Rene always sported her '80s shades like in the air force movies way back when. Both women were breathtaking, no matter what they chose to wear, but this gear made them seem as dangerous and exciting as Ana wished they were. Rene packed all the needed gear in her saddlebags. She had water, snacks, and some extra clothes just in case they got anything on theirs during the feed.

Sometimes Ana felt terrible for the donors, but she knew none of this was avoidable. They had sealed their fate a long time ago. She went, she fed, and she left. They were nothing more than fuel for her engine. Rene had a particular donor that she chose every time she fed. Ana did not. She always tried to pick someone strong and healthy to not cause any ill effects for them. Ana wasn't proud of it, but once, she chose a donor simply for the look of defiance on his face. As her grandmother would say, he was rude and loud and downright too big for his britches. She brought him down a notch or two. She was just as rude and rough and unwilling to bend as he was. Anytime Ana came to feed, he conveniently was nowhere to be found. She looked too because she didn't feel quite as guilty draining that ass hat.

As Rene and Ana pulled through the gate at Virginia Eco Farm number 3, they found a really shady place to park. They walked to the entrance, and Ana realized it never ceased to amaze her. The farm was indeed dome-shaped. It was massive in size. She didn't know how many acres it covered, but she knew it was a lot. It was way up in the mountain on national forest land. The council had camouflaged the entire dome to perfection within the trees. If one didn't know it was there, they would never know despite its size. There was one way in and one way out, as far as Ana knew. There was always someone operating the gate, and immortals were asked to sign in and sign out. A number was assigned to each donor, and the immortals had to add it to their exit sheet. The council did try to prohibit donor use to two times a week, so the numbers helped with that.

Ana noticed a familiar face at the gate. Her friend Rose stood as beautifully as a statute, just staring at the gate.

"What in the world, Rose!" Ana squealed.

"Ana!" Rose yelled.

Ana gathered Rose to her and hugged her tightly. Even though the immortal's appearances never changed, Ana could see that Rose was weak. Rose had one of the saddest love stories Ana had ever heard. She didn't know how she had even survived the pain of it. Rose had a mortal love many decades before, and he had no desire to become immortal. Even though Rose begged him until his dying day, he refused her gift. He was the same as Kat. He wanted to be free of this life and move on to the next. He always told Rose that the only kindness he ever received in this world had been her. They loved each other completely and openly. He never judged her for her immortal life, nor did he envy it. Rose held his hand in the cabin they shared until he took his last breath. She never had and would never be free of the pain. Even if she could never break free to the great beyond, a piece of her had gone. Her love took her heart when he flew to glory. Ana always hoped Rose would feel better, but judging by how she looked, she wasn't doing very well.

Ana and Rose sat and caught up on their lives. Ana told her all their plans and offered her a place in her little town. Rose was very interested and said she would think about it. Ana told Rose she thought being around family would help her. Rose seemed to agree. Ana was excited for her to see everything she had done. Rose seemed depressed and lethargic, which bothered Ana. She made a point to get a definitive time and date that Rose would come to Oak View.

"Okay, let's go inside and get you some nourishment. You are looking a little peaked," Ana said

"Let's do it," Rose said.

The man at the gate was at least 6'3" and had long limbs and a perfect build. His hair was long and black, and he looked to be of Native American descent. The ink that adorned his body was faded and barely visible from many years of sun and abuse, yet he was breathtaking in his own way. He was everything someone would picture a Native American to be. He was a beautiful example of the race.

"Hi, Tom. So wonderful to see you," Rene said, leaning in to place a kiss on his cheek.

"Beauty, always my pleasure. You look lovely as always," Tom answered.

"Thank you. Thank you. You remember my daughter, Ana?" Rene asked.

"Of course, so wonderful to see you, pretty lady," Tom said.

Ana leaned in and kissed his cheek as well.

Rene introduced Rose, and Tom seemed quite taken by her. She paid him little attention. As was protocol, the three ladies signed in and gave a wave to Tom as they went inside.

No matter how many times Ana walked into the gates of a farm, she always felt like a visitor at a petting zoo. It was still uncomfortable, even after all this time. Finally, Rene and Ana agreed to meet at four o'clock at the gate. Ana made sure Rose had her telephone number securely in her back pocket, and she confirmed their visit one more time. Rene knew precisely where to find her regular donor. Rose seemed to have a destination in mind, but Ana did not. She would stroll about as always until she stumbled into someone.

Ana enjoyed the beauty of the farm. The council made sure everything was perfectly maintained. The plants inside the dome served several purposes. They provided oxygen and food, and humans used them for medicinal purposes if the need arose. The immortals took excellent care of their flock, but the humans wanted to feel in control in some small way. They only asked immortals for help when they had exhausted all other choices. There grew gigantic gardens to feed themselves, even though the food was provided. They tended to animals and utilized their milk, eggs, and meat. There was an innate need to be self-sufficient. Immortals were impressed by the humans' ingenuity.

Very few, if any, humans remained that had lived free in the world. It seemed to be only folklore. Human parents told stories to the children, but the humans believed they had been saved due to the kindness of the immortals. They thought they would have all died if not for the farms the immortals created to protect them. It was a half-truth, Ana knew, but it was still half a lie. The humans were programmed to feel grateful and indebted to the immortals. If the immortals instilled fear into the hearts of the humans, they were easier to control. If the immortals could wipe every memory of life outside the farm, they would.

At the beginning of the farm's use, some unruly humans tried to escape. These people were dealt with quickly and with no mercy.

It was a dangerous precedent to set to allow any form of defiance. It was simply not allowed. Over time, the humans accepted their fates and were compliant, willing donors. The entire dome structure was two-foot plexiglass-like material. Tiny wires ran through the surface, and electricity pulsed through the cables. It took only a few humans to die on its cover for the others to understand there was no way out. Groups tried to storm the gate several times, but even a group was no match for the gatekeeper. He begged them to stand down. He was really tired, but they did not stop. He took the actions required by the council in the event of such an occurrence. Sixteen donors died that day on their first attempt. Each subsequent event resulted in more deaths. Over time, the humans learned it was nothing more than suicide to try the gate. If death was the goal, the gatekeeper was more than glad to oblige.

Ana stopped to admire a vast rose garden. She had never seen so many varieties in her life. There were all sizes and colors to admire. Some roses were tiny, and some blossoms were the size of her hand. She smelled each one's fragrance and was intoxicated by its aroma. She sat on a bench inside the garden and thought of all the hard work that went into its design. Suddenly, a small white Pomeranian dog was jumping on her leg. The little fluff ball was thrilled to receive belly rubs and scratches behind the ears. Ana stood and continued her walk down the trail, and her new fluffy buddy bounced down the path with her.

"You are so dang cute. What is your name?" Ana asked, not really expecting the dog to answer her.

"Her name is Sophie," a male voice answered.

Ana turned to see what she believed to be the most beautiful man she had ever seen. He was of average height but was stocky and muscular. His skin was caramel, and his eyes—oh, his eyes— were forest green. This was a rarity in humans as the standard eye color was some variation of brown. When he smiled at Ana, her heart skipped a beat. There was something a little sneaky in his grin. She felt he was a mischievous sort, and she liked it.

"Um, hi," Ana said.

"Um, hi," he mimicked.

Ana blushed, flipped her hair over her shoulder, and walked to this amazing-looking man.

"Is she yours?" Ana asked.

"No, she belongs to the neighbor. I was looking for her. They get worried when she doesn't come back for a while, as you can understand," he said.

"Yeah, I guess so," Ana said.

"I have never seen you here before," he stated.

"I don't come very often, definitely not as often as my mom thinks I should anyway," Ana said.

The gentleman stood and extended his hand out in the direction of a beautiful pond. Ana enjoyed his take-charge attitude. He acted as though they were at his home, and he was inviting her to sit. They took their seats on hand-carved Adirondack chairs placed there so people could enjoy the tranquility of the water. Ducks floated on the pond's surface, and Ana enjoyed watching them.

"Do you have a particular donor you were going to find? Then I could help you," he asked.

"No, I'm not too particular," Ana answered.

She realized how that sounded when it was too late to shove it back into her mouth. She just rolled her eyes and made a low groaning sound as if she were in pain. She was in pain because, at that moment, she was sure one could die from embarrassment.

"I mean I don't visit enough to have a regular donor," she stammered.

"I knew what you meant." He laughed.

Ana quickly tried to change the subject. "So what do I call you?" she asked.

He pointed to the inside of his forearm at a number tattooed there. "22192," he answered.

Ana had always excepted that answer in the past, but this time, it bothered her. She made a mental note of the number for the exit paperwork if she were to need it, but she wanted to know his name.

"Don't you have a name?" Ana asked.

The man stared at her. Ana could feel confusion in his gaze.

"James," he answered.

"James. Well, that is a fine, strong name. My name is Ana. Nice to meet you," Ana said.

She thought this interaction was strange. It felt like she was talking to a regular person and not a mortal. She decided she would ask him things she had always wanted to know about the farm. Since this was all James knew, he wouldn't be as negative about the experience. Ana had tried before, early on, but the human she was speaking with had nothing positive to say at all. It was very depressing to her, and she promised herself she wouldn't ask again, but this was different. James described their living conditions and all the various activities they had. He talked about their jobs and the family units that thrived within the dome. Ana was much more pleased with his description of the farm.

Ana spoke freely with James about her project at home. He seemed to be genuinely interested in every detail. She agreed to bring pictures if ever she visited again. He was thrilled she might. He had always wanted to see what was on the outside but hadn't had the opportunity. Ana knew down deep that she would return. She felt connected with this man. She would dare to say that a friendship was blossoming between them.

"Well, I hate to go, but my mom and I agreed to meet at four. So where has the time gone?" Ana said. She desperately wanted to feed but somehow didn't want just to take it from her new friend.

"Didn't you need to feed?" James asked.

Ana felt her cheeks redden, and she was suddenly embarrassed by her very nature.

"Yes," she answered softly.

This was the only response she could give. She didn't need to explain or apologize for it, but there was still something uncomfortable about the exchange.

"Okay," James said.

He didn't need to give his permission or anything, so there was no suggestion of the sort. The two stood in silence for what seemed like an hour.

"Is there something wrong? Do you need someone else?" James asked.

"No, of course, not," Ana said

"How about you tell me what is most comfortable for you. How would you like me to proceed?" Ana asked.

James had never been given a choice before, so he thought about it for a second. Finally, he tilted his head to the side and exposed his neck to her. The sweat that rolled down his neck was solely due to the heat of the evening, not any sign of nervousness from him. Ana thought he would prefer the wrist, as it was less intimate, but she was definitely pleased by his decision.

"Stand or sit?" James asked.

"Stand if you don't mind," Ana answered. She suddenly became aware that she was asking, but she didn't mind. "Do you want to take your shirt off, just in case?" she asked.

He slipped his shirt over his head and laid it on the chair. She was so glad he made that decision. His body was even more perfect than she thought. His stomach was like ripples, and all she wanted to do was move her hand over its ridges. She didn't dare do it, though.

James stood perfectly still as she approached him. Yes, she was sure this was nothing new for him. Ana tried to control her beast, but it was trying its best to break free. She moved slowly and cautiously to her new friend. She ran her fingers through his hair and tilted his head to the side to gain better access. She tiptoed just a little to nuzzle into his neck with her nose. She breathed in his intoxicating aroma. He smelled like honeysuckle in summer. Ana took his fresh smell of life into herself, and it was overwhelming to her. The way he presented himself to her was like fire in her loins.

James was totally calm. Like a man tied to a whipping post, he awaited her mark. He solemnly awaited the pain. His eyes were closed in anticipation. She heard the steady rhythm of his heart. She didn't ever want to hear it any other way. Ana did something she hadn't done in years.

"Open your eyes," she asked.

James did as she asked.

"You will feel no fear, no pain," Ana said.

She stared into the forest green of his eyes for longer than necessary. Finally, she took a moment and did as Rene had done with her. She memorized his face. She moved her finger across his full lips, and he parted them slightly and was totally at peace. Ana moved back to the valley of his neck and nuzzled once again. She felt her fangs extend, and she could wait no longer. She plunged deep into the skin, piercing the vein underneath perfectly. The blood flowed freely into her waiting body. She drank and listened to his heartbeats. An immortal's heart matched the heart of the donor during a feeding. This connection would not change unless the donor was approaching death. Death was definitely not the goal this time.

Ana tightened her grip on James's arm as her body began to tremble. She moaned in exquisite pleasure. There was a fine line between sexual pleasure and feeding. Ana was sure her body had crossed that line. As the heartbeat of her willing donor began to slow, Ana knew it was time to stop. She pulled back and found his strong arms wrapped around her. He was holding her up onto her feet. She hadn't realized her knees had given way in the grips of this powerful experience. James had supported her so she could feed. He moved her back to her seat and helped her into it. He sat down beside her. Ana felt silly. She should be helping him, not the other way around.

Ana noticed a trickle of blood coming from his wound. She pricked her finger, and a tiny droplet of blood came from it. She moved her finger over the injured area and watched as the healing powers of her blood sealed it. Ana came prepared as she did for everything. She retrieved a bandage from her pocket and placed it securely on the area.

"Wear this for a day or two, so no one tries to feed, okay?" Ana said.

James nodded in agreement. It was dangerous for a human to be fed on too frequently, and with Ana's healing gift, another vampire might not know he had just been fed on.

"I guess I should get going," Ana said.

"Okay," James said, standing from his chair.

"I hope you come back this way soon—I mean, if it's agreeable to you," James said.

Ana blushed as she stared at the very familiar white rocks on the ground.

"Yeah, I will. I need to come more often because of mom and all. She worries too much," Ana said.

"Can I walk you to the bridge?" James asked.

"Sure," Ana said.

Chatter filled the walk back to the bridge. Ana was happy she had come today. The goodbyes were surprisingly difficult. Ana found she really enjoyed her new friend's company. She still believed a friend was a strange title for this man, but she knew it to be true. Ana signed the exit book and placed James's number next to her name. It was exciting to record their interaction, even in this context.

"Hey, over here!" Rene yelled.

"Hey, you ready?" Ana said.

"I hurried, and you just took your sweet time. I have been waiting forty-seven hours for you," Rene said.

She had a way of exaggerating things like time, distance, or how good or bad something was. Ana found it adorable. Rene gathered her water bottle and her snack wrapper and put them in the bin. The two slipped on their gloves and headed home.

The rumble of the Harley sent waves of excitement through Ana's body. She smiled as she realized it was the same excitement she felt with James as he had held her close while she fed. The ride was pleasant, and Ana was euphoric.

"You look so much better, baby," Rene said.

"I feel better too. I think you were right. I need to feed more, I think. You go once a week, don't you?" Ana asked.

"Sometimes more. You just can't feed on the same donor more than once, but you can go as often as you like," Rene said.

Ana tried to act all innocent about the whole thing, but she saw Rene's expression soften a little bit.

"I need a regular donor like you do. I don't want to have to find someone new all the time. That seems exhausting," Ana said.

"Oh, yeah. I don't think I would care for that either. It is hard enough to find regular people you can stand to be around, let alone a human. My donor and I have a lot of fun together. It's not all about feeding Ana," Rene said.

Rene left it right there. She didn't need to explain herself to her grown daughter. She was sure she got her meaning. Ana just looked at her for a second and giggled.

"You are a nut, Mom," Ana said.

The rest of the evening was peaceful. Ana and Rene skipped the evening dinner with the group and chose a quiet night at home. They watched a movie and ate ice cream, donuts, and popcorn. That was another perk of being a vampire, no counting calories. You are always fit and trim and wonderfully attractive, no matter how much cake you ate. Ana was tired from her busy day and decided to turn in for the night. She kissed her mom, thanked her for her pushy ways, and headed to bed. The moment she closed her eyes, all she could see were James's beautiful eyes. She tossed and turned, trying to free herself of his intrusion into her dream, but to no avail. Sleep finally won the battle, and she drifted off.

Kimmy's Stay at Hotel Hell

Kimmy used all her senses to assess her environment. She smelled the damp, musty odor associated with an underground structure. Her eyes adjusted to the dimly lit space, and she saw nothing of importance. There were shelving units on the wall across from her, and there were boxes, paint cans, and everyday basement things. She kept trying to figure out the chains. She couldn't understand the strength they had. Why couldn't she break free? Nothing had ever been able to confine her that way. She was chained to the chair, somehow embedded in the floor's concrete. She could pull it free, but then what? She couldn't break the chains.

She heard something moving around upstairs. It moved back and forth across the floor slowly, like someone pacing on a telephone. She listened closely for anything she might hear that would give her a clue about what the hell was happening. Suddenly, light flooded the space, and footsteps pounded on the stairs. A man she had never seen before came walking into her space. He was humming to himself like she wasn't even sitting in the room.

"Um, hello?" Kimmy said in a very annoyed manner.

The man didn't acknowledge her at all. He moved around the room, peeking in random boxes, and still hummed like a lunatic. Finally, the strange man walked over to her and leaned in close.

"First thing we are going to establish here is that you only speak when you're spoken to," he said.

A quick strike across her face emphasized his statement. Even though she would heal, the pain was still very real. Kimmy could smell no life within this man. She was totally confused by his actions. Immortals were not like this. They were generally a live and let live group. This guy was something different. Kimmy's heart picked up its pace, and he knew it.

"That's right. That's how I like it. It would be best if you were afraid. You have every reason to be. Do you recognize me?" he asked.

Kimmy stared at his face but had no idea who he was. Then a tiny bit of recognition came to her, though still nothing concrete. She scrunched her brows in consideration but still nothing.

"Answer me!" he screamed.

"I don't know your name, but you do seem familiar," Kimmy said.

"Well, I should hope so. I have been around a long time. I was doing this when your little ass was still in diapers," he said.

He paced the floor in front of her with a look of satisfaction at her recognition. After that, she just sat quietly, trying to understand her current situation.

"What am I doing here?" Kimmy asked.

"I'm so glad you asked, my dear. You are a part of a long line of extraordinary women. I handpicked you to be in this little club. You should feel honored," he explained.

"I don't get it. What am I doing here?" Kimmy asked again.

She was growing impatient with this dick with every passing moment. She knew she was going to snap, or he was. She just hoped she was able to do something if he decided to.

"I said don't open your mouth unless I say so!" he screamed.

This time, his words were accompanied by a slash to her face. He had sliced her face from the corner of her mouth to her ear. The blood rushed from the gash. Kimmy screamed in both terror and fear. Real fear was a foreign emotion to her. She had no fear of any-one, mortal or immortal. He grabbed the arms of the chair she was in and leaned close to her face. He licked the blood from her cheek, even as it healed itself. Kimmy couldn't help but gag and pull back from him.

"Where do you think you're going to go, Kimmy?" he asked.

He laughed, and the sound shattered her very core. Kimmy knew she was in for some very horrific shit here. She had no idea how she would ever get free. Her only hope was Lana. She was expecting to find Kimmy in her room the following day. All Kimmy had to do was make it through the night, and she was sure Lana would know something was wrong.

"Let's play a little game," the terrifying man said.

Kimmy tensed. She didn't like the sound of that at all. She wanted to be able to fight, and that wasn't possible. The man slowly began to cut away her clothing, and she was entirely at his mercy. She would close her eyes and go deep into her mind, just as she had done in her mortal years when her stepfather had slithered into her room at night. She would leave her body and hide in her mind. Yes, that was what she would do. She would survive, just like she always did.

Kimmy learned the chains could be moved and positioned any way her tormentor wanted during the night. She didn't understand what the chains were, but she knew that to escape, she had to figure them out. She had no idea when the night ended because she was in the dark, windowless basement. But her captor slept and woke as though morning had come. The torture she endured that night was sexual in nature. It was the same depraved acts any rapist found exciting. Although disgusted, Kimmy was mad. Oh, the ways she would destroy this man when she figured out how to get out of here. The unnamed assailant went upstairs without a word to Kimmy.

She sat in her cold, hard metal chair and ran different rescue or escape plans through her mind. First, there was Lana. She would realize something was wrong, retrace her steps home, and find her purse. She thought she must have dropped it there because she didn't see it anywhere in the room. She would then come and find her. Second, this fool would unchain her. Then believing she was the stronger of the two, she would rip his heart from his chest. The second was the least likely of the ideas she had for escape. Third, Kimmy wondered what would happen if she pulled and pulled until the flesh peeled from her bones and she could slip her hands free. For some reason, she had little faith this would work. The chains had tightened on her wrists any time she struggled to get free. She didn't understand. Nothing had ever acted in this manner before. Kimmy suddenly snapped her head up, and her large eyes became even more prominent in the grips of possible understanding.

The chains were spelled. That was the only explanation. How in the world did he get spelled chains? Any witch who lived in the free world was long dead. The magic would have been broken at the time of their death. Nothing went in or out of the farms without inspection. The gatekeeper would have definitely noticed chains shoved down the front of someone's pants. So how did he do it? And how could she undo it? Kimmy decided since the monster was gone, she would close her eyes a minute to keep up her strength. She had recently fed, so she would be okay for a while. She felt that the monster wouldn't let her starve. He was enjoying this too much.

— ❧ —

Lana

Lana stretched and moaned. She looked over to the neighboring pillow to find a very attractive naked man. She shook him to get him up and moving along.

"Good morning," he grumbled.

"I have stuff to do, so…," Lana said.

She kept an open end to her statement. She didn't want to come out and say, "Get out," but she would if she had to. The man grumbled, but he took the hint. He put on his clothes, thanked her for a lovely evening, and left. Lana showered and got ready for her day with Kimmy. She walked two blocks to Kimmy's house and banged on her door. She was confused when Kimmy didn't instantly open up to greet her.

Lana yelled through the door, "Kimmy, you up?"

No response followed, so she opened the door and peeked inside. There was no need for locked doors in this new world, so Lana just walked inside.

"Kimmy, where you at, girl?" Lana asked.

She took a quick survey of the room and saw that all of Kimmy's things were just as they had been the previous day. She snooped around to see if she saw her purse, which she always carried with her. That appeared to be missing. Lana wasn't overly concerned. She thought maybe Kimmy went down to the coffee shop at the corner. She had never gone ahead of Lana, but it was a possibility. She must have needed her caffeine bad today.

Lana strolled down to the shop and asked if they had seen her. They had not. Lana did think this was strange. She decided to go to the parking garage to see if her car was there. One thing was for sure, Kimmy would never leave her car, not ever. Lana had a sick feeling

138

in the pit of her stomach when she saw her orange baby parked, patiently waiting for her return. Lana checked all the places they usually went in the mornings and found nothing of her friend. She checked the beach and pool and went back to her house one more time just to be sure.

Lana remembered the guy Kimmy had spent the evening dancing with the night before. She made her way to the club, and of course, no one was there until two o'clock. She waited for them to start coming in for the night shift. Everyone remembered the man and the beautiful Kimmy. Thankfully, the man was a local, and she then had a name for him—Brady Richards. They assured her he would be there later. No one had his number or knew where he lived. All they could tell her was that he was a local surfer. Lana walked to Solana Beach, where the surfing was best. She watched all the people milling around but didn't see him.

"Hey, do you know a man named Brady?" Lana asked.

"Yeah, sure do," a young surfer boy answered.

"Do you know how I could get ahold of him?" she asked.

"Sure do, he's right there," the young man said, pointing toward the water.

Lana thanked the young man and moved toward Brady.

"Hey, Brady!" Lana yelled.

Brady acknowledged her with a wave and a smile and jogged over to her.

"Hey, I know you. Kimmy's friend, right?" he asked.

"Yeah, you haven't seen her, have you?" Lana asked.

"No, not since last night. Why?" Brandy asked.

"She wasn't in her room this morning, and she hasn't left. I checked already. She's just…gone. I don't know what's going on, but I have a feeling it's not good," Lana explained.

"What do you think could have happened? I bet she just headed out with friends or something. Don't you?" Brady said.

Lana knew what he was thinking. He was thinking just what she had thought, What could have happened to an immortal? Nothing "happened" to immortals.

"I don't know for sure, but I know something isn't right. Thanks anyway," Lana said, and she turned and started to walk away. She was surprised to find Brady following her up the beach.

"You know her better than I do. Is there anything I can do to help?" Brady asked.

"I have to figure out what even to do. I mean, she didn't just disappear," Lana said.

Brady and Lana took Brady's car back to Kimmy's house, and Brady agreed with her conclusion. This didn't look like she had gone anywhere for an extended period of time. He was more thorough with his investigation of the room than Lana had been. He found a small red book that served as an address book. There were no friends listed in the area. Lana pointed to Ana's name. It had a little heart next to it.

"She talks about this lady a lot," Lana said.

"If we don't come up with something soon, we will have to call and see if they can help, but I don't want to worry them until we have to," Brady said.

"I don't think she is just out somewhere. I really think something is wrong. Kimmy is a really cool person. She wouldn't just leave without saying goodbye. She wouldn't worry someone if she could help it. I really don't think she would do that." Lana said.

Brady just nodded. He didn't seem to like any of this at all, but he tried to keep Lana as calm as possible. Brady sat on the edge of the bed and counted on his fingers what they knew so far, which wasn't much.

"We know she left the club alone. We both know she spent the evening dancing with me and no one else. I didn't even see her talk to anyone else. We both know it would have taken a while to walk home if she took the regular route. I don't believe she would have, though. I think she would have taken some shortcuts. She said she was tired. She would have wanted to get home as quickly as she could. Don't you think?" Brady asked.

"I think so, yes," Lana answered. "There are three or four ways to get here from the club. They are through alleyways and side streets, but she would have had no reason to be afraid to take them. So let's go back to the club and retrace her steps. Maybe we will find something," Lana said.

"That's as good a place as any to start," Brady said.

The new amateur sleuths drove back to the club and went on foot down the first possible route. They made it to Kimmy's front door with nothing. The second route they took on the way back to the club, nothing. On the third trip, they turned down a very dark alleyway. Lana immediately saw something silver lying on the ground. She zipped to it and quickly recognized it.

"It's Kimmy's," Lana announced.

Brady scanned the rest of the alley and found nothing of importance.

"Well, it's official. Something bad is going on here. So what do we do?" Lana said.

"Yeah, something is off for sure. We are going to need help. I don't even know where to start," Brady said. He shook his head and ran his hand through his hair. He scanned the area for anything and was at a loss when there was nothing to find.

"Well, in the old world, when someone was missing, one would have called the cops. They would have done whatever they did, and ta-da, they would have found her by now. We don't have those now. Who would even believe us anyway? There is no one to call," Lana said, panic in her voice.

"I know it's a long shot, but I wonder if the club has cameras for some reason. I don't know why they would, but we could check," Brady said.

"What do we look for?" Lana asked.

"Anything or anyone who seems to be acting suspiciously. I really don't know, but we have to start somewhere," Brady said.

Brady and Lana were surprised to find there were cameras. They were on autotimers, and the club always thought it was a novelty to record parties or other functions for people. The owners were glad to burn a copy for them so they could study it. They did and found nothing. It was getting dark, and Lana knew this would be the second night Kimmy was wherever Kimmy was. Lana was sick about that fact. Brady contacted a friend, who contacted a friend, who contacted a cousin who knew the local sheriff of the area. The council put sheriffs in place to help monitor simple disputes and keep the peace if a tiff arose. The two didn't know what else to do.

Allan Helms called and planned his trip to meet them. Allan was a PD in the old world and carried on in the new world. Lana had wondered what they actually did. Immortals were so laid back and very passive. The council must have deemed them necessary. This made them high on the social and political ladder. Allan was to arrive by the afternoon. Lana was nervous and pacing the floors as she waited. Brady never left her side. He was just as concerned as Lana. He had never heard of anything like this since the humans were confined. This kind of thing just didn't happen to immortals.

Just as Allan promised, he arrived around three o'clock. He immediately began to bombard them with questions. Lana was disturbed that he seemed unsurprised.

"Let me recap," Allan said.

He reviewed all the information the two had given him. He had it all written in the tiny notebook he carried in his shirt pocket. The two nodded their agreement with his recount of events. He put his pen in the pen loop on the arm of his shirt and his notebook back at its home base. Allan rested his elbows on his knees and laced his fingers together as if in prayer. He closed his eyes, and Lana knew he was running the events over again in his mind.

Allan was a very muscular, tall man. He looked to be about thirty-five or forty in mortal years. His build was massive. He had broad shoulders and a narrow waist, leading down to thick, strong legs. Lana knew he was a formidable opponent for anyone. In his mortal life, law enforcement was his calling. Any criminal who had the misfortune of crossing his path was sorry for it, Lana was sure. But as an immortal, he was unstoppable. He was like a train barreling down the tracks. She felt relief that they had called for help and that this goliath had shown up. Allan was skilled in the art of reasoning and profiling. He was their best hope of finding Kimmy.

"I need to make a call, excuse me," Allan said. He retrieved a number from his contacts and hit the call button. "Hey... Yeah, I think we have another one. I may need some backup on this one. Can you spare anybody?" Allan asked.

On the other end, the person must have given an agreeable answer because Allan smiled before he ended the call.

"Okay, I need to see that recording now," Allan asked.

Lana played the recording for him, and he seemed very interested in several points. Brady and Lana had seen nothing of importance on any part of the recording, but Allan scribbled away in his notebook.

"I have a colleague coming. He should be here first thing in the morning. I'm going to need to go to the location where you found the purse," Allan said.

His professionalism was extremely comforting to Lana. She felt all was being done that could be done to find her friend. However, she didn't want to have any what-if moments if this situation didn't turn out well.

"Sure, whenever you want to go," Brady said.

Allan finished reviewing the recording, and the three went to the alleyway. Allan was much more thorough than Lana and Brady had been. His training was evident in his investigation. His notebook gained more notes as he moved from one area to the next. He moved in small sections, dissecting each with great care. Several tiny things were bagged and placed into a small box he had brought with them. All was quiet and gave no hint about what he thought happened to Kimmy.

The group decided to stay in Kimmy's house for the night, just in case anything happened. Nothing did. Before the group had begun to stir for the day, someone pounded on the front door. Allan was there to answer it before the others fully registered the possible threat. A very neatly dressed man stood at the opening. He was of a slighter build than Allan but was toned and muscular. If one had to compare the two men, one was a lion, the other a cheetah. One was strength and size, and the other was stealth and speed. The two men greeted each other with a hug and slap on the back, which men did.

"Hey, Jaxon! Come in. This is Lana and Brady," Allan said.

Lana and Brady nodded a greeting and shook the man's hand.

"Nice to meet you both. I wish it were under better circumstances," Jaxon said.

"You, too, but we don't exactly know what these circumstances are. So what is going on here?" Brady questioned. He was respectful in his questions, but he was impatient to know what they thought they were dealing with here.

"Let me review the finding so far before I give you my opinion. It could be nothing. In most cases, it is. There is no need to get everybody's feathers in a ruffle just yet," Jaxon said.

Lana felt a sense of calm come over her instantly just by the smile on the man's face. He was different from Allan in a bizarre way. She still felt protected and that everything was in the best hands possible, but she felt a calming force emulating from him. Allan moved slowly and with purpose, while Jaxon seemed to be fighting an invisible fire with every step he took. He took two steps for every one of Allan's. Lana felt this was a great pairing. These two represented the best of both worlds.

The newcomer was presented with each piece of evidence. Jaxon had his own little notebook in which to document his findings. They watched the video for the thousandth time, and they noted timestamps. Jaxon got his laptop from his car and started an email to the council forensics team. He sent a list of the timestamps and asked for still shots, zoomed in as much as possible. Jaxon then wondered if the club or any neighboring businesses might have outdoor cameras. Allan told him he had checked the club and immediate places and planned to move farther out today.

This appeared to be the first order of business for the day. An outdoor concert area about a block from the club had cameras outside. The owners were cooperative and gave copies to Allan. The two sheriffs reviewed the recording of the day in question over and over. Both of the men made notes and sent timestamps to the council. Lana felt like they were getting answers. She just didn't know what they were. Lana didn't question their methods; they were the professionals after all.

Images rolled onto the screen of the laptop. Lana and Brady leaned in to see if they could find any similarities. Then there it was.

A face was in both club and venue shots. It was definitely the same person. Allan and Jaxon pointed out his proximity to Kimmy in the club. They pointed out how he seemed to be staring in her direction constantly. The man was at the venue as well, and his gaze was trained on a young woman there as well. The venue owner could not identify him. However, they could identify the woman. When the sheriffs questioned the woman, she had no idea who he was or that he was even there at all. When they took the photos to the club, the bartender and the waitress argued about whether or not that was a man they knew as Theo. Jaxon and Allan thanked them for their help. It wasn't a lot, but it was more than they had before, so they would take it.

"Can you run this information for me, please? Male, Caucasian, medium weight, approximately five feet ten, brown hair, blue eyes, first name Theo or some deviation of that name," Allan asked the forensics team member.

There was a pause on the phone as Jaxon received confirmation of the possible identities of this man. The hunt was on now. This was the part the two men loved. They got a thrill from the chase. The two sheriffs would check every name and turn over every rock until they found Kimmy Coleson.

Kimmy's Ongoing Stay

Kimmy couldn't believe this nightmare. She struggled, bit, and fought as much as her enchanted bindings would allow. This monster had grown bored with the typical behaviors of the mortal kidnapper and sexual assailant. His methods were viler than anything they could have ever dreamed of. He seemed to take enjoyment from inflicting vicious disfiguring assaults on Kimmy. The blood loss she incurred was devastating to her system. She lost almost all her power and strength and couldn't escape the torture. He made long gashes in her flesh from underarm to her wrist, slowly bleeding her almost to the point of no return. Finally, he would give her only enough blood to keep the desiccation at bay.

Kimmy could barely hold her head up, and she began to feel hopeless. Every day he dreamed up a new torment. He cut long strips of flesh from her body, and he was in awe of the healing process. The same healing properties were available in his own body, so Kimmy didn't understand his fascination. He required sick necrophilic behavior from Kimmy. He insisted she lie perfectly still, eyes open, no sound. This man was truly sick and twisted. Kimmy wondered if she would ever get out of this hell.

One day proved to be different for Kimmy. He had taken her chains and led her to a shower. Even though the water was ice cold, it was refreshing to be clean. This seemed to rejuvenate her. She felt stronger just by the rushing water pouring over her abused body. He cut, beat, and mutilated her, just to watch her heal and do it all over again. She was a victim who would never die, and he got a sick thrill out of that fact.

Kimmy's captor took her from her temporary solace and dried her with a towel. He dried her hair and combed it out. He almost seemed caring as he slowly tended to her needs. He spoke gently to her and called her darling and sweetheart. This new development creeped Kimmy out, as she knew she was dealing with more than one personality here. He had never shown her an ounce of kindness up to this point. She hardly felt it was genuine.

He led her out of the basement and to a small sparsely furnished room. He secured her chains to a chair similar to the one in the basement. He asked if she was comfortable. She only glared at him. She wondered what fresh hell awaited her here. He sat behind her in a chair and wiped at her back, ensuring it was free from any water droplets. She began to feel a tickling sensation as he moved an object over her skin. She was too afraid to look around and see what he was doing, so she sat perfectly still. She used her other senses to gain an idea of his actions. She smelled the pungent odor of a marker. He was drawing on her skin with a marker. She had been waiting for pain that seemed wouldn't come.

She was more than curious as to what he was doing, but she didn't care as long as the marker didn't turn into a knife. He took great pains with the outline and began to fill it in with what she could only guess was paint. His work stretch over her entire back, and she could only wonder what he had created. She didn't speak or move during the session.

"You are a very well-behaved canvas," he said.

Kimmy didn't respond.

"Since you are so cooperative, I will reveal my masterpiece to you when it has time to cure properly," he continued.

Kimmy sat with a fan blowing cold air onto her back for what seemed like forever. He never spoke or left his chair. He only sat and stared at her back. Finally, the uncomfortable silence was over as his trance broke, and he stood.

"Okay, Kimmy, are you ready to see it?" he asked.

Kimmy didn't respond.

"Now we have talked about this. You are to answer me when I ask you a question. Let's try this again. Are you ready to see it?" he repeated. He emphasized each word by separating them unnaturally in the question.

"Yes," Kimmy answered.

"Yes, what?" he corrected.

"Yes, sir," Kimmy answered.

The man handed Kimmy a mirror and turned her back to a floor-length one on the opposite wall. Kimmy stood and just stared in amazement at the work on her back. From shoulder to shoulder and the length of her back was a beautiful lily-like flower. He had used dark colors. Blues, purples, and blacks ran through its petals. The background was like a sunset with reds and yellows. The bottom had two tiny letters on the right-hand side. They were TS. Kimmy was impressed with his skill and was confused that he had signed his work.

"I would have loved to have that tattoo on you permanently, but you know we don't take well to that kind of thing," the man said.

Kimmy just stared at every line and detail. As sick as this was, if she could have been tattooed, this would have been something she would have thought was beautiful. Tears welled up in her eyes as she thought of the circumstances leading to this moment. She knew he would never let her go. His work adorned her body, and it would have to be freshened up from time to time. The job would fade and get damaged over time, so he never planned to let her go. This was the clarity she gained from this sitting.

"Awww, how sweet you are. You really like it, don't you? It is beautiful, I must admit, but my beautiful canvas gave an excellent backdrop for my work. One thing about this kind of body art is that it can be changed as often as we like. Don't you like the sound of that, little one?" he asked.

"Yes, sir," Kimmy answered.

"Very good, very good. You're learning quickly. I am very impressed. I think I will give you a treat for your behavior. Let me think," he said.

The man paced back and forth in front of Kimmy. He tapped his chin with his index finger. This nut job was really trying to figure out how to reward her. Finally, after many moments of contemplation, he seemed to reach a decision.

"I think I have a good idea. Let's see what you think about it. How about we don't go back in that old basement tonight? How about I move you to your new room? What do you think about that? Yes, I know it's a surprise to you, but I have a room especially for you. If you act like you have good sense, you will be allowed to stay there, and if you do not, you will go back to the dungeon. Do you understand me?" the man explained.

"Yes, sir," Kimmy answered.

"I think you forget something, don't you? Don't you think you should be thanking me for my kindness?" he asked.

"Thank you, sir," Kimmy said.

This was the first time Kimmy felt any sort of hope. If she were not confined to the basement, maybe she could find a way out of here. She had to play her cards right. She had to continue to gain his trust. He would eventually make a mistake. Kimmy only hoped the error wouldn't cost her, her life. He was very careless with his blood-letting and didn't feed her as much as she needed. She had learned she couldn't ask for anything, ever, or there were severe punishments ahead. She had to take what he provided and be thankful for them. She couldn't wait to hear him beg for mercy, but there would be none given. He would suffer unlike anyone in the history of time. She would see to that.

The man followed behind her, holding her bindings, and led her to a door at the end of a long hallway. Kimmy was beginning to get a feel for her surroundings. It was not a huge house. It seemed to have three stories, including the basement. She took it all in. She looked at the paintings lining the hallway, which caught his attention. His chest puffed out, and he stood a little taller and stopped so she could admire one of the paintings.

"Do you like these? Take your time, little pet. Enjoy," he said.

Kimmy stepped up the paintings, feigning interest. She looked intently at the ones in front of her. She looked up the hallway at the ones they had passed without inspection and then looked at the man.

"Of course, my dear. You can look at all of them," the man answered her unspoken question.

Kimmy stepped slowly back up the hallway. She took her time at each painting. Finally, she stopped in front of a beautiful lily painting much like the one she had on her back. It had lighter colors, blues, pinks, and purples running through it. She turned back to her captor with large expressive eyes.

"You may speak," the man said.

"Thank you, sir. This is quite lovely. It is like mine, but I think the one you gifted me is more beautiful in its own way," Kimmy said.

She lowered her gaze and then raised it to meet his eyes. He seemed utterly taken aback by her comment.

"The one you have is your very own. This one is another memory of mine. I am very pleased you have an eye for the arts. I knew I had made a wise decision choosing you," he said.

He turned Kimmy back toward her room, and he introduced her to her new prison. The room was airy and light. It was painted white and had tiny yellow flowers on the bedding. It reminded Kimmy of the pattern on old feed sack dresses. It was charming despite the landlord. The man took her chains and secured them to an eyebolt on the floor. The length of the chain allowed her to move about some. She was thankful for that. The furnishings in the room consisted of the bed and a chair that sat in the corner, out of reach of her chains.

Kimmy turned to the man and gave him a small submissive smile. He seemed pleased by her response. She knew exactly how to handle men. She just didn't know how much of her arsenal would be helpful with this one. She planned to try it all until she found the key to his damaged lock. Kimmy would play his little game until she either won or died, but she wouldn't give up, not ever. All she wanted was to see her friends again and go home to her mountain. She wasn't going to die by this filthy bastard's hands. She just had to stay his hand and make sure she was worth the trouble to keep alive.

The Call Home

Lana and Brady suggested that it might be time to call Kimmy's friends. Allan and Jaxon agreed, just in case she had contacted them in some way. Lana didn't want to make the call, but she knew it wasn't anybody else's place to do it. So she tapped the contact on Kimmy's phone and waited for an answer.

"Kimmy, how are ya, girl?" Ana greeted.

"Um, hi, my name is Lana, and I'm a friend of Kimmy's," Lana started.

"What's wrong?" Ana said in a panic.

"We really don't know yet, but we felt it was time we called and let you know something wasn't right here," Lana said.

"Where's Kimmy?" Ana said, in a complete panic now.

Lana played out all they knew for Ana and told her she had contacted the sheriffs for help. Ana immediately asked for an address and assured her she would be there ASAP. Lana gave her the information, and for some reason, she felt better just by speaking to the determined Ana.

"Mom!" Ana screamed.

Rene ran in from outside, nearly tearing the door from its hinges.

"What is it, Ana?" Rene asked.

Ana explained it all to Rene and said she was on her way to Myrtle.

"Not by yourself, you're not," Rene said.

"I was hoping you would say that," Ana said.

The two gathered up a few items and headed out the door and on to Myrtle. Ana had never been a fan of the beach, but she didn't hate it either. She had no doubt there was something wrong here, but she just couldn't imagine what it could be. Ana was disgusted with herself that she hadn't paid attention to the fact that Kimmy hadn't called in a while. That was really unusual for her. Ana would have known if she had thought about it. Rene tried to calm her daughter by telling her she would have had no way to know something was wrong, and even if she did, what could she have done about it?

Ana didn't care. She felt guilty for not being a better friend. She would find Kimmy and kick her ass for scaring her like this. Ana had nothing to compare this to other than her days with the Social Service Department. Anytime something like this happened, it usually didn't end well, but this kind of thing didn't happen now. She didn't know where to start, but she was on her way to begin the search.

Ana was thankful for Kimmy's friend Lana. Lana had made the call, and now Ana could help. Rene and Ana had a long history with evil people. If someone had done something to her friend, they would be so sorry they had. Rene and Ana were ruthless in pursuing justice, and with a family member, it would be never-ending. She would find Kimmy or find out what had happened to Kimmy, and she would dish out punishment that more than fit the crime. Whoever had her friend better not have disturbed a hair on her head, or their head would be disturbed for sure. She would detach it from their shoulders. She knew Kimmy better than anyone. If she told her friend she would be there in the morning, nothing would have kept Kimmy from at least contacting Lana with her change of plans. Something was wrong with Kimmy, and Ana knew it.

Rene rode beside Ana and listened to her rant and rave all the way to the ocean. Rene knew this side of Ana. She wasn't sure where she had gotten such rage, but she had seen it many times. Rene then smiled as she remembered she had stood beside Ana during every hideous thing she had done. She smiled while the blood drained from her victims. The people were guilty sinners of the worst kind. They deserved every punishment Ana delivered them. Rene remembered she had delivered some of her own, too, so it wasn't all Ana. They were both capable of vengeance. Whoever it was, this person better hope the sheriffs found them before Ana did, or there would be hell to pay.

They pulled into the driveway of what was Kimmy's home here. Ana looked around and took notice of the three vehicles in the driveway. She walked quickly to the door. She couldn't get there fast enough to begin her search. She knocked twice and turned the knob.

"Hello," Ana said.

"Hey, come in. You must be Ana," Lana said.

"Yes. Lana?" Ana asked. "This is my mom, Rene."

Everyone shook hands and introduced Brady, Allan, and Jaxon.

"Now, Ms. Reed, we don't know what is going on yet, but we are doing everything we can to find Kimmy," Jaxon said.

"It's Ana, and I do know what's going on. Somebody has her. She wouldn't just leave, and she hasn't called in a long time. That isn't something she does. Not in all the years I have known her has she ever not called with an update in a reasonable amount of time. She knows I worry about her running around by herself. She knows," Ana said.

"I know you have been acquainted for a long time. We just want you to know we are taking this seriously. This isn't the first time we have seen something like this in both the old and new world. People feel safe since the humans are confined, but there are still those out there that mean to do harm to others. So we won't stop until we find her, okay?" Allan explained.

"We have a list of names of people in the area that have a some-what less-than-desirable past. We have what we believe to be a photo of the perp and a first name, so that is a lot to go on. We just have to take it one step at a time and follow all the leads. It may take some time, but we will find her," Allan continued.

"What if she doesn't have time? What if, while we are running down all these clues, someone is killing her at that very moment? We can split up and cover more ground that way," Ana said.

"I agree, but everyone needs to work in pairs. No one travels alone. I think that is fair, don't you?" Jaxon asked.

Jaxon planned to give Ana, Rene, Lana, and Brady the least likely leads to follow. He and Allan would follow the ones that could possibly lead them to Kimmy's dangerous captor. Both sheriffs had grown more confident that Kimmy wouldn't just disappear without letting anyone know. They believed this was the same man they had been looking for in two other cases. The MO seemed the same, and the suspect's description was similar. All the participants needed to feel useful. They couldn't just sit and wait while their friend was in danger, and the sheriffs knew that, so they would direct the traffic out of harm's way if they could.

Each group was given several names to check out. Ana was very unnerved that there were so many immortals that the sheriffs believed should be investigated. The fact that the news didn't report incidents between immortals might be a bad thing, Ana thought. This might have led people into a false sense of security. Ana thought there definitely were not as many cases of wrongdoings among the immortals, but now she was beginning to believe it was much more prominent than she imagined it to be.

Ana and Rene started with the first name on their list, Robert Celos. They went to his home and found him lounging by the pool. He had just got back from a vacation trip to Arizona. He was happy to produce his ticket and gave them phone numbers to confirm his visit. They thanked him for his cooperation and moved on to the next name, Barthalamuel Hinsdale. They finally located Mr. Hinsdale on the beach with his wife. They both said they had visitors during the time of Kimmy's disappearance and hadn't left home or the beach during their stay. They did give their guests contact information, but Ana felt it wasn't necessary. She would circle back to this couple if none of the leads panned out, though.

The remaining names were as fruitless as these had been. Night was approaching, and the groups met back at Kimmy's house for an update. No one had any promising leads, and only four names remained unchecked. Everyone agreed they would beat the bushes until they found these four men. Ana didn't sleep at all that night. She was sick to her stomach. Images of Kimmy in various deadly situations kept creeping on her mind. She could hear Kimmy saying, "Don't give up on me." Ana knew under no circumstances would she ever give up.

Morning came, and Rene and Ana took their names and headed out.

Ross Clemons worked in a dress shop near the beach. He wasn't a man one would ever believe had done anything at all to a woman, but they would question him just the same.

"Hi, so nice of you to drop by," the glamorous Mr. Clemons greeted. "Won't you have a look around?"

He was over-the-top feminine, and his makeup and nails were much better than Ana's had ever been. He wore loose-fitting linen pants and a short-sleeved button-up with tiny starfish all over it. He had on leather sandals, and Ana couldn't help but notice that his pedicure was done to perfection and that his feet were as soft as a baby's behind. This guy couldn't catch a cold, let alone Kimmy, so she asked him random questions just in case. She asked if he knew Kimmy or had seen her before. He was very attentive to the photos Ana showed him, and he said he was truly sorry he couldn't help. He asked that they let him know their findings. Ana knew he was just a nosey nelly, but she agreed. He was so uplifting and happy that he made Ana feel better just in that short amount of time.

Ana decided to call Lana and see if they had better luck.

"Hey, ours was a bust. How was yours?" Ana asked.

"I was just going to call you. This Theo Sails isn't living at the address we have for him. Actually, it isn't even a house. It's part of a shopping mall. It looks like an art gallery or something. We went inside and looked around but didn't find anything. What do you want us to do now?" Lana asked.

"Text us the address. We will be right there," Ana said.

Lana did as Ana asked and called Allan to see if he could help with the address.

"I'll make some calls and see if I can get another address for him," Allan said.

"Okay, let us know," Lana said.

Ana decided to check with some of the neighboring businesses. She wanted to see if anyone knew this guy. So she started with the shoe store two doors down.

"Hey, I was wondering if you could help me. Do you know the man who used to be at the art place next door?" Ana asked.

"Yep. Theo. But he hasn't been open in a long time now," the nice lady answered.

"Oh no, you wouldn't happen to know where I could find him, do you? We had a piece we wanted to see if he could do for us," Ana lied.

The lady thought about it for a second then answered, "I had to think about where he said he lived. He told me once he had a house up on Ocean Side. He uses it for a studio, too, I think. He does excellent work. I had something done myself. I was very pleased," the lady said.

"Oh, that sounds great. I waited longer than I had told him to get it done, so I was so disappointed for him to be no longer be here. Ocean Side, you say? Is it the white house on the right?" Ana asked.

She tried to act like she was familiar with the man and knew just exactly what she was talking about, though she did not.

"No, it's the yellow one with the little fence around it, I think," the woman corrected.

"Thanks so much for your help," Rene said, trying to rush Ana along.

"Yes, thank you so much," Ana said.

"You are so welcome. Tell him Racheal says hi when you see him," the lady said.

"Oh, I will," Ana said.

The two left and headed for Ocean Side. They didn't bother letting Allan know because they had been let down so much already. Rene suggested they park down several streets from the house, and Ana agreed. There was no car in the driveway, and the garage door was open, showing no car parked there either. Ana went up to the front door and knocked. She figured she would come up with something should someone answer, but no one did. Ana turned to Rene and shrugged her shoulders. Rene simply reached down and tried the knob. It was locked. This was suspicious because no one ever locked a door. The two moved to the open garage door and found the door leading into the house was unlocked.

They cautiously went inside, trying to be as quiet as possible. They looked around the kitchen, and Ana noticed a well-used paint pallet in the trashcan. She knew they were in the right place. Ana saw a door and took it down to the basement area of the house. They flipped on the light switch and immediately knew they were in the right place. The room was cluttered with everyday basement things, but a chair was embedded into the floor's concrete. The chair legs were bent as though someone had strained against them. Ana couldn't breathe when she noticed a pile of tattered clothing lying on the countertop. Kimmy had for sure been here because the cut-up shirt was Ana's. Kimmy and Ana often exchanged clothes, and she remembered Kimmy taking this one with her.

Rene gasped. "What is that?" she asked.

She knew full well what she was looking at—it was blood splattered on the concrete blocks—but she needed Ana's confirmation. She was terrified and felt like she was going to throw up. Rene had never fully gotten over her fears for Ana's safety. So anything evil in the world was a threat to her child, and she didn't tolerate those.

Ana saw what Rene had pointed to, and her face grew pale before the heat of rage flushed her cheeks. Ana heard the door open upstairs. She took the steps two at a time and burst through the basement door into the kitchen. She planned to beat her friend's location out of whoever was standing there. Unfortunately, familiar faces stood in her path.

"What are you doing?" Jaxon said.

"She was here. I know for sure she was. We haven't checked the house yet. Kimmy! Kimmy!" Ana screamed. She raced from door to door, checking for her friend. Then she heard a faint reply at the end of the hallway.

"Down here!" Ana yelled.

The door was locked. Allan moved Ana to the side and hit the door with his shoulder. The door gave way quickly, and they were inside. Sitting on the bed, bound in silver chains, was Kimmy. Tears streamed down her face, and she erupted in laughter.

"I have never been so glad to see you in my life. Get me out of here!" she screamed.

"Why didn't you break the chains?" Ana said. She started to touch the chains to break Kimmy free, but Jaxon suddenly stopped her.

"No, don't touch those. Let me do it," Jaxon said.

He moved Ana back and slowly unwrapped the chains from Kimmy's wrists and ankles. He laid them on the floor, and Kimmy was free. She jumped into Ana's arms and hugged her tightly.

"We have to get you out of here," Ana said while pulling her friend from the bed.

Kimmy pulled back from Ana. "No, I can't just leave. He will do this again to someone else, or he will find me. No way I'm going to live the rest of my life wondering where he is. I am out of the chains, which is something else we have to figure out later, and I'm not about to let this piece of shit get away with this," Kimmy explained.

Ana looked from Allan to Jaxon and back again. She waited for them to say they had to leave, but they didn't. Instead, they just stood there like knots on a log.

"Would you please tell her we have to go? She is weak, and she needs to get out of here," Ana said.

"Forever is a long time to live in fear, Ana," Rene said.

Ana looked back at Kimmy and studied her face. She knew this had changed her forever, but she couldn't stand the thought of her being scared for the rest of forever.

"Okay, I get it, but if you're staying, so am I. You can't fight him on your own, not the way you are right now. We will do whatever you want to do," Ana said.

"If you're staying, I'm staying," Rene stated firmly.

"This guy is nothing without those chains, but I'm not telling you to go. No way," Kimmy said.

"You understand why we can't be here when he gets here, I hope. We are the sheriffs, and vigilante justice is frowned upon in the council, but I get it," Jaxon said.

"We will be right down the street. We will wait in the car until you talk this out with this man and get him to apologize. I know that is what you're going to do," Allan said.

"Well," Ana started.

"Nope, nope, that's what you're going to do, right?" Allan asked.

Ana finally got his meaning and nodded in agreement.

"Just tell him he needs to leave town, and no one ever needs to hear from him again, not ever. Do you understand?" Jaxon asked.

"Yeah," Ana answered.

Jaxon has that right, Ana thought. *No one will ever hear from him again.*

She didn't know what had happened to Kimmy here, but it didn't matter. He was going to pay. Jaxon and Allan took the chains with them and said they would find out what was up with them. Rene, Ana, and Kimmy sat like spiders in a web, waiting for their prey. Kimmy explained that this man had a routine he never deviated from, ever. He would walk through the door at five on the dot. She didn't know where he went every day. But he would be home at five—no ifs, ands, or buts.

Ana went to the car and got Kimmy several bottles of BB to help boost her strength. It made Ana sick at how Kimmy drank it like she was starving to death. Ana suspected that she was starving, and oh, how he would pay for that. Neither Rene nor Ana asked Kimmy any questions until they saw her back.

"What is on your back?" Ana asked.

"He painted that on me. That wasn't too bad. I kinda like it," Kimmy said. She was such an upbeat person. Even in this horrific circumstance, she found a silver lining.

"We will be scrubbing that off as soon as we get you home," Rene said.

Just as Kimmy said, they heard a car pull into the garage at five o'clock. They listened to this thing pilfering in the kitchen and opening and closing drawers. They silently waited for him to find a new set of problems in his day. They planned on being the last problem he would ever have. Ana wondered why people had to pee whenever somebody was hiding or waiting. Every time she had hidden behind a couch to scream happy birthday to someone or anytime she stayed in a long line, she had to pee every single time. This was no exception. Ana's excitement was over the top, and she could see the devil in Rene's eyes as well.

Kimmy sat on the bed, just as they had planned. Her chains were gone, and she wondered how long it would take him to figure that out. He was so self-absorbed that she thought he wouldn't even notice for a minute or two. She wasn't wrong.

"Hello, little one. I hope you have had a good day," the man said.

Kimmy didn't respond. The man did turn and look in her direction but didn't notice her new freedom. He was the definition of a narcissist. It was all about him. He couldn't care less if she had those chains wrapped around her neck. He would just be annoyed that he had to find a new audience for his annoying stories. He began to take off his tie and unbutton the top button so he could breathe better.

Kimmy thought, *You better breathe now, you shit.*

He sat on the edge of the bed, started to untie his spotless shoes, and slipped them off. This was when the first of many assaults would have taken place, but Kimmy had other plans. She was getting more and more anxious about him not even looking at her. She considered running her hand through his hair or some other out-of-character behavior, but she didn't. Instead, she quietly sat as she had been taught to do. Ana and Rene waited in the room across the hall. They couldn't stand the thought of him this near to Kimmy, but they promised they would stay put until she called for them.

"Now, little pet, I am all yours for the evening. What do you think about that?" the man said. He turned to see her response, and only then did he notice that the chains were gone. "What the hell?" he yelled.

Kimmy jumped forward and struck the man directly in the mouth. Blood poured from the split lip she just gave him. He quickly regained his footing, dove across the bed, and grabbed Kimmy's leg. He clawed and pulled until she was almost underneath his weight. Kimmy started to scream for help.

"Ana! Ana!" Kimmy cried.

Ana wasted no time bursting through the door. She and Rene grabbed the tyrant and pulled Kimmy free of his grasp. Ana's fangs had descended from her gums, and she wanted nothing more than to rip out this bastard's throat, but she wouldn't deny Kimmy the satisfaction. Rene and Ana held him tightly, and he was no match for their fury. Finally, Kimmy rose to her feet in front of him and spat in his face.

"It's my turn to speak now. What do you think about that?" Kimmy said.

She looked this monster dead in the eye and told him everything she wished she had time to do to him. Unfortunately, he was no different from all the other schoolyard bullies in history. He was weak in the face of opposition, and he cried. He begged for understanding and even tried to blame Kimmy for his actions. This crazy person tried to convince Kimmy that he wouldn't have had to do all this if she had only been less of a snob and showed a little common decency.

"So all this was my fault. Is that what I am hearing coming out of your mouth? Are you really this twisted?" Kimmy asked.

This line of questioning infuriated the man, and he flung his head back and caught Rene right in the nose with the back of his head. Blood flew out of her nose and mouth. Ana immediately retaliated with a swift punch to the side of his head. She continued to pound away at his head. She hoped it would cave in, but she stopped before it did. She wanted him fully aware of his fate. Ana wanted him to know that Kimmy got her revenge. Kimmy walked up to the man toe to toe. She unbuttoned his pants and let them fall to the floor. Ana was a little confused, but she let it play out.

Kimmy pulled his pants off his body and ripped the shirt from his back. He stood completely naked. She hoped he felt as uncomfortable and scared as she had been. He would be scared very soon. Kimmy was sure of that much. Kimmy had taken the liberty of retrieving some things from his toy box, as he called it, and when she produced the shining blade, he screamed. He knew justice was about to be served, and he could do nothing to stop it. So Kimmy's first order of business was to make him weaker than he already was. She sliced his arms from pit to wrist and watched as the blood soaked the carpet. Next, she removed huge strips of flesh from his thighs to his calves, and the blood pooled, just as she had fantasized. He was limp in the arms of Rene and Ana. Their need for blood seemed insatiable.

Kimmy saved the best for last as she lifted his limp appendage and relieved him of it. The screams were ear-piercing as she let it fall to the floor. Kimmy was grateful the object of her torment was gone, and its owner soon to follow. The only thing she could see was the smirk on his stupid face whenever he hurt her. She planned to rid him of that as well. She took the blood-soaked blade and gave him a new smile. This smile went from ear to ear. She cut it to the bone. She wanted him to know the pain she felt every time she saw him smile. Kimmy stood and admired her work. She watched as his life force drained from his body. He would heal but not fast enough. Somehow this was still not enough. Kimmy stood in front of him for one last bit of vengeance. She placed her hands on each side of his bleeding face and let him know what she planned to do next.

"You once said you wanted to give your heart to someone, but we were all just bitches. Do you remember that? Well, I'm going to take it," Kimmy calmly said.

She punched her fist through the man's chest and felt his heart beating in her hand. She kept her grip on the organ while he writhed and whined in pain. Finally, when she'd had enough, she pulled it from his body. She held it in her hand, and she watched as it disintegrated into dust. Ana and Rene dropped the dead husk to the floor, and they watched as it appeared to melt away. Finally, there was nothing left but dust on the bloody carpet. Kimmy simply turned to the door and walked out.

"Let's go home," she said.

No one spoke a word as they made their way to the house where Kimmy had been staying. Lana and Brady were there to greet her. Kimmy hugged her friend and cried real tears of joy. She thanked Brady for all he had done for her. She couldn't believe he had done so much for someone he barely knew. Kimmy hoped she would have done the same, but she didn't really know. She did notice the way Lana and Brady looked at each other. She hoped this was a good sign. Maybe something good would come of this nightmare after all. Jaxon and Allan had to send in reports on their findings. They simply said Kimmy was found safe and that no further investigation was needed. Kimmy guessed that was true. She was safe, and that garbage would never hurt another soul.

Ana encouraged Lana and Brady to come to the mountain with them for a while. She thought everyone could use a break from

Myrtle. To her surprise, they agreed, and everyone packed up and headed home. Kimmy knew one thing was for sure. "Home" was the nicest word she had ever heard in her life, and it would be a long time before she left it again if she ever did.

Oakview's Newest Residents

I t didn't take the group long to get on the road. Ana did take the time to call the man at the dress shop and let him know all was well with Kimmy. She could almost see him standing with one hand on his hip and the other over his heart in an overly dramatic manner. He said he was delighted everything was okay and wished us well. Ana really did wish that strange little man well. He was one of the good ones. She could just tell that about him.

Lana and Brady loaded into Brady's truck, Kimmy and Ana took Kimmy's precious car, and Rene led the way. Music was pumping from every vehicle. Everyone was glad to be out of Myrtle. Kimmy looked back once at her vast blue friend. She knew she might see the ocean again sometime, but it would never be this one. She was thankful to leave it behind her in the rearview mirror.

"Hope you can keep up," Rene said.

She peeled out in the Camero she was driving, and smoke bellowed from the tires. Kimmy laughed wholeheartedly as she put the pedal to the floor. She laid on the horn as a final goodbye to her former place of refuge. Lana and Brady pulled away, shaking their heads at their traveling companions. His 4 x 4 truck wasn't built for speed. It was more a bull than a racehorse. The happy train moved steadily toward the rolling hills of home. Many phone calls passed between the vehicles, so everyone felt like they rode together on their trip.

As Kimmy saw her mountain just up ahead, her heart leaped with sheer joy. She remembered a song she had once heard and quoted the lyrics to Ana.

"There is nothing like the green, green grass of home," Kimmy quoted.

"You got that right," Ana said. She patted Kimmy on the knee and smiled.

Both Lana and Brady had traveled almost everywhere in the world, but somehow they had missed this place. It was so beautiful Lana could hardly believe it. Everything was lush and green, and the air was fresh and full of life. It was just as Kimmy had described it. The very mountain itself felt alive, and it seemed to be waiting on its children's return. The quiet, simple country life would be in stark contrast to Lana's party scene, but it reminded Lana of her youth. It would be a welcome change for her.

Brady was a man who enjoyed the great outdoors. He loved to ski, mountain-climb, hike, and of course, surf. Unfortunately, this place didn't offer surfing, but it had so much else to offer. He would find great happiness in this environment, he was sure. Brady had grown very fond of Lana, and he knew that anywhere she called home would be where he wanted to be as well. He hoped Lana felt the same connection. Their meeting just seemed too strange to be a coincidence. It was like fate had a hand in it.

Kimmy was confused when she saw Rene pass the road that led to their house.

"Where is she going?" Kimmy asked.

"Oh, I forgot to tell you. We use that for office space and storage now. We live up here just a bit," Ana answered.

They traveled about three miles down a very narrow road and drove to a beautiful brick two-story house. When Kimmy was younger, she dreamed of living in a house like this one, but only people of a particular class could afford that, and she wasn't part of that club. She felt it was a case of the haves and the have-nots. Those who had kept it, and those who didn't never have. Kimmy was a farmer's daughter, and the women who lived in these grand homes were the daughters of the wealthy.

Kimmy never dreamed of being more than a farmer's daughter turned into a farmer's wife. Thankfully, someone saw more in her spirit than she ever did. He granted her the gift of immortality. After all the time she had walked the earth, Kimmy never really got the hay out of her hair. She would always be a farmer's daughter, and of that, she was proud. She watched the wealthy stomp on the heads of the poor and build their wealth on the backs of those in servitude. If that was what it took to be wealthy, she would happily do without it.

There was plenty of room for everyone in the massive estate. Rene's was on the first level, and each guest found their rooms among the six upstairs. Ana had turned the old carriage house into her own apartment. Even though it was still in the same yard as her mother, she felt more independent. She had always lived in the same house as Rene. To even go into the backyard was a big step for her. She felt free to make changes or do anything she wanted to do. It was not like Rene would have ever minded anything she did in their home, but she just felt better about making changes to her own. It was just different to live in the CH, and Ana loved it.

Kimmy stayed with Ana most of the time. Ana felt that it made Kimmy feel more secure, and she was all about her feeling safe. Kimmy kept most of her things in the big house, but she had her PJs and toiletries at Ana's. Ana never asked Kimmy about her ordeal in Myrtle. She knew she would talk about it if she needed to. So at night, the two sat in front of the TV and talked about everything but the trauma.

"You think we can go to the farm sometime soon? I still don't feel like I'm hitting on all cylinders," Kimmy asked.

"Yep, sure can. I was going to see what you thought about me asking my donor some questions about any fishy business going on in there," Ana answered.

She didn't even want to mention the chains or any magic behind the dome. She knew they needed to wrap up the loose ends, but those subjects were intricate parts of Kimmy's nightmare. So Ana chose to tread lightly on the subject. Kimmy looked to the floor and totally ignored the question. The two ate chips and drank wine until they were giggling like teenage girls. Kimmy kept her eyes downcast and finally responded to Ana's question from two hours prior.

"I think we should try to figure out whatever we can about the magic. I want everyone involved to pay," Kimmy said.

Ana simply shook her head and shoved more chips in her mouth. "Let's see if everybody wants to go tomorrow," Ana suggested.

Everyone agreed to meet at nine sharp. Ana was excited to see James as much as she was excited to get the answers they needed. Everyone piled into the shopping van, and they went toward the farm. The trip was fun. Lana and Brady told stories of their lives and helped everyone get to know them better. Ana liked them right away. They were just regular people living regular lives until this nightmare with Kimmy had happened. Both of them had stepped up to the plate, though, and worked tirelessly to find Kimmy. Ana could never repay them for that kindness.

When arriving at the farm, Ana noticed that a different gate-keeper was on duty. He was the complete opposite of the last one. He was more of a business type. He was clean cut and well groomed. Ana knew he was probably the more vicious of the two if the truth were told. Everyone signed in and headed off in their own directions. Ana was glad Kimmy took off the other way. Feeding was a private matter, and Ana always wanted to do it alone. She wanted to find James, not just to ask him the questions, but just to see him.

Ana glanced in the direction her mother had gone and saw her embracing a very tall handsome gentleman. They clasped hands and headed off down the path. Rene had embraced him like one might embrace a long-lost companion. Ana really loved the idea because that was just how she felt about James. They had met only once, but she knew she had to have more. Ana would have no problem finding a willing donor, but she didn't want just any donor. She didn't even want to refer to James as a donor. He was her friend.

Ana considered taking another path, but she couldn't bring herself to do it. She had met James on this path, and she hoped to do the same today. She waited for a little white fluff ball to bound up to her, but none ever came. She stopped and smelled the roses in the garden, which were beginning to come to their end. She walked over to the pond and watched the duck, and she remembered her time with James there. It felt like butterflies fluttering in her stomach as she remembered the feed. No one came along the path, so she continued farther.

Every so often, she could see tiny houses nestled among the trees. Some were ornately decorated with lawn ornaments and birdhouses.

Hand-carved wooden yard furniture and statues adorned the yards of the cottages. Some houses were just as they had been when brought into the sanctuary. There were barn-shaped roofs and A-frame roofs, all in different colors. There were red, green, tan, and silver. Each had its own personality just by the subtle changes. All the homes were wood-sided and appeared to be cozy and well maintained. What they lacked in size was more than made up for with character.

Family units were kept together, just as in the mortal world. Men and women were allowed the freedom to love and have children on their own terms. Ana suddenly stopped in her tracks. She had never considered the fact that James might have a partner. He could have children as well. They never spoke of it, but she never asked. Maybe he was protecting his family from her. The thought of James sharing a bond like that with a mortal woman made Ana feel queasy.

"Stop it, Ana," she said to herself.

She knew she was making something out of possibly nothing, but her insecurities were front and center.

Up ahead, Ana heard a sound *tap, tap, tap*. A young man was repairing a fence surrounding a small paddock, where he had several goats.

"Good morning," Ana called.

"Good morning to you," the young man answered.

"Looks like you have a busy day ahead," Ana said. She pointed to the fence that seemed to be getting the best of the young man.

"Yeah, old stinky there keeps breaking into the doe pen," he explained.

Ana laughed as she noticed a giant very agitated, stinky male goat in the paddock to the side of the house.

"You'll have that, though. Can I help you with something?" he asked.

Ana was too embarrassed to ask the stranger about James, so she just kept talking.

"No, I'm just here with my family today. I was just looking around," Ana explained.

"Well, I'm Bryon. Nice to meet you," Bryon said.

He slipped off his work glove and extended his hand to Ana in greeting. She excepted his hand and smiled warmly at the polite young man.

"Ana. Ana Reed," Ana greeted.

Bryon stood for a moment as if he were trying to remember something important.

"Ana? Are you James's Ana?" Bryon asked.

Ana was so shaken she couldn't speak. She knew she must look like a complete idiot with her mouth hanging open for the flies to come in. After a few seconds of silence, Bryon continued.

"Do you know James?" he asked.

"Um, yes, I know him. I thought I would say hello, but I haven't seen him yet. I'm sure he is busy," Ana answered.

"He would kill me if I didn't call him and let him know you were here. Would you come and sit until I get ahold of him?" Bryon asked politely.

"Sure, I'm in no hurry. Take your time," Ana said. She walked up to a chair sitting in the shade of an old oak tree and took a seat.

"I will be right back. I will get the word out, and he will be here lickety-split. Would you like some tea?" Bryon asked.

"That would be very nice. Thank you," Ana said.

The council had installed old landline phones between the houses for the residence to use. Ana remembered it being somewhat of a roll of the dice, though. You were at the mercy of a phone cord, and someone was actually hearing it ringing. Nevertheless, Ana had full faith in Bryon. He seemed very motivated to find James, and Ana was glad he was. She grew more impatient as time moved forward, but the breeze blowing through the trees was helping her relax a little.

It had been a long time since their one and only meeting. Ana thought James would have given up on her by now, but this man, Bryon, seemed to know who she was. He had referred to Ana as "James's Ana," and she felt a rush of heat rising in her body at the thought. He must be close to Bryon to confide in him about her unless it was of no great importance to him, and he was just making idle conversation. Maybe he told him of a foolish immortal who made a fool of herself with him. Perhaps he told him she wasn't that special but whatever. Ana quickly stopped the negativity before she bolted out of her chair and left.

"You must have made quite the impression on James, and he is on his way now. He asked that you not leave. He is coming. 'Please wait,' end quote," Bryon said.

He had a crooked smile, and that only made his innuendo more awkward. Ana didn't respond. James had made quite the impression on her as well. However, she had learned long ago not to open up too much. Opening up left one vulnerable to ridicule and embarrassment when things didn't go as one had hoped. Bryon and Ana chatted about Bryon's farming projects, and Ana learned more than she ever wanted to know about Nubian goats. She pretended to be interested, though. She didn't want to appear rude or anxious for James to arrive.

Ana saw James walking up the path briskly. She wanted to jump up and run to him, but she held her seat. "Eagerness isn't becoming of a young lady," would be what her mother would have said. She remained focused on her discussion with Brayon but did peek from time to time. James moved like a man on a mission, and his eyes never left Ana. He started to jog when he reached the yard, and when he got to Ana, he pulled her to her feet and wrapped his arms around her in a big bear hug. It took Ana by surprise, but she hugged him right back.

"I have been so worried about you. What kept you away so long?" James asked.

Ana felt him nuzzle his nose in her hair, and she heard him take a deep breath. Her heart melted at his evident caring for her. Ana couldn't understand this feeling between them, but she just knew she couldn't ignore it. He was a magnet to her steel, and the pull was too strong to fight.

"I know. We had an...uh, a situation, but everything is okay now," Ana explained.

"What kind of situation?" James asked.

He had a very dominant personality. His very aura demanded respect from everyone. So even though he was the inferior species here, he carried himself with pride. Among other things, Ana admired this about him. She drew back from him and glanced toward Bryon. James took the hint and figured a way for them to make their exit.

"Thanks so much for getting in touch with me. I'll come back later and help you finish up," James said.

"No problem. Come on back, and we will get into something. I'm about to wrap this up, I think," Bryon said.

James took Ana's hand as she had seen her mother's friend do, and they walked down the path.

"These houses are so cute," Ana said. She studied the different hidden gems and again wondered about his living arrangements.

"Thanks. We like it," James said.

Like she had before, Ana felt a sense of ownership from James. She understood this was all he knew the world to be, so he kind of took pride in the place. It was his prison, and he had no idea he was an inmate. She was thankful for that. She never wanted to see him defeated or hopeless as the first residence of the farms had been. She always wanted that royal quality to exude from his very soul.

"Is your house nearby?" Ana asked.

"Yep, not too far," he answered. "I really was worried about you. Then I thought, maybe I had just been crazy to believe we made a connection. Where did you go?"

Ana didn't hesitate in telling James a broad outline of her trip. She left out the part about the chains and the magic but didn't leave out the brutality done to her friend. She was completely surprised by the level of concern he showed Kimmy.

"It could have turned out so much worse. We are so thankful we found her in time," Ana said.

James shook his head and gritted his teeth. He was angry and helpless. Ana saw his face redden and his grip tighten on her hand.

"We're okay now, no worries. That ass will never, and I mean never, hurt another person again," Ana consoled.

"Tell your friend I send my love and hope that she recovers soon. I know immortals heal and everything, but that's not what's broken with your friend. It may take her some time to deal with it all," James said.

Ana felt such adoration for this man. He showed genuine concern for her friend merely because Ana loved her. One afternoon in
this man's company sparked a fire in Ana she didn't know was even
possible. She was interested to see if a second encounter would lift
the veil of infatuation she had with him. Then, of course, he would
likely do something or say something stupid, and the illusion of perfection would evaporate. She hoped he would, then again; she was
desperate for him not to.

As the two moved down the path, they took their time. They
stopped and sat at the many seating areas along the way. Ana noticed
a plaque with a single name engraved on it attached to the benches
and random statues.

"Who are these people?" Ana asked.

"Those are mortals who did great deeds for not only our kind
but yours as well. People teach their children about each person so
no one ever forgets their contributions," James explained. He ran his
fingers over the name with great respect for this unknown person.

"Do you know this one?" Ana asked.

"I know the story. Adam developed some of the vegetation here
on the farm that proved to be beneficial to us humans. The plants
encourage healthy blood production. When immortals feed, as you
know, there can be significant blood loss, but the plant life he developed allows the body to rejuvenate much quicker," James explained.

Ana nodded and found it quite strange how James was so mat-
ter-of-fact about immortals taking the blood from their veins. It
seemed to be such an invasion, just out and out theft, of their person.
The mortals had no choice of whether or not they gave their dona-
tion. It was taken, just as it had been before the farm. Only now, the
donors were brainwashed not to mind it. Ana knew in the old world
there were willing donors, but who had actually fed on them? She
didn't know any immortals who would have fed on a mentally defi-
cient person, and anyone who chose to be a blood bag had to be nuts.

James, however, knew no different way of life. On the contrary,
he was programmed to believe this was natural and the least the mortals could do for their benefactors. They returned to their walk, and
Ana asked James about every plaque they came across. One was a

doctor, another helped the immortals during a bloody uprising, and one was an extraordinary animal breeder. This man developed not only natural animals but superspecies. These creatures produce more of whatever they were bred to produce. Whether it was milk or meat, they were superior in their design. Ana asked if James could show her some of these animals sometime, and James gladly agreed. Her request left him with the hope that she planned to return for future visits. He was overjoyed. He smiled as he thought of all the things he could hold back in showing her so she would have to come back to see them. He would have to make a list.

"Are those people still here on the farm?" Ana asked.

"No, all of them are gone on to the next life, I imagine. They only get a plaque of acknowledgment after they are gone," James said.

Reality hit Ana like a ton of bricks. Everyone behind these walls would one day be nothing more than a memory or a name engraved on a plaque somewhere. They were all mortal and would suffer the natural death of man. The thought sickened her. She knew she had to get the image of James's corpse out of her mind.

"Well, this is it," James said.

He extended his hand in the direction of a little barn roof cottage on his right. There were beautifully hand-carved chairs and a bench on the porch out front. A mama bear and three cubs strolled across the backrest of the bench, with pine trees as their backdrop. On the backrest of one chair was a carved bobcat's head, and the other had a majestic wolf staring through her soul. They were so delicate and beautiful Ana couldn't find the words to express how much she loved them. The craftsmanship and expert execution of the pieces were like nothing she had ever seen outside these walls.

"These are so beautiful," Ana said.

"Thank you. They were fun to make," James said.

"What? You did these," Ana asked.

"Yeah. I needed something for out here and thought I would just make something. I know it's silly when there are tons to choose from at the warehouse, but I wanted something different," James explained.

Ana realized the carved pieces at Bryon's home were done by the same artist, and this artist was her James. Her James, just as Bryon had referred to her as "James's Ana." He was hers. She didn't know how or why, but he was hers. No matter the cost, she would enjoy him for as long as she could or as long as he could stay with her.

"Would you like to sit? I will get us some lemonade," James asked.

Ana sat in the bobcat chair and left the wolf for her wolf. James went inside, and Ana heard him switch off something she believed to be an air conditioner. He was quick to return. Ana was very impressed with the lemonade. It was perfectly sweet and sour, and she loved it.

"Did you make this? If you say you did, I'm going to believe you're some sort of magician," Ana said.

"No magician here. My friend Brenda made it. She makes big batches, and it was my turn to get some. I'm so glad you like it," James explained.

Immediately, Ana wondered who this Brenda was. What did she look like? How old was she? She had questions. Ana couldn't stand a rival for James's affections. Ana knew jealousy was an ugly emotion, but she couldn't help how she felt. She had always been a victim of the green-eyed monster. She wouldn't apologize for that either. She thought she had the worse end of the deal. She was the one in pain and insecurity. It was everyone else's responsibility to shield her from that kind of grief. She knew it wasn't rational, but it was her lie, and she was sticking to it.

Then as if James could read her thoughts, he continued, "Brenda and her partner live up that way. They were friends with my mom."

Ana smiled and was surprised at how relieved she was by his explanation. She tried to be inconspicuous as she peeked through the screen door into his home. James noticed, and he smiled.

"Would you like to come inside? I will turn the AC back on if you want to," James asked.

"I'm sure you're warm out here. That's fine with me," Ana said.

She was so nosey. She wanted to see everything James surrounded himself with inside his home. The house was small, so whatever he had was precious to him for one reason or the other. She wanted to know the story of every piece. She wanted to know what made James sentimental because she wanted to be valuable to him as well.

She sat on a small couch and scanned the room. Across from her was a TV on a stand, with carved figures surrounding it. The walls had beautiful paintings of nature and landscapes, but on a prominent space, visible from all areas, was a portrait of a woman and a small boy. Ana immediately recognized the forest green eyes of the boy.

"Aww, it that you?" Ana asked.

"Yes," he answered.

"Your mother?" Ana questioned.

"Yes," he said.

"She is beautiful," Ana said.

"Yes, she was," he corrected.

Ana noticed the past tense and dropped the obviously painful subject.

To her right, taking up precious real estate in the home was a large bookcase. The shelving was so full that James had the rows doubled on each shelf and had books stacked on the rows. Ana believed she had found his loves. It was clear his mother held the number one space, followed by literature, then his art. She wanted desperately to fit into just a small section of his heart.

"I love your collection," Ana said. She pointed to his books lining the wall.

"Thanks. I love to read. I read as much as I can," James said.

"I love to read too," Ana confided.

"It is hard for me to imagine the things I read about, but I guess that's what an imagination is for," James said.

Ana realized it probably was overwhelming to read about things outside these walls. She always enjoyed fantasies, like *The Lord of the Rings* and *The Hobbit*. Maybe James viewed the marvels in his books as Ana did Falkor in *The Neverending Story*. Ana sipped her drink slowly. She didn't want her time with James to end. They sat quietly at times, but it wasn't an awkward silence. Both were contemplating the other.

"Can I ask you something?" James asked.

"Of course, you can. Anything," Ana said.

"Where do you live? What is it like? Who lives there with you?" James fired in rapid succession.

The questions seemed to Ana to be rehearsed. He spoke as if he were reading from a questionnaire. Ana smiled as she thought about all the questions and his curiosity.

"Well, I will take those one at a time. The first, I think, was where I live, right? I live in a little town called Oak View here in Virginia. Number two was, what's it like? It is a very close-knit place. Everyone knows everybody else and knows all their business whether they want them to or not. It's cool, though, because there is always a friend around if you need to talk. Then there was number three. Who lives there? My mom, Kimmy, Lana, and Brady live on the estate. Did I get them all?" Ana said.

She noticed his reaction to Brady's name and hoped she wasn't reading too much into his seemingly concerned look.

"Yep, that was all of them, for now," James said.

Ana decided to rescue him from his uncomfortable feelings as he had done for her earlier. She explained everyone's relationship to her and went on to say that she believed Lana and Brady were involved but hadn't come out with it yet. James seemed visibly eased by this information. Ana was paying close attention to all his body language during her explanation.

"It sounds great. Honestly, I can't even imagine how it would be out there. Do you know what I mean? Everyone knows everyone else here, and no one would hesitate to help someone out if they needed it. You seemed surprised by Lana and Brady's willingness to help when it came to Kimmy. Here, that is just a given. There are some benefits to our society after all. Maybe," James said.

"Yeah, there really may be," Ana said.

She wasn't lying to him either. She truly believed there was a lot to be said for this way of life. The human race had come a long way. It came from a time of greed and selfishness to one of kindness and mercy. It had emerged like a butterfly from its prison cocoon.

"Can I ask you a question too?" Ana asked.

"Hit me," James said.

"Do you have family here? What is your contribution zone on the farm? What is your favorite book?" Ana asked. She spat out the questions so quickly she could see James's mind reeling to keep up.

"Haha! Okay, here I go. Number 1, I have an aunt and her partner and three cousins. Second, I work here as a carpenter and amateur electrician. Last, I have so many I couldn't pick just one. There is one book of poetry and short stories my mother and I read from when I was a child. If I had to choose one, I guess that would be the one," James answered.

"I love poetry too. I have too many favorites to pick just one. But I have always loved Poe and Stevenson," Ana said.

"There is one poem my mother and I read regularly. Would you like to hear it?" James asked.

"I would love to," Ana said

James began to read a poem about a Christmas morning and a woman named Lame Carter. She had been an apparition visiting her friend who wasn't yet aware of her death. It was a beautiful, sad tale. Ana was glad he had shared it with her.

"Oh, I love that. The friend didn't even know she was gone. A sad lover's tale," Ana said.

"Yes, it is, but do you know why I like it? It's the part about the snow. Where you coming from so airily over the snow? I have seen snow through the barrier, but we do not need it here, so we don't have it. I think it is so beautiful, and I wonder what it would feel like to catch a flake on my tongue like in the books. When I read about rain, I picture it like the systems used to water the different areas under the dome, but it is never everywhere all at once. It is so amazing you get to experience all that on the outside," James said.

Ana noticed a faraway look in his eyes like he was picturing it all in his mind. She felt guilty all of a sudden at how many times she took a beautiful snowfall for granted or fussed because her hair got wet in the rain. She wanted him to have all these things but knew it would never be. So many things in the world were out of his reach. They were right on the other side of that glass, and a lie kept him from them. A small piece of Ana was selfish, though. He was always there for her to visit. He would never go so far away as she couldn't find him, but how terrible was that of her? Fear of losing him made her want him to be here. That was just a horrible thing even to think.

"I have an idea. How about I tell you anything you are interested in learning, and you agree to make me one of those figurines?" Ana suggested.

James glanced over to the TV stand, where all this art was sitting.

"You have yourself a deal, Ms. Reed," he said.

Ana was impressed he remembered her last name. But as Ana looked out of the screen door, she was surprised to see that it was late afternoon. The group hadn't set a time to return to the gate, but she felt like she should go before they came looking for her.

"I didn't even realize how late it was getting to be. I really should go. Everyone will be waiting for me," Ana said.

She was very sad that their time was over today. She wanted nothing more than to sit in his company and share poetry for the rest of her days, but she didn't want anyone coming to look for her. Ana stood as if she were leaving.

"Did you need to feed?" James asked.

"Tell you what, how about I come back tomorrow if you're not busy?" Ana asked.

"Oh, I'm never too busy for you," James said.

Ana blushed and smiled. She was so happy to hear him agree to another meeting. James reached out and took her hand and gently guided her back to her seat.

She sat on the edge of the seat. She didn't want to get too comfortable and want to stay longer than she should. She felt like she might have already visited too long, but she couldn't help herself. James brushed her hair from her face and cupped her cheek in her hand. Ana melted from his intimate touch. He leaned in slowly and kissed her cheek. An innocent, sweet kiss sent passionate waves rolling through every pore of Ana's skin. She didn't understand her reaction, but she wasn't complaining. She turned her face a bit and leaned in, taking his lips in a soft, slow kiss. She felt his body tremble next to her. She rested her forehead against his as she said her goodbyes.

"I really have to go, or they will come looking for me," Ana explained.

"But you will come back tomorrow?" James asked.

"I don't want to go now, but yes, I will for sure be here tomorrow. I promise," Ana promised.

"Okay," James said.

This was the hardest, shortest goodbye of Ana's life. Why was it so hard to be apart from him? She didn't know, but she did know that if she had to just stay inside this prison with him, she would do it. She never wanted to leave his side. None of her fears of disappointment came to pass, but tomorrow was another day.

James walked Ana back to the bridge again and kissed her hand as she said goodbye. When Ana got to the gate, to her surprise, her mother was still not there, so she was safe from the questions she feared would come. Everyone else sat under the tree at the picnic table, chatting away. Ana joined them, and they waited for Rene. Patience was a skill quickly learned by immortals. After all, eternity was a really, really long time. Patience was a skill best learned early on, so one wouldn't die from anxiety.

Rene didn't make them wait much longer. She arrived with a smile on her face and a sheen on her skin. She was positively radiant with nourishment and happiness. Everyone climbed back in their transportation, and off they went for home. Ana wasn't sure what excuse she would have to come up with to get out of there alone, but she would. The night would be long and lonely as she waited to see her prince in the morning.

Discovery

The night was sleepless for Ana as her mind raced from one thing to another. She thought about her interaction with James and couldn't wait to see him in the morning. She knew she shouldn't be too eager, but she didn't care how she looked anymore. She was going immediately when she could escape. She made her plan. She would tell everyone she would investigate the possibility of the craft being used within the farms. She knew her mom would be concerned, but she would convince her she would just ask some questions. Ana would make sure to tell them she would be home about 10:00 p.m. That would give her plenty of time to investigate and to be with James.

The sun finally poured through her window. Well, poured was a stretch. It peeped through her curtains. Ana then showered and prepared for her day. She took extra time with her makeup and hair. She put her hair in a high ponytail and curled it to perfection. She still chose to wear shorts and a T-shirt, but she picked walking shorts instead of denim and a new V-neck T-shirt instead of her usual ratty dirty one. Ana had been known to wear clothes that were threadbare and all stained. So she chose to present herself a little better today. She hoped James would be impressed by her, not feel sorry for the seemingly homeless girl she represented.

Ana's plan worked just as she thought it would. Rene gave her a list of dos and don'ts and tried to get her to agree to take someone along with her. Ana finally won the battle. Kimmy could tell there was an ulterior motive, so she didn't insist on accompanying her. Lana and Brady had made plans for the day, so she was in the clear. Rene offered to go, but she had a meeting during the morning hours and knew Ana wanted to go early, so she didn't argue.

"I promise I will be careful and not push too hard," Ana said.

"Okay, call me at lunch just to check in, okay?" Rene asked.

Ana agreed. She thought her mom suspected something, but Rene never asked, so Ana never offered any information.

She took the hummer, as her sandals were not conducive to the bike. The closer she got to the farm, the more nervous she became. Never in all her years had she been this affected by the opposite sex or either sex for that matter. She found a parking spot and took the time to check her makeup in the visor mirror. When she felt she looked as good as she would get, she headed to the gate.

"Good morning, beauty," the gatekeeper greeted.

"Good morning. So nice to see you again," Ana said.

She recognized the man as the one from their first visit. His go-to greeting must be "beauty," as this was the greeting he used with her mother too. He kissed Ana's cheek after she signed the book. Then she passed through and headed in the direction of James's house.

Ana didn't stop at any of the usual spots along the way. Instead, she hurried along until she saw the familiar cottage ahead. She expected to see James emerge from inside, but he didn't. She started to knock when she saw a note sticking from the screen door with her name on the front. Ana's heart sank, and her insecurities rushed her. Had he changed his mind about see her today? She slowly opened the letter, fearing its contents.

It said, "Dearest Ana, I'm sorry if I am not here upon your arrival. There was a situation at my cousin's house with his bull, and I needed to help. Please, please don't leave. Feel free to go inside and make yourself at home. There are snacks and more of Brenda's lemonade. Please don't leave. I will be back as quickly as I can."

It was signed, "With all my love, James."

As tempting as the lemonade sounded, there was no way Ana was sitting here, bored and nervous, waiting for him. Maybe she could be of some help. After all, she was stronger, faster, and more resilient than the mortals. That beast could hurt one of them. It could hurt her James. She wasn't going to sit back and wait for that to happen. Nope, no way. She remembered the direction James had pointed out when he spoke of his cousins, and she was on her way. She stuck the note in her pocket. She was silly that way. She would date it and keep it for as long as she lived. It was, after all, his first letter to her. She giggled as she thought of him saying, "Please, please don't leave." It must have been heart-wrenching to leave home knowing she would arrive and find him gone. She refused to give him any cause for doubt or pain of any kind. She would, at the least, show up and show him she wouldn't leave. She would never leave him, not ever.

It didn't take long before she knew she was heading in the right direction. She heard several voices screaming "Get him!" "This way, run him this way!" Then she heard "No, be careful!" "Get out of the way!"

She turned around a bend, and there, standing right in her path, was the biggest, meanest-looking black bull she had ever seen in her life. It wasn't like she had much experience with these animals, but she did know they meant business when they were mad. This thing looked pretty pissed off. She wasn't sure where it was supposed to go or in what direction, but she knew she wanted it gone. It was dangerous and massive.

The bull stood perfectly still, staring directly into her eyes. He blew and snorted but never moved. The bull was mad, but he wasn't stupid. He knew she was a predator and that she could end him in a minute if she wanted to. Suddenly, running up behind the massive beast was a group of sweaty, ill-prepared mortals. The bull turned its muscular neck to see the group standing motionless behind him. It turned back to face Ana and decided his best chance lay with the group of humans to his rear. He turned and walked calmly back in the direction of the people. They parted like the Red Sea, and he walked right between them toward his home. He found the same break in the fence through which he had broken free, and hopped right back into his barbed-wire cell.

All the humans just stood with their mouths hanging open. They had expected this to be a fight and that someone would indeed be injured in the recapture of their bull, but he gave up and returned on his own. Then all the eyes landed on Ana.

She stood silently, and with nothing left to do, she waved. "Um, hi. Is that where he was supposed to go? If not, maybe I could help get him where he needs to be."

James came running from the group's rear, took Ana by her hands, and kissed her cheek. "Are you okay? He didn't hurt you, did he?"

Clearly, he didn't understand the relationship between immortals and the animal kingdom. Most animals knew they were inferior, and they complied with the wishes of the immortals. However, she did find it sweet that he was so concerned about her well-being. She decided to play along.

"Shew, yes, I'm fine. He just about scared me to death," she lied.

"Well, you're okay now. Let me help him with the fence. Is that okay?" James asked.

"Of course. Can I come too? Or would it be too weird for your family?" Ana asked.

"You better come," James said.

He had a huge smile on his face and beamed with pride with her by his side. The bull moved to the very backside of the fenced-in area. This made the fence repair much safer, and Ana just acted like she didn't know he would do that when she approached.

"That is the biggest bull I have ever seen in my life," Ana said, staring at the massive goliath in the field.

Every muscle on the bull's massive frame glistened with sweat. He snorted and pawed at the ground, but Ana knew this was bravado. He would never confront her in a threatening manner. She continued to act like a girl, which was way out of her comfort zone. She wanted the men to be men here. They kept telling the females to stay back until the bull was secured behind the barrier. She let them have that. It didn't hurt anything to let James feel like her protector for a while. At some point, he would know he wasn't, but she didn't want that taken from him just yet. It kind of felt good to have someone other than her mother want to protect her.

As Ana stood watching the men fix the fencing, an older woman walked up beside her.

"Hello. I'm Nelly, James's aunt," the woman said.

"Hello. Ana Reed. It looks like you have had an eventful morning so far," Ana said.

"Yes, I wanted to say thank you. I know you caused that hardheaded bull to come back, so thank you. I'm so afraid the boys are going to get killed fooling with him, but they don't hear reason," Nelly said, shaking her head.

"I didn't do a thing. I was just at the right place at the right time, is all. I'm glad he went in with no problem," Ana said.

"Well, the two men working on the fence are my sons Kirt and Kyle. The blond woman over here is Violet, Kirt's partner, and the other is Tilly. She is Kyle's friend, and we hope she is to be his partner sometime soon. Then there is my James. He is my sister's son. I raised him after she passed. He is the sweetest boy in the world," she explained.

Ana thought, *Maybe Nelly is trying to tell me, "He's sensitive. Please don't break his heart."*

"That has been my experience with him so far as well. He is a really nice person," Ana said.

She stood staring at the sweat-covered back of her James, and she noticed the muscles growing and deflating as he worked. She saw the similarity between the men and that bull. They were both hot, sweaty, and aggravated with one another. Both were fighting for the alpha male position in the relationship, and due to Ana's assistance, the humans had won this one. But she still understood that without her there, that could have ended much differently. The humans would have still won the war, but at what cost? Angry humans could have killed the bull after it took the life of one of the precious mortals. The fight for dominance would have been for nothing.

Nelly noticed the way Ana watched James, and she smiled a knowing smile. She had seen this look before. It was the way she looked at her partner. It was full of wonder and respect. She hoped this young immortal would be the way James repaired his damaged heart. He had never been the same after the death of his mother. He loved his extended family. He always joined in on family affairs, but he missed his mother fiercely. She wanted him to feel like he belonged somewhere, to someone. Ana's look made her feel hopeful that it would be a great one, even though this would be a difficult pairing. Nelly watched James peek up every now and then to see Ana staring at him. He always made a point to stretch or lift something to make his male attributes more prominent. The men made quick work of the fence. They watched the old bull closely, but Ana knew he wouldn't come anywhere near her. She stayed close enough to make sure he didn't.

"Okay, I think we got it now," James said.

"You two don't rush off. Come up and get some water. You are burning up," Nelly said.

Everyone made their way up to Nelly's little cottage and sat on the covered porch. Nelly gave everyone tall glasses of ice-cold water and reminded them not to drink it too fast. They did anyway. Ana sipped hers, as her mother would have instructed her to do. She would always say, "You can tell a lady's character by how she drank and ate." James gulped it down and wiped the sweat from his brow with the back of his hand. Everyone talked for a while and laughed about the bull's antics.

"How is Kaleb doing?" James asked.

"He's much better. He is just really sore. That will teach him," Nelly said.

James remembered Ana didn't know Kaleb, so he explained that Kaleb was Nelly's third son. He was messing with that same bull, and it had won. It had rolled him around on the ground and stomped at him but thankfully hadn't dealt a fatal blow.

"Oh, that's terrible. I'm glad he is feeling better now," Ana said.

She looked over to the massive bull in the field and knew this thing was a killer. He would have been glad to take Kaleb's life. All he wanted was to be free. He, unlike the mortals, knew he was a prisoner here, and he would never accept it. She feared the beast, not for what it could do to her, but what it could do to James or her new friends here. Mortals had risked their lives for as long as they had used animals for work or food. It seemed like too great a risk when one could easily be killed. Time had taken her memories of being mortal, so it was beyond her understanding.

"Does he have a name?" Ana asked.

"Who?" James asked.

"The bull," she answered. She hoped she didn't sound foolish, but she really wanted to know.

"Oh, yes, his name is Titan," Kyle answered.

James snickered a little, and Ana turned to glare at him.

"What? He needed a name if he didn't have one," Ana explained.

"No, no, it's just cute, is all. You wanted him to have an identity. Oh, he has one, all right. He is an ass. Titan fits him, though. I mean, just look at him. He is a titan," James said.

"That he is," Ana agreed.

After visiting for an appropriate amount of time, Ana and James set off for his home. They held hands and talked all the way back to the cottage. Finally, he stopped underneath a beautiful maple tree in his yard, whose leaves were barely hanging on to the branches. He took Ana's face in his hands and kissed her. He kissed her with passion and fire. It felt as though his life poured through the softness of his lips. She stared into his eyes and embraced him tightly. She held him as if she never wanted to let him go, and she didn't.

Ana noticed the sun's position in the sky and told James she needed to call her mother to check in. He gave her some privacy and went inside to cut on the AC.

"Hey, Mom," Ana said as her mother picked up on the second ring.

"Hey, are you having a good time? Have you found out anything yet?" Rene asked.

"No, not yet, but I will," Ana answered.

"Call before you leave for home, okay?" Rene asked.

"Sure will. Love you," Ana agreed.

"Love you, baby," Rene said.

Ana opened up the squeaky screen door and went inside. She saw James cutting a sandwich diagonally and putting chips on a paper plate.

"I made us some lunch. It's just a ham sandwich and chips, but it will fill your holler tooth," James said.

"Sounds perfect," Ana said.

She hadn't realized she had her phone on speakerphone, so James had heard her conversation with Rene.

"I'm sorry. I wasn't eavesdropping, but I couldn't help but hear your mom ask if you had found out anything. So what are you trying to find out?" James asked.

"First, I want to make sure you know that is not why I am here. I do have some questions, but if you don't want to answer them, that is fine. I just like being with you," Ana said.

She was scared he might think she wasn't being honest about her feelings for him. She didn't want him to think she was being covert in any way.

"Does this have something to do with your friend Kimmy? You know I will help if I can, and you came here before that horrible nightmare, so I know you might have liked me a little before your questions," James said.

He held his fingers apart as if he demonstrated how much a little bit was and had that sneaky look in his eyes.

"I just don't ever want you to think badly of me. I really want to see where this goes between us," Ana explained.

"Me too. I really like you, Ana. I think we have a weird connection. I can't explain it, but I don't ever want you to go. Of course, you can ask me anything you want. I will do my best to answer. If I don't know, I will find someone who does. How does that sound?" James said.

"Remember when I said Kimmy was abducted? Well, did you ever wonder how someone could abduct an immortal?" Ana asked.

"I did," James said.

"The man used chains that were spelled. I don't know if you understand what that means, but it was chains she can't break. No female can ever break them. The only problem with that is, no immortal can do witchcraft. Humans can, though. So how did he get them? They were new for sure. They weren't ancient, so we are investigating if there are any witches practicing magic on the farm. I don't know if you know there are many farms all over the world, but there are only three between here and where she was taken. So we thought we would start here and work our way out to the others. He could have gotten them anywhere, but this is our best bet for now. Do you know anything about that kind of stuff?" Ana asked.

James sat for a few minutes and seemed to be weighing the situation out. He took Ana's hand in his, and they were locked in a trusting circle.

"Do you remember how I told you about the people on the plaques?" James asked.

Ana nodded.

"Those are not the only stories passed down from our ancestors. People tell their children stories of a time when we were free. Most mortals understand the reasons why we are here, but others don't. I heard of mortals who practiced the craft, hoping to undo the magic barrier spell that keeps us here," James explained.

"Barrier spell?" Ana asked.

"The story goes that when mortals were first placed inside the farms, they were defiant and crafty. They kept finding ways to break through the walls. They went under it once from what they say. The immortals explained the importance of human confinement to the witches inside the walls. They explained the poison in the air and water. They told them that the human race couldn't survive on the outside. The sorceress developed a spell to seal the dome. So if the stories are true, then it is possible that there are witches here, but I don't know anyone who practices it anymore," James said.

Ana took a moment and thought about everything he had said. She had never heard of this before, but that wasn't surprising. She didn't need to know such a thing, so she had never asked. Suddenly, a thought came to her.

"Do you know the family of witches that helped do the spell?" Ana asked.

"There are four different plaques with two different sire names down in the square. They are supposedly the families responsible for the boundary," James explained.

"Can you take me there?" Ana asked.

James nodded, and they went to find the names of these women.

The area where the plaques were displayed was far more ornate than any of the other locations Ana had seen. There was definitely something special about these four women. A white gazebo with miniature pink roses climbing its walls housed the statues. The statues of these women had been created from beautiful white stone. Each figure was different, so Ana had no doubt that they were actual depictions of the women themselves. The statues held stone baskets and floral bouquets, where the plaques were fastened. The surnames of two women were Johnson, and the other two were Maines.

"Are there any of the Johnsons or Maines families here anymore?" Ana asked.

"Yeah, I don't know them very well. They live on the other side," James said.

"Can we go there?" Ana asked.

"It will take some time to get there. But if you're not in a hurry, we sure can go," James answered.

"I'm not in a hurry. We can take our time," Ana said.

James smiled and was excited she wanted to stay with him for a while. The trip would take several hours, and James was going to enjoy every moment he had with Ana. They took the gator on their journey. James packed up some snacks and bottled water. He took a blanket for them to sit on while they ate. He wanted to make her day special, even if it was a semiwork trip.

Ana saw humans doing all sorts of activities on the way. A group of ladies stood stirring a large cast-iron kettle dangling over an open fire. They mixed with what looked like a wooden boat paddle. Ana could smell apples, cinnamon, and cloves. James said they were making apple butter, and Ana thought how delicious it must be with all the wonderful smells pouring from the mixture.

James said the residents prepared many things for the upcoming winter months. Farther down the way, she saw a group of people collecting pumpkins from a field. Further on, she saw giant sunflowers being harvested for their seeds. The humans insisted on self-reliance to the degree that they were capable of doing. Everything could be simpler and easier for them, but they wanted to do things for themselves as much as possible. The time of laziness within the human race appeared to be over. Ana was impressed by all she saw.

James slowed the gator and pulled to the side of the path. He clicked off the engine, and they waited. Ana saw three horseback riders approaching. She loved the fact that James was taking every precaution to ensure the safety of the riders. The hum of the gator could have spooked the horses, leaving their passengers in danger. Ana felt a little nervous. She was afraid her presence might scare the timid animals as well. The horses slowly and lightly walked past the gator. The riders had to encourage them to move forward with gentle kicks to their ribs. Ana sighed audibly as nothing had happened that would have left her to blame.

Long stretches passed with no signs of settlement. Then small groups of tiny homes would spring up like mushrooms on the forest floor. Ana guessed these were family units who wanted to stay close to one another. Ana heard the sound of clucking chickens, bleating lambs, and bawling cows. She could smell the pig lots long before James ever knew they were there. It wasn't long before Ana saw the houses emerging from the woods. Each space was a small farm all its own. She thought it was amazing how well they utilized every inch available to them.

"There they are," James said.

The couple pulled up to the first home and walked hand in hand through the yard. A lady about fifty popped out of the front door and went onto the porch. She squinted her eyes, trying to see who her visitors might be.

"Can I help you, folks?" the lady asked.

"Hi, my name is James, and this is my lady, Ana. Are you Ms. Maines? We were wondering if you had the time to answer a few questions for us?" James said with the utmost respect in his tone.

Ana's heart flooded with happiness when James referred to her as his lady. No title had ever given her so much joy. She had been a daughter, sister, social worker, and friend. She had been the violent deliverer of justice and the gentle hand of comfort, but never had she been anyone's lady. To be his lady was the highest honor she had ever been given.

They sat on the porch with Ms. Maines. She insisted that they have some of her fresh lemon meringue pie and a tall glass of milk. It was amazing. Ana could taste the love and experience in every bite. Ms. Maines had probably made this so many times she could do it with her eyes closed. Ana hoped that someday she would be able to do that too.

"We know some subjects are taboo up here, so we understand if you don't want to talk to us about anything. I just wanted to put that out there for you. Ana's friend Kimmy was abducted and tortured by another immortal. He was in possession of special chains, which he used to detain her. The chains were new. They weren't something from the old world. Ms. Maines, these chains were spelled to hold an immortal woman. I don't need to tell you how devastating the experience was for her friend. Do you happen to know of anyone here within the walls that would be practicing that kind of magic?" James asked.

Ana sat and only spoke if either of them asked her a direct question. She knew some humans were suspicious of her kind, and with good reason.

"I haven't heard of anything directly relating to the chains, but there are stories. You know what I mean?" Ms. Maines said in a hushed voice.

"What kind of stories?" Ana asked.

It didn't take long for her to forget her own rule of speak only when spoken to, but this was important. She couldn't help herself. Thankfully, Ms. Maines showed no signs of being offended and answered her question.

"Well, I have had my own experiences with immortals regarding magical favors. They will offer just about anything to get the spell of their choosing. It's usually something dumb, like a love potion or a locator spell. Most mortals I know don't think it's worth the risk. You know we aren't supposed to practice the craft anymore, don't you? When it comes to magic binding chains, I don't know anybody who would do that kind of art, no way," Ms. Mains said.

James thought this would be the answer they'd get, but it didn't hurt to ask anyway.

"Are there any Johnsons left up this way?" James asked.

"Nope, there haven't been any in a long time. The last died out about ten years ago, I guess," Ms. Maines answered.

"I will tell you this, James. I know you know already, Ana. There are other farms out there in the world. We are not the only ones. The only reason I know was that many years ago, a fella came around, asking for favors, and when I declined, he said he would just go to another farm. He was really nice, and he understood why I chose not to do it for him. Maybe they were spelled somewhere else," Ms. Maines said.

"Can I ask, Ms. Maines, how would one spell the chains? Wouldn't they have to have the chains to spell them? The gatekeeper checks us on our way in and on our way out. I am pretty sure they would have noticed huge chains," Ana asked.

"Well, the only thing I can think is that he slipped in a link from the chain. That is all it would take. Just one link to spell and connect it to the rest of the chain, and it's all spelled. So if I needed something like that done, that is how I would do it. I doubt the gatekeeper would have thought much of a link of chain on a man's keyring or left in his pocket by mistake," Ms. Maines explained.

"That makes sense to me," Ana agreed.

She offered to help Ms. Maines with the plates and cups, but Ms. Maines refused. She said she was just happy to see some young folk around. The two told the lady they would come again to visit and let her know if they found anything. She seemed delighted that they might return. Kisses and hugs with their new friend sent them back home.

A slight breeze cooled the afternoon air. Ana loved this time of year. Most people loved the spring and summer months, but Ana preferred the fall. There was something cozy about the change of the season. Spring through summer seemed so long. She loved the deviation in her eternity. She didn't understand why anyone would choose to live in one climate. There was no hope for anything new. She craved that in her life. She always looked forward to changing from her flip-flops to boots and from tank tops to flannel. She enjoyed picking wildflowers but also building snowmen and eating snow cream from freshly fallen snow. She loved it all.

James picked the most beautiful spot for their snack. He spread their blanket on the ground underneath a towering oak tree. They had apples and cheese with crackers. He even made peanut butter crackers and chips to go along with it all. She was impressed with how quickly he threw it all together. Ana and James told stories about their lives and learned so much just in that short amount of time together. Several times James leaned in to brush the hair from Ana's face or simply stroke her hand. Ana had many, many stories to tell James compared to his one lifetime, but she managed to hit the high spots for him.

"I wish you didn't have to go," James said.

"I don't have to go yet," Ana said.

"I mean, I wish you didn't ever have to go," he confessed.

Ana knew precisely how he felt, and it made her heart ache to think of leaving him even for a short time.

"We could make this work if you wanted to," she whispered.

"I don't care what we have to do. If you say you want me, I do so want you, forever. I know it seems dumb and fast. I can't explain it, but I can't think of anything but you ever since we met. I can't sleep at night thinking of you, and when I finally fall asleep, you are with me in my dreams. I wake with a need for you that you can't understand," James explained.

"Oh, I understand, all right," Ana said.

She hoped she knew what he meant by need. She knew if it were like the need she felt for him, it was all-encompassing. It burned in her loins and made her stomach lurch in her belly. It was physically painful to miss him. How was this possible? How did she need this man so much after such a short period of time? She didn't know, but she didn't care either. She was complete by his side, and she wouldn't lose that feeling. She had waited several lifetimes to feel it.

Ana rose to her knees and moved even closer to James. She leaned in and kissed him. Her tongue danced across his lips slowly, seductively. She felt James's body tremble until he gained control of himself. He flipped her quickly onto her back on their makeshift dining table and kissed her passionately. He trailed kisses across her cheek and down her neck, making goose pimples appear on her skin. His hands roamed her body like he was starving to know every curve. Ana was so delirious with desire she could only submit to his will.

She ran her hands across his shoulders and traced the muscles along his back. Every muscle was tense with anticipation. Everything was comfortable and natural between them. There was no awkwardness at all. Ana had always been so insecure in intimate situations, but not with James. Somehow she knew it was real, that there was no need to be embarrassed or try to hide from this man. He owned not only her body but her mind, heart, and soul. The pairing of the two was nothing like anything either had ever experienced. Ana's tears ran down her cheeks, and waves of exquisite pleasure flooded her body. James's body was as still as stone when he came to fruition. They lay in the comfort of their bond for what seemed like forever, soaking in every memory of each other.

They lay together in the lazy autumn air and talked more about intimate moments in their lives. Even though Ana never wanted to leave this spot, she thought they should go back to James's house before it got dark. She was no better than her mother. She worried incessantly about his safety. He was well equipped to handle this mountain, but she still saw him as a fragile human. He would just have to get used to her being that way. She knew she loved him, and love was many different things, one being worry.

They reluctantly gathered their things and headed back to the cottage. James immediately went to the tiny bathroom area and began laying out a towel and a pair of his cozy sweatpants and shirt. He let the water run so it would be good and warm for Ana. Ana's emotions were overwhelming. She had never known anyone who was as thoughtful as James. His level of care for her was unbelievable. Maybe she had just picked losers in the past, and this was how it was supposed to be. Ana didn't know, but she would never stop feeling grateful for it.

The warm cascade of water was so refreshing. She enjoyed using James's shampoo and body wash because now his scent would linger a little bit longer with her. She towel-dried her hair the best she could. She still looked like a little drowned rat when she came from the bathroom. She found James cutting vegetables on the counter.

"Next," Ana said playfully.

"No way. Are you nuts? I may never shower again," James said with a chuckle.

"Oh, I hope you do," Ana said. She made a smelly face and held her nose for emphasis.

"Well, not today," James said defiantly.

Ana blushed. James had put a notebook and pen on the counter across from him. He kept preparing their dinner while she jotted down all the details they had collected about Kimmy's case so far. Of course, they knew very little, but anything was better than nothing. Ana gave her mom an extra call just to stay in her good graces. Rene was very pleased she had that much respect for her delicate feelings.

James prepared pork chops and grilled veggies outside on the deck, while Ana put together her mom's famous chocolate layer cake. She had always watched her make it but never attempted it herself. She hoped it was fit to eat. James assured her it would be delicious. She knew he would never hurt her feelings. He would lie if he had to. It felt like they were a little family while they did the mundane task of cleaning up the kitchen after their meal. Ana washed, and James dried the dishes. Ana paid close attention to where everything lived in the kitchen so that he didn't have to help next time. Finally, the couple sat and watched a movie while snuggled up on the couch. It was a perfect day.

Time flew by much too quickly for both James and Ana. It was approaching time for Ana to go, so she sent a quick text to her mom, letting her know she was on the way. The goodbye felt as though Ana's heart broke even though she knew she would see him soon. James wanted to walk with her to the bridge as he had done before, but Ana insisted he stayed home.

"It's going to be hard enough to go as it is. If you walk me there, I won't want to go at all," Ana said.

"Then don't go," James said. He wrapped his arms around her waist and held her tightly. His devilish grin was adorable.

"No, no, there will be none of that," Ana said.

Ana wiggled free from his grip and giggled like a child. She smacked at his hand playfully. She kissed him lightly and headed to the door.

"I will be back in the next day or two, I promise," Ana said.

"Please do. I miss you already," James said.

He did the thing again where he breathed her in before she left. She felt loved and full of hope. She couldn't wait to see him again. She missed him already.

Back to the CH

Ana stopped in the big house to touch base with her mom. She did have a few things to update her on regarding the chains. Rene suggested she call Allan in the morning and let him know what she found. Ana agreed. She kissed her mom good night and headed for the CH to fill Kimmy in on her exciting day.

"Well, I was wondering if you were going to come home or not," Kimmy said.

Ana sheepishly grinned at her.

"Spill it," Kimmy said.

She sat up cross-legged and pulled the blanket over her legs. She handed Ana a glass of wine she had waiting for her. Ana flopped down on the couch and dramatically sighed.

"I'm in so much trouble, girl," she began.

"From the looks of you, it's the good kind of trouble," Kimmy said.

"I hope so," Ana confessed.

"I'm not going to drag it out of you, but I might beat it out. Come clean," Kimmy said.

She took a couch pillow and hit Ana with it playfully.

"There is this man," Ana started to say.

"I knew it! I knew it!" Kimmy interrupted.

"He has got to be the most beautiful man on the entire earth. He is so thoughtful and caring. I think I may have really fallen this time, hard. What am I going to do?" Ana asked.

"What do you mean what are you going to do? Is it because you're immortal and he isn't? People have been doing that for ages. That's nothing new. If you want to make it work, you will. The only thing that worries me is that he will grow old and leave this world but you won't. That is the basic problem we all face when we love a mortal. He will die, and you will be left with unimaginable grief. I think it's too late for this talk now, isn't it?" Kimmy asked.

She was a hopeless romantic, and this love story was right up her alley—hot, spicy, and doomed for heartbreak.

"Maybe he can get out sometime, though. There is always that chance," Kimmy said.

Ana's head snapped up, and she snapped at Kimmy.

"What? There are no mortals on the outside, are there?" Ana asked excitedly.

"No, no mortals, Ana," Kimmy explained.

"What do you mean? What are you saying?" Ana asked.

"Don't you know about the exceptions?" Kimmy asked.

"What is that?" Ana asked.

"Mortals who do extraordinary things get a choice. They can stay on the farm and die a natural human death or be turned like us and be free. There are lots of exceptions out here. Didn't you know that?" Kimmy asked.

"Are those the people whose names are on the plaques?" Ana asked.

"Yep," Kimmy said.

"I thought they were all dead," Ana said.

"Of course, the immortals told the humans they were dead. They couldn't let them know they were turned and are still living free. It would cause too much upheaval in the farm," Kimmy explained.

Ana's mind raced. She couldn't believe the news she was hearing. Maybe she wouldn't have to watch the love of all her lives die.

"How do they become an exception?" Ana asked.

"Those people did great deeds or were capable of doing great deeds if they were free. Therefore, if the immortals saw the potential for greatness in a human, they gave them immortality to achieve the excellence they saw in them," Kimmy explained.

"I can't believe this," Ana whispered.

"I can't believe you didn't know. You need to get out more, Ana Reed," Kimmy said.

Ana felt like a complete idiot. She knew nothing about the world around her. This huge thing was unknown to her simply because, until now, it didn't affect her. She was one of those people, she guessed. She only cared to know what was beneficial for her to know, and that sucked. She made a mental note to be more interested in a broader array of subjects. It was far better to know a little about a lot than a lot about a little. She was figuring this out the hard way.

Ana told Kimmy every juicy detail about her day with James. Kimmy gasped and swooned and said "Oh, how sweet!" too many times to count. Ana couldn't agree more. He was so very sweet. Ana knew that her mission would forever be to get James out of there. She would fight for his freedom for as long as he breathed to fight for it. It never crossed her mind that James might not want to go. He might not want to live as she lived. He had family inside the walls. Ana only hoped he would value their love enough to be free to be with her.

Kimmy and Ana sat up giggling and talking half the night until, finally, they decided to go to bed. Ana stayed in James's T-shirt so his smell would linger just a little bit longer. Then sleep found her, and she lay in James's arms in her dreams. Their love transcended time and space. Ana hoped he dreamed of peaceful rest with her.

James's mortality was limiting for him. He was exhausted both mentally and physically from the day. He smiled as he lay on his bed and thought of Ana. James knew he was in love with this wonderful woman. He knew the difference between infatuation and love. Nothing in his life had felt this way before. She had burned herself into his very soul. James knew he would give his life for her. She was his queen, his beautiful angel. He couldn't allow fear to come into his heart. He was inferior to her in every way, yet she still wanted him. He hoped she never grew tired of their time together. After all, she had the whole world to enjoy. She was free to explore it with someone like her. But no, he couldn't think that way. Ana wanted him, and that was all there was to it. He would love her as long as she let him and mourn her if she ever decided to go, but for now, he would wallow in his happiness for a little while. Sleep finally came, and his thoughts were replaced with dreams of his Ana. He could feel her wrapped in his embrace as they peacefully slept.

James was woken up suddenly by a rustling outside. He thought it was an animal on his porch, but it was a big one if it was. He slipped from the bed and went to the window. He kept the light off so he wouldn't spook the creature. He peeped through a crack in the curtains and was surprised by what he saw. There was what appeared to be a woman standing beside the bushes next to his porch. She wasn't doing anything. She was just staring at the house. James watched her for several moments and decided it was just too weird not to see what was happening here.

He jerked the door open quickly and yelled, "Hey!"

The woman shrieked and jumped from fright. She quickly turned and began running away from the cottage. James jumped from the porch, ignoring the rocks and sticks as they abused his bare feet, and gave chase. He was much quicker than the girl and soon had her arm on his hand. He spun her to face him for questioning.

"Why are you sneaking around my house?" James asked.

He wanted to appear tough and scary, but the girl's tiny frame and obvious terror limited his ability to fake it. So he loosened his grip a little and asked again. "Why are you sneaking around my house, young lady?"

"I...I...I'm lost," she lied.

"Okay, little girl, nobody gets lost here. What are you doing here? I won't ask you again. Maybe we should call upfront and have the gatekeeper tell me where you belong. What do you think about that?" James asked.

"No, no, please," the girl begged.

James gave her a stern look and pulled her back to the cottage.

"Please, just let me go. I won't bother you no more," the girl pleaded.

James sat her in the chair on the porch more forcefully than he had intended. As a result, she hit her head on the back of the chair. It made a sickening plunk sound.

"Are you okay? Ugh," James said.

"Yeah, just let me go," the girls said again.

"Please just tell me why you are here, okay? I'm not mad. Really, I'm not," James explained.

"I saw you today in the woods with that lady," she explained.

James's face burned with red hot embarrassment. He hoped she hadn't seen their moment under the oak.

"And?" James asked.

"I know you went to Ms. Maines's today. I know what you wanted too. Why are you trying to stir up trouble for somebody? Ain't nobody bothering you," she stammered.

"Hey, hey, we aren't trying to stir up trouble for anybody. We just had some questions for Ms. Maines, is all. Why? Who you worried about getting into trouble over our questions?" James asked.

"Me!" the girl screamed.

The girl jumped to her feet and tried to run away, but James swiftly retrieved her and put her back in her seat.

"First, can I at least get a name to call you besides 'young lady'?" James asked.

The girl stared at him for a few seconds and realized she wasn't leaving here until he was satisfied. All she could do now was hope his humanity would win and he wouldn't tell on a fellow mortal. She had heard of mortals taking the side of the immortals before, but she never knew one that would have done such a thing. She hoped this wouldn't be her first time.

"Tana," she whispered.

"Okay, now that's a start. Nice to meet you, Tana," James said.

He extended his hand to this girl who was maybe fourteen years old girl and smiled. She took it and shook it with vigor. He couldn't help but imagine this was her first actual handshake, and she overdid it just a little bit.

"Tell me what's going on, and I will tell you why I went to see your friend Ms. Maines," James bargained.

"She ain't no friend to me," Tana argued.

"And why is that?" James asked.

"She's into some bad stuff, and if she keeps it up, she will get us all into trouble. I really came to talk to you, but I chickened out before I could knock," Tana said.

She started to have a slight waver in her voice, and it broke James's heart.

"Well, no worries now. We are friends here. Just tell me what the problem is, and I will help you fix it," James assured.

"You was asking her about the Johnson family, weren't you? I'm a Johnson, and my mom and dad are Johnsons, and my five sisters are Johnsons. So she lied right to your face. She does terrible magic up there and blames it on other folks. When I heard her say there weren't any of us left, I knew she was planning on that very thing for us. Do you know what they do if they catch you practicing the craft in here? You disappear. There really wouldn't be any more Johnsons then, would there?" Tana explained.

"Well, I expect not. Tell me what she has been doing, okay? My friend and I can help you, and we wouldn't have to tell anybody about the little magic you all use. I know people still do a little here and there, and I don't believe the immortals have a problem with that," James said.

"All I know is, there are a lot of shady characters that go up there to see her. That is why I followed you and that lady. I wanted to hear what she was telling you in case I could use it later," Tana said.

"Smart thinking," James encouraged.

"I heard you say something about a binding spell. I know she knows how to do one 'cause she used it on her cow when she kept getting out," Lana said.

"That is really good to know. If I could show you a picture, could you tell me if you have ever seen that man at her house? I don't have it right now, but I think I could get one," James asked.

"Yeah, you won't tell on us, will you? My folks would kill me if they knew I was here right now," Tana said.

"Where do they think you are?" James asked.

James knew the houses were too small to sneak out unnoticed, so he was interested to learn how she had done it. Tana smiled proudly and showed him. She waved her arms in the air and said some nonsensical words, and there were two of her on the porch. James was taken aback. He didn't know what to say. He just sat and stared at the apparition.

"See, I'm peacefully asleep in my bed," Tana explained.

"Can you come back tomorrow when it's appropriate for you to be out?" James asked.

He tilted his head and gave her a fatherly look of scolding.

"Yeah, I will. I'm sorry I was sneaky like I was," Tana said.

"How about you come over at lunch? Bring your parents or sisters or whomever you want, and we can talk and have some watermelon. What do you say?" James asked.

"Okay, around twelve then?" Tana asked.

"Sounds good. Let me take you back. You shouldn't be out in these woods alone, young lady," James said.

He smiled at the reference of his previous name for her, and she smiled back. Then he saddled up the horses so they wouldn't make too much noise returning her home. They rode without incident to the path that led to her house, and they went the rest of the way on foot. James watched as she slowly opened the door and went inside. Before she closed the door, she gave a quick wave to the black night where she had left him standing. James had a long way back home, and he was excited to tell Ana what he had learned. He wished he had a way to contact her, but he would just have to wait for her return. That would seem like forever to him now. However, he thought he was on to something with Ms. Maines and couldn't wait to investigate further.

Noon arrived, and the whole family showed up at James's home. As promised, he provided the watermelon for their visit. Tana's father had insisted on a public apology from Tana regarding her late-night intrusion. James was gracious in his acceptance and told her father he was thankful she had come.

"Could I speak to you in private just a moment, Mr. Johnson?" James asked.

The two walked around to the horse lot, and both leaned against the fence, staring at the mares.

"I didn't want to get into too much detail with the young ones around, but if that Ms. Maines is responsible for the binding spell used on those chains, she is a dangerous person. My friend knows a woman who was abducted using those chains, and the result was horrific. She was tortured and almost killed. If my friend hadn't found her, I just don't know what might have happened to her. So you can understand why we need to lay this to rest, can't you?" James asked.

"Yeah, just one thing worries me, though. How are you going to ensure the immortals don't believe anything she tells them about my family? What if she tells them my girls practice? What then?" Mr. Johnson asked.

James could see the fear in his eyes at the thought of his wife and daughters. James knew it was dangerous for them to be involved, so he would have to think of another way.

"I'm not going to mention your family at all, not even to my friend. It's not worth the risk. Kimmy is free now, and mentally, she is healing from the ordeal. So there is no need to bring any of you into it. I need to see if any of your family has ever seen the man at Ms. Maines's house, though. How about next time she comes for a visit, I ask for a photo? If she can't leave it, we can ask about it, but all of you must lie even if you know he was there. Then, later, I will come and find out the truth, okay?" James explained.

"I don't know how I can ever repay you for protecting my girls. They are my life. They can't help what they are, you know? We will do everything in our power to help you find the truth, I swear," Mr. Johnson declared.

James's Mistake

James was at peace with his decision to keep the Johnsons' name out of it. He knew the price for practicing magic, and these were good people. They had a fun day visiting. They ate watermelon and laughed as the kids got more on them than in them. Mr. Johnson said it was okay, though. It wasn't good if you didn't get it all over your face. The children played in the creek and caught minnows and crawdads. James found a bucket with a lid so they could take them home with them. The girls promised to release them into their section of the creek when they got home, and James acted relieved by their promise. He was disappointed that Ana hadn't come today, but he knew she was working on her own leads in the case. He believed she would come, just like she promised, in a day or two.

The evening ended, and the Johnson family headed for home. James had no idea how they managed all those children. He was exhausted from playing all day and answering endless questions. Once, one of the girls had even asked why frogs were green. James was sure he could find out, but he just said it was because green was their favorite color. This seemed to be an acceptable answer to her, and she jogged away. He fixed himself a thick peanut butter and grape jelly sandwich, poured a huge glass of milk, and rested on the couch until it was time for bed.

There were no dreams, either good or bad, for James that night. He believed he was too tired to dream, so he was well rested when the light came through his window. He stayed around the house until lunch. He was convinced Ana wouldn't show today. He put a note in the door, just in case, and headed to the barn. He saddled up Betsy and headed out for a ride. He thought he might ride up the mountain and do a little digging. He might run into Ms. Maines again and see if he could find out why she had lied about the Johnsons. James wanted to get ahead of this fast-moving train if he could.

James took his time traveling to the top of the mountain. It really was beautiful up here, on top of the world. It seemed strange to him how different it was from the bottom to the top. He found the air was crisper and cooler the further he rode, and fall was more evident in everything. James slipped on a jacket from his saddlebags to ward off the nip in the air. The wildlife he saw was bustling around and preparing for the approaching winter. He saw squirrels with their cheeks full, scampering to their homes with their treasures. The deer flicked their tails, and the bucks had their noses high in the air, searching for a mate. Fall mating meant spring fawns, so the deer were intent on their missions. They barely glanced in his direction as he passed. The leaves were almost gone from their branches, and James knew the seasons were fighting for dominance.

He rode to the road that led to Ms. Maines's house. He had to decide right now if he would go and talk to her or not. He knew it probably wasn't a wise decision, but he turned Besty down the path, and off they went. As he approached, he saw Ms. Maines in her yard, hanging clothes on the line to dry.

"Well, so nice to see you in my neck of the wood so soon, James," Ms. Maines greeted.

James was surprised that she could tell it was him at this distance. There was no squinting or shielding her eyes from the sun as she had done previously. She wasn't even wearing her glasses today.

"Yes, ma'am. My friend and I had such a good time the other day. So I thought I would come and find some new places for us to explore the next time she visits. I thought you might know of some good places, like caves or, you know, stuff like that. I'm sorry if I'm keeping you from your work," James lied.

He trotted his mare up to the fence Ms. Maines was working near and slipped down from the saddle.

"I'm sure you did have a nice time the other day," she said.

James noticed her off-colored tone and wondered if she knew how nice it had really been.

"That's a beautiful animal you got there," she said.

"Thanks. She's a good one, a real friend. She doesn't think much of these long trips, though," James said.

He patted the horse's shoulder and rubbed her face lovingly.

"I'm sure she doesn't. I have an old mare up there in the barn. She's been under the weather here lately. She's been lame on her front right for several days. I can't seem to find out what is ailing her. It might just be weather or old rummy coming to visit her old bones. It's a shame too. She is a really good companion to me. Sure-footed as any horse you've ever seen, I can promise you that," Ms. Maines said.

James was willing to do anything to keep her talking. He knew she had forgotten more than he would ever know about a horse, but he would try his luck anyway.

"I would be glad to take a look if you would like me to. I have had to fix up my girls more times than I can count. But it's true what they say. Sometimes two sets of eyes are better than one," James suggested.

Ms. Maines smiled an off-putting smile and nodded. "Would you? That would be great. I have done all I know to do. I hate to watch her suffer."

"Sure, lead the way," James said.

The two walked behind the house to the barn where the horse was stalled. The moment James entered the barn, he knew something wasn't right. The only horse he saw was a very young, very healthy chestnut mare. Before he could even ask a question, Mr. Maines threw her hands in the air and screamed out a phrase in Latin. The only reason James thought it was Latin was that it sounded like some of the medical jargon he had read before.

"Circulus!"

James tried to run to the door, but something invisible blocked him. Ms. Maines laughed so hard she had to bend down with her hands on her knees to catch her breath.

"Shew! Oh, I forgot to tell you you're about a month too late to help old Sugarfoot. There was no fixing that old girl. So I got myself a new one. We will see how she fares on the old mountain. Now what in the world am I going to do with you?" she asked herself.

Maines paced back and forth in front of James, tapping her index finger on her pursed lips.

"What are you doing?" James asked.

"Cut the shit! I know what you're up to. You're up here, being a nosey ass. Don't you know snitches get stitches, boy? Nosey little boys get their noses shaved off. That's what I have heard. I tried to get you to stay away. I tried to tell you, but no, you had to come back. You just had to see if you could see what you wanted to see. So now I have to figure out what I am going to do with you," she said.

"I think there has been a misunderstanding. Really, I do. I don't know what you're talking about. I didn't even know this was a thing until you just did it. If anybody is at fault here, maybe it's you. I was just trying to help. Now let me out of here," James demanded.

"Oh, you are a liar too! Isn't that lovely? You should have left this sleeping dog lie. That is what you should have done. There are three things I hate. A liar, a thief, and a nosey ass. It looks like I got all three with you. You don't need to know nothing about me. Nothing! Do you hear me?" Ms. Maines screamed.

She clenched her hands into fists and screamed another piece of Latin, "Non caeli!"

James knew instantly what she had said. His lungs constricted in his chest. He couldn't draw a single breath. He fell to his knees and dug at his throat. His chest ached from the weight crushing his lungs. As the black cone of death started drifting over his field of vision, he used his last breath to beg.

"Please..."

James didn't beg for himself. He begged for Ana. He knew she would be devastated if this ended the way it looked like it might. He couldn't even imagine what she would do to the whole place if this played out the way it was headed. Maines unclenched her fists and undid her magic with one word.

"Caeli."

Air flooded James's burning chest. He gasped for the sweet nectar of life. Finally, his vision was restored, and he regained his footing.

"I can't just let you go now. I think you know that's true, but I can't have any more accidents up here either. So let me think now. Be quiet," Maines stated.

She paced, tapped, and hummed, trying to find a solution to her problem. This woman was crazy as a bed bug, and James knew it. What was he supposed to do with a crazy, unbalanced witch?

"I won't tell a soul, I swear it. I won't say I saw a thing, and you will never see my face on your side of the mountain again. I'm sorry. I really am. I shouldn't have come here, being nosey. You are right. I'm sorry," James lied.

Maines walked up to the circle's edge and stared into James's eyes. "I know you're not sorry, little boy. You would be, though, if you knew what you were trying to mess up for me—hell, for all of us."

"I am sorry, but if you don't believe me, make me understand. Did you spell those chains? That is all I wanted to know. I'm sure you had your reasons. I just wanted to know," James said.

He figured if he were going to die, he would just lay it all out there and see what she chose to do with it.

"I've done a lot of things. I don't know if that particular spell belongs to me or not. Business is business, my friend. What people do with the trinkets I make has nothing to do with me. I don't care. I'm trying to do something great here, and you won't get in my way. You best believe that, boy!" she yelled.

"What are you trying to do? Maybe I could help you," James said.

"I doubt that. You look like a fan of those bloodsuckers to me. You wouldn't like what I'm going to do," Maines said.

James didn't like the sound of "going to" instead of "trying to." This woman had a plan, and she was sure it was going to work.

"I don't guess it would hurt to tell you about it. After all, you're not going to remember it in a few moments anyway. I plan on erasing, oh, about the last six months of your life," Ms. Maines explained.

James snapped his head up and stared at the woman. "You don't have to do all that. I'm not going to say a word to anybody."

"Oh, I know you're not. I guess there is no harm getting some of this off my chest, even if you won't remember it," Maines said.

She pulled up a stool and sat. She motioned for James to do the same. He sat in the middle of his circular prison and waited to hear her story. He was upset that this crazy person planned to erase Ana from his memory, but he was sure Ana would figure it out.

"Aren't you tired of being weak? Don't you want to be able to say no and defend yourself when the monsters come around? They steal the very blood from our veins and steal the hearts of anyone they chose with their lying faces and perfect bodies. It makes me sick that we have no choice in anything," Maines explained.

James knew these were rhetorical questions, so he just remained quiet. She emphasized her statement by slapping at the veins in her arm. She pulled at her shirt that hid her heart. James wondered if heartbreak had broken this woman. Something had to have made her so cold. She had no compassion for anyone affected by the items she created. She just didn't care.

"I have designed the perfect spell. Of course, it has to be done in stages. You can't rush it. Do you know what I mean? I have started it a little at a time, and I believe it's working. I can make us mortals the most powerful beings on the planet," Maines tried to explain.

James looked at her like he was already confused, and she just started explaining her brilliant plan.

"Ugh. Okay, I'll take it slow so you might understand me. Do you know how immortals can't do magic, and witches can't be immortal? Imagine an immortal being able to practice the craft. Their abilities would be limitless. They would have eternity to learn and study and grow in their power. The restrictions time places on us witches would be gone. We could try and try and try again if it were necessary to get something right. There would be no time limit, no clock ticking down on our existence. Powerful magic requires extraordinary ingredients. No immortal would just say, 'Oh yes, here's my blood.' They want something in return, and that's where I come in. I am quite the entrepreneur, if I do say so myself. I got myself a booming little barter business going on here. They supply a little blood, and I do the spell of their choosing. Bingo-bango, everybody wins," Maines explained.

The woman twirled and danced to the music inside her own head.

"Some of the magic is hurting people, though. I bet you didn't even know that," James said.

"No, it's not hurting people. It's hurting those monsters, and I could give a rat's ass about that," Maines raged.

James knew her need for power or revenge or whatever this was, was far greater than anything he was equipped to deal with.

"I get that," he lied.

"You don't get shit! I saw you. You're in love with one of those abominations! You don't get anything!" Maines screamed.

James could almost see good and evil raging inside of her. However, this battle had been won by the dark side long ago. He just wondered what that meant for him.

"Everyone here is so brainwashed. Not me, no way, I know the truth. I can harness the power of the immortal through their blood. I will transfer that power into the body of a witch, and voila, immortal witch! And that witch will be me! I will be the most powerful being on the planet. If you were going to remember any of this, you could say, 'I knew her when...' But sadly you won't. Shew, do you know how good that feels? Have you ever had a secret and couldn't tell someone but it felt like a ton of bricks was lifted off you when you could? Even if you don't remember, I will. Well, I have things to do, so let's get to it, shall we? This looks like it hurts quite a bit when I have done it before, but maybe you will remember the pain and not be so nosey next time," Maines said.

James knew this was it. As crazy as this lady was, she might fry his brain completely. He took a moment to say goodbye to his Ana and prepared for the pain. He shut his eyes as tightly as he could and bit down on his bottom lip. His hands he turned to fists, and he sat rock solid on the floor.

"Obliviscatur," Maines said.

Under her breath, she mumbled more words James couldn't hear. He felt the pressure build behind his eyes until the pain had blinded him. He held his head with his fists and screamed in pain. She continued her chant in perfect rhythm, but James could not hear it as blood trickled from his ears. The pain paralyzed him. He tried to hold Ana's name in his mind, but then there was nothing but the black void of torment.

James thought he heard a banging sound, but he couldn't open his eyes to see. Then as if a light switch had been flipped, the pain subsided. The pounding in his head started to dull. He tried to pull his hands from his eyes so he could get a look at what had happened. Black dots clouded his vision, and the more he rubbed at them, the worse they became. Finally, he decided to sit quietly and let them clear on their own if they ever would. He slowly peeped through his tear-soaked lashes and could see the faint outline of a tall red-haired lady standing right in front of him.

As his vision became clearer, he saw the crumpled body of Ms. Maines lying at the feet of the woman. James saw the woman's fangs, and every vein in her body was visible through her skin. He could see her rage in her eyes. She was a terrifying, beautiful vision of rescue. He started to question the rescue part of it all when she approached him, and her form didn't change. James said nothing. He just stood and accepted his fate. He preferred this means of death over the slow explosion in his brain. Then the woman's face suddenly fixed itself into human form, and James started to breathe.

"Are you James?" the woman asked.

"Yes, ma'am," James answered.

He always showed respect to the immortals no matter if they looked to be his junior. They had the gift of youth. James felt the respect should lie in their wisdom, not their appearance. James tried to move out of the circle and found the barrier still in place. He started to panic.

"It's okay. She's still alive, so her magic is still active. Don't worry. We will get you out of here. By the way, I'm Rene Reed, Ana's mom. Nice to meet ya," Rene said with a chuckle.

She raised her finger to James in a "Wait a moment" gesture and put her phone to her ear.

"Yeah, I got him, but we have a problem. We need the gate-keeper to come up here. Where are we anyway?" Rene asked James.

"Maines's place," he answered.

"Maines's place. Okay, okay, he's fine. Come on," Rene said, shaking her head.

James's head still hurt and felt fuzzy, but everything seemed to be intact. He knew his name and the name of his love, Ana.

Rene knelt next to the woman on the floor and felt her pulse to make sure it was strong enough to keep her alive. "I hate I had to do that, but I really didn't see much else to do at the time. We can't have her waking up and doing anymore hocus-pocus around here. I won't kill her just yet until the gatekeeper comes to question her," she explained.

"I don't care what you do with her. Thanks for coming to find me," James whispered.

"Now I couldn't have my baby all sad and crying because I wouldn't go on a little hike today now, could I?" Rene said.

She smiled. Then she found a piece of twine and bound Ms. Maines's hands behind her back. She then stretched it down her back to her feet and hogtied her. It seemed fitting to both her and James.

The door to the barn burst open, and James saw the most beautiful sight he had ever seen—Ana. Rene grabbed her just before the barrier sent her flying backward in the hay.

"We have to wait a moment, okay? Is the gatekeeper coming?" Rene asked.

"Yeah, he is on the way. Why can't he get out?" Ana asked.

"I'm right here. You can ask me if you want to," James said.

Ana ran over to the circle and stared into the eyes of her love. There were no words needed between the two. Their love was evident to anyone who saw them. Rene was both happy and sad. She didn't want to share her daughter, but she didn't want her to be without love either.

"Are you okay?" Ana asked.

"Nothing but a little headache. I will be just fine," James said.

The dashing man from the gate strolled in like this was just an ordinary day. This pricked Ana just a little bit. Didn't he know James's life was in danger? Surely this didn't happen every day.

"Hi, I'm Jack. What have we got here?" Jack asked.

Everyone started talking at once, and Jack raised his hand in the air to make them stop.

"One at a time, please. Who called me?" Jack asked.

"I did, but I just got here. Ask her," Ana said.

She pointed to her mother, who in turn rolled her eyes in true Rene fashion. Then Rene told Jack all that she knew and turned the story over to James. As James recounted the day's activities, he was surprisingly detailed. He kept his promise to the Johnson family and never mentioned their names. Ms. Maines began to groan and wiggle around a bit. Rene politely knocked her back out again. Jack shook his head and laughed at her openness.

"It seems pretty straightforward if you ask me. We were looking for a person who could do binding spells. We needed to find out who supplied the chains to my friend's abductor. We felt like that person needed to pay for their crimes. Without the chains, the man would have never been able to torture my friend as long as he did, so whoever supplied them to him was as guilty as he was. This woman conveniently used a binding spell to kidnap my James, and who knows what other magic she was doing to torture him? It seems open and shut to me," Ana explained.

"Ms. Maines said she didn't know if she had spelled the chains or not, to be honest. She said she had done a lot of favors for people, and until she saw a picture of the man, she just didn't know," James said.

Jack started pecking on his phone. It was just a few seconds, and he held the phone out for Ana to see.

"Is this the man in question?" Jack asked.

"Yep, that is the dirtbag," Ana answered.

"Okay, stand her up. And, Ms. Reed, try to refrain from knocking her out again," Jack said.

Rene snapped the rope that tied Ms. Maines's feet to her wrists and stood her up. Ana slapped her face, found a cup of nasty stagnant water, and threw it in her face. Ms. Maines started to groan and roll her head like a drunk trying to gather himself.

"Wakey, wakey. Time to open your eyes," Ana taunted.

Ms. Maines slowly began to wink her eyes open and was startled by her new guests. Ana shoved the photo close to her face and demanded answers.

"Do you know this man?" she asked.

Ms. Maines stared at the photo and shook her head no.

"Are you sure you have never seen him? Think it through. It's imperative. It could save your life right now," Jack asked.

Ms. Maines righted her head and gritted her teeth in defiance.

"I have never seen that man in my life. Turn me loose, you monster!" Maines screamed.

Jack was quick in his delivery. He walked up to face the woman. He placed his hands on each side of her head, and with one quick snap, she was done. The spell was immediately void, and James raced to Ana's side. Ana understood there was nothing to learn from this woman, and she was glad Jack had taken her out. Ms. Maines's body fell to the floor, and Rene backed away as if it were poison.

James was shocked by the speed at which Jack delivered his punishment. He wondered if they could have learned anything from this woman. He wondered if they could have made her tell the truth. He knew in his heart she would have never given them any information, though. So all there was left to do was take out the threat, and Jack had done so quickly and with no remorse.

"James, your methods were indeed reckless and dangerous, but your results are undeniable. You have uncovered the viper in our midst. It is hard to say how many lives you have saved by your actions today. It will be noted and will not go unrewarded," Jack explained.

He shook James's hand. James was a little confused by his praise. James believed anyone would have done what he had done. Wouldn't anyone have tried to find the truth, if not for Kimmy, for all the other possible Kimmy's in the world?

"I'm just glad it ended well. It was touch and go there for a second," James said.

He rubbed his head and rolled his eyes, trying to lighten the heavy mood of the room. He had never taken compliments well, and this one, he felt, was undeserved. Ana wrapped her arms around James's neck and cried. She knew how volatile this situation had been. She knew she was too close to her worst fear, which was losing him forever.

"Aww, now, stop that mess. I'm fine, and we made it. I really think she was responsible for everything. Kimmy can sleep a little better now," James consoled her.

"I know, but that was too close. Don't you ever do anything like that again!" Ana yelled.

Rene couldn't take Ana's pain any longer, so she went and wrapped her arms around her sobbing daughter. She stroked Ana's hair and whispered, "Shhh." Ana stopped shaking and gulped in air.

"Dry it up, little lady. He is fine," Rene said.

"As I'm sure you all understand, nothing that happened here can ever leave this room. Only the people who need to know will know. Something like this could cause a panic in both the mortals and immortals as well. Do you all understand?" Jack asked.

Everyone nodded in agreement.

"There is a reason the craft is not encouraged anymore. For one, it is too dangerous. Secondly, it promotes greed. No one has ever had enough power, and they will always try to have more. There is never enough, not ever. People will trample on anyone or anything in their path for it. That kind of greed destroyed mankind once before. Immortals see the need for strict adherence to the rules. No one wants another disaster," Jack explained.

Rene and Ana remembered the time before the tremendous devastation, and they knew every word Jack spoke was the truth. Having never seen another kind of world, James could only trust that what Jack said was true. His world was one of helpfulness and unity. He couldn't picture a world where others were so vicious. What was the point of power if everyone around you was gone even when you had it?

"I need to make some calls. James, I will return with the determination of the council. I have a cleanup team on the way if you don't mind staying until they get here. Thank you so much, Rene, Ana. I will see you soon," Jack said. He kissed Rene's and Ana's cheeks and shook James's hand.

"Sure, we will stay. Thanks for everything," Rene said.

With that, Jack was gone back down the mountain to tie up the loose ends.

James sat on the stool, and Ana stood guard over him, running her fingers through his hair. As Rene watched, she knew Ana would never leave him again. She would want to shelter him from every storm, just as Rene had done for Ana.

"That wasn't much of a first meeting, if I should say so," Rene said.

"No doubt," James agreed.

"I'm so glad you came with me today. I might not have made it here in time. I don't even want to think about what could have happened," Ana said.

"All's well that ends well. Isn't that what they say?" Rene said.

"Didn't end very well for her, but if she spelled the chains, that wasn't enough of a punishment for her," Ana said.

The cleanup team arrived, and Ms. Maines's body was bagged and tagged. They reviewed the cover story with Ana, Rene, and James. The story would be that James came to help with Ms. Maines's young mare and found her dead of a massive heart attack. The reason for her death was open and shut. There was no reason for anyone to think otherwise. Ms. Maines would be nothing more than a memory to her mortal neighbors until the sands of time buried even her memory.

"I think I'm going to stay at the farm for a while," Ana said.

"I kind of thought you might. Do you know what I'm going to do? I'm going to do what I came here to do in the first place. I'm going to find my own friend. How do you like that? I think I have filled my quota of good deeds for the day," Rene stated.

She leaned in and kissed her daughter, then hugged James tightly.

"I'm glad you're okay," Rene whispered.

"Me too. Thank you," James whispered back.

James felt warmth flood him as he thought of his own mother's hugs. This one felt the same. Ana made a call to Jack and inquired about Ms. Maines's young mare. He quickly encouraged them to take her if they wanted her. James and Ana welcomed the newest member of their family. He didn't know what Ms. Maines had called her, but he did remember she said her older horse was called Sugarfoot, so Sugarfoot she would be. James was a tender-hearted soul, and even in the wake of truth about Ms. Maines, he felt sympathy for her too. Even though Ms. Maines was greedy, cruel, and selfish, James thought maybe something had made her that way.

The young mare was surprisingly calm while Ana held its lead on the way home. Betsy tried to move anywhere but beside Ana on the path. Ana would have to work on a more trusting relationship with the other "lady" in James's life. They made it back to the cottage right before dark, and they were quick to unsaddle, brush, and stall the two horses. Being the silly person she was, Ana told the animals good night before shutting the door to the barn. Besty threw her ears back in protest and snorted.

"Let me go turn the water on for you," Ana said.

James was so tired he couldn't even argue with her about it. He started untying his boots and threw them haphazardly in the corner. His shirt was filthy, and he stank from the fear-based sweating he had done. The shirt followed his boots to the floor. Ana laid out a towel and a washcloth just as he had done for her. All she wanted to do was make him comfortable and safe. She turned to find him standing at the bathroom door in his underwear.

"Let me get out of your way," Ana said.

"I think not. You're gonna stay right here with me," James said.

Ana smiled, lowered the toilet seat, and watched her beautiful man undress and melt under the warm flowing water. She sat in silence while he washed away the day. He let all the fear, pain, and grief go down the drain with the dirty water. She picked up the washcloth and opened the shower curtain and began to move it slowly across his back. James knew that was the best thing he'd ever felt in his life. His muscles ached from the tension, and her touch left them fluid and free. The water washed away the bubbles, and Ana got his towel, spread it out, and stood waiting for him to wrap himself in it.

As James tucked the towel into the top, he leaned in and kissed Ana's full pouting lips. He felt something he hadn't felt in many years. He felt tears falling from his eyes, down his cheeks. He tasted his salty sadness in the passion of their kiss. The adrenaline his body had produced was gone, and what was left was overwhelming. He held Ana tightly and cleansed his soul in the curls of her hair.

Ana took his hand, and they made their way to the bed. She turned it down, and James fell into it and sighed. Ana slipped off her shoes and her shorts and slipped in beside him. She snuggled up to his warm, perfect body and soaked in the bliss of his safety. They didn't move from their positions for the entire night. He held her next to him, and she was more comfortable than she had ever been. Morning came accompanied by the crow of a feeble old rooster. Ana stretched and wiped the drool from the corner of her mouth. She quickly wiped at James's chest. She would have died if she had drowned him in spit after everything he had survived.

"Good morning, angel," James said.

"Good morning," Ana said.

"Have you been awake long?" Ana asked.

"Just a little while, not too long. I'm dying for some coffee. Do you want some?" James asked.

"I would love some," Ana answered.

The coffee breathed new life into them both, and they couldn't wait for a more peaceful day today.

James's Deal

James sat carving at a piece of beautiful chestnut wood, while Ana read one of his books she had never read before. She thought they were like an old married couple already. She had made some lemonade, and even though it wasn't as good as Brenda's, she was rather pleased with how it turned out. Neither she nor James was dead from her efforts, so she ranked it pretty high on the success meter. Ana heard a vehicle coming up the path.

"Somebody's coming," Ana said.

James looked up the path and saw nothing. He strained to hear whatever it was she heard, but he heard nothing. He waited another moment or two then he heard the buzz of an ATV coming their way. Sometimes James forgot Ana's unique abilities because he was blinded to anything but her soul. Jack was their visitor, and Ana wondered what he had come to tell them.

"James, Ana, so good to see you. I'm glad it is more favorable circumstances today," Jack greeted.

"Nice to see you. What can we do for you, Jack?" James asked.

"I told you yesterday that I would be around to speak to you about the determination of the council. They were quick in making their ruling this time. It appears they believe you to be a good candidate for exception status. Not only from your actions yesterday but many small deeds you have performed over the years. They have a detailed list. I didn't feel it necessary to have it. I am on board with the decision merely based on your actions as of late." Jack explained.

Ana couldn't speak. She remembered what Kimmy had said about the exceptions, and she was nervous and excited to hear what James would decide to do. She promised herself that no matter what he chose to do, she would love him for as long as his life would let her.

"I'm sorry, sir, but I'm not sure what any of that means. I just did what any decent person would do. I do thank you for your kindness, though," James said.

"Of course, you wouldn't understand, James. No mortal would. That's why I am here. The council has given me the authority to offer you an extraordinary gift. It will come at a price, as most truly wonderful gifts do, so you will be given time to think it through. As a reward for your past good deeds and future deeds we will require from you, we offer you immortality," Jack explained.

James sat on the stump where he had been before and just stared at the ground. He finally broke the silence.

"I'm sorry... What?" he asked.

"We can grant you eternity, but there are some things we will require from you as well. The maniac who had your friend is not the only one like him in the world. If the need arose, you would be required to render your services in tracking and dispatching justice to said persons. There are many situations where your skills would come in handy for us. Then, of course, Ms. Reed would be in the employ of the council as well if you were to decide to come aboard," Jack said.

James looked at Jack, then back at Ana, who looked nervous and excited all at once. He got up and paced back and forth in front of Jack, running his hand through his hair, as he did when he was thinking hard on something.

"So let me get this straight. You are saying the council will make me like you in exchange for me ridding the world of parasites like the man who took Kimmy?" James asked.

"In a nutshell, yes," Jack answered.

"You must understand this would be for the duration of your existence, but it would be scattered sporadically through the years. We have many just like you, so we wouldn't be calling on you all the time. It would be but a small block of time in your endless sea of it," Jack explained.

James again looked to Ana. She didn't even move. She didn't even breathe. She was in shock by this turn of events.

"Where do I sign up?" James asked.

Ana ran over to him and threw her arms around his neck. She was the happiest she had ever been. He would be hers forever.

"James, there is one downside to this that you may not have thought about in the two seconds since I presented it to you. Everyone here must think you perished. You will cause grief to the ones who love you. They will always and forever have to believe that you died within these walls," Jack said.

James returned to his stump, and the happiness was drained from his face. His aunt and his cousins, who were like brothers, would have to mourn a lie.

"If that proves to be an obstacle you can't overcome, I will simply mesmerize away all you have seen in the past few days. You will continue to live out your days as a mortal and die a human death. But if you chose to go in the other direction, I promise to come and relieve the suffering of your family with the same mind control. They will be sad and grieve, but there will be no guilt or torture in it for them. They will feel your absence in everyday life, but they will find peace knowing you are with your mother," Jack explained.

And that was it. That was the real choice here. If James chose to go the immortal path, he would forever give up the chance to be reunited with his mother, but he wouldn't get the chance of happiness with Ana if he didn't. He thought of his mother's warm smile and heard her gentle laugh in his ears. He remembered her calling him her happy little boy. She would want him to find happiness and do good with his life. With this gift, he could do good for many lifetimes. He felt his mother was at peace wherever she was and that no sadness dwelled in the place she lived now. His choice was simple. He chose Ana every day, all the time, and forever.

"Let's do it," James said.

"Well done. I'm glad you have seen the reason for all this. I will make the arrangements, and in one week's time, we will make it so. That's the twenty-first day of the month, I believe," Jack said.

He smiled and shook James's sweaty palm. Then he pulled him in for a manly hug, kissed Ana, and was on his way to let the council know James's decision.

Both James and Ana were in shock. They spent the rest of the day talking and laughing and planning their life outside the confines of the wall. Ana had so much she wanted to share with James. She would show him everything she loved in the world, and she hoped he loved them too.

Whatever business the council had for them was well worth the trade. Ana had always been one for dishing out the justice, so this was right up her alley, and they agreed to let her go along too. It was crazy and wonderful and perfect. Ana didn't know what she had done to deserve this, but she was thankful for it. One week… One week, and he would be free. Not only would he be free, but he would also be safe.

She couldn't wait to see how the transformation touched him. She couldn't imagine him more perfect than he was right now, but she knew he would be. Her body ached for it. Ana noticed James looking at her strangely.

"Are you okay?" he asked.

She covered her mouth with her hand and quickly turned away from him. She knew why she felt the need she felt. She hadn't fed. Her body was aching for him in more than one way. She could smell his blood and hear his heart pounding in his chest. She fought the sensation and brought herself back to her normal human state.

"I'm sorry," Ana said.

"Why? No, don't ever be sorry, Ana. What's wrong? Can I help you?" James asked.

"I haven't fed. Ugh, I'm so embarrassed," she said.

"Don't ever be embarrassed, ever. Come inside with me," he said.

James took Ana's hand and led her inside. He sat her down on the sofa and slipped his T-shirt off. He sat beside her and wrapped his arm around her shoulder. He leaned her head on his shoulder and snuggled into her.

"Drink," he whispered.

Ana had no embarrassment left in her, only thirst. She sank her fangs into the recess of his neck and drank. Her body did as it had done before. She trembled and panted as if they were in the throes of passion. This only proved to excite James further. He loved the way her need for him was released in this extraordinary way. She pulled and tugged at him like a baby suckling its mother. She listened to the sound of his heartbeat, and when it was one beat slower than it had been, she pulled away.

Ana's body was radiant with nourishment and the heat of the exchange. She so consumed James that nothing would stop them from completing the connection they shared. She would take him into her as she had taken him into herself. She would give him the release he so obviously craved. Yet this encounter was totally different from the last. There were no tender moments in this animalistic affair. Instead, they enjoyed each other in a way only the truest of lovers did. They lay in exquisite bliss, and no one said a word until sleep invaded them both.

The Longest Week

Ana and James began the longest week of their lives. Ana never asked James how he felt about the decision he had to make. She only enjoyed the prospect of forever with him. They spent lazy afternoons in the special places within the farm. They spent as much time as they could with James's family without them realizing that something was different. He hugged them more and told them everything he wanted to say to them. He thanked his aunt for the unconditional love she gave to him. He could never thank her enough for stepping in and being his fill-in, bonus mom when his own mother was gone. Ana hoped this was a good sign for her.

On the evening of the last night before Jack's return, James left Ana in their bed and went to enjoy the crisp evening air. He weighed out everything and found nothing outweighed his need to be with Ana. He would miss the only home he had ever known. He would miss the familiar smells and sounds of his life. The silliest things were burdening him the most. He worried about his precious horses and what future they would have without him. He wished they could join him in freedom. Maybe he would ask about that later.

James couldn't stand the thought of leaving his mother's portrait behind. It had been a constant source of comfort over his lifetime, and he really didn't know what to do without it. James had an idea. He tiptoed back where Ana had her phone. He borrowed it for a moment. He began with pictures of the portrait and then went outside. He captured his memories within the small black box. He knew Ana would know what to do with them, but even if she didn't, he had them there on her phone's screen.

Ana heard him stirring about but thought this was a private time for him. She lay in their bed and listened to him go from room to room, then outside. Finally, James put her phone back and slipped into bed. Ana pretended to be asleep and felt him cuddled up next to her. Ana couldn't imagine the pain of this goodbye. It did seem to be dishonest, but it was really the only way. She hoped he could understand.

Daybreak came, and Ana and James sat on the front porch, drinking their coffee. A rumble of a motor filled the quiet morning. A large gray Chevy truck that long since should have been in the scrap heap came plowing down the path. Tom, the gatekeeper from Ana's first trip, popped out the door and waved to them.

"Hey, guys," Tom called.

He paced back and forth while they talked. He was seriously hyper, and Ana almost got dizzy watching him. Tom was charming but feral. He was what the history books might have called savage.

"Are you ready, buddy?" Tom asked.

"Don't really know what we are doing, but yeah, I'm ready," James answered.

"It's gonna be great in a month or two, but that first little bit's gonna kick your ass," Tom said.

"I got good help to get me through," James said.

He took Ana's hand and smiled.

"We need to go inside, if that's okay," Tom said.

Everyone piled into the tight space of James's cottage. Ana noticed Tom stayed near the door, and he left it ajar. He didn't let it latch behind him. She wondered what the story was behind that, but endless days left room for endless trauma. What trauma broke his spirit? What made him afraid to stop moving? What made him fearful of latched doors? That was clearly his albatross around his neck. Ana would hope someday he would be free of the unseen tormentor and find peace.

"First, we need to give you some meds that will give you the appearance that you are no longer living. So roll up your sleeve, please," Tom said.

This was moving so quickly. James didn't have time to process anything or even ask a question. Tom retrieved a syringe from his jacket pocket with an ugly green fluid inside.

"One, two," Tom counted.

He was obviously one of those people who believed three was the number you didn't say, that three was the number when the action took place. James sucked in his breath as the needle pierced his arm like a bee's sting. The fluid was hot, and he could feel it running the course of his body with every inch it traveled through his veins. He felt sleepy, and then there was nothing but black.

Ana laid James back onto the couch. She could hear his heart slowing to a faint whisper. It terrified her to the core. Her doubts poured over her as she imagined every possible way this could go wrong. Every way would leave her mourning her lost love. James's breath was so shallow no mortal could have heard it. Ana was having a hard time breathing herself.

"Okay, that's done. Now the part you won't like. We can't very well say this strong, healthy young man dropped dead from natural causes. It has to look like an accident. He is going to need a head injury to make it look convincing. The question is, will you do it, or should I?" Tom asked.

"You do it. I don't think I can," Ana answered.

Tom was quick and inflicted an injury that looked life-threatening on the right side of James's head. James's head bled above his eye, and a knot began to form on the side of his face.

"You hit him too hard!" Ana screamed.

"Calm down. I have done this like three times. He will be fine. I will take him down to the barn and turn out the mares. The drug will keep him out quite a while, but you have to go now. You will be notified when James is safely inside the council center," Tom instructed.

Ana didn't want to leave James, but she knew she had to go. Had she been there, James's family would have wondered why she didn't just heal him. So Ana kissed his lips and whispered "See ya soon" in his ear. Ana left with love and excitement for their new lives blooming in her heart. She would wait not so patiently at home for the call that would reunite her with her king.

Tom's slight arrogance was simply his way of hiding his insecure nature. His outward confidence hid a small boy with a heart too big to ignore the hate in his father's eyes. Abuse and neglect formed the mortal he was and the immortal he became. Even though no one could guess it, he felt pity for anyone who suffered. He spent quiet moments reflecting on others' pain. He cursed their tormentors and worried irrationally about their fates.

Tom placed James safely in position in a barn stall. He made sure James blocked the gate so nothing would happen to his vulnerable body. Sugarfoot was set free within the confines of the barn. Tom saddled Betsy and led her down the path toward James's aunt's home. He knew the horse would know her way and go right up to the front door with a bit of persuasion. Tom counted on someone realizing something was wrong. They would find him just as they had planned and call the front for assistance. The council would remove him from the farm, and it would be done.

Kyle worked in the yard of his mother's home. Betsy did her part to perfection. She trotted away from Tom as he stood in his complete vampire form in the middle of the path. Betsy couldn't wait to get away from him and to the safety of her familiar extended family. She trotted to Kyle and kept glancing to see if the threat was following her.

"Whoa, whoa, old girl! What are you doing here?" Kyle asked. Then he yelled to his mom, "Hey, Mom, come out here!"

"What is it? Oh, ain't that Betsy?" Nelly asked.

"Yeah, something must be wrong. I'm going to go check," Kyle said.

"Take Kurt with you," Nelly instructed.

Kyle and Kurt made good time but didn't feel a sense of panic. Instead, they expected to find James on his ass in the yard, and they would get the pleasure of laughing at him for his troubles. So when he wasn't in the yard, they went out to the barn. Time stood still for them as they found the lifeless body of James.

"Go get Mama. James! Wake up, buddy," Kyle yelled.

Kurt ran full force all the way to his Nelly's house.

"Mama, come on! Help us. It's James," Kurt screamed.

"What is it? Oh god, no!" Nelly yelled.

Kurt and Nelly ran as quickly as the older woman could. Finally, they made it to the barn and found Kyle sobbing like a baby beside the body of his adopted brother. Kyle grabbed his mother as she ran toward James.

"Mama, he's gone. He's gone," Kyle cried.

James's replacement mother screamed and clawed at Kyle's shirt. He turned her and moved slowly to the door.

"What do we do?" Kurt asked.

He paced, cursed, and pulled at his hair. He had never had anyone die before, and he didn't know how to process it.

"No, no, not like this," Nelly cried.

She quickly straightened herself for her children. There were things to be done, and she had to do them. But first, she had to call the front. She slowly went to James's home and dialed the number. She explained all she knew, and they immediately said that help was on the way. Nelly replaced the phone on its cradle and turned to see the portrait of her sister. She cried, and her heart felt as though it were breaking in her chest. The only comfort she could find was in the knowledge that the mother and son were now reunited in another time and space. There was a kind of peace in that fact.

Tom came quickly and assured the family that the greatest care would be taken with James's remains.

"I'm so sorry for your loss. If there is anything you need, please don't hesitate to ask," he said.

And with that, it was done. All that was left was the grief and pain of loss. James was whisked away to a new life. Removing the dead was typical protocol within the farm, so there were no questions about the immortals retrieving his body. The memorial service was beautiful. There was an outpouring of love and respect from everyone in attendance. People told stories from James's past that left them laughing or in tears. Nelly wasn't surprised Ana hadn't come. She knew that immortals' emotions were heightened. If her pain was this great, she could only imagine the level of Ana's grief. She pictured Ana in bed with the pain of a thousand mortals to endure. However, Nelly knew Ana would come someday and that they would spend the day talking and celebrating James.

James's Hospital

As soon as Ana received the call, she was on her way to the council center. When she arrived, she found James in a standard room, peacefully sleeping. Ana was glad she made it before he woke. She wanted him to feel safe and protected, always. While she waited, she watched a documentary on TV and held James's hand. After a few hours, Ana felt James squeeze her hand. His eyes were still closed, but she could hear his heartbeat as it picked up in rhythm. Consciousness was trying to break through his fog of sleep.

"Ana," James whispered.

"I'm right here. Take your time," Ana said.

James moved his head toward the sound of Ana's voice and slowly opened his eyes. He saw his personal angel and smiled.

"Hi, my love. Let me get you some water," Ana said.

It wasn't long before James was sitting up in bed, talking and fully alert. Then the door to the room opened, and a man in a white lab coat came into the room. The man was one of those people who instantly made anyone feel more at ease. He had one of those faces that made you smile and relax.

"Well, you're awake. That's wonderful. I'm Dr. Taylor, and I will be assisting you today," the doctor said.

"I'm Ana. So nice to meet you," Ana greeted.

"Very nice to meet you, young lady. James, your transformation is going great, but there is a decision you will need to make before we can move forward. There are two choices you will need to consider. To complete the transformation, you will need to ingest immortal blood. The question is, do you want an anonymous donor or someone you are comfortable with to do it? There is a difference between the two. You will have what we call a sire bond to whomever your donor is going to be. There will be certain controlling factors your donor will have in regard to you. Your donor will be able to mesmerize you, where no other immortal will have that ability, and you will also have a strong sense of loyalty to them. There is no way to explain the sire bond to someone who has never felt it. If you choose an anonymous donor, you may never know who that person is. You may never be in the company of your particular donor, so you would never have to be concerned with the bond. If you choose a person you know, they will have these connections with you for as long as you both remain in this realm of existence. There are pros and cons both for and against the sire bond. I personally enjoy my bond with both my donor and the people I have assisted in changing. I will give you some time to think about it and come back in a bit. Do you have any questions for me?" Dr. Taylor asked.

James stared at Ana, trying to read her thoughts.

"It's up to you," Ana said.

"Don't you want to?" James asked.

"Of course, I do, but I don't want you to feel like you have to choose me," Ana explained.

"I have never wanted anything more in my life. I choose you forever. You just need to make sure forever is what you have in mind because it sounds like I won't have much of a choice but to love you for eternity," James said.

"Forever is just what I had in mind too," Ana said.

With tears streaming down her face, she leaned in and kissed James.

"Okay, Doc, I want her to do it. I'm ready whenever you are," James said.

"My job is done here for now. So I will leave you two to do the hard part," Dr. Taylor said.

As the doctor heading to the door, he turned and gave Ana a wink. She had spoken to the doctor about all she would need to do if James wanted her to be his donor. She was so thrilled she would be the one to bond with him for eternity.

"Have you done this before?" James asked.

"No, but I have talked with the doctor about what we need to do, and it seems pretty straightforward. I drink, you drink, then well, you know… Then you wake up like me. I'm ready," Ana said.

She sounded way more confident than she actually felt, but she wanted James to be okay with his choice. She wanted him to feel safe and secure with her.

"I'm glad to hear it. I'm a little possessive now when it comes to you, and it sounds like that is about to get a whole lot worse. I wouldn't be too happy if someone else shared the bond with you that we are going to share," James said.

"No, silly. It's only you. I will always be only you," Ana assured him.

"You tell me when you're ready, and we will do this thing," James said.

"You tell me," Ana said.

"No time like the present, I always say," James said.

He was very aware that the only alternative to the transformation was death, and he had come too far to chicken out now. He was going to be okay. Ana would see to it. James could see the veins in Ana's face more clearly now, and he knew she was fighting the desire to feed. It looked painful to him. Was this how it was going to be for him? He imagined it would be, but he would learn to control it just as Ana had done.

"Okay," Ana said.

She moved over to the side of the bed and sat down. She took James's hand in hers and kissed it gently. She raised her own wrist to her lips and her fangs extended. She bit into her flesh, and blood started to trickle out. Her wound starting healing almost as soon as she placed it on James's lips. He did drink, but Ana wasn't confident with the amount he had ingested. So she bit into the flesh of her wrist again, making a much larger incision. The blood flowed freely this time.

James drank from her wrist and held it close to his waiting mouth. He, too, wanted to make sure not to fail due to some technicality. He clearly had enough this time as it dripped from his chin and puddle on the sheets. Ana felt terrible about the mess they had made on the bed linens, but she would worry about that later.

The next stage of the transformation would satiate Ana's hunger. She cradled James's head in her hand and tilted it so that she could gain access to his beautiful neck. She sank into his flesh with ease. She drank from the well of his body, and total satisfaction flooded hers. She listened to the rhythm of his heart as the doctor had instructed her to do. She counted every beat.

The beats grew more erratic. They were one, two, skip, one, two, skip. Then they skipped two beats. That was just what the doctor said she wanted to hear. She pulled back from James before death dragged her into the void. Now was the hardest part. Ana had to wait and watch as James gave in to the blackness of death. She knew he would fight it because that was his nature. Had he been conscious, he would have known falling further was what he needed to do, but unconscious, he was a warrior. His body clung to precious life, even though immortality awaited it.

Finally, the door creaked open, and Dr. Taylor came inside.

"You did so well, Ana. Everything looks just as it should. We can speed this along so his body doesn't have to suffer, if that is okay with you," Dr. Taylor said.

Ana nodded and moved out of the way. Her emotions were everywhere. She was thrilled and scared all at once. She would leave this to the doctor. Dr. Taylor took a scalpel from a tray and a plastic tub from a cabinet. He laid James's forearm in the curvature of the tub. Dr. Taylor ran the scalpel up the length of his arm from wrist to elbow, allowing the contents to drain into the tub. Ana listened to James's heart as it ticked down like an unwound clock. She listened to the last beat and watched as his body completely emptied of life.

"Aww, he will be fine. Don't cry," Dr. Taylor said.

Ana hadn't noticed her tears until that moment. The doctor stroked her hair and gave her what she imagined to be a fatherly hug. Ana wouldn't know about anything like that, though. This was the closest to it she had ever been in her many lives. She wiped all of her confused emotions onto the tissue the doctor handed her and sat in her seat.

"Now that's much better, pretty girl. Let me send someone in to clean up everything. The most aggravating part right now is the waiting. You just sit, and before you know it, he will be awake," Dr. Taylor said.

"Thank you so much. Is it okay if my mom comes to wait with me?" Ana asked.

"Sure, I will let them know she is coming," the doctor said.

Ana picked up her phone and called Rene. She couldn't wait to tell her everything. Not only was Rene her mother, but she was also her best friend. Time had done nothing but make their bond stronger.

"Hi, Mom. We did it," Ana said.

"That is so great, baby. Did you ask if I could come to wait with you?" Rene asked.

"Yeah, they said it was fine," Ana answered.

"Okay, see ya soon," Rene said.

"Okay, love you."

"Love you more," Rene said.

No more than ten minutes passed, and Rene was standing, holding her daughter.

"Yeah, I know, I know, but I wasn't going to make you wait two hours for me to get here. I have been in the parking lot," Rene explained.

"You're the best mom in the world," Ana said.

"I know, I know," Rene said.

Ana and Rene sat by James's bed and ate every snack they could find. They finally called in a pizza and some breadsticks. They watched every dumb TV show that could stand until they both slipped off into sleep. A stirring of covers woke the two sentries from their guard posts. Ana was shocked to find James's hand outstretched as if he were looking for her. Ana took his hand and cooed and kissed his face. His skin was flawless caramel silk, and his hair was lush and beautiful. He would awake from his sleep a new creature, and they could begin their forever together. Ana could hardly wait. She wanted to shake him and scream his name until he woke, but she didn't. She suffered in silence.

Slight movements and small groans were signs of progression. James was fighting to regain his place in the world. Ana admired his warrior spirit and knew the transformation would benefit everyone who would ever need this great man. If anyone deserved power, strength, and immortality, it was James. He would wield them like a sword to defend the innocent and punish the guilty.

James fluttered his eyes, and the first sight he saw was his angel. Ana saw the forest green of his eyes now danced with gold dust. It was her James, but it wasn't her James. This version was even nobler than the other. He was amazingly perfect in every way.

"Hi," Ana said.

"Hi," James croaked.

Ana hugged him tightly and kissed his lips.

"Hi there, sweet boy," Rene said.

"Hi," he answered.

— ❦ —

New Life

James's stay at the center was a short one. The council recommended a two-day stay for monitoring mental health, but they deemed James sound and ready to proceed. Some "baby" vampires had a difficult time with the transition. Ana was thrilled to take him back to Oak View. She couldn't wait to introduce him to everything she had told him about on their visits to the farm.

James wasn't ready for the vulnerable feeling freedom gave him. Even though he knew his new form protected him much better than his mortal form did, he still felt anxiety about there being no barrier between him and the outside world. Having heard so many stories about the effects of the environment on people, he found that it really did, except that he was in no danger. Before the big double doors opened, Ana noticed his apprehension, and she squeezed his hand.

"You're okay. I'm right here. It's great, trust me," Ana said.

James squeezed her hand for added confirmation and walked beside her through the doors and into freedom.

The air smelled different, and the sun felt as though it were sitting right on his shoulders. Ana explained that it was the difference in location. She assured him that it would seem more like what he was used to when they got on up to the mountain. The two climbed into the pearl-white Camero and rolled the windows down. James was in awe of the sights and sounds that were speeding past him.

Two hours of travel was almost overwhelming to him. He saw things he had only read about in books. He knew the outside world was different, but this was more than he ever imagined it to be. Inside the walls of the farm, no car could have gone so fast. The endless roadway was open and welcoming. Who knew speed would be James's new obsession?

Ana pointed out the road that led to her childhood home. She said they would come and look at it one day when they were out and about. When James saw the house he was to call home, he was amazed. The warehouse inside the farm wasn't even this big, so he seemed a little more at ease when he saw the carriage house. It was still ten times bigger than his cottage but nowhere near as massive as the brick monstrosity on the hill.

They went inside and closed the door behind them. This instantly gave James a more secure feeling, as there were boundaries around them. He hoped this weird sensation of weightlessness would end soon. It was unnerving not to know exactly what his role was here in this new place. He didn't know what to do or how to act, so he let Ana take the lead.

"Have a seat. This is your home. Relax and get comfortable. Do you want something to eat? Would you like to change out of those clothes?" Ana asked.

James stared at her in confusion. He had nothing to change into here. He had nothing, period. That feeling alone was scary and heartbreaking to him, but he nodded and smiled. The clothing he had worn the day he was removed from the farm had been returned to his family. The clothing the hospital provided was itchy and stiff. He really wouldn't mind finding something else to wear.

"I don't have anything yet," James said.

Ana smiled, took his hand, and dragged him into their bedroom, which was almost the same size as his whole cottage.

"Yes, you do, silly," Ana said.

She opened a drawer in a large chest and took a T-shirt, sweats, and undies from it. Next, she opened a large closet in the room and handed him a pair of comfy slippers with plaid fluff on the inside.

"Right over there is our bathroom," Ana said.

She pointed to the bathroom, and James took a peek inside. It was amazing. There was a tub sitting right at the center of the room, and there was a separate shower too. The regular necessities of a restroom were available, but James couldn't help but think how much space all this took up. Life within the farm was compact, and only what one needed was allowed a precious place in the home. He couldn't help but imagine how wonderful it would be to stretch out in the large bathtub and soak. His small cottage only had a tiny shower tucked away in a corner in which he could bathe. It all seemed amazingly indulgent, but James supposed this was the way of the outside world. He would have to adapt to it.

"Are you hungry?" Ana asked.

"I'm starving," James answered.

She was thrilled with his more open response and joyfully turned to leave the room.

"You get changed, and I will go make some coffee to start," she said.

"That would be great. Ana?" James began.

Ana stopped dead in her tracks.

"Yes?" she answered.

"I love you," James said.

"I love you too," Ana said.

James changed out of the uncomfortable clothing from the hospital and slipped into the new cozy clothes Ana had prepared for him. The shoes were something else. They were fluffy and warm and kind of silly, but he loved them. He stared at his feet many times, wondering if this was really what men on the outside wore or if this was something they just happened to find for him. He didn't care. He would hide them if anyone came around, but he wouldn't stop wearing them.

James made his way down to the kitchen and smelled the wonderful fragrance of coffee brewing on the countertop. He stepped behind Ana and hugged her around the waist. He put his nose in her hair and breathed in her essence. She was the most amazing, perfect creature that had ever been created, and he was sure of that fact.

"Let's see what Mom stock us up with," Ana said.

Both James and Ana were shocked by the amount of food that filled the cabinets. He had everything he had ever heard of to sample. He wanted to try it all, but the couple chose old standby ham-and-cheese sandwiches with chips and a pickle. The two sat and just relaxed for the rest of the afternoon. Ana had so many surprises for James but didn't want to overwhelm him with everything all at once. Even though the family wanted to welcome James and get to know him better, they gave the couple their privacy during this delicate transition.

Night came, and the couple made their way to their room. They laughed and played and made love until the wee hours of the morning. Ana knew there was no better feeling in the world than being in his capable hands. He knew her body like his own and pleased her beyond anything she could imagine. She hoped he felt the same satisfaction with her as well. His insatiable desire for her left her to believe that he did. She was a thirst he couldn't quench unless she fully enclosed him. She was a sculpture of desire for him to create over and over again.

James slept more peacefully than he ever had in his life. Perfect slumber replaced the tossing, turning, and worry of before. Ana quietly left the room and went to the kitchen. She wanted James to feel comfortable and happy in his new home. All she wanted was for him to feel like he was the king, alpha, lord of his domain. She wasn't a Suzie Homemaker, that was for sure, but she would learn. And she would give to him all he deserved.

James woke to a note on Ana's pillow. It said, "Good morning, my love. I'm in the kitchen. I hope you slept well. I put your things in the bathroom if you would like a shower before breakfast. Love, Ana."

James rolled over and buried his face in Ana's pillow. He loved her smell. He could bathe in only her for the rest of his life and be completely happy. He tucked the note into the bedside table drawer, made a mental note to date it, and found a place to keep such keepsakes.

In the bathroom, he found jeans, a white T-shirt, and a flannel to wear. On the floor was a pair of new boots with socks stuck into the top. Ana was over the top. She had a towel and washcloth ready on the sink. Everything was perfect, right down to the toothbrush in the holder by the sink. Ana had written James's name on his with a black fine-tipped marker, and James thought that was extra cute of her. She was even more impressive than he even realized. James knew his job would be difficult if he planned to make her feel even a portion of how special she made him feel.

James followed his nose to the kitchen, where, just as he thought, bacon sizzled in a pan on the stovetop.

"Good morning, love," Ana said.

"Good morning. It smells amazing in here," James replied.

He stuck his nose over the pan and sniffed. He slowly tried to slip a piece from the draining plate, but Ana quickly slapped at his hand.

"Not yet. I'm waiting for the toast. Have a seat," Ana said.

James sat at the table, and Ana poured him a cup of hot coffee. He heard the familiar pop, and the toast jumped from its hiding place. Ana made two plates with bacon, toast, and eggs. There were homemade strawberry preserves and tall glasses of orange juice and milk. The two sat and chatted about their day's plans and enjoyed the beauty of the morning.

"I have to say, you outdid yourself with everything you did to get ready for me. You thought of everything," James said.

"Okay, well, most of that was Mom. I told her sizes and a vague description of what you like, and she took the ball and ran with it. Trust me. I'm sure there are a ton of things that you will hate in your closet. In her defense, though, it's not every day you get to play dress-up with a real-life Ken doll," Ana said.

James didn't understand the reference, but he could tell it was meant as a joke.

"Oh, you're so funny," he said.

"I have a surprise for you when we are done with breakfast," Ana confessed.

"Oh yeah? What is it?" James asked.

"It wouldn't be a surprise if I told you now, would it?" Ana said.

James made quick work of his food and began to clean up the dishes from the table. Ana washed, and James dried. Ana thought this was the best way to do tedious chores.

"Okay, are you ready for your surprise?" Ana asked.

"Yep, can't wait," James answered.

He couldn't help but giggle as Ana pulled on tall black mud boots and a floppy straw hat that was way too big for her head.

"Oh, hush. This is all the rage in Paris," Ana scolded.

She strutted out the door like a runway model, and James obediently followed her.

They walked hand in hand through a field behind the CH. James noticed a huge red structure up ahead that he could only believe to be a barn. Surely it wasn't, though. It was bigger than even the warehouse on the farm had been. Huge silver metal roof vents spun round and round, and a large horse weathervane sat between them.

"Time to close your eyes now," Ana said.

James did just as Ana instructed and felt her take his hand and lead him inside the massive structure. James could smell the familiar smells of his own barn. He smelled hay, grain, the unmistakable scent of leather, and horse sweat. He felt a twinge of sadness for his companions on the farm, but the prospect of a place for new horses was exciting. Ana positioned him directly in the middle of the floor while Rene, Brady, Lana, and Kimmy led six horses out of their stalls. There was one for each of them to enjoy.

"Okay, open your eyes," Ana instructed.

Not only were there three of the most beautiful horses in the world standing in front of him but there were also three very familiar ones as well. Betsy, Sugarfoot, and Baby had made their way to freedom too. All neighed in recognition. James quickly hugged Betsy and kissed her long face. She was definitely just as excited to see her friend. Every animal got cuddles and love before James could even speak.

"I don't even know what to say. I can't say thank you enough. This girl right here has been my friend—no, family—since she was a foal. It broke me to leave her. Thank you so much," James said.

"I love you," Ana said.

"I love you so much," James said.

"Thanks to all of you for everything you have done to make me feel so welcome. I promise I will find a way to repay your kindness someday," James said.

As he addressed the group, he only saw one familiar face—Rene's.

"Let me see if I get this right. You're Brady, obviously, little Lana, and you must be the infamous Kimmy," James guessed.

He pointed to each in turn, and each one's smile answered his questions of correctness. Everyone took turns with warm, welcoming hugs for their new brother. Brady extended the utmost gratitude for James's testosterone on the estate. He confessed he was beginning to feel a little outnumbered here. James laughed and pleaded allegiance to his new brother. James did feel like he belonged among these new people. Ana's detailed descriptions of each had left him feeling as though they were not strangers at all. If they were important to Ana, then they were important to James. That is all there was to that.

James spent several hours grooming and loving all the four-legged family members. He organized and cleaned the tack room. No one in the family was versed in equine management, so they must have brought everything they could find on the subject. There were items of which James had no idea their purpose. He was so excited to learn. He began to daydream about training and conditioning horses to accept and trust immortals. He imagined there was a need for such a skill in the world. He would have to talk to Ana about it.

Ana sat on top of hay bales and helped polish the silver and oil the leather. Ana had the most fun watching James enjoy himself so much. She couldn't wait for him to realize the world was at his feet and that nothing would be denied him. Everything he ever dreamed of was attainable. She wanted him to have it too. She wanted him to feel joy and fulfillment in all things he touched. Her sole purpose was to make him smile, and she promised herself that she would do just that.

Besty was a little shy. She could tell James was different, but it didn't take long to realize he was still her friend. James left her loose in the barn, and she followed him as a dog would follow its master. There was no need for a lead or a tether of any kind. She was utterly content to stay right by his side. He did have to move her from time to time if she were where he needed to be, but she graciously complied. Years of tender care had left their mark on Betsy, and she loved James with all her heart. Ana had no doubt Betsy would gladly follow him into death if he needed her to go.

Rene called and asked the two if they would like to join everyone for lunch, and as their stomachs were growling, they gladly accepted the invitation. This wasn't any lunch like James had ever seen before. There was a table full of delicious food waiting on the big house's dining table. Everyone sat as though they had assigned seats, and there was a new place setting right beside Ana's. James quickly took the spot. Everyone talked, laughed, and made plans for the remainder of the day.

"Have you talked to James about the dogs yet?" Kimmy asked.

Leave it to Kimmy to just bring up any subject to get the ball rolling, Ana thought.

"No, I haven't gotten the chance yet," Ana answered.

"Dogs?" James asked.

"You might think it's silly, but I was thinking, maybe it would be fun to raise dogs. You know, dogs that wouldn't be afraid of immortals. If I raised them from pups, they would feel more accepting and trusting. That was just what I was thinking," Ana explained.

James laughed, and Ana seemed a little hurt by his response.

"No, no, I don't think it's silly at all. I was going to talk to you about the same thing, only with horses. Maybe we could do both, if it is okay," James said.

Ana jumped into James's arms and squealed in delight.

"Yes, that sounds perfect," she said.

"Sounds like you might need some backup then," Brady asked.

"I wanna help too!" Lana yelled.

"I'm in," Kimmy said.

James held out his hand, and everyone laid their hands on top of his.

"Sounds like a plan to me," he said.

"We can start tomorrow," Rene said.

She was already asserting her authority in the project. Ana thought Rene viewed herself as management in everything that involved her children, both biological and adopted. Rene was overjoyed by the fact Ana had no desire to leave the estate. She knew the couple would go for council business or little sightseeing adventures, but they would always return home. Oak View would always be their home base. Rene would allow her baby birds to fly, but she would always prepare the nest for their return.

Time flew by quickly. Ana and James loved their little slice of heaven. Even though the work was long and hard, both felt it to be rewarding. Ana started with three breeding pairs—Labrador retrievers, Corgis, and Chihuahuas. They were three distinct breeds with three very different personalities and sizes. James started with the six mares in his care and found the most beautiful black and white paint stud to add to the family. The first colt was due in late summer, and everyone was thrilled.

Lana and Brady learned everything they could from James and took it upon themselves to study all the material available on equine studies. Lana even learned basic vet skills to assist with the canine companions. Everyone had an active role in this endeavor. Kimmy loved to ride. She had ridden horses in her mortal years, but there was never the freedom the world provided now. She exercised all the horses and helped in their training. Rene took the calls and book reservations for people who wanted to travel to Virginia to visit the animals. This new adventure pulled many more people into the sleepy little town, and that was just what Ana had wanted to happen. The diner stayed busy, and the rooms at Rose's boarding house stayed full. Everyone was doing what they loved to do. Ana had this vision when she first arrived home, and here it was in action. She had only not envisioned James in her dream. He was an added bonus.

Rene was busy all the time with one thing or another. She cooked and cleaned and loved her children with all her heart. Her table was full, and her cup "runneth over" with love. Rene wouldn't have minded forty more children, but the four extra would work for now. She hoped others who felt lost and alone would find this place and choose to stay with them. She couldn't bear to think of any child being motherless and unloved in the world. Even if they were grown, one was never too old for their mother. Maybe that was something she could look into in the future herself.

Evening dinners were full of chatter. Rene thought of how different it was now compared to when it was just her and Ana against the world. She had more to fuss over and more to love. She never thought she would feel so loved and protected again after losing her mother, but this little group of misfits had shown her she could. She had never felt more complete.

Holiday Time

The cool air of winter was soon approaching. Their newfound family made plans to celebrate the old tradition of Thanksgiving. James had read about the feast of Thanksgiving but had never celebrated it within the farm walls. He understood it to be a time of gratefulness for a new world provided to the settlers. He found it fitting for his circumstances. He definitely had a new life and a new world to be grateful for. Rene spent weeks preparing the menu and gathering all the ingredients for the many dishes she planned to make. There were a few special order ingredients, but everything came in just in time.

All the ladies offered to help Rene in any way they could, but she wouldn't hear it. She wanted to do it all by herself. "Too many hands in the kitchen make for a disorganized chef," she said. Everyone insisted that she ask if she needed anything, and she agreed. Rene knew her recipes like the back of her hand, and all the magic was in a pinch of this and a dab of that. She couldn't teach those girls how to cook that way, especially not on the biggest day for a meal of the year, Thanksgiving. Nope, nobody was going to sabotage her special day. She would do it by herself.

Everyone looked so beautiful as they gathered for the feast. The ladies had the most fun picking out just the right dresses for the occasion. The gentleman wore what Ana and Lana picked for them to wear, and they looked dashing and timeless. Rene looked like a goddess in her white gown trimmed in gold. She wore her hair in a bun, and tiny tendrils flowed down her cheeks. Ana wondered how Rene managed to prepare everything and still look flawless. She imagined it was a trick only mothers knew; she would never be in that particular club.

Ana in pale yellow, Kimmy in purple, Lana in sky blue, and Rose in her signature blush pink adorned the room like jewels. The dashing princes could only marvel at their perfection.

"Let us raise our glasses in thankfulness for our bond and strength of family," Rene stated.

The group did as she asked, with a round of cheers rising in the room.

"Let's go around the room and say one thing we are all thankful for," Ana suggested.

"Yes, please," Rene agreed.

"I'll go first. I'm thankful for every single person here this evening. I am thankful for the new lives we are building as a family," Ana said.

"Cheers!" everyone said.

"Me next. I'm thankful for finding my place in the world with all of you. I have been on my own too long," Lana said.

"Cheers!" everyone said.

"Um, well, I'm grateful for the good food and family," Brady added.

"Cheers!" everyone said.

"I'm thankful for all the love I have found here and for all the love I have lost through time," Rose said.

"Cheers," everyone said more solemnly.

"I'm thankful I have enough love in my life, that you all came to find me when I needed you. I am grateful for you all," Kimmy said.

"Cheers!" everyone said.

"I'm thankful for my new life and the chance to live it with my love, Ana," James said.

"Cheers!" everyone yelled.

"I'm thankful for my daughter. I live and will live to love and protect her always. But now that I look out over this beautiful assembly, I realize I have many children to cherish. For this, I am truly grateful," Rene said.

"Cheers!" everyone erupted.

"Let's eat," Brady said.

"Yes, let's," Rene said.

The glow of the candlelight illuminated the faces of all the happy guests. The clanking of silverware and the gurgle of wineglasses being refilled was joyous. Everyone basked in the company and the pumpkin pie. Everyone felt whole and complete, some for the first time in a very, very long time. They felt included and part of something bigger than just them. They remembered the feeling of belonging. Everyone remembered the love of their mortal families and was truly thankful for their new chance at a family.

The group sat and chatted long after their bellies were full. Rene could only smile at her blessed fortune. Everyone changed from their formal attire to casual and helped Rene with the cleanup. Many hands made for light work, Rene always said, and it was true. The kitchen was straight, and all the leftovers found their home inside the big silver fridge.

The group met in the theater room to watch a Thanksgiving classic. Rene remembered it playing every Thanksgiving day during her youth, and she loved it. *The Legend of Sleepy Hollow* blared from the speakers. Everyone laughed at the clumsy Ichabod Crane and cringed at the horseman.

"I met a Hessian once. He was every bit as cruel and sadistic as the horseman," Rose simply stated.

Ana often forgot just how long Rose had walked the earth. She wondered how many spectacular tales she had in her repertoire. Ana was determined to one day sit and listen to her friend and learn more about her life. Rose was quiet, but behind her eyes was a fire that Ana could see. Ana wasn't sure what caused the blaze, but she hoped Rose would trust her enough to share it someday. By being a counselor in the old world, Ana knew that sometimes pain was eased by the sharing of grief. She hoped she could help Rose with hers.

"That is so crazy," Lana said.

Everyone else returned to the movie without a second thought to Rose's confession. It spoke volumes to Ana, though. How many centuries could one endure suffering and grief before they simply shut out their emotions altogether? How much laughter and happiness would go undocumented without a witness to one's life? Ana wanted to be that witness for Rose. She would have to see about that.

Lana really loved history, and she learned all she could about the people who were now absent in the world. Customs and traditions were of utmost importance to her, so this day of celebration was glorious. Kimmy loved the history of the Wiccan culture. She supported a clean existence with as little footprint on the earth as possible. She studied crystals and the zodiac. She lived in balance with nature. Each member of this motley crew had a different attribute to contribute to the family. Each was as different as night and day, but their core values were the same—love and loyalty.

The world was soon covered in a crisp white blanket of snow. The trees glistened with crystals of ice, and their branches drooped under their weight. Ana could hardly convince James to come inside to eat. The wonderful winter wonderland around him enchanted him. He ran like a child, catching the snowflakes on his tongue. Ana showed him the delicate skill of making the perfect snow angel, and their snowman was bigger than both of them. She found a top hat, scarf, and pipe for their frosty friend. She told James the story of frosty the snowman but couldn't find the beloved childhood favorite for him to watch.

Ana loved James so much that his joy was her joy. Her favorite activity with him was saddling the horses and hearing Betsy's jingle bell harness. The winter wonderland was breathtaking, and Ana never remembered a time she enjoyed the icy landscape so much. Ana found a new sense of excitement for the thing she had taken for granted as she saw James's childlike wonder.

Christmas was fast approaching, and everyone brought traditions from their mortal lives into the home. Ana felt that the most beautiful were the hand-cut snowflakes that Rose made from tissue paper. Rose explained that wasn't exactly how they had done them, but it was close enough. James carved ornaments, and Ana stained them. Kimmy painted scenes onto delicate glass ornaments depicting important events in her life. She represented her milestones on the tiny spheres of glass.

Ana never mentioned one in particular. It had a lone lily painted in its center. It was an exact representation of the one her abductor had painted on her skin. Ana thought it was a reminder of a horrible yet life-altering event in her life. Kimmy had changed since the incident. She was not quite as free as she had once been. Family and home replaced people and places. She realized the value of stability and the comfort that lay within it.

Every night in the month of December leading to the big day, Rene planned some kind of activity for the family. There were specific nights for cookie baking, candy making, stocking decorating, and Ana's favorite, movie watching. Rene picked a different holiday classic, and everyone piled up in their favorite PJs to watch. Ana was thankful immortals didn't have to worry about gaining weight because she was sure she would weigh five hundred pounds by now.

The boys hung so many lights around the estate that there was no corner free from the glow of the holidays. James, having never experienced anything like this, couldn't believe how wonderful it was. The tree they chose towered ten feet high, and every branch held its own story. He told Ana it was a magical time of year because he could feel it in the air. Ana totally agreed.

Christmas Eve dinner was to be a grand affair. The ladies all wore tones of red and green. The entire estate was in holiday overload. The table was full of everyone's favorite dishes, and Rene emptied a china cabinet to display the assortment of confections she had made. There was ham, potatoes, broccoli casseroles, sweet potatoes. Anything anyone could have desired was present and accounted for on Rene Reed's table. Everyone clinked their glasses and ate until no one could hardly budge from their seats. Then came the fun part—the presents.

"Okay, everyone, if you will all adjourn to the sitting room, we will start the opening of gifts portion of the evening. I'm sure you all are anxious for that, aren't you?" Rene asked.

Everyone pushed back their chairs and lazily made their way to the sitting room. The tree was a glow, and the presents seemed to have multiplied since earlier in the day. Some gifts were handmade. Others were items found that would suit another. Everything was precious and perfect, just like Christmas should be. James made carved statues of each person's horse, and Ana painted them to match their companion animals. James had carved the names of each animal into the saddle with the date of this special day. Ana still was amazed by his talent.

After all, the gifts were unwrapped, and the boxes and bows were tidied up. James asked if everyone would stay just a little bit longer. He handed Ana a package that had been hidden from sight. Ana couldn't imagine what it could be in such a big box. Everyone fell silent as she pulled the ribbon and lifted the lid to her gift. Inside was the most beautiful carved angel Ana had ever seen, and on the base was her name and the date. The likeness to Ana's face was amazingly perfect.

"Oh, James, I love it so much. Thank you, baby. I love you," Ana said.

Ana choked back the tears and stared at her gift. No one moved from their spots as James pulled another box similar to the last from his pocket. He dropped to one knee and began to speak.

"Ana, I think this is a custom from your mortal life that was very important to people in love. The contents of this box represent a pack between the giver and the recipient of the gift. This agreement states that they will remain loyal and in love and will live as one soul upon the earth as long as they live. There is nothing or no one in my heart but you, Deangela Dawn Reed. Will you do the honor of wearing this symbol of our covenant?" James asked.

He popped open the box, and a perfectly set diamond surrounded by three smaller diamonds on each side stared back at Ana. Two plain gold bands sat behind the ornate diamond ring. Ana couldn't breathe because of her tears. She reached for the ring, and James pulled it back playfully from her reach.

"I think I kinda need an answer first," James said.

"Yes!" Ana squealed.

James took the ring from the box and slid it on Ana's finger. All the ladies gasped and held their hands over their swooning hearts as if it were too much to take.

The couple decided to forego the old tradition of a wedding ceremony. They felt that the spiritual connection they shared needed no public display. Their rings were a mere outward display of their inner emotion. It was enough for them. In the past, this would have been a terribly difficult time for Rene. She would have feared this man would take Ana from her, but now she knew that wasn't the case. Instead, she was genuinely happy for them both.

Before anyone could blink, springtime was upon them. New life sprang from every corner of the estate. Everything came alive in a sea of green where the brown of sleep had been. The trees began to bud, and pink and white balls of fragrance hung on every branch. Spring showers infused the earth with life. The immortals were fueled in a way that the cold of winter had not fueled them. They planned exciting new projects and new ways to help the community integrate with the landscape around them.

Ana oversaw the building of more kennels. James added more horses to the ranks of the family. Kimmy added chickens, ducks, and geese to the estate. She took great pride in providing the family with their bounty. This was a way for her to feel as if she were contributing to the home, even though her contribution was simply being her sweet self. Rose came often, offering her experience in many different areas. Her long time wandering the planet had given her much knowledge, and everyone thirsted for it.

James worked on his new riding ring project. As he dug the holes and set the posts into the ground, someone called out to him.

"Hello, friend," a man said.

James looked down the path that led to the house where he last saw Ana. Panic rose in his chest as this stranger approached.

"Hello. How can I help ya?" James said.

He still stared in the direction of the CH until he saw Ana step onto the back porch, munching on an apple. Relief flooded him as he took in her beauty.

"I sure hope so. My name is Rowland Hatchet, and I heard about your operation here. I was wondering if you might be in the market for another hand to help out 'round here," Rowland said.

James stretched out his hand in greeting and introduced himself to Rowland.

"There's always more work than there is time. That's for sure," James said.

"I know. That's right. See, I have been just drifting around for a long time now, and I thought the sound of your group was maybe something I could get into," Rowland explained.

"We are a family here. Any of us would die for the other. That my friend is not for everyone, but it is for us. We take our bond seriously, and we are always looking for like-minded people to join us. My mother-in-law always says many hands make for light work," James explained.

"Your mother-in-law is right. I have missed that kind of connection with folks," Rowland said.

"I'm working on this fence here. I could use some help if you feel like getting dirty," James said.

"Sounds like fun to me," Rowland agreed.

The two worked for hours on the ring. They dug holes and tamped posts and marked off where the boards would go. Before long, the bones of the structure were complete. The help cut James's work in half, and he was grateful.

"You guys hungry?" Ana called out.

James looked up to see Rene and Ana coming up the path to the barn. They carried a giant basket and a jug of something with them.

"Starving. Rowland, this is my wife, Ana, and my mother-in-law, Rene Reed. They're the best cooks in the county, so you have to eat with us," James said.

"Rowland Hatchet. And I would love to." He smiled.

Ana and Rene cleared off a work table and laid out their goodies. There were chicken legs, potato salad, baked beans, and homemade rolls. To wash it down, Ana fixed the best sweet tea with fresh lemons Rowland had ever tasted.

"This is delicious. Thank you, ladies, so much," Rowland said.

Ana caught a distinct Southern drawl in his voice that was somewhat different from her own.

"Where are you from?" she asked.

"Originally, I'm from a little town in Texas right outside of Houston. But that town isn't even there anymore. The city done swallowed it up," he answered.

"You worked with horse a lot there then?" Rene asked.

"Yes, ma'am. I used to be a hand on a ranch in my younger days, and I really enjoyed it. If someone had told me that lazy fishing days would get old, I would have called them a liar," Rowland answered.

"I totally understand that. There is only so much boredom a body can stand," Rene said.

"Yes, ma'am," Rowland said. "I know it seems odd for someone to just show up at your door and ask to stay, but I promise to pull my weight around here and work hard. Maybe someday I can earn my place in the family too. I didn't realize how much I missed it until I heard about the Reed clan in Virginia and how they had an honest-to-goodness family going on," Rowland said. "I just wanted to see it at first. Then I thought, 'Heck, why not ask? All they can do is say no.'"

"We don't say no to somebody who can build a fence like that," James said. He pointed to the perfectly spaced posted evenly distributed around the circle.

"I have done it a few hundred times," Rowland laughed.

"We have an extra room in the big house. So you're welcome to it if you want to stay for a while," Rene said.

"Oh no, ma'am. If it's all the same to you all, I wouldn't mind fixing up one of those old bunkhouses over there," Rowland said.

He pointed to a group of six tiny structures to his left. Bunkhouses were a nice way to describe the places where the unwilling workers had spent their lives, but he didn't want to call them what they were. He felt it gave power to the past and their suffering, and he wouldn't give it that.

"Are you sure? You could stay with us until you have made it livable at least," Rene said.

"Yes, ma'am, I can bunk right here with the critters until I get it fixed up to suit me, if that's okay with y'all," Rowland said.

James understood Rowlands's apprehension. His own fear of the open air was what Rowland feared in uncomfortable places and with unfamiliar people. However, he was comfortable among the animals and felt a kinship with their spirits. Maybe with the love and support of family, he would gain more confidence around other people and find the same kinship with his own kind. James felt that Rowland had liked and trusted animals way more for a very long time than he did people. He hoped he could help him with that.

"Whatever is the most comfortable for you. You are welcome here for as long as you want to stay," James said.

"I will eat you out of house and home if these ladies keep up with this good cooking," Rowland said.

He ate his fill and then some, and the two hard-working men decided to take a short break and ride for a while. They saddled up two of the younger horses and rode up the fence line to check it all for breaks. This didn't even seem like work to Rowland. This seemed like home. He could almost imagine his brother by his side, humming some silly song he had just made up. He smiled at the thought.

Time passed, as time did, and Rowland, James, and Brady worked side by side on many projects. Each contributed knowledge and ideas that were beneficial to the common goal. People came from every corner of the globe to visit the animals and to see the family. No one would have guessed they were to be the envy of their neighbors, but here they were, killing it. Rowland soon became another of Rene's children, and his heart was free and thankful for their acceptance.

Almost a century had passed with nothing but grief and fear reigning in Rowland's heart. He had never allowed anyone to climb his walls of emotion. His fear of loss was just too great, but now this new family filled his heart with joy. When he realized they were rooted deep inside him, the fear paralyzed him. But he thought about the amount of happiness he had within the family, and he knew it was worth it.

Council Business

O ne Sunday morning, the buzz of the phone woke James and Ana. The caller ID showed that it was Allan, and they stared at the phone for three rings before James answered it.

"Hello," James answered.

"Good morning, James. Sorry to call so early, but I wanted to give you enough time to get things in order before your flight," Allan said.

"Flight? Where am I going?" James asked.

"You will be flying to council headquarters first. We will fill you in when you get here. Your flight leaves Hillsboro Airport at six this evening. Just tell them Ana's name and yours, and they will send you straight to us," Allan explained.

"Okay, we will see you later then," James said.

Ana could hear the conversation, and she wasn't as excited as she had once been to fulfill their agreement.

"Well, here we go," James said.

"Yep," Ana said.

The couple got up and made their bed. They had no idea when the next time would be that their heads would rest on their own pillows. Ana called everyone to the barn for a group meeting. James explained what had been said. Everyone was on board and ready to pick up the slack in their absence. Rene cried and held Ana close to her. She stroked her hair, and all the fear of her everyday life rushed back into her heart.

"Mom, it's okay. James and I will be careful, and we will come home as soon as we can. I know if we need you, you are a phone call away. Don't think I won't call either. We are partners in crime. I want to help. We have to do what we promised to do. It has to be important, or they wouldn't have called us. So don't worry, okay? We will stick together, and we will be just fine," Ana explained.

"I know," Rene said.

This was all Rene could say at the moment. She would think about it for a while and figure out a way to manage her unstable thoughts.

James and Ana spent the day making notes and reminders for everyone. They really didn't need them, but everyone agreed to follow them to the letter. James was thankful for Rowland's experience with the horses and knew they were in capable hands. They each took one small bag with toiletries and a change of clothes. They figured they could get anything they needed when they reached their mystery destination.

The flight to council headquarters was uneventful except for the butterflies doing swan dives in Ana's belly. She wasn't worried about herself or James. Instead, she was concerned about her mother. Rene would suffer, worry, and cry until they returned home, which broke Ana's heart. She felt a lot better knowing everyone was around her mom to comfort her and keep her mind occupied. Ana asked everyone to try to include Rene in anything they could so she could stay busy. Everyone assured her that they would take care of Rene, and Ana had nothing to worry about while she was away.

A black Escalade took the couple straight to the front doors of the large white headquarters building. Allan stood waiting on the step for them. He ushered them inside before the hugs and slaps on the back were issued out to them both.

"You look well and happy," Allan said.

"Very much so," James said.

"Let's go meet up with Jaxon and the team for a quick briefing on the case," Allan said.

The three walked down long hallways with turns to the left then to the right. Ana was sure she could never find her way back out if she didn't have a guide. Jaxon and two others were seated in a large conference room. Jaxon jumped from his seat and greeted the two like family.

"It is so nice to see you again. This is Nathan and Wilma Rilley. They are here to help with the briefing. This is James and Ana Reed. The young lady here is the one I told you about, the one who helped with the Lilly case," Jaxon stated.

"So very lovely to meet you. We have heard wonderful things about you, Ms. Reed. I know your specific brand of investigation and seizure will be nothing but beneficial to us here. James, we're so happy to have you on board. We really needed the help here. If you don't mind, we will jump right in," Wilma said.

"We have binders prepared for you to take with you with the information we have on the case," Jaxon said.

The two opened their binders to the first page. It said, "1888 to Present."

"As you can see, this particular suspect has been active since the late 1800s. His victims stretch over the entire globe, and decades pass between them. That's why we haven't been able to fix his location yet. There have been two victims in the last week who follow his pattern. This culprit, for lack of a better term, dissects his victims. He seems to be searching the remains for something. In 1888, he killed five women on the streets of London. Those victims, minus the fatal blow of decapitation, showed the same MO as the current woman. We feel you may be able to locate him since this is the quickest remains we have ever found," Nathan explained.

"There is a map with the location of all the victims we have tied him to in case you see a pattern we might have missed. The only hypothesis we have is that the clues lead us to believe that the person is male and has extensive medical knowledge. He uses surgical precision in his assaults, and in two instances, there were marks left from a possible injection of some kind," Nathan continued.

"We know it's not much to go on, but it's all we have. There are so many open cases, and we can't afford to use the resources needed on more dangerous suspects to find one who kills once or twice every three decades or so. No life is more valuable than another, but this one is so sporadic that it's hard to focus on it as much as is needed to end it," Wilma said.

"I would suggest you start at the area where the last body was found and work back from there. Just follow the leads as you go. When a job is done in steps, things pop up from the most unexpected places. If you can take the time, you may find something we haven't been able to find. Any resources you need are at your disposal. All you have to do is ask," Allan added.

In the old world, this area of the desert was known to house the seedier characters of society. In this new world, it isn't much different. People tend to hold on to the same vices they had in their mortal lives long after they transition. If a person was a person who liked to gamble or run the horses, they still enjoyed the same pastime in their immortal life. If they wanted the company of different types of women or men, they felt the same in their new life. So many of the things that made this city famous in the old world still kept it popular even now.

Ladies of the night were still sought out for their original purpose, but there was just as great a demand for simple companionship. At some point in their lives, both women and men felt the need for someone to talk to and spend time with. Both client and associate filled the void of family with this temporary fix. In 1888, the victims of this culprit worked the same profession as these current victims did. They were found in back alleys and were hidden in empty structures. They died horrific deaths, and then their bodies were mutilated and studied. These current victims suffered the same fates.

James and Ana would start among the members of this social sect and see where it took them. They started at the location of the first victim and worked their way through the businesses on the block. There was no shortage of gentlemen's clubs in the area, but they had to start somewhere. The first three businesses were clothing shops, and no one there recognized the ladies in the photos they were shown. Or at least they didn't admit they had known them. The third was a club called the TopHat Club.

The TopHat Club specialized in BDSM, and leather and chains were everywhere. It was the middle of the afternoon, but it was dark as night inside the club. There was only creepy red recessed lighting on the ceiling and a few strategically placed lamps with red illumination on some booths in the back. Ana felt utterly uncomfortable in this environment, and James had no idea at all what the draw was for this particular fetish. Everyone proved to be quite nice and helpful when they answered James's questions. However, they did not know the ladies or who could have done this to them. The club manager insisted they return for a drink later on, and James and Ana said they would try to come by, even though they had no intention of doing so.

The next club was the Silver Dollar Gentlemen's Club. They had better luck here, as one of the ladies spent her evenings here regularly.

"Yes, that is one of our regular ladies. It's such a shame," the owner said.

"Yes, it sure is. Were you working the night she was killed?" James asked.

"Yeah, I was here all night by myself. My help didn't show that night. I remember because we were so busy I could barely keep up," he answered.

"You don't happen to have cameras here, do you?" Ana asked.

She remembered the help the cameras had given them in Kimmy's case, so it was worth a shot.

"The only cameras are on the stage so the dancers can review their performances. I'm not sure if they were on that night or not. Let me get Diamond, the dance manager, for you," the owner said.

"Thanks so much," Ana said.

The owner made a call, and the most glamourous woman Ana had ever seen came from the back. Even though the lady was wearing nearly nothing, she carried herself with a confidence Ana only wished she possessed.

"Hey there, sugar. How can I help you, folks?" Diamond asked.

"Thank you for coming to speak with us. We are looking into Lacy's case, and we were just wondering if you knew whether the cameras were on the night Lacy was killed," Ana asked.

"What happened to Lacy was such a shame. I don't have many real friends, but she was one of the few. I already checked about the cameras, and that was one night we didn't have them on. I could have kicked myself too. I thought I should turn them on all night and just never did. I want to find the asshole as bad as anybody. All of us girls kind of look out for one another around here, and with the humans gone, we got lazy. You just don't see our kind doing crazy shit to one another much, so we just didn't think it would happen. It makes me sick," Diamond said.

"Oh, I totally understand. I didn't even know this kind of thing happened anymore until it happened to my friend. We were lucky, though, that we found her in time. I'm sorry that didn't happen for Lacy," Ana said.

"I'm glad it worked out for your friend too. I just wish there was something I could do to help. Say, if you find out anything, would you please let me know? I just want to know who the animal was that did this to Lacy. Everyone needs to know so we can keep our guard up better," Diamond asked.

"We definitely will. Do you have a card or something so I can call you with any updates?" Ana asked.

"Sure do, sugar," Diamond said.

She grabbed a card with her name and number on it and handed it to Ana. The two said their goodbyes and moved on to the next stop. They had no luck, so they decided to stop and get a bite to eat. They were trying their best to wrap this one up quickly so they get back home, but it wasn't looking very promising. Everyone in this part of the world seemed to be very nice, and they had formed their own unique family units, but if you were not in, you just weren't in. Most people were polite but not forthcoming with any information. Ana felt they really had none to give, but their blasé attitudes left her a little annoyed.

The restaurant they chose was called the Rensdale, and it was a very high-class joint. Neither James nor Ana felt like they belonged in this fancy place. Nevertheless, they were seated and ordered their meals with little difficulty. The trouble came later when the desert they ordered was set ablaze right beside their table. James didn't know whether to cheer or grab his water glass and douse the thing. They thanked everyone for the amazing experience and headed back to their room to construct a new strategy.

Just as James pushed the door open for Ana to exit, a familiar face greeted them. Ric Robins from Channel VAA stood on the other side. Ric recognized Ana immediately. She couldn't believe that, given the great number of people he met, he still remembered her.

"Ana Reed, how lovely to see you," Ric said.

"Mr. Robins, yes, it is," Ana said. "This is my husband, James."

The two men shook hands and exchanged customary greetings with each other.

"Please join me for a glass of wine," Ric said.

"We would love to, but we have some business to attend to this afternoon, I'm sorry to say," Ana said.

"Oh, pity, will you be in town long?" Ric asked.

"It's looking that way," James answered.

"Here's my card. I would love to get together once you are finished. Maybe diner?" Ric asked.

"That sounds wonderful," Ana said.

"I know you probably don't know your way around yet, so we can meet here if you like, say, around eight?" Ric asked.

"We should be ready to eat again by then," James said.

He patted his belly to show how stuffed he was.

"Good, I'm so glad. I will see ya then," Ric said.

Ana and James left the restaurant and headed to their room. They didn't really know what to do next, so they needed a plan. Ana plopped down on the bed and opened her binder. James sat next to her, and they went over some of the basic information.

"You know what I was thinking? I was thinking how odd it was that Mr. Robins remembered my name. It has been a long time since we were on his show. It just seemed a bit odd. Don't you think?" Ana asked.

"It is tough to forget a face a beautiful as yours," James answered.

He leaned over and kissed her cheek and tickled her a little until she giggled.

"You're a little bit biased, I do believe. I just think it's strange, is all. I got a weird feeling, and you know what mom says about your gut. You have to follow your gut feeling about things. It won't lead you wrong. Hey, wait a minute, look at this," Ana said.

She pointed to a photo of the deceased unnamed woman. There was a tattoo of an angel on her shoulder that was very distinct. It was your average angel right down to the angel wings and halo, but the face was the dead girl's face. Ana rummaged through the book until she found a photo of Lily, and on her calf was a similar angel, only this angel's face was Lily's face.

Ana tapped the photos and nodded. "Look, it has to be the same artist. We may at least get the name of our second girl. It can't hurt to follow up on it. We don't have anything else. How can we find out who did it, though?" she asked.

"Let's call Diamond. If she was as close to Lily as she said, she might know who did the tattoo for her," James suggested.

"Good idea," Ana said. She found Diamond's card and punched in the numbers.

Diamond answered on the second ring. "This is your Diamond girl. How can I help you?" she answered.

"I'm sorry to bother you, ma'am. This is Ana Reed. We met earlier today. I had a question for you," Ana said.

"You're not bothering me, sugar. What can I do for you?" Diamond said.

"Do you know the tattoo that Lily had on her calf, the angel one? You wouldn't happen to know where she got it done, would you?" Ana asked.

"Sure do, sugar. I have one myself. Slick done them for us. His shop is called Dragon Inc. It's up on the corner of Fifth and Maple. He's a good dude. I have known him for years," Diamond said.

"Oh, no, it's nothing like that. It's just that both girls had a similar tattoo. We were hoping he might identify the second victim. It's all we have to go on so far," Ana explained.

"I'm sure he will be glad to help ya. Just tell him his Diamond girl sent ya, and he will be glad to tell ya anything you want to know. Don't hesitate to call me anytime you need to, okay?" Diamond said.

"Thanks so much. Maybe the next time we call, we will have some news for you," Ana said.

"Okay, you be careful," Diamond said.

"Always," Ana said. Ending the call, she turned to James. "Got it. Let's go."

James gathered his keys, and they headed out. Ana felt the same thrill of the hunt that she once did. She wanted to make this bastard pay for killing those girls. Admittedly, the ladies were just dead girls to Ana until she met Diamond. Now they were all Diamond. She represented this desert world to Ana now, and every life meant something to someone. Lily was Diamond's friend, and she was someone's daughter, sister, or lover. She was important and deserved to be avenged.

They found Dragon Inc. easily, and Slick sat staring at his artwork on a canvas of flesh.

"Be right with you, just finishing up here. Have a look around," Slick called out.

"Thanks so much. Take your time. We are in no hurry," Ana said.

Slick sprayed the man's back with an alcohol-based liquid and whipped it clean of the excess ink. He studied and studied his work. It was as if he was looking for imperfections he was not going to find.

"I think you are all finished up," Slick said. He held out a mirror to the seated man and turned him to see the beautiful tiger crouched on his back.

"Perfect as always, Slick," the man said.

"Cool, I'm glad you like it," Slick said.

The two men shook hands, and Slick started to clean up his area.

"Now what can I do ya for?" Slick asked Ana and James.

"Actually, your Diamond girl said you might know the answer to a question I have. Do you know this woman?" Ana asked. She showed Slick a photo of the deceased lady.

Slick was obviously taken aback by the image. "Oh no, what happened to Kylie?" Slick asked.

"Kylie?" Ana said.

"Yeah, that's Kylie Noland. I just did a piece for her not too long ago," Slick said.

"We are looking into the deaths of your friend Kylie and another lady that happened last week. We were hoping someone could shed some light on them," James said.

"You wouldn't happen to know anything about Kylie, would you? Like where she worked or lived or anything that would be helpful?" Ana said.

"Damn, who's the other girl?" Slick asked.

"Lilly. She worked at Diamond's club. You knew her, too, didn't you?" Ana asked.

"No, not Lily! She was the sweetest little thing I've ever met," Slick said. Then he gave them information about Kylie. "Yeah, Kylie worked up at the little motel on second, right there at the light. I can't remember the name of it, though. It's one of those fancy things. I couldn't have gotten in the door in the old world or this one. She wasn't a working girl or a dancer. She was just a regular sweet girl."

Ana could tell that the death of this girl left a hole in this seemingly tough man's heart. She wondered what their relationship had truly been. She figured, *Why not ask?* He would either tell them or say it was none of their business. Either way, she would have her answer.

"Can I ask you a personal question?" Ana said.

"Yeah," Slick answered.

"What was your relationship with Kylie? I mean, you said she wasn't one of the ladies that worked on this block. So how was it that she met you and came to you for her artwork?" Ana asked.

"What you're really asking is why she was with someone like me if she was a good, sweet girl, right?" Slick said.

"No, no," Ana said.

"It's okay. I never really understood it either. I was the luckiest man in the world the day I met Kylie. I was standing right outside the door, puffing on a cig, when she walked past. She had on this ridiculous hot pink '80s number and heels she could barely walk in. I couldn't help but ask her where she thought she was going. When she turned around to face me and I saw the thick blue eye shadow and bright pink blush, I couldn't help but laugh. She got mad. Oh, she got mad. She asked me what the hell I was laughing at, and I didn't help it any much when I started singing that '80s tune 'Oh Mickey, you're so fine.' You know that one, right?" Slick said.

Ana nodded because she vaguely remembered the tune. Unfortunately, James had no idea of the reference, so he just continued to listen.

"Kylie said she was ready for a change. She heard the girls down here were like family to one another, so she wanted to see if she could work here. All she wanted was one true friend. That was all she wanted. I asked her to come in for a drink, and she did! I couldn't believe she did, but she did. Every day after her shift, she came by just to chat and rest and watch me work. I can't believe this shit happened!" Slick said.

"How come you didn't know about her death? It's been a couple of weeks now since it happened. Didn't you miss her coming by and go ask about her?" Ana asked.

"Well, first, Kylie said she was going to go see her mom. She didn't say when, so I thought she had gone and just didn't say goodbye. But really, I wouldn't have gone to look for her in that place. Those are just not my kind of people. Maybe I should have, though," Slick said.

"Do you remember Kylie saying anything about anybody acting weird or anything?" Ana asked.

Slick sat and really thought about the question. Ana could see the pain in his eyes and how hard it was for him to keep his emotions in check.

"The only thing I remember her saying that seems odd now is that there was a person in her building that was a long-time guest and that they were rude every time she had to deal with them. She said they jumped down her throat once for sending housekeeping up to their room when they hadn't called for them. I remember how mad she was. Whoever it was got completely twisted with her, and she didn't know why," Slick said.

"That's good. That's really good. Do you remember about when that was?" James asked.

"Yep, it wasn't too long ago, about three weeks or a little more, I guess. I'm so sorry this happened," Slick said.

He paced the floor and ran his fingers over his bald head. He stroked at his long beard and seemed beside himself with grief. Ana thought he had had enough for right now. But if they needed to, they would come back and talk to him again. They left their number for him to call if he remembered anything else. He agreed, and Ana and James went to the room to get ready for diner.

Ana stopped at a dress shop and picked up a little black wrap dress and strappy heels. The attendant insisted she took a diamond pendant necklace to complete the look. James grabbed a white button-up shirt and jacket. Finally, they got to the room and threw their new treasures onto the bed. They showered together as they had done every day, and passion soon took over the task.

James couldn't help but feel the grief Slick must have felt in the loss of his Kylie. He held Ana a little bit tighter and caressed her a little bit longer. He couldn't imagine a day without the love of his life, and he hoped he could stop anything like this from happening to anyone else. If he could stop this person, he could save someone like Slick from pain and suffering. James knew he couldn't stop until he found them.

Seven-thirty came, and the two set out for the restaurant. They felt a little more prepared for the upscale atmosphere in their new and improved gear. The attendant seated them, and they ordered two glasses of the house wine and waited for Ric to arrive. He showed up promptly at eight and joined them.

"Ric, so glad to see you," James said.

"You, too, Ana. You look lovely," Ric said.

He took his seat and ordered a dark draft beer, which was his favorite. He seemed nervous and preoccupied. He wasn't his cool, collected self from earlier in the day. He spun his glass nervously in his hands and seemed to be at a loss for words.

"Ric, are you okay, buddy? You don't seem yourself this evening," Ana asked.

It wasn't that she actually knew Ric, but it felt like she did from the many hours of broadcasts she had watched where he paraded like a king in front of the camera. This nervous, agitated version of Ric was very easily detected by anyone who had ever watched Channel VAA.

"To be honest, no. I haven't been completely honest with you. I knew you were here in the city. I wanted to talk to you about a few things," Ric confessed.

"Okay, I'm confused. What's up, Ric?" Ana asked.

"I know you are here on council business. I know you are looking into the deaths that happened here a couple of weeks ago, and I want to help. I have my reasons. Believe me, I do, but I wasn't sure you would be receptive to my help if I just came out and asked," Ric said.

"I'm not sure I follow," James said.

"This person you are looking for is very important to me. This isn't the first time he has made his way into my path, and I'm not going to let him get away this time. I had to make sure you two were on the up and up before I talked to you. I have been tailing you since you got here, and you have already learned more than I could ever learn because of who I am. People don't want to answer any questions I have. They don't know if it is for VAA or me," Ric explained.

"I get that, but what's your connection to this person?" Ana asked.

"My wife, Racheal, that's my connection. In 1964, this same animal killed my beautiful Racheal. I know it's the same man because I have a connection in the council who showed me the other victims' photos. Either of those women could have been my Racheal. The wounds were the same. Even the positioning of the bodies was similar. Sometimes he doesn't pick a woman from the street. Sometimes he chooses a woman like my Racheal or the lady from the hotel. I haven't figured out what makes him choose his victims, but I do know he isn't fixated on just working girls. There have been many women who were not from that background but suffered the same fate. I want to help you. I want to look into his eyes and tell him why I am going to kill him. I have to, for Rachael," Ric explained.

"We will take all the help we can get, but you do understand we can't let this get out into the public, right? You can never let this become public knowledge," James said.

He and Ana were nervous about Ric knowing their business, but it seemed he had known all along, and nothing terrible had happened. The council made it plain that they didn't want anything leaked to the press about any cases, but this wasn't leaked. Ric openly came to them with information. There was no way the council would be upset at them for that. Ana believed Ric could prove helpful if the council would allow it.

"I understand, and I totally agree. People don't need to know about this kind of thing. It would just lead to a lot of vigilante justice and overly cautious people. That isn't why we did all we have done. Immortals should feel safe and secure. They shouldn't have to worry about some sicko killing their families. I will never breathe a word to anyone about what we find or how we handle it. I promise you that," Ric said.

"Of course, we will have to talk this over with the sheriff, but I don't see why they wouldn't want your help here. There are things, right now, that we can't access, and I believe you could be a great help to us on that front," James said.

"You just say the word. Then whatever you need, we will make it happen. But first, can we eat? I'm about to starve to death over here," Ric said.

"Yes, please, my stomach is trying to eat my backbone," James said.

Ana laughed and thought, *You can take the boy out of the country, but you can't take the country out of the boy.*

Ric took this dinner as an opportunity to talk about his wife. He explained how she was the best person he had ever known and that her death was a loss for everyone she had known. He spoke as if he were trying to convince them of his cause. Ana and James needed no convincing.

They wanted him to find answers. They wanted him to have closure. Sometimes just knowing why helped people in a small way to heal. James agreed to call Allan and see what he thought of Ric's help in the case. He promised to call as soon as he had an answer. James and Ana then returned to their room, and Ana went to change into her comfortable clothes. James took this time to give Allan a call.

"Hello," Allan answered.

"Hey, Allan," James said.

"Hey, what's up?" Allan asked.

"We may have a problem here. Do you know the news anchor, Ric Robins? Well, he is here, and he knows who we are. He also knows why we are here. Apparently, his wife was killed in the '60s by this same guy. He's been following us for a while now and wants to help. We just didn't know what to do here," James explained.

"I thought he might show up. He has done so two times already since his wife was killed. We have done a background check on him and can't find any real reason not to let him into the circle. He could prove helpful to you. His status could give you the in you need in certain social circles. The only thing I ask you to keep in mind is his mental state. In 1964, his world was turned upside down. This monster took his wife. So you can understand why his rage and grief could be dangerous for those working with him. I will leave that decision up to you. We can't make it for you. I know you will use your head and not put yourself or Ana in unnecessary harm," Allan said.

"Your wrong about one thing. I don't understand his grief, and I don't want to. I don't know what I would do if someone hurt Ana. I wouldn't rest until they were wiped off the face of the earth. I want him to be able to have as much peace as he ever will have. He deserves that much. We will be careful, of course. We just wanted to make sure it was okay first," James explained.

"You're a free agent here, James. No one is going to retaliate against you for any decision you make. Our arrangement was for you to try to help if we asked. We don't expect perfection. No one is standing over you, micromanaging you in any way. You contact us anytime you need anything or if you have any questions at all. Nobody's gonna revoke your vampire card if you make a mistake. Hell, I would have been put down decades ago if that were the case," Allan said.

"That's cool. We just want to do our best here. I can never repay the gift I was given, but I want to make a difference somehow," James said.

"That is the reason you were chosen in the first place. You are loyal and strong. We knew immortality would suit you," Allan said.

"Thanks, man. We will call ya when we find anything," James said.

"Talk to ya then," Allan said.

James filled Ana in on all Allan had said, and she plopped down on the bed.

"I was thinking about something. How about we get a room in Kylie's hotel? We could see if we could find out who the hateful guest is. I know it's not much, but we are kind of hitting a brick wall," Ana said.

"Sound good to me," James agreed.

Ana picked up her phone, looked up the number, and put on her best highfalutin accent. "Hello, my name is Ana Reed, and my husband and I were needing to reserve a room if we could."

"I am so sorry, Ms. Reed, but we are booked solid for a few weeks. However, I would be glad to call you if something becomes available before then," the receptionist said.

"Oh, no, we were so looking forward to it. Yes, please, if you wouldn't mind giving me a call," Ana said.

"No problem at all," the receptionist said.

Ana gave her number and thanked the nice lady. After ending the call, she asked James, "Well, now what?"

"All we can do is wait on that lead, I guess. But, hey, I am going to call Ric and tell him what Allan said, okay?" James said.

"K," Ana said.

Ana pulled a giant chocolate bar from her bag and broke off a piece to offer to James. He rolled his eyes and laughed. Ric answered and was thrilled by the news. He agreed to meet the couple in the morning so they could get to work. Ana snuggled close to James, and he wrapped his arm around her tightly. She couldn't seem to get close enough to him. Ric had broken her heart talking about his wife. All she wanted to do was help him get rid of some of the pain.

When the phone rang a little after three in the morning, James answered on the first ring. It was usually never good when the phone buzzed that early in the morning.

"Hello," James answered.

"Hey, I'm sorry to call at this hour, but you said to if anything happened," a lady said.

It took a moment for James to recognize Diamond's voice on the other end.

"No problem at all. What's up?" he asked.

"This may be nothing, but a lady came by tonight, acting weird. She was asking if anybody had come by lately, asking questions about Lacy. I didn't know what to say, so I lied. I don't think she bought it, though. She kept saying how people needed to mind their own business and keep their noses out of things that didn't concern them. I thought you should know," Diamond said.

"That's weird. Did you recognize her or get a name?" James asked.

"No, I sure didn't, but the cameras were on. So at least you will know what she looks like if you were to see her. I stepped outside to see if I could see what she was traveling in. She got one of those pick-up cars. You know, the green ones? I don't know the name of the company, though. I couldn't see it. I hope that helps," Diamond said.

"You're the best. We will be right down. Is there any way we could get a copy of that video?" James asked.

"Already have it ready for you," Diamond said.

"Okay, great. See ya in a few moments," James said.

"Okay, later," Diamond said.

Ana was up and pulling on her boots before James ended the call. The two went to see what Diamond had for them. On their way, James called Ric to know if he wanted to meet them there. He said he would be there in five minutes. Ana and James started to review the video before Ric arrived. In the video, they saw a woman in her thirties, with long straight black hair and bright red lipstick waving her arms as she spoke. This woman was clearly agitated, and her body language suggested she was trying to be intimidating and confident.

Ric arrived, and they backed up the video so he could see the twenty minutes of straight-on video the woman had provided. Unfortunately, Ric didn't recognize the woman either. James made a call to Allan.

"Hey, if we send you a video, do you have a way to maybe ID the woman in it?" James asked.

"We can try for sure. There are some pretty innovative things going on with that kind of thing these days. Send it to my email, and

I will let you know as soon as I know. Who is this woman?" Allan asked.

"She was asking a lot of questions about Lacey and was pretty aggravated that we had come by," James said.

"Sounds like a solid lead. I will get back to you soon," Allan said.

James thanked Diamond and promised to let her know what was going on. The trio decided to wait in James and Ana's room for the call from Allan. It didn't take long before he sent an email with old photos attached. The old images looked like they dated back to the 1800s. The same woman in the video stared back at Ana. She wore a high-necked white top with a lace collar and diamond broach at her neck. Her hair was pulled back in a tight bun, and her eyes were lifeless, her face emotionless. Allan added the information that he had gathered on the woman.

Her name was Nora Rilley. She was born in 1856 to Ronaldo and Wilamina Rilley in Eastern London. Her father had been a doctor. He passed away in 1886. Her mother passed in 1856 after her birth. Nora had one sibling, a sister named Helen, who passed away in 1884.

Nora had traveled, as all immortals did, to every corner of the globe. She was last known to reside in Burbank, California, but that had been a couple of decades before. Her whereabouts were unknown at this time. Ana knew exactly where she had been just a few hours before. She had been at the Silver Dollar, harassing her friend. Now the question was, where was she now? Ana knew she hadn't gone far, and she was determined to find her.

"I think we should go see Slick again. Maybe he would remember Kylie saying her name. At the very least, he might know if the mean guest was a man or a woman. We just never expected it to be a female, so we didn't ask," Ana suggested.

"Yeah, that's good," James agreed.

The trio made their way to Dragon Inc., and it was locked up tight. James banged on the door, and everyone was surprised to see Slick's sleepy face as he opened up for them.

"Hey, man," Slick said. He had clearly just woken up, and he wiped the sleep from his eyes.

"I'm sorry to come by so early, but—" James started to say.

"No, come on in. Let me make some coffee so I can function," Slick said.

Ana and Ric followed James into Slick's shop, and everyone took a seat. Slick threw back a curtain and went into the back room. It wasn't long before Ana smelled strong coffee brewing away. Slick joined them and sat in the reclining tattoo chair.

"What's up?" Slick asked.

"We just had a few questions we were hoping you could answer for us," Ana said.

"Shoot," Slick said.

"Do you remember if Kylie ever said if the rude guest Kylie had mentioned was a man or a woman?" Ana asked.

"Yep, it was a woman for sure. Kylie used to say; I'm going to slap that bitch's head off if she keeps it up," Slick said.

"Did Kylie ever say what she looked like?" Ana continued.

"Got one better. I saw her myself," Slick said.

"She was about thirty and had long straight black hair. She had it pulled back in a ponytail. She had a face so sour it could curdle buttermilk," Slick explained. "I don't know her name, though. I just saw her one day when she passed by the window here, and Kylie pointed her out. I offered to kill her for Kylie, but she said if anyone got that honor, it was going to be her."

"Pretty sure we know it," Ana said.

"You think she did this to Kylie?" Slick asked.

"Not sure, but it looks like she might have had a hand in it," James said.

"Hey, you're that TV guy, ain't ya?" Slick asked.

"Ric Robins," Ric said. He extended his hand and shook Slick's hand.

"Cool, cool! Well, sorry I couldn't be of more help to ya," Slick said.

"No, you gave us just what we needed," James said.

"Now what do we need to get that room?" Ana said.

"What room?" Ric asked.

"We tried to get a room where the woman is staying, but they are booked. We won't be able to get one for weeks," Ana explained.

"What hotel?" Ric asked.

"The Wineburg on Second," Ana said.

A smile spread across Ric's face, and he held a finger up in the air. He dug his phone from his pocket and entered a number.

"Hello, this is Ric Robins, Channel VAA. Can I speak to Matt, please?" Ric asked. He sat patiently for a few seconds and then resumed his conversation. "Matt, how are ya, buddy?"

Ana watched as Ric's personality changed from one of a serial killer stalker to a mild-mannered reporter. She was impressed by his ability to change at the drop of a hat. All he was missing was Clark Kent's curly-cue hair and glasses to complete the transformation.

"Yes, I'm fine, thanks for asking. Look, I have a favor to ask you. I have a couple of friends of mine here on business, and they really want to stay with you for a while. They were so disappointed to find out you were all booked up. Is there anything you could do to get them a room?" Ric asked. There were a few moments of silence before Ric spoke again. "Oh, that's great, man! Thanks so much. I will let them know. They should be in town this afternoon. Is that okay?"

The gentleman must have said it was because Ric thanked him again and ended the call.

"Check-in is at four. If you have any problems, tell them to call Matt. They have your name. Everything is set," Ric said.

"How in the world?" Ana said.

"When Matt first opened up, I did a few stories on his hotel. I've known Matt for a very long time. I knew he had something special here. His place isn't the same old seven and six you see on every corner. He knows the Wineburg wouldn't be what it is today if it weren't for me, so he always helps me out when I'm in town," Ric explained.

"I knew you were good for something," James said. He punched Ric's arm playfully, and Ric rolled his eyes.

Ric helped Ana and James all morning, helping them fit into the more affluent society they would join. They picked out entire new wardrobes. Ana got a bag so expensive in the old world it would have taken three months of her salary just to pay for it. Finally, they fancied up and headed to the hotel.

Check-in went smoothly, and everyone was courteous and extra friendly due to the Reeds' connection to Mr. Robins. Several of the women on staff asked if Ric would be joining them on their trip. Obviously, they all had major crushes on the TV personality, but Ana knew this would go totally unnoticed by Ric. Ric had one focus and one focus alone, and it was to find and eradicate the monster that took his wife from him. No woman would ever take the place of his love.

Several days passed with no sighting of the mysterious Nora. James and Ana spent countless hours in the lounge or restaurant or just roamed the hallways. They were beginning to suspect she had gone already. So Ana, having absolutely no patience, jumped into investigating Nora's whereabouts.

One day, the couple took their usual seats in the restaurant area and continued their conversation even as the waitress walked up.

"I just don't know where she could be. She said she was going to be staying here. She wouldn't have just left without a word, dear," Ana said.

"I know. It's a shame," James said.

"But how will we ever get the papers to her now if she isn't staying here?" Ana asked.

"I didn't mean to eavesdrop, but maybe I could help you find your friend," the waitress said.

"Oh, maybe you could. Our friend was supposed to meet us here to pick up some papers, but we can't seem to find her. Her name is Nora. You wouldn't happen to know her, do you?" Ana asked.

The waitress looked puzzled. She had an expression that suggested she didn't believe Nora had any friends.

"Nora Rilley?" the waitress asked.

"Yes, yes, that's her. Is she staying here?" Ana asked.

"Yes, she sure is, but I'm afraid she hasn't been here for a couple of days now. She works at a research facility somewhere outside the city. I heard her talking about it one day," the girl said.

This only confirmed Ana's suspicions that eavesdropping was in this young lady's DNA.

"Well, bother. She is going to be terribly upset if she doesn't get these documents. It is council business, you know," Ana whispered.

The young lady leaned in close in order to catch every word. This girl was a true busybody, and Ana planned to use that to her advantage. Maybe the girl had never heard of the saying "Curiosity killed the cat" before.

"Council business?" the girl whispered.

"Shhhh, yes, very important business," Ana said quietly. "If you could find out where this facility is, I'm sure the council would love to know what a huge help you were. I mean, Ric wanted to come himself, but he said he just couldn't make it in time, so the council sent us instead," Ana continued.

"Ric, like Ric Robins from VAA? Oh my god!" The girl said.

"Shhh, yes, Mr. Robins is in deep with this project. I would be glad to tell him how helpful you were. I bet he would even stop by to thank you personally. Right, dear?" Ana asked James.

"You know he would. He is nice like that," James said.

"You sit tight. I will be right back," the girl said.

Ana shook her head and thought, *This is why you don't change sixteen-year-old girls. They are dumb as mortals and apparently just as dumb as immortals.*

Ana watched through the open restaurant doors as the waitress began tapping on the front desk computer. She jotted something down on a yellow legal pad and headed back to Ana and James's table.

"Here you go, Ms. Reed. She had it listed as her primary residence. The last thing I saw her driving was a red Range Rover," the girl said.

Ana took the paper from the young lady and tapped it with her finger.

"Well, look at you. You're a regular Nancy Drew, aren't you?" Ana asked.

"Nancy who?" the girl asked.

"She was a famous young lady detective just like you," Ana said.

The girl beamed with pride, and Ana kind of felt guilty for playing on her ignorance.

"Now you make sure you keep this hush-hush so no one can know we asked about Nora, okay? You're in the loop now, so you just keep quiet until you hear from us," James said.

The girl's wide-eyed innocence was almost funny if it hadn't been kind of sad, but she had given them answers. Ric would have to thank her for that when this was all over. The two headed back upstairs and changed into their normal clothes. Ana was glad to get back into her blue jeans and T-shirt, and she knew James would favor his boots over these dress shoes any day. They called Ric, and he met them at the edge of town. No one was sure yet how Nora tied into the whole mess, but they planned to ask her just that very question.

They decided to go on foot for a mile or so, so they wouldn't draw attention to their arrival. The address the girl had written down didn't look like any research facility Ana had ever seen before. Instead, it looked like an abandoned warehouse of some kind, and not even a very big one. They circled the building to check out all the ways in and out. There was one door in front, one on the side, and one in the back. James rolled fifty-gallon drums in front of the doors. They appeared to be full of what Ana suspected to be water. It wouldn't stop a determined immortal, but it might slow her down.

The three went to the front and saw no dramatic way to do it but to just do it. So they opened the door and walked right inside. The door wasn't even locked. Ana found that to be odd if this, in fact, was the murderer. The inside was almost empty. Concrete floors, fluorescent lights, a musty sofa, and a coffee table were all that occupied the front entrance space. Music played from a section to the backside of the building, so they followed the echo of sound. The music originated from a room where the walls didn't quite reach the ceiling. A large window covered the front section almost completely. Everyone clung to the shadows so as not to be noticed.

There she was. She wore a white lab coat and had her hair pulled back in a severe bun. She shook a tube of liquid between her fingers and set it aside to grab another. She flipped through a notebook lying on a table in the center of the room and made some notes inside. She definitely was working on something, and Ana thought there was no time like the present to find out what it was.

Ana slipped quietly under the widow, out of view of her target. Her heart pounded in her chest just as it had always done right before an encounter. She stood by the door and slowly started turning the knob. She watched James and Ric for signs of the woman's activity, but she seemed not to notice her guest. When the latch clicked, Ana sprang into the room. Nora jumped back, clearly startled by her presence, but she quickly regained her footing. She ran headlong toward the open door and to what she thought was freedom. Little did she know that there was no freedom awaiting her. James grabbed her after she knocked Ana to the side and ran through the doorway.

"Let me go! What are you doing?" Nora screamed.

"Calm down. We just want to ask you a few questions," James said.

The woman never stopped struggling. She kicked and bit and scratched until Ric came from the shadows. As soon as her eyes met his, she melted in James's grip. She stood perfectly still as if she watched death itself approaching.

"What do you want?" Nora asked.

"You know what I want. I want answers," Ric said.

"You want answers? Well, so do I!" Nora screamed.

Ana came from the room, stepped up to Nora, and smacked her face so hard it made her hand sting.

"Calm down now, or so help me I will beat you to death," Ana said.

James saw a look in Ana's eyes he had never seen before. She had blood in her eyes. She wanted to end this woman right then and there. Yet he wasn't afraid or sickened by her fury. On the contrary, he was proud and envious of it. He wanted to be more like her and have no hesitation. He wanted to do what was necessary without a second thought. He was sure he would get there in time, but for now, he would watch his wife exact vengeance swiftly and without regret.

"We know you had something to do with Lilly's and Kylie's deaths. We want to know what and why," Ana said. "You will have one chance to tell the truth before I start 'encouraging' you to tell it."

Suddenly, bottles and papers began to fly through the air in the room Nora had been working in. A creepy smile spread across Nora's face, and all eyes watched as the room destroyed itself. Ric ran to the door, expecting to find another person hiding inside, but he only saw the glass container as it whirled past his head.

"What the hell? There's nobody in there," Ric yelled.

"What's going on?" Ana screamed.

"You are making Daddy angry," Nora said.

"Who?" Ana asked.

"Daddy, he's in there, and you interrupted our work," Nora said.

Ric slammed the door closed, and Nora laughed.

"Do you think that door is going to help you?" Nora asked.

The door blew off its hinges and landed five feet from the opening. Nora laughed hysterically as unseen hands lifted Ric's body into the air. As Ric dangled helplessly in the air, he clawed at his throat. Ana didn't really know what to do. She had never seen anything like this, ever.

"Okay, you have one chance to save his life. You can let me go and leave here unharmed, or you can have this little fight and watch Daddy rip his head from his shoulders. It's your choice," Nora stated.

No one had any idea what they were dealing with here at all. Ric gasped and scratched but couldn't break free.

"Don't let her go," Ric gasped.

"I'm going to do it, Ric. Is that okay?" Ana screamed in panic.

Ric closed his eyes and nodded the best he could. Ana wasted no time. She punched right through the breastbone of Nora Rilley. She found her target and pulled it free from its cage. She held it in her hand in front of the woman's face. The last seconds of life for Nora Rilley was spent watching Ric fall to the ground, free of her father's grasp.

Every immortal's end was different. Some burned, some exploded, and some simply turned to dust. Unfortunately, this one was a burner. Her body burst into red hot flames until nothing remained but a silver locket among the ashes. No one spoke or moved for what seemed like an hour until James finally spoke.

"We need to call Allan. I don't know what just happened here. Maybe he will," James said.

James called Allan and then explained everything to him.

Allan just said, "Yep, uh-huh, okay over and over." He put James on hold for a minute, and then Jaxon came on the line.

"Hey, listen, don't touch anything, okay? Do you see anything that the woman had on her person? A piece of jewelry or something like that?" Jaxon asked.

"Yeah, a necklace. It's the only thing left. It's in the ashes. Do you want me to get it?" James asked.

"Don't touch it. Is there a container around there anywhere that is metal?" Jaxon asked.

"Okay, get something to pick it up with, but don't let it touch your skin. Just drop it inside the container," Jaxon instructed.

"Okay," James said.

He searched the room for a container of some kind and found an old metal toolbox. He got a pair of forceps-looking pinchers and, after many attempts, picked up the necklace and dropped it inside.

"Cover the necklace with the ashes, and bring them to your room. We will be there shortly to retrieve them from you. Whatever you do, do not open that box again. Is that clear?" Jaxon said.

"Crystal," James said.

The trio did as instructed and went to wait in the room for Jaxon. However, it didn't take long before there was a knock on the door. James answered it to find Allan and Jaxon on the other side.

"Do you have it?" Allan asked.

"Well, hello to you, and yes, over there," Ana said, pointing to the desk.

"Can you tell us what the hell just happened?" Ric asked.

"We had a team go to the facility and clear out everything. We hope to get more answers after we go through it all, but we did dig up a few things. In the late 1800s, an immortal found Nora dying on the streets of London. She had been robbed and beaten and was on her way out of here. He felt sorry for her and tried to heal her, but he was young and didn't think it through. She was too far gone and died with the immortal's blood in her system. When he realized what he had done, he took her to an abbey nearby and left her for the nuns to find. When she woke, she was hungry and scared, not a good combination. She destroyed everyone in that refuge. She went home, and as you can imagine, her father, the good doctor, was not thrilled to see her in her new state. He worked until his death, trying to free his daughter from this plague of sin that was forced upon her. There were rumors that when he died, Nora went completely insane. Immortals said she sought out the help of the voodoo priestesses in New Orleans to help her bring back her father so that she could be free. We will never know why she didn't just kill herself, but an insane mind can't be understood. Maybe she thought she and her father wouldn't be reunited in the afterlife or something. I don't know, but we believe the soul of her father is inside that locket. When she died, he was trapped back inside the locket because the magic was tied to her. This is all speculation, mind you, but we just don't know for sure until we read all the journals. I wish things had turned out differently today, but some things can't be helped. You did a great job. You saved Ric and stopped a killer. Not too shabby for a day's work," Allan explained.

"So you're telling me that was a ghost? I mean, a real ghost? That's what you are saying right now?" Ana asked.

"Yep, your run-of-the-mill everyday phantom," Allan explained.

"Run-of-the-mill? Who knew there was even such a thing?" Ana squealed.

"We thought you knew. You didn't think we were the only supernaturals out there, did ya?" Allan said with a wink.

"I am so over this day. We will have to have a pamphlet or a newsletter or something to get caught up on all things crazy. Just not today, not today," Ana said.

"You two go home, and, Ric, thanks so much for everything you did," Allan said.

The men shook hands and said their goodbyes. Ric promised to make a trip to Virginia in the next month or two for a visit.

Ana and James rounded up everything, even the new fancy clothes they bought for the hotel. They loaded them in the car and headed home. They were so excited to get back to the estate and all their loved ones. The desert turned into city, the city turned into country, and the mountain soon loomed before them.

They hadn't told a soul they were coming home, so everyone was surprised and overjoyed by their return. Day-to-day operations at the estate soon became the norm again, and James and Ana couldn't have been happier. The foul arrived two days after they made their way home, and they named him Doc. It was rather creepy but fitting all the same. Time would tell when they would have to leave again or what new crazy they would face. The dynamic duo decided to live each day to its fullest and to love hard and work harder. They wanted to grow their little piece of heaven, and with determination, they would.

Nature being what nature was, she took pleasure in the fact that these unnatural beings were tending to her creations. She also found it humorous that these immortals thought they were the only mystical, magical things in the world. She would watch as the world changed again, as it had done since the first day of its rotation. The once-powerful would switch places with the weak, and the meek would live like kings. That was the way it always had been and the way it always would be. But now there were two immortals to balance the scales between good and evil, and nature watched.

About the Author

Julie Troutman lives in a rural community in Virginia called Baywood. Many generations of her family have called this area home. Julie has never wandered far from her mountain, as she calls it. Her rural upbringing fueled the flames of her imagination. She credits her mother for her love of literature and her drive to be the best she could be with whatever task she undertakes. Many snowy days sitting by the fire with her mother, reading from her vast collection of poetry and short stories, gave her a passion for the craft of writing.

She now lives within a rock's throw of her home place with her supportive husband and many rescue animals. Her son is the light of her life and has helped develop her sense of wonder and fantasy. Her debut novel, *The Farm*, started as a dream in 2018 and was completed in 2021. With the prompting of friends and family, she took a leap of faith and finished the work. This will undoubtedly be the first of many tales to be told by this aspiring new author, and she hopes to take you along for the adventure.

CPSIA information can be obtained
at www.ICGtesting.com
Printed in the USA
LVHW011055150322
713472LV00001B/59